W9-BTA-231

BANG, YOU'RE DEAD

With a deep thrumming resonance, the gate between dimensions spit him out of nightmare, rolling across the ground in bright sunlight. He woke like a frightened tomcat, hair on end, and scrambled staggering to his feet, grabbing for a rifle that wasn't there. So he snatched at his holster and looked around wild-eyed. Four men stood a little way off, watching him and laughing, talking some foreign lingo he might have heard Varia speak once.

The men started toward him, and bracing his legs against residual dizziness, Macurdy drew his revolver. His wits began to adjust, and he was aware they carried short spears pointed his way. He pointed the revolver back at them, and when they kept coming, jabbed it in their direction. They stopped eight or ten feet away, spears at the ready. A stride forward and thrust, by any of them, and he'd be meat. One, the leader, said something to him, he had no idea what.

"Stay back," he answered. "I don't want to hurt no one."

The man spoke more sharply, and jabbed the spear at him, its point almost reaching him. Macurdy jumped backward and pulled the trigger—and nothing happened. He felt the hammer release and strike, heard it click, but no shot fired. He pulled again, and again nothing. Staring around, he finally spied the rifle—lying in the grass too far away....

BAEN BOOKS BY JOHN DALMAS

THE LION OF FARSIDE

JOHN DALMAS

BAEN

THE LION OF FARSIDE

This is a work of fiction. All the characters and events portrayed in this book are fictional, and any resemblance to real people or incidents is purely coincidental.

Copyright © 1995 by John Dalmas

All rights reserved, including the right to reproduce this book or portions thereof in any form.

A Baen Books Original

Baen Publishing Enterprises
P.O. Box 1403
Riverdale, NY 10471

ISBN: 0-671-87674-0

Cover art by Paul Alexander

First printing, July 1995

Distributed by Simon & Schuster
1230 Avenue of the Americas
New York, NY 10020

Printed in the United States of America

This book is for
Jerry Simmons and Sarge Gerbode
and for the
Spokane Word Weavers

◆◆◆

My thanks to (alphabetically) Eileen Brady, Mary Jane Engh, Jim Glass and David Palter, for their perceptive critiques. And most especially to Hank Davis at Baen Books, for a critique which will prove of lasting value to me as a writer.

PART 1
To Waken The
Lion

1

Varia

None of my family knew where Aunt Varia really came from. Evansville, we figured—that's what she'd let on. Uncle Will had met her at Salem, at the Washington County Fair, and it was love at first sight, he told me once. For him, anyway. "And at second sight and third," laughing when he said it. He claimed she was the best wife a man ever had.

Sometimes she seemed a bit peculiar, but of course she wasn't the only peculiar one in Washington County. Not even the only peculiar Macurdy. Fact is, she had to be a little strange to have married Will. For one thing, from his eighteenth birthday on, the only time he stuck his nose inside church was for his own wedding. Unless you count his funeral, and I don't think he had any nose then. Of course, Ma and Gramma were the only ones in the family that were really churchy; most of us were semi-churchy.

Plus he'd get strange notions from time to time. One time Max tells about, before Varia came on the scene, he and Will were helping Dick Fenton butcher steers, and Will caught some hot blood in a tin cup and drank it down like milk. Said it was good for the muscles and glands. Dick said considering how Will didn't have any girl friend, his glands weren't doing him much good anyway, unless he was servicing the livestock. Strong as the Macurdies are, especially Will, we had a reputation as easy going, which no doubt was why Dick figured he could get away with saying that. But just then Will took another notion: He punched Dick right between the eyes, which also broke his nose.

3

But whenever the family gathered on a holiday, or Ma and Gramma would be feeding a harvest crew, Aunt Varia would be in Ma's big kitchen, or sometimes Julie's in later years, helping do the things women do when a big feed is getting fixed. Fact is, Gramma and Ma both said Varia was a magician in the kitchen. And she was always easy to get along with. When folks were gathered around the table or in the sitting room, Varia would sit there not saying much. Not shy; only quiet and watchful. She'd just sit there, the really really pretty one, listening and smiling.

She had two smiles, actually. The usual one was purely friendly and cheerful, but the other one, which I'd only see now and then, seemed kind of spooky to me. As if she knew things other people didn't, and sometimes I wondered what they might be.

I wasn't the only one. I remember Ma saying once she wondered what Varia thought about behind those peculiar eyes. Not the Bible, she'd bet; Aunt Varia didn't go to church any more'n Will did. She did read a lot of books, though. Library books about history and science, Will said. I remember once he laughed and said that if he died, she could go off to Bloomington and be a professor, after all she'd read. He told me she'd even read Darwin's book on evolution, but not to tell Ma or Gramma or he'd kill me.

Another thing about Varia—she wore her hair long. Not braided, but in two bunches like a pair of shiny copper-red horses' tails, only kind of out to the sides. That was a time when women hardly ever wore their hair long. Some old ladies Gramma's age let theirs grow long, but they tied it up back of their head in a bun. Ma wished she'd wear it different; the way it was showed her ears, which were kind of pointy. I always thought it looked pretty, though I didn't say so, and her ears went with her eyes just fine.

When I was young, I always thought that what was oddest about Aunt Varia was how she'd laugh, now and then, when no one else did. I remember once we had a new preacher over for supper, and he was standing up saying the blessing when Varia laughed like that. First thing he did was look down to see if his pants were unbuttoned or anything. Most of us saw him look, and Frank and me laughed. Couldn't help it. Threw the reverend off his prayer so bad, he just sort of limped on through to the amen. A lot quicker than he might have, which was fine by Frank and me.

Varia was still pretty young then. I mean actually, in years. But what folks noticed first about her was her eyes. She had two, just like the rest of us, but they were different. Big and leaf green—leaf green!—and tilted up at the outside corners. Made her look foreign. She was a pretty woman though, the prettiest around, and those eyes were part of it. They suited her just right, as if any other color or size or shape would have spoiled her looks.

Along with her eyes, her build was what caught the eye most, even among women I think. A little slim, maybe, for some tastes, but not where it counted. When I was thirteen, fourteen years old, sometimes I'd get a hard-on when I looked at her. Whenever I did, she'd look at me and laugh, as if she knew. That killed it every time.

Not that it was a mean laugh. There wasn't any meanness to Varia at all.

I said earlier that she had to have been strange to marry Uncle Will. As a farmer, Will was seriously short on judgement, though otherwise he seemed reasonably smart. He'd take a notion to do the darnedest things. His place was right next to ours, with his northeast forty up against our northwest forty, and right in the middle of the two forties was a thirty-acre clay pocket too heavy and wet for growing anything but hay. So that's what we'd always used it for, a hay meadow. Anyway, this one spring day I was fixing fence and saw Will out there plowing his half of it, turning over that nice stand of grass. His team had all it could do to pull the moldboard through it.

Naturally I was curious, so I went over and asked how come he was plowing it. "Gonna plant potatoes," he told me. Potatoes in clay! Was it anyone else, I'd have thought he was fooling. What he ended up with was a worn-out team, busted up harness, and twelve acres of ground that, when the top dried out, was like a cobblestone pavement. Afterward, when he tried harrowing it, the disks just hopped along the top. I was only fourteen at the time, but I sure as heck knew better'n to do something like that. When Pa saw it, he just shook his head. So far as I know, he never said anything to Will about it. Wouldn't have done any good.

But if Will was a little short sometimes between the ears, he made up for it further down. The Macurdy men were well known for their strength, but Will was almost surely the strongest man in Washington County, and fast-moving. He could outwork most two men. Even if he didn't have hair on his chest, or any whiskers beyond a little peach fuzz. That was typical of Macurdy men, too, and a little embarrassing when I was a teenager.

Anyway he got so he did a lot of work off the farm, which was just as well, considering the kind of farming decisions he sometimes made. Most of his land he rented to Pa, and didn't keep much stock to tend to. A few pigs, a couple of cows that Varia milked, and a team of horses he used logging. He worked for the barrel works a lot of the time, logging white oak cooperage, and cutting up the tops for the Barlow brothers' brick kiln.

And it wasn't just Will's muscles that were big. The Bible says you mustn't show yourself nekkit to folks, but we all figured that rule didn't hold down by the Sycamore Bend. That's where us boys used to swim. And Harley Burton used to have easily the biggest one of all the kids that swam there. (Course, I was only nine, ten years old then. By the time I turned fourteen, and seemed likely to beat him out, Harley was off to France in the Army, helping teach the Kaiser a lesson.) Anyway, when I was about ten, I mentioned to Pa how big Harley's was, and Pa said he'd be surprised if Harley's was near as big as Will's. Said there was someone like that in every generation of Macurdies, but Will had outdone himself. After that I was always a little curious to see what Will had, but of course I never did.

Will was the youngest of three boys, Pa being the oldest. (The Macurdies had always been cursed with what folks around there considered small families; I'd find out more about that later.) I was a little kid five years old when he married Varia. Will was about twenty-five at the time. Even then, I wondered why such a pretty girl would marry someone strange as Will. Some months later she got with child, and when she was supposedly about five months along, Will took her into town. She'd take the train to Evansville, she said, to get cared for and midwifed by her gramma on her mama's side. Some folks thought that was an insult to the Macurdy clan, and to Doc Simmons, and it seemed awful soon, only five months along. But Will was content, so no one in the family said anything. Us Macurdies have always been easy going; let folks pretty much be what they are. And Varia'd said the women in her family had a lot of trouble carrying to full term and birthing, so she wanted to be with her own gramma.

She was back about six weeks later, her belly down to normal, which on her was flat. And didn't have any baby with her. No one was surprised at that, of course; she hadn't carried it long enough. Miscarried, she told Mamma, like she'd been afraid she might. No one troubled her to tell more; didn't want to grieve her.

Melissy Turnbuck told Julie she wondered if the baby hadn't been the victim of an orangewood knitting needle. Julie slapped her face for that; I saw her do it. The only one more surprised than me was Melissy. Years later, Julie told me that Varia having an abortion at five, six months wouldn't make sense anyway. Julie worked for Doc Simmons then, and explained that five months is too far along for that.

Afterward, Varia got with child about every other year— pretty remarkable in our family—and always went off to her gramma, and never came home with anything more than her suitcase. After about the third time, we came to expect it, but she and Will kept trying.

By then we'd come to know that she was strange in other ways than her miscarriages, her tilty green eyes, and laughing at odd times. Because us kids were growing up, and Will didn't look all that young anymore—but Varia didn't look any different. In fact, when I was twenty-five, she still looked twenty, though she had to be around forty by then, at least.

That's the year a big old white oak barber-chaired on Will— split up from the stump, kicked loose about ten feet up, and fell on him. White oak's treacherous that way; the main reason folks log it is, it's the only tree that's much good for wet cooperage, so it's worth a lot. The one that got him had a butt

better'n three feet across. He'd chained it and all before he
ever picked up the ax, and tightened the chain with wedges,
but the grab hook broke off! Ed Lewis, on the other end of
the saw, said all he could see of Will was his left boot and
right arm; the rest of him was under that big oak butt, squashed
flat as pie crust. It shook Ed so bad, he quit logging; got a job
at Singleton's, delivering coal and hogged stovewood. After
they got the tree off Will, Byron Haskell, the undertaker, said
he never before saw anything looked like that, and hoped never
to again. The casket was kept closed, of course.

Pa said one thing about it was, Will died too quick to suffer.

Ma commented on how brave Varia was, what a strong front
she put up, though she did look a little pale and drawn for a
while. Afterward a couple of fellas around there tried paying
court to her. Pretty as she was, the prettiest woman in
Washington County, you might have thought there'd be more,
quite a few more, but there was only the two. Unless you count
old Lennox Campbell drooling on his vest. Could be they were
scared off by how young she looked for her age, plus when it
came to giving birth, she seemed sterile as a freemartin.

Or maybe they knew without knowing that she wasn't
shopping for a man.

She stayed on the farm for more than another year, all by
herself. Didn't seem right, even when you knew she was forty
or whatever. A new Watkins man was going around, and when
she answered the door to him, he asked if her mother was home.
She did her own milking, dunged out her barn, gardened, fed
her cows and chickens—stuff like that. Sold her team to Pa,
though, and her hogs, and Pa agreed we'd farm her land for
her on shares. She helped with things like shocking corn and
oats, the way she'd always done. Even slim as she was, she was
strong, and no one ever knew her to get sick, not even a cold.

At first Frank and I took turns going over and doing whatever
heavy work there was to do; it was less than forty rod from our
place to hers. But after a little, it seemed like it fell to me to do
most of it, which I didn't mind. It was all family. We kept expecting
her to get tired of being alone like that. Figured she'd either
marry or go someplace she had blood kin. Evansville, probably.

Finally, after more than a year, she asked Pa if he'd like to buy her place. If the terms weren't too hard, he said, so they sat down together and worked out an agreement. That was in February; she figured to leave in April. And suddenly the whole family realized how much we'd miss her—Ma, Pa, all of us.

Right after that, I was over there with the spreader, getting her manure spread before plowing. I was pitching on a load when she came out to the barn and told me she was driving into town. (Will'd bought a Model A truck.) She said if I wanted to take a break, there was half a peach pie in the pantry; eat all I wanted of it. Then she left.

That sounded all right to me. Matter of fact, I got so excited, I couldn't hardly hold myself till she drove off. And it wasn't the pie I was excited about, it was the house! I didn't even finish loading the spreader, just put the pitchfork aside and went out with half a load. Soon as I got back with the empty spreader, I went to the house, left my barn boots on her porch, and went in. I didn't know what had got into me, but I was practically shaking.

I'd lived just down the road from it all my life, but never seen much of the inside; I'd hardly gotten farther than the kitchen. Our house was a lot bigger, so all the family get-togethers were held either there or at Max and Julie's over on the Maple Hill Road, turn and turn about. Now, alone inside, I asked myself why in the world I was so shaky-excited about a chance to snoop around Varia's house. I walked all through it, just walked through it looking around, and I realized that what I was looking for was pictures: family photos. Not of the Macurdy family, but *hers!* Seemed to me there ought to be some, and I wanted to see what they looked like. Wanted to see so bad, my chest felt all tight.

I didn't find any on the walls, so I started looking through dresser drawers and closet shelves for albums, or maybe boxes that might have pictures in them. Not mussing anything up; what I surely didn't want was for Varia to know. And when I didn't find anything downstairs, I went up in the attic.

The first thing my eyes hit on up there was a chest. Unlocked. I opened it, and right on top was this big brown envelope that I knew had to have pictures in it. I went over by the window with it, and took out what was inside.

On top was what looked like a letter, a letter I couldn't have read if I'd stood there all week. Could have been Chinese for all of me. Under it was pictures, snapshots. And if I hadn't thought before that Varia was peculiar, the pictures would have done it for me.

They were of children. The first showed four little boys alike as twins—looking a bit like Will, but with Varia's tilty eyes. The next was of five little girls, like twins again, and there wasn't any question who the mother was: Varia. In fact there was five—litters, I guess you could call them, the youngest of them looking about two years old. And written under each child, real small, was what might have been a name.

I didn't have any doubt at all that they were Will's and Varia's kids. Twenty-three little Macurdies, except I doubted they thought of themselves that way. Five litters. But Varia'd gone off pregnant probably eight or nine different times—more than five, anyway. So all told, it seemed to me she'd given birth to some forty. Having litters and a short term explained why she'd started to swell so early, but even so, they couldn't have been much bigger than squirrels when they were born. I was amazed they'd lived. Seemed like with Varia, Will was more fertile than all the Macurdy men since God knew when.

And if all that wasn't enough, they were dressed strange, in little coveralls about half snug, like they were tailor-made. Tucked into little black, pull-on boots coming not much above the ankles. Looked like they were dressed for Sunday, but not at the Oak Creek Presbyterian Church. The little girls had Varia's long hair, fastened like hers in twin horse tails that hung down over the front of their shoulders. The boys' heads were just about shaved, and they stood there at attention like grinning little soldiers. All of them, boys and girls alike, would have their mamma's green eyes, I had no doubt, and they looked to be standing in front of a low building with white stone pillars. Didn't look like any studio backdrop, either. Looked real. Those pictures—kids and building—gave me chill bumps like a plucked turkey.

And there was one other picture, which I took one glance at and covered up quick as I could. Then I put them all back in the envelope in the same order they'd been in, and put the envelope back in the chest the way I'd found it. Closed the lid, and went back downstairs, all of a sudden scared to death that Varia might come back before I got out of there. Because she had a big big secret, and I'd found it out.

I went right back to spreading manure; didn't have the nerve to stay and eat any pie. When I heard the eleven-forty train whistling for the Ramsey Road crossing, I unhitched the team and drove them home. Halfway there, Varia passed me in the Model A. I didn't even wave; I was afraid she'd stop to talk. When she drove by, I could feel those bright green eyes right on me, and it seemed to me she knew what I'd done, what I'd found out. My mouth was drier'n dust. I didn't know how I could ever face her again.

That night I dreamt about Varia. I dreamt I was over to plow her garden patch and couldn't get the plow in the ground, which was all paved over with brick. Then she came out to me wearing only a shirt, one of Will's, the tails scarcely halfway to her knees, and unbuttoned down far enough at the top, I could see the roundness of her titties. I was sure she wasn't wearing anything underneath it. She invited me in for pie. Her tilty green eyes were bigger than ever, and smiling, she asked me what the trouble was. I said I couldn't get it in, that it was too hard, meaning the plow and the ground. She laughed and put her fingers on my cheek, and said it couldn't ever be *too* hard. My face got hot as a depot stove, and somehow we weren't in her garden patch anymore, but in my bedroom. And I wasn't asleep anymore, it seemed like. Nor was Varia there, really, but only her ghost, so to speak. I could see right through her. But I could still feel where her fingers had touched my cheek.

"Haven't you ever wanted to be a daddy, Curtis?" she asked. Her voice was soft when she said it, not at all like a witch.

I swallowed and told her I'd never thought about it.

"Well then, have you ever wanted to be in bed with a pretty woman?"

I couldn't more'n nod. Frank and me'd been to see the Linzler sisters a couple times, on their farm outside Salem; they charge two dollars. And I screwed Maudie Hodge a few times in her daddy's hayloft. Wearing a French safe, except the first time with Maudie. I didn't want to have to marry anyone, surely not Maudie Hodge, and you couldn't know but what the Linzler sisters might have the clap, or worse. None of them were really pretty; nowhere near as pretty as Varia. Of course, they didn't drop whole litters of strange, smiling little kids, either.

Anyway she took me by the hand and we walked out of the house together, her transparent in the moonlight. And somehow I didn't have my pajamas on, but my regular pants and shirt, and my barn boots. Which about three-quarters decided me I was still dreaming. I've looked back on that night more times than I'd care to count, and I'm still not sure.

When we got to her house, another her was waiting on the back porch, this second Varia not transparent at all. She wore what looked like the same shirt, plaid flannel. The first Varia stepped up to the second Varia and they melted right into one another, while I found myself taking off my barn boots. Then, chuckling like she does, she opened the storm door. And the hinge squeaked, making me start like someone waking up.

And there I was, really on her porch, like I'd sleepwalked there. I mean *really on her porch*. No way was this a dream any longer. "You didn't eat your pie," she said softly, and chuckled again. I walked through that door like I was bewitched—I couldn't have stayed out any more than I could have flown by flapping my arms—and she closed it behind us. Then, in the kitchen, she put her arms around me and kissed me like nothing I ever imagined, and led me by the hand into her bedroom.

"Curtis," she said softly, "since Will died, you're the strongest of the Macurdies, and you're smarter than Will. A lot smarter; you have no idea yet how smart, how able. Perhaps you never will. Although your uncle was more intelligent than people gave him credit for, and a nice nice man. I became very fond of him."

I only about half heard what she was saying, because she was unbuttoning my shirt while she talked. "You'll give us fine children, Curtis. More than fine. They'll be pleased about that." *They?* I thought. Then she kissed me again, and stepped back and smiled at me. "Will and I did have children, you know. The ones you saw in the pictures this morning."

I stared at her. She knew all right, just like I figured. Then she stepped around behind me and pulled off my shirt, put her arms around me and unbuckled my belt—and felt around inside while she kissed my back. Now she knew what I didn't— how I sized up with Will. I couldn't hardly breathe, and my knees like to have buckled. When she'd finished undressing me, she shucked out of Will's old shirt, and I'd never seen anything like her. So sweet and pretty, it made my throat hurt just to look. Then she pulled me onto the bed, and after that— no way could I describe what it was like. Between times, she told me she wanted me to marry her. I told her that's what I wanted, too. At least part of me did, no doubt of that, but I wasn't so sure about the rest of me, and I guess she knew what I was thinking, because she said there wasn't any hurry. Then she chuckled again and said next week would be soon enough, and started wriggling around on top of me and eating my face.

After another hour or so, I washed up and got dressed, and the transparent Varia led me back home. I was worried that someone would see us, but she said there wasn't any danger of that. That's the first I ever knew of invisibility spells.

The next day I finished off her manure pile, and while I was forking manure that morning, I got to worrying. She hadn't aged for more'n twenty years, while I'd gone from a bitty little boy to six-foot-one, and two-twenty-four on the creamery scales with my clothes on. In twenty more years, I'd be forty-six and she'd still be twenty. And in forty years . . . Folks already talked; some were even a little scared of her. That was one reason she didn't go into town any more than she needed to. First Will and then ma had done most of Varia's shopping in recent years. They even went to the library to get books she wanted.

No doubt about it, being married with her would be somewhat more than just thrashing around on the bed together. And by the light of day, riding behind a team of Belgians spreading cow manure, it seemed to me we needed to talk about that. So when I heard the eleven-forty train whistle, I left my pitchfork there and went up to her house and knocked.

She let me in, then cranked up Ma on the phone. Asked if I could stay for lunch and help her eat leftovers before she had to throw them out.

Ma didn't answer right away; there was half a minute there I couldn't hear her voice. Maybe she wondered if I'd started doing more at Varia's than just work. But she said that'd be fine. Anyway I sat down at the table, and we began talking while Varia rustled up a meal. I told her what was bothering me, and she just smiled. "We won't stay here," she said.

"Where—Where would we go?" I wasn't sure I wanted to hear the answer to that. Because suddenly I wanted to be with Varia the rest of my life, and was scared her answer would be something I couldn't live with.

"Where would you like?"

I thought for a minute. "Since the Depression hit last fall," I reminded her, "lots of folks are out of work. It's hard to get a job nowadays."

"We'll get a farm," she said, reasonable as could be. "Somewhere well away from here; maybe some black land in Illinois."

I shook my head. "That'd cost a lot of money. Especially that Illinois black land."

"Land prices are way down. I talked to them at the bank before I sold out to your father. And my grandmother's got money that belongs to me."

Her grandmother. I supposed I'd meet her. I wasn't sure I wanted to.

"She looks a lot like me," Varia said without my asking.

"Just as young?" I was a little scared of what the answer might be.

Varia laughed. "A little older. Maybe twenty-one." Light danced in her eyes when she said it. She was so bright and lively, I couldn't help thinking she'd be a wife like no one ever had before, except Will. But still—

"How about when I'm fifty," I said, "and you still look twenty?"

She looked at me a long time before she answered. "You won't need to look fifty, if you don't want to. Not you. You can look just as young then as you do today."

The first thing that hit me was, I'd have to sell my soul to the devil. I've never actually believed in the devil, but that's the thought that came to me. I set it aside. "Will aged," I reminded her.

"Will never had the choice. I tried. He was a nice man, a gentle man, and he had some unusual genes we need. But not the talent; not enough. I planned to stay with him till the situation here got dangerous—from my not aging, I mean—have sixty or seventy children by him, then disappear. I'd leave a note that I was afraid to stay, because I wasn't aging. That I was going somewhere where people thought I was twenty."

I guess I must have looked troubled, because she put her hand on my cheek again, soft as goose down, and said: "I never actually loved Will, as fond of him as I came to be. It's you I've loved. For a dozen or more years now, since I realized what you might be. Or who."

For a dozen years! That was a stopper. But she wasn't done. "And in the Sisterhood," she said, "we learn self-control." Her mouth twisted a bit. "Self-abnegation, really. It's not always easy, even though we're from selected stock. There's a lot about a person that's not genetic."

It's funny how much I remember of what she said, considering I didn't understand half of it then. The biggest puzzles were who this *we* was she talked about. And Will's jeans? I never knew him to own a pair of jeans. He'd always worn overalls, like most farmers.

Anyway, the upshot of it was, we'd tell Ma and Pa that we planned to get married and go somewhere else to live. And when we got there, we'd tell folks I was twenty-five and she was twenty. Then, in twelve, fifteen years we'd move again. Might be interesting to live different places.

We got married ten days later. The family didn't announce it beforehand; Varia asked them not to. We just got the blood tests and license, and one evening after supper, my folks went with us to the parsonage. Took Reverend Fleming totally by surprise. I suppose he thought I'd got Varia pregnant. Anyway he took us next door to the church, turned on the lights, and married us in our coats, it being cold out and no fire in the furnace. When it was over, we all went home—Ma, Pa, Frank and Edith to their house, Max and Julie to theirs, and me and Varia to ours. Varia Macurdy. She didn't even get a new name out of it, nor much in the way of wedding gifts. The ring was the one Will gave her.

I said something about it when we went inside. She said none of it mattered, that she'd got me, and that was what counted. Then we went upstairs to bed. We hadn't been to bed together except that one night, but we made up for it before we went to sleep.

We'd already packed most everything she wanted to take with us—not a whole heck of a lot. The week before, I'd hammered together sort of a shed for the back of the Model A, with stakes for the stake pockets, that we could use to move. So by ten the next morning we were sitting in the cab together, headed south for the Ohio River, happy as two worms in an apple.

We didn't have a notion of what we were getting into.

2

Idri

Evansville actually was where her gramma lived, except her gramma wasn't her gramma. More like her cousin. And almost as good-looking as Varia. The big difference was their personalities; I could see that right away. Idri's eyes were mean and hard, not laughing like Varia's. As if she held grudges; I recall thinking that. She didn't seem to be married—didn't wear a ring, anyway—but I smelled and saw cigar butts in an ashtray. Maybe a brother, I thought. Not knowing Idri at the time.

After Varia introduced me as her new husband, Idri looked me up and down and scowled. The first thing she said was, "You'll have to take him through! He's needed there right now!" Not "It's nice to know you," or "Welcome to the family," or "I suppose you'd like to meet your stepchildren." Just giving orders: "You'll have to take him through." Whatever that meant.

Varia's eyebrows shot up. "I have no intention of taking him through," she said. "We're moving to Illinois. I just came here to let you know, and draw five hundred dollars from the contingency account."

Idri raised more than her eyebrows; she raised her voice. I don't know what she said, because they started talking in some foreign language. But she sounded as mad as anyone I'd ever heard, ripping Varia up one side and down the other. Varia looked shocked at first, but after a minute she snapped something sharp and hard at Idri that stopped her in mid-snarl. Called her something, I suppose. Then she took my sleeve and dragged me out the door, and right on out to the truck.

When we'd got in the cab, she started shaking, and I asked her what was wrong.

"There's a lot I didn't tell you," she said. "It didn't seem important. Now it is."

I didn't say anything, just nodded and sat listening, my eyes on that beautiful face.

"Idri and I are not—Americans. And not from some place in Europe. We're from another world entirely, a world called Yuulith." She looked at me as if begging me to believe. "It's as if it's right beside this one, and now and then, in a few special places, openings develop between them for a few minutes. We call them gates. We can go through them from one world to the other. The nearest is across the river in Kentucky; that's the one we use."

I'd heard or read some strange things in my life, but this was the strangest. Yet somehow I believed. For one thing, the name Yuulith gave me chills. No, she was telling the truth, and she knew I knew. "I can't tell you everything about it all at once," she said, "why we're here, why I'm making babies here—except that it seemed very important. In our world, there's a land with very bad people—soldiers, and lords of magic—evil, and very powerful. But recently—recently they sent an army into our country and killed most of us."

Her voice was quiet while she told me all this, but her face was drawn up tight. "Idri and I belong to a Sisterhood that over the past three hundred years has worked to develop our power. But when the gate opened, the time before last, Idri learned what the enemy had done. The ylver, they're called. They'd captured our Cloister—our town—and destroyed it, taking most of our Sisters captive."

Varia'd cried the edge off her grief a couple months earlier, though none of us knew it then, but the tears were running again. "Then they killed the children," she said, "and their soldiers raped the Sisters over and over, making the people watch. Finally they set their war dogs on them, on the Sisters that is, to tear them apart."

I sat staring at her. "And Idri wants us to go *there*?"

She nodded, and her voice took new strength "But I'm not. It's over with there, it's all turned evil, and this is my world now. You and I are going to Illinois and make babies, beautiful babies, one or two at a time, and bring them up ourselves, and love each of them. And each other."

What could I say? I kissed her right there in the cab in broad daylight, then put the truck in gear and headed out of Evansville, bound for Illinois.

3

The Blackland

Within a week we'd moved onto 120 acres of blackland in Macon County, Illinois, north of Decatur. And it was ours as long as we kept making the mortgage payments. Varia made the down payment, $600, from money left her by Will, and what Pa had paid down on Will's place. And had enough left over to buy a team and harness for $80, and equipment we hadn't brought with us, plus seed and some house furnishings. Everything secondhand, of course, but lots of people were selling stuff, good stuff, to keep food on the table. We weren't bad off, compared to them. We still had money for potatoes and beans, bacon and oatmeal, and salt and sugar and flour. Buying livestock would have to wait though. Except for pasture and hay, I figured to plant most of the ground to corn—corn and a big truck garden—and enough oats for the team next winter, and for the cow I figured to buy when I'd made a crop. In the barn there was already hay and oats enough for the team a few months, while the woodshed had wood and cobs for the stoves awhile. Even a couple sacks of coal for the kitchen.

The buildings were pretty decent, and the house was more than big enough for the two of us. They all needed paint, but that'd have to wait. The five hundred dollars Varia hadn't been able to get from Idri would have made a big difference—except it wouldn't have, the way things turned out. But anyway, it seemed to me we'd get by in good shape.

You never know entirely what to expect, working a new team, but when I brought them home, Varia talked to them awhile, and they worked out real well. She was always good with horses, riding or handling them. I started plowing that same day.

I even got a job milking eight Brown Swiss cows for a neighbor, morning and evening. Given the hard times, it paid pretty decent—fifty cents a day—and each morning I took home a big jar of milk and some fresh butter, worth another twenty cents or so.

It also meant I got up at four every morning, to eat before going to Morath's to milk, and finished up there at seven or so in the evening. Between milkings I walked a furrow behind the team all day, keeping the plow where it belonged. So I made a point of being in bed before nine, and I'm talking about in bed for the purpose of sleeping.

Nonetheless, we had time to sit around a little before bedtime, and the very first night, Varia told me she wanted to lay a spell on me. Naturally I kind of backed off from that. "What for?" I asked her.

"So you'll understand me better."

"Hon," I said, "I understand you pretty well already."

She didn't say anything for a minute, just sort of chewed on her lower lip as if she was thinking. Finally she said, "Why do you suppose the Macurdy family was chosen to father my children?"

I stared at her without knowing a thing to say.

"Where do you think the Macurdies came from?" she asked.

"What d'you mean? From Kentucky, way back when James Madison was president."

"And before Kentucky?"

It seemed to me right then that I was going to learn something I didn't want to know. I shook my head. "Grampa said we're Scotch-Irish. In school they told us that means from Scotland by way of Ireland."

"Let me put a spell on you, and afterward I'll tell you. It will make it easier for both of us."

I squirmed in my chair. "Will it take long? I thought maybe the two of us could go to bed early."

She laughed, the same young-girl laugh I'd heard since I was a little boy. "It won't take long. And it's as good as an hour's sleep anyway."

It took me half a minute to say yes, but I knew right away I'd do it. I mean, I'd trusted her so far, and she'd trusted me, and we'd bound ourselves together till death us do part. And what was I scared of? She'd never do me any harm. Besides, it seemed to me she'd spelled me that night she'd taken me to her house, and that had worked out just fine. "Okay," I told her, "I'll do it."

"Thank you, darling," she said, and pulled her chair up closer. "Now look in my eyes."

That was always easy to do, but this time was different. It was like they drew me right in, and I went limp, but after what seemed like ten, fifteen seconds I came back to normal again. "Sorry it didn't work," I said, thinking she'd be disappointed. But she laughed.

"Look at the clock."

I looked, and my mouth must have dropped open. We'd sat down at ten to eight, and now it was a quarter after. "What happened?" I asked.

"You and I did what was necessary. Told your body not to get old; that it's got the ylvin genes. And got you ready to start learning." She came over and knelt down beside me, and kissed me sweeter'n honey. Old Junior started to swell up right away, and Varia began to purr. "Do you still want to go to bed early?" she asked me.

We both of us stood up then, her laughing, and off we went. I didn't get to sleep by nine that night, but I felt fine when she woke me up at four. I'd been dreaming up a storm, and none the worse for it. Part of the dream was being a hundred years old and still young. Strange dream, but not near as strange as it would have been if I wasn't married to Varia.

The next evening we did something different. She laid a lighter spell on me that left me awake but relaxed. Then she taught me to do what she called meditate. I'd always thought "meditate" meant to think about something, but this was different. She told me afterward she hadn't thought it'd go that well, first time. The spell had helped, but she told me my breeding was showing itself. It turned out we'd sat like that, straight-backed in two kitchen chairs, for half an hour.

When we were done, she began telling me things. I listened,

but I didn't really believe. I mean, part of me said she wouldn't lie to me about things like that, but what she told me was flat-out unbelievable. My great-great-grampa had come from her world, she said, where her Sisterhood was breeding up strains of people for special purposes, like we breed up hogs and cattle and horses. This was because they were always in danger from "the ylver," who had a lot more power than the Sisterhood, and the only way her people could survive was to get stronger and smarter, and be better at magic.

Anyway, Great-great-grampa had been an experiment, and it'd worked real well. Except for one thing: he hadn't wanted to do what they told him. He was to breed a lot of different sisters, but he'd fallen in love with one of them, and her with him, and he didn't want to keep on living as a stud horse. So the boss sister took her away, sent her off somewhere.

To make a long story short, he ran off to the nearest gate and went through it into Kentucky, coming out in Muhlenberg County. Afraid of being followed and caught, he headed north and crossed the Ohio River into Indiana, where he got work deadening timber long enough to make a stake and get married. Then he went on north again to Washington County, where he homesteaded the land our family's worked ever since.

They'd bred up other studs besides him, but back in Yuulith where'd he'd come from, his progeny proved out specially good, so they tracked him by following his trace in what Varia called the Web. That was something they'd just learned to do; only a few knew how. Then they sent her to bear children by Will.

That's what she told me, and knowing what I know now, I know it's true.

Only now, she told me, it had all gone to waste. Most of the Sisters had been killed and the rest scattered. She didn't know if any of her children were alive. The whole story seemed a little more real to me when she said that, from the way her eyes welled up. She'd never seen her children beyond a couple weeks old, except in the pictures I'd found, but they were hers, all she had.

After that she spelled me often, and did drills with me, twenty or thirty minutes at a time. To open up my magical powers, she said. I told her that'd be a waste of time, that I didn't have any to open up, and anyway I didn't want magical powers. I had my brain and my two hands and my muscles, and everything else I needed. She was magical enough for both of us.

She looked at me long and seriously. I'd never seen her more serious. "Darling," she told me, "you do have them. They showed up more when you were little. Do you remember once when you were seven or eight, and you looked up at the corner of the ceiling, where I'd looked? Before Idri, my Evansville contact was my favorite sister, Liiset, and now and then she'd look in on me. Something Idri couldn't do.

"She wasn't there physically, but you sensed her spirit and translated it to her physical appearance—her face. You couldn't have done any of that if you didn't have the talent."

I remembered, for the first time since that day. It'd been too spooky. "Seems like I've lost it since, though," I said.

She shook her head. "How did you find the pictures? How did you even know enough to look?"

"But what if I don't want magical powers?" I asked her.

She didn't answer right away. Then she said, "If you were blind, and didn't entirely believe in sight, you might be uncomfortable if I said I wanted to open your eyes."

I didn't have anything to answer, so I nodded and told her fine, let's do it. It would make her happy, and I figured she wouldn't do something bad for me. My problem, I told myself, was I was scared of what I didn't know. I'd been scared that night the transparent Varia took me home with her, too, and look how much I'd liked that after we got there! But I still felt uncomfortable about "opening my magical powers."

Over several weeks, I couldn't see we were making any progress. Varia said it was a little like putting a pot of water on the stove to boil: You wait and wait, and nothing seems to be happening, and suddenly there it is boiling. I couldn't help wondering, though, if maybe the wood in my firebox was piss elm, and wouldn't burn.

One evening when we'd finished, her eyes didn't have their usual steadiness, and I asked her if anything was wrong.

"Not with you," she said.

"With what, then?"

"I guess I'm just tired."

"Looks like more than tired. Looks like worried."

She smiled. "See? Your powers are coming back. I was thinking about my children; all forty-one of them."

Yeah, I thought to myself, *maybe my powers are coming back, 'cause I can tell you're lying to me.* I really didn't believe they were; just a look at her face told me. But I wasn't going to badger her. "I'll have the plowing done tomorrow morning," I said. "Maybe you and I ought to take the rest of the day off. Go in to Decatur and walk through the stores. Buy some ice cream, and celebrate. Maybe Morath will even divide my cows up between his daughters to milk in the evening, and we can blow twenty cents on a movie."

She came over and kissed me, tears in her eyes. "Curtis, you're so nice, I love you more than you know. If anything ever happens to me, I want you to remember that. Regardless of anything. And tomorrow—tomorrow I'd love to go to Decatur with you when you're done plowing."

That's Varia for you, always thinking, always trying to do the right thing. I still didn't realize how well I'd married. A good good woman.

Anyway, when tomorrow got there, and I'd milked and had breakfast, her tune had changed. "Before we blow any money on ice cream and a movie," she said, "there are things I need to do to this house. Let the plowing wait till this afternoon." She handed me a list. "I want you to get these things for me right now. I need to civilize this kitchen."

I stared at her. She was standing there kind of like Ma did in front of Pa sometimes, when she didn't want any argument. I looked at the list: red and white checkered oil cloth, paint, and eight or ten other things she had every right to want, or even have. But none of it seemed very important, and I'd have to chase all over town to get it. "Okay," I grumped. I'd never been grumpy before with Varia; I didn't even give her a kiss, sad to say. How many times I felt bad about that.

I went out to the truck, gave it a crank, and drove off to Decatur.

It was almost noon when I got back. By that time I'd convinced myself she'd gotten pregnant; I'd heard how women can get notional when they're pregnant. When I walked into the house, she wasn't in the kitchen, and I felt a little pang. "Honey!" I called out, "I'm back! I got your stuff!"

She didn't answer, and I got a sick feeling. Two weeks before, I'd have told myself I was scared she'd gone off and left me because I hadn't given her that kiss, but now I hardly glanced at the idea. It was something a lot worse. "Maybe she's out in the privy," I muttered, but didn't believe that either, not even enough to go out and call to her. Instead, somehow or other I went into the pantry, and there on the counter was some folded tablet paper held down by a stove-lid handle. I unfolded it and started reading, though somehow I knew what had happened—not the details, but the main thing.

Sweet darling Curtis, the gate is going to open again soon, and they are coming to take me away, Idri and some men. The Sisterhood still exists. It's been butchered and forced to flee, but it still exists. Idri must have tracked me, and then gone back to Evansville for help.

I sensed them coming yesterday, and this morning I felt them again while I was cooking breakfast. They'll be here very soon. It wouldn't do any good for us to run away. They would only follow. That's why I sent you to town. I'm sure she's supposed to take us both, but she'd find an excuse to kill you. I know her too well.

Don't forget to take the money out of the honey jar. It's yours.

Darling, it hurts so much to leave you like this. But you'll get over it. It was beautiful to be your wife this short time. I'll remember you and love you forever.

Reading it, it was like I'd been there watching her write it, tears running down her face like mine were, and for a minute, when I was done, I felt helpless, like a wooden man. But only for a minute.

4

Conjure Woman

I stopped at Morath's long enough to tell Miz Morath I wouldn't be able to milk for them awhile. That my wife's relatives had come and stolen her away, and I was going after them. I left my team there; Morath could use them or rent them out, to pay for their keep. Then I headed south on Route 51, and before I got forty miles, the truck quit on me. I figured it was the carburetor—I'd had trouble with it before—but fooling with it didn't help, so I gave up and hiked on into Assumption, where I hired myself a tow. The fella at the garage there fussed with it awhile, and I ended up getting a new one put on. All in all, it cost me more than three hours. I didn't know whether to swear or cry.

I'd never before felt the way I did then: dangerous. Never knew I could. I didn't feel at all like the Curtis Macurdy folks knew back in Washington County.

Then I drove on. North of Vandalia it threw a rod, and there wasn't a thing in hell I could do about that. Not in the time I had. I wondered if Idri'd cast a spell to keep me from following them, and told myself if she had, it wasn't going to work. Leaving the truck by the road, I started walking. Each time a car came along, I stuck a thumb out, and after a while a moving van went on by me a little way and pulled over. I took off running and climbed in.

"Where yew a-headin'?" the driver asked me. A southerner by the way he talked.

"Kentucky," I told him. "Muhlenberg County."

He laughed and slapped his leg. "Talk 'bout bein' in luck!

I'm deliverin' this load to Central City; that's in Muhlenberg County." He reached under the truck seat, took out a clear glass bottle three-quarters full, and handed it to me. "Have a swig," he told me.

I handed it back. "Thanks," I said, "but my family's all teetotalers. Been that way as far back as anyone remembers."

He didn't take offense like some might. Just pulled the wooden stopper with his teeth, raised the bottle, took a big swig, and about strangled. "Good stuff," he said with his eyes watering. "Not like most of the rotgut folks sell these days. My uncle makes it hisself."

He started the truck then and drove on, talking about how he wished he was headed for home instead of Kentucky. After a while I started dozing, off and on. Woke up when he stopped the truck for gas. It was beginning to get dark out.

"Yew gonna git a crick in yore neck, yew sleep like that," he told me. "I'm figurin' to drive all night, if I can, but I'm apt to git sleepy. Can yew drive a truck?"

I told him I could.

"I put a sofa crosst the back of the load, so's I can go back there and sleep if I need to. Why don't yew go back there? Then if I git too sleepy to drive, yew'll be all rested, and we can change places. Git there quicker."

Anything to speed things up. I went around back, opened the doors and climbed in, latching them behind me. After a minute the truck started again. The sofa felt good enough, but laying there, I didn't feel sleepy any longer. I kept wondering how in the world I'd find the gate, once I got to Muhlenberg County. Finally I told myself, *same way you found the pictures*. However that was. Anyway it settled my mind enough that I got to sleep.

When I woke up, it seemed like I'd slept a long time. A long time full of dreams. Dreams with Varia in them. Laying there, I felt them slipping away, and they were gone, just like she was. The truck wasn't moving, so I got up, felt for the latch, and opened the doors. It was night out, moonlight, and a little spooky feeling, but nothing bad. I hopped down.

We were on a country road, stuck in a mudhole. I went to

the cab; the driver was inside, laying against the steering wheel asleep. The door was locked, which surprised me, and so was the one on the other side, but moonlight on the seat showed the whiskey bottle laying on its side without the stopper. I decided he'd finished it off after he got stuck.

There was a little field across the road, but otherwise it seemed to be all woods around there, and a big big hill on the other side. Didn't look like any place I'd seen in Illinois or Indiana, the hill was too big, so I decided I was in Kentucky.

The moon was full and low in the sky, which meant it was near daybreak. I set off down the road with the moon at my back, not liking to leave the driver like that, but I needed to find that gate. I felt pretty optimistic. I'd made it to Kentucky in under a day, even though I'd lost my truck.

Right away I left the field behind, woods crowding the road on both sides. The night was mild, and in a little bit I started enjoying the hike. The leaves were coming out, and it smelled like spring. I must have walked a mile or more before I came to another cleared field, not more'n six or eight acres, with a little shack at the far end, just back from the road. By that time, morning had started lightening the sky a bit.

The whole shack turned out to be made of shakes, walls and all. I heard a dog woof inside; a minute later the front door opened and an old woman looked out.

"Who's out there?" she yelled.

"Name's Curtis Macurdy," I told her. "I'm lost. I'd appreciate if you could tell me where I am."

She cackled like a hen. Her old hound came out past her and down the steps, to sniff my legs without making a sound. "Yew ain't from nowheres 'round yere," she said.

"No ma'am. I just left Illinois, headed for Kentucky."

"Kentucky?!" She cackled again. "Yewr in Missoura!"

Now I realized who she sounded like. Her accent was like the truck driver's, only thicker. He must have drank enough, he decided to go home, and these hills must be the Ozarks. From what I'd heard and read of the Ozarks, it could be a month before the van company found out where their truck was, if they ever did.

"How far to Kentucky?" I asked.

"Don't rightly know. But yew ain't goin' to walk there today. Tell ya what. I got to go fetch water. If'n yew'll tote it fer me, I'll feed ya breakfast."

She didn't have a well, but across the road just three, four chains, was a spring in the hillside, with a wooden trough for the water to run out of. She had two buckets hung on a shoulder yoke, and I carried them for her. If it'd been me living there, I'd have built a house on the other side of the road, and run the trough on down to it. Or better, put a pipe under the road.

While she fixed breakfast, she chattered on like someone who didn't have anyone to talk to very often. "I'm a-goin' up on the knob, when the sun comes up," she said. "I staked out a young cockerel up there last evenin'."

"Staked out a chicken?"

"Oh, that's right, yewr from up Illinois way. Yew don't know 'bout Injun Knob. It's a spirit mountain, and every full moon, the spirit comes a-hootin'."

"A-hootin'?"

"Yep. At midnight. Most folks cain't yere it, but I can, 'cause I'm a conjure woman."

"Really!"

"Yep. And it's good to give it a little somethin' now and then. I'll go up there, and the chicken'll be gone. It always is."

"Mightn't a fox have taken it?" I asked. "Or some other animal?" I'd read they still had wolves in the Ozarks.

"Not up there. Ain't no critters go up there on the night of the full moon. Fact is, up on top they ain't no critters anytime, not even birds. They know better. A couple times been young fellas went up there on a dare, the evenin' of a full moon, and they ain't none of 'em ever come back down. Then, eight, ten years ago, a perfessor come yere from the university with another feller, both of 'em wearing big ol' pistols on their side, and they never come back, neither." She cackled again. "The sheriff come with a posse, a day or two later, and combed the woods, but couldn't find hide nor hair of 'em."

The hairs on my neck started to bristle, and the old woman grinned at me. "Yew wanna go up there with me?"

I nodded. Varia had said there was more than one gate. After breakfast, we started up the mountain on a little footpath. Most of the birds were back for the summer, and the woods was full of their singing. I saw gray squirrel and chipmunks and rabbit turds, and lots and lots of oaks and clumps of pine. It was a long steep path, with lots of stops for the old woman to rest a minute, till finally I could see the top close ahead. There was lots of bedrock showing by that time, and the trees were sparse and small. And there weren't any more birds or squirrels or chipmunks. I'm not sure what they felt that kept them away, but I was feeling something that had my neck hairs bristling again. Either that or I was imagining.

We took one last rest, the old woman breathing hard, and frowning.

"Anything the matter?" I asked her.

She didn't answer, and after a minute we went on. At the top, she knelt down by a knee-high pine seedling with a leather thong tied to it: the tether she'd tied the chicken with. But there wasn't any chicken now, nor feathers nor blood, like a possum or bobcat would have left. Just the leather thong, which was either awful short to start with, or something had shortened it.

She still wasn't talking, and the frown was still there. She stood up and closed her eyes so tight her whole face skrinched together, and she began mumbling something I couldn't make out. Cold chills ran down me from the top of my head to my feet. After a minute she started to talk.

"Some folks were up yere last night, in the dark. Two men and two women, folks o' power. And the mountain took three of 'em—not et 'em; received 'em—two witchy women, young and perty, and one of the men. I'm a-goin' back down, right now."

We went. She didn't have anything more to say all the way to her cabin. I didn't either, but my brain was going a mile a minute.

I knew just what I was going to do: get me a job around there somewhere, on a farm or in the woods. It wouldn't need to pay cash; bed and board would be plenty, and the bed could be hay in the barn. I had twenty-seven dollars in my shoe, more than enough to buy a pistol and a good rifle, and plenty of shells. And I'd be back on top of Injun Knob before dark, on the night of the next full moon.

PART 2
The Twice-Stolen Bride

5

Xader

The top of Injun Knob appeared ordinary in the moonlight, half bald, its scrubby trees scattered. The gate hadn't opened yet, but Varia could feel it. Chuckling, Xader put his arms around her from behind, groping her through her housedress: "Might as well enjoy ourselves while we wait," he murmured, and kissed her neck. His inborn psionic talent was sufficient that, unless she took him by surprise, he could hold off whatever magic she might try with handcuffs on. So she stamped hard on his instep, and swearing, he let her go, stepping back from her.

Abruptly the three of them were swallowed into a deep bass indigo nothingness, a nothingness with a gut-wrenching, mind-numbing sense of distortion, followed by a moment of suspension while the gate examined them. Then Varia found herself running like someone who'd just jumped from a moving car. As if the gate had spit her out. Unable to windmill her manacled arms for balance, she fell headlong onto grass. A minute later, hands raised her to her feet, a small hand on one side, a larger on the other.

She stood not in midnight now, but in sun-dappled high noon, and looked about her. They were no longer on the mountaintop, but in a cathedral-like grove of large old basswood trees. The grass was lawn-like, almost without saplings, as if grazed between the monthly openings of the gate. And in fact, on this side, in the world called Yuulith, animals and humans could enter the site freely until the first distortion of the matrix, the Web of the World, when the gate began to regenerate. Then it physically repelled them.

35

Several rough-clad men with spears had been waiting to collect anyone or anything that came through. They held back though, recognizing that these were part of the Sisterhood. Ignoring them, Idri first untied the bandanna that held Varia's mouth shut, then removed the gag from between her teeth, leaving the handcuffs on. For just a moment she watched Varia work the kinks from her jaw, then turned and slapped Xader, the sound almost like a small-caliber pistol. Idri, like Varia, was considerably stronger than she looked.

"She's still a Sister, Xader," she snapped, "and don't forget it. Keep your hands to yourself, and remember who you are."

Remember what *you* are, Varia corrected silently. *A cull.* Occasionally a guardsman clone was flawed in some unacceptable way, and the whole batch was either kept for labor or quietly disposed of. It occurred to Varia that the Ferny Cove disaster might have left so few guardsmen alive, culls were used more widely now.

Xader had flushed with resentment. But it wasn't the slap that had stung him, Varia knew. He'd harassed her before, in the Packard, with the curtains drawn and Armik driving. And Idri had allowed it, to a point. Perhaps she rationalized it as punishment for Varia's deserting the Sisterhood, but basically she had a sadistic streak. Sitting in front, she'd ignored Varia's muffled complaints, grunted through her gag, but when Xader's hand went into his victim's pants, as it invariably had, Idri had turned as if she had eyes in the back of her head, slapped him, and chewed him out. He'd laughed and stopped—in his brutal, offensive way he was good-natured—but in an hour or two resumed his harassment.

No, what stung him now, Varia told herself, were the witnesses, the tribesmen who'd seen it. And no doubt he considered himself entrapped, for this time he'd been slapped without even putting his hand up her dress.

Varia wondered if this meant the end of his abuse. With her gag out, she could complain in words, and Idri could hardly ignore her.

The tribesmen at the gate had been respectful enough. At Idri's order, one had led them to the village headman, who'd loaned them horses and an escort. There Idri had removed Varia's handcuffs, and both had dressed themselves in tribesmen's breeches, for riding. Then they'd ridden to Oztown and the chief's compound, arriving at dusk. Idri wasted no time; made arrangements that same evening for a squad of warriors as an escort. They left the next morning at sunup, riding eastward through mildly rolling wooded hills, and occasional large openings with farms and villages.

Xader left Varia carefully alone, though from time to time she felt his eyes.

They traveled till dusk before camping. The new escort were swaggerers, warriors of the chief's own elite. Undoubtedly they'd heard of the rape at Ferny Cove, for they eyed the Sisters appraisingly, without the respect they might once have shown. But they'd said or done nothing more offensive than look. Then Idri started the supper fires with simple hand gestures, reminding them of the Sisters' reputation for dangerous sorceries.

The escort ate separately from its charges, except that Idri invited their sergeant to sit beside her. When they'd eaten, the escort and Xader had laid down their beds a little distance from the Sisters, screened by undergrowth. The men, including Xader, had warm sleeping robes against the night chill. The Sisters, with their powers, used only a pallet and a single light blanket.

Varia was awakened by a powerful hand clutching her throat, cutting off her air. The voice that murmured to her was Xader's, and she smelled whiskey on his breath. "There's a knife in my other hand," he said. "One sound and you're dead." He let go her throat then, threw the blanket aside, fumbled with the drawstring on her breeches and began tugging them down. She could sense the knife an inch from her throat; it move to her belly as he got her breeches off her buttocks.

"Idri will crucify you for this," she whispered.

Xader chuckled, seemingly without rancor. "Idri's over by the creek bank, bobbing up and down on that sergeant's pole. And when she's done with him, she'll sleep like a sow—like the sow she is." Again he chuckled. "I know."

Her breeches were down to her knees now, down to her ankles. She struggled, twisting from side to side, intensely conscious of the knife. *Idri pushed you too far yesterday,* she thought panting. *When she wakes up, I'll be dead and you'll be gone. Sarkia will chain her in a Tiger barracks for that, but it won't do me any good.* He pricked her waist with the knife tip then, numbing her will, and using a bare foot, freed her of her breeches. Then, bare from the waist down, he forced himself between her knees. *The Sisterhood must be in bad shape,* she thought, *or you wouldn't dare do this. Sarkia would set Tomm himself on your trail.*

Once more he chuckled. "Put it in for me," he said. His face smirked in hers, his breath reeking. "I'll show you what a good man's like."

She might have cooperated—it seemed her best chance for survival—but his boast was an affront to Curtis. Reaching down as if to comply, she found his testicles, and willed a powerful jolt of electricity through them. The knife which had jabbed her waist, she fully expected to plunge into her guts, but in his agony, he lost it. As he screamed, she squeezed, with hands that had milked cows for years.

With all her strength, she rolled him off, still clutching, willed another jolt, then tore his scrotum half off, cords stretching and giving. His body doubled with spasm, then went slack. She didn't entirely trust his unconsciousness, and held on grimly while scanning with her cat vision for the knife. Someone, a sentry, had grabbed a torch and hurried over, stopping a few yards off to stare. Glancing back over her shoulder, Varia's large green eyes caught the man's and held them, dominating him even as she crouched over Xader with her buttocks bared. "Never try to rape a Sister," she hissed at him, "or you'll end up like this one."

Round-eyed, the sentry said nothing. The whole camp had wakened at Xader's scream, but they kept back. Except for Idri, who arrived only partly covered by the sergeant's long, unbuttoned tunic, his saber in her hand. Xader's eyes were open again, wide and glazed with shock, and sweat greased his forehead, though the night was chill. Varia sent another jolt through him, not as strong, bringing a thin whinny of pain.

Idri cursed. "Let him go!" she ordered.

Varia did, snatching her breeches from the ground. "Go ahead, Xader," she said. "Here's your chance to tell her what you told me: that she's a sow in heat."

Psychically Varia felt the crackle of Idri's rage, but it wasn't aimed at her. The Sister stepped and thrust, the saber striking Xader beneath the ribs and riding in. He squawked like air released from a bladder, then went slack again, and blood stained his twill shirt, purchased at J.C. Penney's in Evansville, Indiana, in another universe. Idri wiped her blade first on his bare thigh, then on his sleeve. "Leave him here," she told the wide-eyed sentry. "Let the vermin clean his bones." She turned her gaze to Varia. "Put your breeches on. You have my apologies, for what they're worth. I should have known he'd try something like this."

Their gazes met and briefly locked, and it was Idri's that turned away. *Yes,* Varia thought as she pulled her breeches on, *you knew what he was like. Probably he'd been in trouble for bothering local women at Ferny Cove, and you saved his skin. You'd love having power over an oversexed fool like that.*

But she said none of it. They had hundreds of miles to go, and she was Idri's prisoner.

6

Welcome Home!

On the third day after crossing the Great Muddy River, they rode down out of wooded hills into the broad east-west valley of the Green River, an extensively cleared plain. At the edge of vision to the north they could see high hills dark with forest. The country they traveled through was new to Varia, though not to Idri, who whenever they crossed into a new kingdom, arranged for local escorts.

Unlike the west side of the Great Muddy, the people here lived under kings. The highway the Sisters rode was dirt—mud after rains—and along it, the farmers lived in tiny hamlets at intervals of a mile or less, half a dozen to a dozen cottages in each, plus outbuildings. Every few miles stood a village, and about once a day they came to a real town, with a reeve's palisaded fort. On a few occasions the party slept in inns, but more commonly, Idri obtained space for them at some manor house.

Clearly the Sisterhood retained some part of its old reputation and respect here, for nowhere were they refused an escort, or food or lodging. Though the obsequiousness common before the disaster at Ferny Cove was reduced now mostly to courteous or sometimes grudging compliance.

As they rode, Varia had abundant time to think. She and Idri had little to say to each other; their antagonism dated from long before Varia had arrived at Evansville with Curtis Macurdy. As girls, they'd vied for a coveted executive apprenticeship in the Dynast's office, and Varia had been chosen on the basis of a higher responsibility score, superior

40

7

Tigers!

She slept through breakfast and most of the morning, wakening slowly, aware finally that she'd slept the clock around. *Up!* she told herself. *Up and face the day!* Then burrowed deeper into the security and comfort of the thick feather mattress.

But when she peeked again, the clock (which bore the name *Westclox* on its face and had been made in Norcross, Georgia, in another universe) said 11:32, and she discovered she was hungry. So dragging herself from bed, she washed and dressed, and by noon had joined a growing crowd of attractive women, ages twelve to perhaps ninety, in the dining room. She was among the earlier arrivals, and there was room beside her, but somehow Liiset, when she came in, took a seat at the other end of the room. Without acknowledging her wave or meeting her eyes.

A guardsman intercepted her as she left. (Recognizing identities among look-alikes was a talent that turned on early in the Sisterhood, with both girls and boys, even among those like Idri who did not see auras.) His face told her nothing, and his aura scarcely more, for this errand meant little to him, but she followed with an empty feeling. To the Dynast's office.

When she entered, she knew at once that here was trouble, the trouble she'd avoided thinking about. Two persons awaited her. One was Idri, with a look of hard-eyed satisfaction. The other was the Dynast, older than any other Sister, ever, by at least a century. A Sister of awesomely long life and memory. She'd been Dynast when Curtis's great-great-grandfather had run away. Yet she could pass easily for twenty-five, if you ignored her eyes and aura.

"Welcome home, Sister Varia," Sarkia said amiably. "I see you're pregnant."

It didn't show physically yet, but any Sister who could see auras could tell.

"You realize why you're here, of course."

Varia nodded. This would be her hearing for refusing an order, and perhaps for desertion. "Yes, Sister Sarkia."

"Very well." The Dynast recited the charges in an almost kindly tone. "Do you deny either of them, in kind or in spirit?"

"No, Sister Sarkia."

"Can you cite extenuating circumstances?"

"Only that the events at Ferny Cove were described to me as much more drastic than they actually were. It seemed to me that the Sisterhood had been destroyed."

The Dynast's eyes and aura showed no agitation. "But obviously it was not," she said. "You lacked faith, no doubt because of your long separation from us. Well. We must get you back into the spirit of service and discipline. Yours is our most fertile clone, and you and Will Macurdy much our most fertile pairing. You should have brought his nephew through, as ordered." She paused, seeming to consider. "I'm assigning you to duties in the crèche; this will go well with your pregnancy. Meanwhile you'll maintain your physical health by participating in the morning drills."

She stopped there and sat wordless for a minute, her eyes holding Varia like a bug on a pin. "Then, after a suitable post-partum recovery, you will be assigned to a Tiger barracks for re-impregnation."

A sudden stone sat heavily in Varia's bowels. The Tiger clones had been bred and culled for a hardness of spirit, and they were notoriously infertile. And there was more, she realized; the Dynast was not done.

"During your assignment in the crèche, you will be supervised by Sister Maliv. During your assignment in the Tiger barracks, Sister Idri will see to your welfare, and make sure you are properly chastened and corrected."

Varia had never seen Idri smile before.

✧   ✧   ✧

While living and working at the crèche, Varia managed mostly not to dwell on her sentence. Only occasionally did she think of it, sometimes at the sight of a Tiger striding lithe and hard down some path. And sometimes when she wiped and washed some boy infant, or awakened from nightmare. Gestation seemed scarcely to take weeks, though she'd been in the Cloister more than four months when she was taken to the lying-in ward. To her surprise and dismay, Sarkia was there, and Idri.

She was delivered of two boys, about two and a half pounds each, but vigorous. When infants and mother had been cleaned up, and the babes taken to be fed (they were too small to nurse), Varia's eyes went to the Dynast, and stuck on her gaze. Sarkia's lips had thinned and twisted.

Because she'd borne only the two, Varia realized. Had only willed two, those first hours after fertilization, when in her self-induced trance, she might have willed half a dozen. Like their ylvin progenitors, most Sisters were relatively infertile. Which meant spending several nights in a breeding room each month, with selected partners. Usually the experience was enjoyable, for typically their partners were skilled and pleasant, and it was how things were done in the Sisterhood. And when a Sister became pregnant, she was expected to produce as large a litter as was safe. Five was usual.

But conception with Curtis had taken place in a different world, and the future she'd had in mind had been a different future.

Sarkia turned to Idri and muttered: "Do what you will with her."

For the second time, Varia saw Idri smile.

Over the following two months she continued in the crèche, nursing infants of mothers who had other duties, and after a bit, her own. After the first six weeks her nursing duties were gradually reduced till in the third month she went dry. And knew her sentence would soon begin.

Even so it began with a shock. Two grinning Tigers banged into her room one evening, running her roommates out. While one held her arms painfully behind her back, the other chopped her hair off with scissors, then shaved her head, leaving numerous nicks behind. When he was done, they stripped her roughly, put a coarse woolen shift on her, and hustled her from the building, arms behind her back again. That sack-like shift, which fell short of her knees, was all the clothing left to her.

Tiger barracks were different from Sister barracks—temporary squad huts with bath and latrine. Normally two half-sibling clones made a squad, and eight grinning Tigers were waiting when Varia was propelled into their breeding room. For a minute she was pushed-thrown back and forth among them like a beach ball, staggering, reeling around the small ring of naked Tigers, never allowed to fall. Then the shift was pulled from her, and the sergeant, exerting his prerogative, threw her on the bed and took her roughly.

The first round was quick. The sergeant took perhaps a minute, while the others, having watched, were mostly quicker, and she'd begun to feel hopeful that this wouldn't be as bad as she'd feared. But though their fertility was low, they had the sexual energy of youth. Thus those who'd finished, restimulated by watching the others, had a second round which took much longer, and in some cases sadistic forms. Long before that round was done, Varia was weeping silently in blind desolation. She wasn't really aware when the still longer, much rougher third round began, and was unconscious well before it was over.

She awoke in the empty bath. Awoke when the Tiger sentry threw a bucket of cold water on her, then threw her shift at her, and watched grinning while she pulled it on. A sober-faced guardsman waited outside, and led her to the kitchen, barefoot and in only her wet shift, through twenty degree cold and two inches of snow. She was hardly aware of it, though she shivered violently. Most of the Sisterhood had the power to produce additional body heat by mentally controlling cellular respiration levels and circulation. In Varia's state of shock, only shivering was available to her.

At the kitchen, a younger Sister waited, an adolescent. Big-eyed at what she saw, the girl showed Varia her duties, demonstrating and helping, while Varia emerged somewhat from shock, becoming more aware, watching and duplicating:

Fires were laid, then lit, in the dining room stove, the stack of ovens, and the great ceramic cookstove, and replenished in the large ceramic water heater, for the hot springs weren't hot enough for kitchen needs.

It was now that Varia, hobbling and unable to stand straight, realized fully how sore she was. When the instructions were finished, and Varia, outside in the cold, had begun splitting the day's firewood, the girl vanished. Meanwhile, with the exertion and the partial return of her mental faculties, Varia had stopped shivering.

Fifteen minutes later the chief cook arrived, the Sister in charge of the kitchen, a large, strong-looking woman, handsome instead of pretty. Arrived well ahead of her usual hours, and came out to the woodpile to peer at Varia in the darkness. The woman's lips were as thin and twisted as Sarkia's had been at Varia's delivery.

Her voice was rough. "What's wrong with you?" she demanded.

Voice dead, face wooden, Varia told her, and began shivering again, violently. The woman took her arm and steered her brusquely into the kitchen where there was light, squinted at the black eye, the split and swollen lips. "Take off your shift," she ordered.

Varia did, without emotion.

"Good God!" The cook looked at the myriad black bruises and bloody spots on thighs and buttocks, arms and breasts, for when Varia had gone into shock, the Tigers had pinched and struck her, even jabbed her with knife tips, trying to elicit movement. "Here, girl," the woman said, and helped her onto a table. There, by the light of an oil lamp, she examined her as a gynecologist might have. Varia was literally raw, fore and aft, despite being slimed with semen, and undoubtedly had vaginal and rectal lesions that could become infected. Swearing, the woman turned to the now-shivering girl who'd fetched her.

"Go outside and bring me the guard."

The girl ran, and the guard came in, looking worried.

"Where did you get her?" the cook demanded.

He told her.

"*That* clone! Go back there and wake up the sergeant." The

guard blanched; he was scarcely out of adolescence himself. "Tell that pile of shit his mother wants him in this kitchen within ten minutes, or I'll see his balls on my butcher block."

She hadn't raised her voice, but the intensity behind it allowed no noncompliance. As the guard reached the door, she shouted after him, "Make sure you tell him exactly what I said."

Then she sent Varia with the adolescent girl, hobbling off barefoot to the infirmary.

She was in the infirmary for three days. On the second, the chief cook came to see her. "I talked to the sergeant," the woman said. "He's one of my sons. He said Idri told him they should do whatever they wanted with you, the rougher the better. So when Idri came in to breakfast, I was waiting for her. I took her to the woodpile and shook hell out of her. She took it, too." The woman's smile was grim. "I was bred to produce Tigers. I could twist her head off if I wanted, and she knew I was on the edge. All she could say was, she was going to report me to the Dynast."

The cook laughed, a dry bark. "I'm eighty-eight years old, girl. At my age you don't have many years left before decline, and you think a bit, some of us, most of us, of how your points will balance after death; what penalties and penances might await you. Makes it easier to take the bull by the horns. In midmorning the Dynast called me to her. I told her what you'd looked like, and what my son had said.

"She didn't say a thing, but I saw her jaw tighten. Later her secretary stopped to tell me not to worry about anything Idri might want to do." Again she snorted. "As if I would. Sarkia told her she'd wanted you punished, not killed. And ordered her to latrine detail for a week; she'll love that, high and mighty as she sees herself.

"Then she had your sergeant in. Not that she raked him over the coals like I did; he's just a Tiger, the way she designed him. But she set him straight. You'll find things better when you go back."

The cook left then. And of all she'd said, the words that stuck in Varia's mind were four: "When you go back." She'd have to go back to that place.

8

A Plan Enacted

When Varia left the infirmary at the end of the third day, she was in better condition physically than she'd expected to be. She'd been enough years on Farside that she'd come to judge healing by the standards there. In the Cloister, what they lacked in science, they more than made up for with healing touches, and formulas spoken instead of manufactured.

She left wearing more than her shift, too. The healer had found a pair of work breeches for her, and mittens, and ill-fitting boots, all shabby enough to fit her punishment status, but far better than only the shift, which now became her shirt.

At the barracks, the sergeant had already given orders orally, rules of conduct toward their woman. The first was short term: she was not to be bothered that night. The second was, she was not to be struck or pinched or otherwise hurt. The third, she was not to be sodomized again, or anything done to her that could not result in pregnancy. Further, no man was to take her more than once every other night; a schedule would be posted. *That still means four each evening,* she told herself, and felt desolation wash through her again. The best she could do was remind herself it wouldn't start for another twenty-four hours.

That was the first night she thought of escape. She didn't let her mind dwell on it though; the difficulties would seem insuperable. Something she did look at was the season. She'd have no chance at all, fleeing through the wilderness, before spring came. Late spring. The mental power to warm herself was limited by her level of biological energy. On a winter night

51

it would protect her for only a few hours, leaving her famished. It worked best when the temperature stress was moderate.

Till then she'd survive, she told herself, grow strong, and hopefully come through this without getting pregnant. Given the Tigers' low fertility, she could be optimistic.

The next morning she built and lit the kitchen fires, split a pile of wood, then during breakfast helped the adolescent scullery girls who washed the breakfast dishes, scrubbed pots and pans, and cleaned the kitchen. Before noon she ate lunch, again with the scullery girls, and went "home" for the rest of the day, sleeping most of it. Home to a room kept for breeding, its windows barred against the rare maverick like herself who might think of escape.

Supper too she ate in the scullery; ate lightly. Then, half brave, half terrified, returned to the Tiger barracks and what awaited her there.

At seven that evening, the first on the day's breeding roster entered her room, finished and left in brief minutes. Then she washed herself and sat mentally frozen, waiting on her chair. The next appeared at seven-thirty, and the next at eight. None of the three spoke. Two of them, though not blatantly abusive, were surly and rough. As if she'd wronged them, she thought bitterly; as if they blamed her for the schedule. As if it were their right to enjoy a violent hours-long orgy every night, with her the sole victim.

At eight-thirty the sergeant walked in, closed the door behind him and paused. His angle of erection was about 135 degrees. "I'm sorry about that other night," he said.

She stared. *Sorry? That helps some, I guess. After the last two it does.* "Thank you for telling me," she said quietly. "I— I appreciate that."

He came to her then and stood over her. "I don't know your name," she said.

"Skortov."

But when he mounted her, he was nothing more than a machine, driving hard, finishing, and leaving without another word.

❖   ❖   ❖

A few days later, another woman was assigned to the squad. Each evening two of the Tigers went to a breeding room in a women's barracks. This too was a punishment action, less severe than her own but still punishment, for the Sister would be receptive to impregnation only briefly each month, yet she'd be used each night, and now only two men an evening visited Varia. But the reduction in her breeding schedule was brief. With rare quickness the other Sister became pregnant, and again Varia took on four of them each evening. When they'd finished, a tide of desolation would sweep over her. To keep from weeping, she'd daydream herself to sleep, daydream of escape, and reunion with Curtis.

Only one of the Tigers, named Corgan, treated her with blatant cruelty, masturbating before his turn, then humping her long and violently, painfully. And when his stint as sentry coincided with her time to leave for the kitchen, just before 3 A.M., he'd stop her on the doorstep, groping and kissing her roughly before he'd let her pass. She didn't report it to Skortov; didn't want to cause dangerous resentments within the squad, resentments that inevitably would worsen things for her.

Once she'd asked Skortov why sentries were posted outside the barracks door. It was standard for Tiger barracks, he said. To Varia it was apparent that he'd never before wondered, and it seemed to her that something was lacking in the Tigers— this clone at least—lacking in either their genes or their training or both. They ought to wonder about anything as pointless as that.

Winter's occasional snows and ice storms ended, and spring flowers bloomed. In the nearby human community, oxen pulled plows through wet soil, followed by the plowmen, and by crows that feasted on the worms and grubs exposed. On the shrubs, buds swelled and broke. Her head was shaved again. Trees began to green, lilacs bloomed, and Varia began to plan how she'd equip herself and get over the palisade. Once outside she'd have to improvise, steal a horse or maybe just walk. Afoot she'd leave a harder trail to follow.

She didn't deceive herself that her prospects were good. Guards would be sent after her, perhaps even Tigers, and if she were caught . . . Thinking of that, she almost changed her mind. If she stayed, she told herself, surely she'd get pregnant before too much longer. Then she'd will sixlings, be moved out of the Tiger barracks and in with her clone. Sarkia would be pleased with her, perhaps let her work in the crèche, or the ceramics shop.

It was that thought that renewed her resolve. She realized she didn't want to live with Liiset, who'd abandoned her. And especially she didn't want to please Sarkia. It was Sarkia who'd told Idri, "Do what you will with her." In effect, who'd caused that terrible night. She should have known.

Or had she? Did she use Idri to do her evil, the evil that Idri was so attracted to, then step forward to rescue the abused? Gaining the victim's gratitude and devotion, even adoration? The thought was like a blow to the stomach.

No, she'd definitely go, at an hour that would give her a long start. About midnight, for like all her clones, she could see in the dark like a cat. A night of hard rain would be best; it would wash out her trail. Then she'd have to keep ahead of any tracker sent after her. It was Tomm who frightened her most, Sarkia's best tracker. She'd heard he could follow a psychic trace as readily as tracks; she'd have to cast a web of confusion whenever she changed direction or paused to rest.

And move fast; that was important. Stay off established trails, head north and west, make her way to Ferny Cove, and go through the gate to Curtis. They'd go somewhere far from Evansville. To Oregon, a land of fertile valleys. They'd talked about Oregon before.

But she'd have to avoid recapture, or God only knew what Sarkia might have done to her. She wondered if she could survive a week like that first night.

Over the next weeks she varied the time she left for her morning duties. Normally she started for the kitchen just before the twelve to three sentry got off, but now she sometimes left just afterward, when the three to six sentry was on duty. That way if she didn't show, each would assume she'd leave, or had left, on the other's watch, and she wouldn't be missed until the cook and her assistant arrived at the kitchen about five-thirty. Cook would no doubt be furious, assume she'd overslept, and send the guard running to have her wakened. There'd be confusion then, and a search would hardly be started much before seven.

The last half of May was unusual, rainless. Finally, on the first of June, late evening brought thunder and wind. Near midnight the rain began, beating on the roof.

And suddenly fear stuck the breath in Varia's throat, for this was the time, if it was to be. For several long minutes she listened to the drumming. At last, pushing out of her paralysis, she put her boots and breeches on, and the leather belt she'd asked Skortov for. Then, from beneath her mattress, she took a stolen meat knife sheathed in a tough oven mitt she'd taken. Fumbling, hands trembling, she strung it on the belt through the slits she'd cut. Finally she put her shift on over it, hiding it.

She snuffed out her oil lamp, then opened her door a few inches to peer into the men's sleeping room. For a long minute she watched and listened, gathering her nerve. Then the latrine door opened, and she was looking at the bright yellow flame of the latrine's oil lamp. She froze. Her eyes, adjusted to the dark, were briefly dazzled by the lamp, and she didn't recognize the man who stepped out.

It seemed to her he must have seen her, seen her eye peering past the doorpost, but somehow he hadn't. Turning away, he started for the front of the barracks, fully clothed, and she realized what was happening. It was midnight; he was relieving the watch. *Good God!* she thought. *How could I have overlooked that?* Her stomach churned. Was this an omen? If she'd been challenged crossing their sleeping room, she'd have been in serious trouble. Her lie wouldn't convince them all.

Through the barracks door, she saw the two Tigers' backs as they exchanged murmurs on the front stoop. Then the man off watch came in and went straight to the latrine. As soon as its door closed behind him, she swallowed her fear and slipped out, moving quietly, trying to seem legitimate. Opening the barracks door, she stepped onto the stoop—and it was Corgan who stood on guard with his spear at port arms. Her heart nearly stopped as he turned and scowled, but she had enough presence of mind to close the door behind her. The rain still fell, cascading noisily from both sides of the small roof sheltering the stoop.

"What're you doing out here?" he growled. "It's not three o'clock."

My God! If he gropes me, he'll find my belt and knife! "I've got a boyfriend."

"A boyfriend? You?"

"What's the matter? Don't you think I can have a boyfriend? All you Tigers do is hump me. I need loving from time to time." She stepped off the stoop into the rain, pausing to peer back at him. He stood puzzled, confused: The concept was beyond him. "Tell you what," she said. "When it's your turn tomorrow, if you'll take the time to stroke me a little, and kiss me nicely enough, I'll give you a special treat."

She turned then and trotted off through the downpour toward the kitchen, giggling on the edge of hysteria. When she got there, she refastened her belt on the outside of her shift. Cook had set aside two large loaves of yesterday's bread to make dressing with, and she tucked them inside her shift. The belt would keep them in. She followed them with a large slab cut from a cheese. It occurred to her then that the bread, if it got too wet, might come apart inside her shift, and looked around for something to repel the rain. *The oil-cloth in the vegetable room!* she thought. *I can wear it back-side out so the white won't show.* She took it from its table, but the rough back side was a pale beige, still too visible in the dark. With one of the knives hanging there, she cut a hole in it for her head, then smeared lard on the rough side, the beige side. That done, she opened the soot door behind the stack of ovens, and smeared soot into the lard until the oil cloth was black. *Now if the rain doesn't wash it off . . .*

She slipped it on black side out, then washed her hands. The lye soap didn't lather much, but it removed the sooty lard. She gave one last look around, thinking of the problems she was leaving for the cook—the nearest she had to a friend; Liiset had avoided her since their reunion. Clenching her teeth, Varia laid and lit fires beneath the oven stack and in the stoves, and replenished the fire in the water heater. It took a few minutes, but she would not wrong the cook by leaving them cold.

Then she went into the rain again. It had eased considerably, and that worried her. If it stopped, instead of her tracks being washed out, they'd be conspicuous in the rain-softened ground. For a moment she considered cancelling the attempt. She could hide the oil-cloth under the floor, for the kitchen was built on blocks, then sleep in the kitchen for two hours, and do her job as if nothing was wrong.

Swearing, she shook the thought off and trotted toward the palisade. Who knew when a better time would come? Besides, tomorrow evening that damned Corgan might be pawing and kissing her, expecting his special treat.

The next question was, did any of the sentries on the east side of the palisade catwalk have night vision. Most clones didn't. The Tiger clones did, all of them she thought, but her impression was that they didn't pull sentry duty except in their own barracks. The sentries' attention should be outward, but in a time and territory of little threat, who knew where one of them might look. And surprised at seeing someone out in such weather, might track her with their eyes.

When she got near enough to see, all of them were huddled in the widely spaced watch shelters, out of the rain. Temporary log buildings had been built backed up against the inside of the palisade, some with ladders leaning against them. Choosing one well removed from any watch shelter, she climbed to its roof, which put the archers' catwalk within reach. In another moment she was crouched on it. The rain had intensified again, reducing visibility. Without hesitating she tossed her knife over the side, then clambered gingerly over the sharp-ended palisade logs, let herself down to arm's length and let go. The impact buckled her knees, and she sprawled heavily in weeds and mud. It took only seconds to find her knife. Threading it on her belt again, she trotted off northward, staying close to the stockade so she wouldn't be seen from above.

And despite the danger, and the cold rain that must gradually drain her energy, found herself suddenly exhilarated. She could do this! She really could! She could make it work, make her way to Ferny Cove, and to Macon County, or wherever Curtis was! Her dreams could come true despite everything.

9

The Lion Arrives in Oz

Curtis Macurdy hiked up the slope through deepening dusk. He'd lost the conjure woman's footpath, but it wasn't that which worried him. On a hill like Injun Knob, you couldn't miss the top. If you kept going uphill, you got there.

He wore a sheepskin jacket tied round his waist by the sleeves; he'd want it later to keep warm with, sitting or lying on the ground waiting for midnight. Just now, though, sweat slicked his forehead and he breathed deeply, not entirely from climbing. For there was fear, not of the gate, but that there would be no gate. That Varia was gone beyond finding, beyond recovery. It had been a month already. What might have happened to her in that month? Given how Idri hated her.

The fear had been kindled the night before, when he'd hiked that same slope, and spent the night on top in mists and drizzles, sitting, standing, dozing on the wet ground. And shivering despite the heavy jacket he'd paid two dollars for secondhand. When dawn had come with no gate, he'd hiked back down and asked the old conjure woman what had gone wrong. She'd cackled her brittle laugh and said he'd come the wrong night; come again the next.

The calendar in the sawmill had been for 1929, useless for 1930, so he'd judged by how the moon looked the night before: nearly full. When she'd told him it was the next night, he'd asked to see her calendar. She'd laughed at that, too. "Ain't

58

got no calendar," she'd said. "Know in my bones when the moon is full."

In Washington County, every kitchen had a calendar, and every calendar the phases of the moon. Lots of people planted, castrated pigs, and dehorned calves by the phases of the moon.

When he reached the top of Injun Knob this second try, it was dusk, the sky clear and the moon already up, its round fullness reassuring. After a night as wakeful as the one before, he expected to fall asleep nearly as soon as he sat down. But he sat anyway, almost exactly on the top, leaning against the largest tree available, a scrubby shortleaf pine. After a few minutes, he got up and put on his jacket, then sat back down. He felt ready for whatever happened—anything except nothing at all. A Smith & Wesson .44 hung on his belt, and a Winchester .45-70 buffalo gun lay across his lap, its thick octagonal barrel feeling heavy as a Model-T axle. Spare shells for both guns were buttoned in his jacket pockets.

The moonlight played tricks with his vision. Things moved in the shadows, images formed and shifted. And when his eyelids slid shut, Varia met him in a garden, a garden surrounded by a palisade like the pioneer forts in his history book. They walked into a house with a windmill by the back porch—it was Will's— and inside were three other Varias. "We're your wives," one of them said, and they pushed him down on a bed and undressed him. He was compliant, but when they pulled his underwear off, there was another set beneath them, and a set beneath them . . . Then he was on his feet. "Varia, he said, "this isn't going to work. It's got to be just you and me. I like your sisters all right, but . . ."

"I'm not Varia, I'm Liiset."

He looked around at the others, then back to the first. "No," he said, "you're Varia. Why are you trying to fool me like that?"

She started to cry, and they sat down on a fallen tree by the Sycamore Bend, he with his arms around her. "Honey," he said, "it's not going to work with all four of you. It's not. You're the only one I want." Still weeping, she started to fade out of his arms, less substantial than the transparent Varia back on the farm. "Don't go away!" he cried. "I came all this way to get you back!"

He awoke shouting, lunging to his feet, the heavy buffalo gun clopping against bare bedrock. He didn't notice, his mind still caught up in the dream. *Oh God!* he thought, *don't let it be like that!* Then blinking, looked around, breathing hard. It was quiet and peaceful, the full moon shining down between sparse trees. This was still Missouri in the U.S. of A., he was sure of it. Had midnight come and gone? The only directions he knew for certain were up and down. The moon could still be east of south, or . . . He found the dipper and the pointers, then the Pole Star faint in the moonlight. Not midnight yet; not for a while. He bent, picked up his rifle and sighted on the moon. The sights were undamaged, hadn't struck the rock. With a sigh he turned up his collar, sat back down against the pine, and letting his eyes close again, slept.

With a deep thrumming resonance, the gate spit him out of nightmare, rolling across the ground in bright sunlight. He woke like a frightened tomcat, hair on end, and scrambled staggering to his feet, grabbing for a rifle that wasn't there. So he snatched at his holster, drew the .44, and looked around wild-eyed. Four men stood a little way off, watching him and laughing, talking some foreign lingo he might have heard once before, when Varia and Idri had lashed each other that day in Evansville.

The men started toward him, and bracing his legs against residual dizziness, Macurdy drew his revolver. His wits began to adjust, and he was aware that they carried short spears pointed his way. He pointed the revolver back at them, and when they kept coming, jabbed it in their direction. They stopped eight or ten feet away, spears at the ready. A stride forward and thrust, by any of them, and he'd be meat. One, the leader, said something to him, he had no idea what.

"Stay back," he answered. "I don't want to hurt no one."

The man spoke more sharply, and jabbed the spear at him, its point almost reaching him. Macurdy jumped backward and pulled the trigger—and nothing happened. He felt the hammer release and strike, heard it click, but no shot fired. He pulled again, and again nothing. He knew he'd loaded all six chambers. Staring around, he spied the rifle lying in the grass too far away.

The man had been saying something more. Now the others moved behind Macurdy, who looked at the revolver and swung the cylinder out. From each chamber, a center-fire cartridge peered back at him, two of them indented by the firing pin. The spearmen watched curiously. Reseating the cylinder, he tried again, and once more it clicked, so he slid the weapon back into its holster. Then a spear jabbed his left buttock, and with a yell, Macurdy jumped forward. Once more the leader spoke, beckoning, and Macurdy followed him.

On this side, the gate was in a grassy grove of large old basswood trees. The place looked nothing like Injun Knob; there wasn't even a knoll, a hump. Within a couple of minutes they were out of the woods, crossing open pasture. Several times more the spear jabbed one buttock or the other. Limping now, Macurdy felt blood trickling down the back of both legs. At each jab he jumped, and someone laughed. Glancing over his shoulder, he identified his tormentor, then the leader snapped another order and the jabbing ceased.

The pasture ended at a wide potato field. Macurdy could see a crew of men hoeing some distance away. He trudged between the potato hills, three spearmen spread behind him while their leader walked ahead. Across the field was a considerable village of log buildings.

His captors took him to a small hut, one of numerous surrounded by a twelve-foot palisade. The leader opened the door, and—Macurdy turned abruptly, grabbed the shaft of the spear that had jabbed him, wrenched it free, and doing a horizontal haft stroke, struck his tormentor on the side of the head with the hard hickory shaft. The man staggered sideways and Macurdy was on him, grabbed him by his waistband and his wadmal shirt and slammed him head first against the log wall. Then let him fall, and stood with his hands raised above his own head in submission.

The leader barked rapid words, then strode over to the fallen man, and bending, spoke to him. When the man didn't move, he kicked him, and made some rough comment. Briefly he looked Macurdy in the eye, then grunted an order to the remaining two spearmen. One jabbed their captive hard in the belly with a spear butt, and Macurdy doubled over. The other struck him above an ear, and he fell to his knees. Moccasin-like boots began kicking him, and he dropped the rest of the way, curling up in a ball. Someone rolled him onto his back astraddle of him, fists striking at his face. Except to shield himself with his forearms, Macurdy made no resistance, and after half a minute, the leader barked another order. Reluctantly, Macurdy's pummeler got to his feet.

Macurdy got slowly to his own. Hands grasped him, frog-marched him to the door of the hut and propelled him inside, where he fell sprawling on the floor. A moment later his sheepskin jacket was thrown in after him.

The floor he lay on was dirt. The only light came through the door, and through foot-square windows, one each in three of the walls. Beneath one of them was a trestle table with a bench on one side and a water bucket. The place smelled of wood smoke and damp ground.

An old man stood in a corner, and after a moment spoke to him—in American! "You're wearing Farside clothes!"

Macurdy got to hands and knees, then stood up, fingers exploring his face gingerly. "My name's Curtis Macurdy," he said. "From Washington County, Indiana originally, but I've been working at Neeley's Corners, in Missouri." He examined the old man, perhaps six feet tall once, now gaunt and somewhat bent, with one shoulder carried lower than the other. And bearded. Macurdy wasn't used to beards, hadn't seen half a dozen beards in his life.

The old man sat down as if weighted by Macurdy's gaze. "Did you just now"—he waved vaguely—"arrive through the, ah, aperture between universes?"

"I came through the gate on Injun Knob."

"How do you feel?"

Macurdy reached back, feeling his behind. "Not too good. That sonofabitch I slammed against the wall had been jabbing my rear end with his spear all the way from the woods." He stepped to the door and peered out. The unconscious man had been taken away, but one of the others had been left on guard. The man scowled at Macurdy, and gestured threateningly with his spear.

"Okay," Macurdy said placatingly in his direction. "Okay.

I'm not looking for trouble. I don't doubt you're good to your wife and mother, and all I want to do is get along."

He backed away from the door, bent painfully and picked up his jacket, then straightened and looked the cabin over. It was about twelve by twelve feet, and low roofed. On one wall hung two sleeping pads, long sacks of straw. A pair of split-plank shelves had been built on another. At the windowless end was a mud and stick fireplace; a copper kettle and ladle hanging beside it. Embers glowed beneath a blanket of wood ash.

"And you just arrived?" the man asked. "Just now?"

"Yep."

"You don't feel ill?"

"Nope."

"Remarkable. When my companion and I came through, eight years ago, we arrived desperately ill. I had a fever, cramps, and severe diarrhea for two days. My companion was so ill, I feared for his life. I've been told that two young men died after coming through, some years before we did."

"How about two women and one man, a month ago?"

"What did they look like?"

"The women looked young, like maybe twenty years, one of them pretty, the other one twice as pretty. The prettiest one had red hair, the other reddish brown."

"And green eyes?"

"Green and tilty. What happened to them?"

"I understand they were provided with horses and an escort, and left. I didn't actually see them. They're said to belong to a powerful, um—it translates to Sisterhood, but actually it seems to be some sort of politically influential power group." He paused, curious. "What do you know of them?"

"I'm married to the red-headed one. Her name is Varia. She's a sort of witch, but nothing bad. No deals with the devil or anything."

"I've heard," the man said, "that one arrived manacled."

"That's her. That's my wife. They came and took her away while I was in town. I followed them to get her back, but didn't catch up with them, so I got me a rifle and pistol, and waited till the gate opened again." He drew the .44. "Lost the rifle when I came through, and this didn't work when I tried to use it."

"Ah. Ours didn't either. We'd thought perhaps it was the ammunition, but if yours didn't . . ."

"Maybe guns don't work in this world."

The old man shook his head. "Our human biochemistry functions properly here. I can't imagine why nitrocellulose wouldn't explode." He sighed, got up carefully and held out a hand. "Excuse my lack of manners. I am, or was, Doctor Edward Talbott, a professor of psychology at the University of Missouri. Just now my profession is slave, and normally at this time of day, I'd be working at some sort of hard labor. Yesterday, however, I was quite ill, with a fever, so I've been given a day to recover. My health has been surprisingly good here, so far as infections are concerned. My problems have been structural: arthritis, actually."

"Mine is that sonofabitch's spear. I don't suppose you'd look at my rear end and see how bad he stabbed me?"

"I can look, but I'm afraid I have nothing for bandages. Just a moment." A fat stub of candle squatted on the table. He took it to the fireplace and lit it at an ember, then came back. Macurdy pulled down his overalls and trousers and bent over a bit. "They don't seem severe," Talbott said. "The bleeding has stopped, though obviously there was quite a bit of it earlier."

Macurdy pulled his trousers up and sat down on the bench, hissing with pain as he did. Then they talked. Macurdy didn't have to pump Talbott; the professor was starved to talk with someone newly from the other side. Mostly he talked about this side; things the newcomer needed to know. He also speculated that the sergeant who'd brought Macurdy in might suspect him of connections with the Sisterhood. "That would account for your arriving functional," he added, "and for his treating you with restraint, despite what you did to one of his men."

He changed the subject. "You referred to your wife as a witch. What does she do that seems 'witchy'? I'm very interested in the paranormal; it's what drew me to Injun Knob."

"What she does ain't any kind of normal," Macurdy answered. "For one thing, when I was five years old, she could pass for twenty. And when I was twenty-five, she could still pass for twenty, just as easy. And she can lay a spell on you, at least if you're willing.

"She says I've got the blood line for magic, too—that my great-great-grampa ran away from the Sisterhood. For a couple of weeks she spelled me about every evening and had me doing drills. To 'open up my powers,' she said. Which might be why I didn't get sick, crossing over. But I never showed much sign of magic powers."

Macurdy got off the bench, wincing again. Going to the candle, he took a cartridge from his pistol and pried the bullet out with his jackknife, planning to toss the powder onto the embers, to see if it flared up. But when he shook the cartridge case over his palm, nothing came out. He peered inside it. Empty! They'd worked when he'd taken target practice. He tried another, then went to his jacket, and from a pocket took one of the large cartridges for the .45-70; it was empty too.

Grunting, he turned to Professor Talbott. "No powder. They were fine, three, four days ago."

Talbott said nothing, just sat staring at his hands, which lay folded on his knees. For a moment Macurdy stood thoughtful, then tossed the brass case into the ashes and sat down again. "You know what you never told me?" he said. "What they call this place. Not Missouri, I don't suppose."

"Oz." Talbott pronounced it *Ohz*. "Imagine it being spelled as in *The Wonderful Wizard of Oz*, but pronounced with a broad *O*."

"I remember that book. We had it in school." Macurdy grinned. "I didn't know you could get to Oz from Missouri. Thought you had to start from Kansas."

"Hmm. O-Z, but pronounced like in Ozark. I expected there'd be Ozarks on this side, too; expected to come out on something like Injun Knob."

"There are mountains not very far west of here," Talbott answered, "considerably higher than the Ozarks. You can see them in the daytime. They may be why the forests are so thick. We seem to have an orographically-enhanced summer monsoon here, off what they call the Southern Sea, which I suspect is less landlocked than the Gulf of Mexico. And the winters are wet, with frontal storms out of the west. Though the moisture for them might be from the Southern Sea, too, brought in by cyclonic circulation around the storm front."

Macurdy only half-listened, not comprehending at all. And at any rate seeing something more interesting to him. Talbott was a gaunt, bent, oldish man, his hair and beard mostly white but with black streaks. The lines in his leathery face reflected weather and hardship. His rough wadmal breeches were ingrained with dirt; his homespun shirt had been snagged and darned. His callused hands hadn't known soap for years, and their nails were black and broken.

But as Macurdy looked, the scarecrow figure became a tallish, lanky man in brown tweed and a green bow tie, clean-shaven and with his hair parted neatly in the middle. Dirt and calluses had no part of the image. He saw it plain as day, and it occurred to him that this kind of seeing was a magic power. Maybe, he told himself, going through the gate had jarred it loose for him.

They continued talking until Macurdy, who'd gone abruptly from midnight to noon, got sleepy. Talbott took down one of the straw-filled sleeping pads. Macurdy lay down on it and went to sleep.

To waken wide-eyed from some bad dream. Talbott had snuffed the candle, and the fire had burned down to embers again. Macurdy got up painfully and felt his way to the door, to stand outside gazing up at the sky. There was the Big Dipper, there the pointer stars. And there the North Star; in school, Mr. Anderson had called it the Pole Star, Polaris. Same stars, it seemed like, but a different world beneath them.

It struck him then that there was no longer a guard at the door. But there remained the palisade, and according to Talbott, a spearman who patrolled the night with a large dog on a leash. Escaping now made no sense anyway, Macurdy told himself. He needed to learn the language here, and something of the people, or he'd have no chance in hell of finding Varia.

10

The Shaman's Apprentice

When the slaves were mustered for the day's labor details, Macurdy and Talbott were put to work digging a large pit in stiff clay, the worst kind of pick and shovel labor. Brought up to work hard and fast, Macurdy impressed the overseer, and on the second day his ration was increased that evening.

Macurdy tried to share with Talbott, who would not accept it. "You need it. You're a much larger man," Talbott said, "and you work harder. But I appreciate your generosity. In a place like this, it's good to have a friend." On the other hand, Talbott insisted that Macurdy share the herb tea he made, with water heated in the small kettle.

Talbott had shared the hut for several years, but recently the other man had become unable to work, and died. Talbott wouldn't say of what. Macurdy guessed he'd been taken out and put down, like a crippled horse.

A man always worked with the man he lived with, Talbott went on. When larger crews worked together, only those who lived together were allowed to talk to each other. He assumed it was to prevent escapes or uprisings being planned. That fitted with the spearman and dog who circulated at night, looking into slave huts. No one was allowed in any but their own. And the guard at the single large slave latrine, who allowed no talking.

For his first months in Oz, Talbott had shared the hut with the young man he'd arrived with. Charles Hauser had been a doctoral candidate in physics, an ex-farmboy from up north in Marion County. Charles had learned the language here quite quickly, and that, along with his energy on the job, had impressed the Oz tribesmen. He learned fast and worked fast, and his practicality had resulted in job improvements. The Ozmen weren't generally open to suggestions from slaves, but they'd become receptive to Hauser's.

"Then," Talbott said, "he somehow became assigned to the local—uh—call him a shaman. Who . . ."

"What's a shaman?"

"He's a medicine man and magician, influential in local politics. Charles collects herbs for him and does routine chores. He also blows glass for him, not only bottles but crude lenses; he even made him a crude, low-powered microscope. And a simple, treadle-powered lathe, drill, grinder and tool sharpener, all in one, with hand-carved pulleys.

"They moved him in with the shaman. He sleeps in the workshop he built, and is allowed to do errands around the village. Charles comes to see me rather often. Usually he brings meat, especially fat pork in winter to help me through the cold weather. And the herbs I dutifully use to retain my health. He even got the shaman to see me one evening; the man actually helped me. Markedly. My arthritis had been severe enough then, that I felt in imminent danger of being done away with as useless."

He gestured at the kettle and its accessories. "Charles gave me those, to make the herb tea with. He also tried to get me easier work, but my particular talents aren't valuable here. And Charles is still a slave himself. He has no influence except through the shaman."

That night, Macurdy lay thinking he needed to get a special assignment like Hauser's. Not that he disliked physical labor; he enjoyed exerting his strength. But it seemed to him that working and living with Talbott, he'd learn little more than the language.

A few evenings later, Hauser came to visit, bringing a new supply of herbs. He was able to stay only minutes, and Macurdy, who'd gone to the latrine, missed him. Three days later at muster, instead of being sent to work with Talbott, he was turned over to a spearman who'd come to take him somewhere. They arrived at a long low house stuccoed with some sort of clay, and whitewashed. Moss and grass grew on its steep roof, and there were rather numerous windows, their shutters closed against the early morning chill, for they had no panes. Four chimneys marked four fireplaces, suggesting at least four rooms. It was one of the two or three most imposing structures in the village of Wolf Springs. The spearman knocked firmly but politely with his shaft.

The door opened almost at once, and Charles Hauser looked out. The spearman left Macurdy with him, and Hauser shook Macurdy's hand, then led him into an end room. The shaman looked up from his work table to gaze long and intently at his visitor before speaking at some length to Hauser. Hauser, in turn, spoke to Macurdy.

"Professor Talbott tells me you're descended from a Sisterhood breeding on one side."

"On my Dad's side, according to what my wife told me. And I guess on my Ma's, too, because her dad was a cousin of my dad's dad."

"He also told me your wife is one of the Sisters, and considered you to have a latent talent for magic. A talent that hadn't shown itself to you."

"Actually I guess it had. Only I hadn't recognized what it was—what was going on with me."

Hauser regarded him for a moment, then turned and gave the shaman a résumé before asking Macurdy what, specifically, those experiences had been. Macurdy told him of seeing Liiset in the corner of the ceiling, and finding the pictures in the attic. And finally of looking at Talbott and seeing a younger version in brown tweed, wearing a green bow tie.

Hauser nodded thoughtfully. "Green leather. It was probably the only tie he owned."

He and the shaman talked for two or three minutes then, Macurdy watching with no emotion stronger than interest. Finally Hauser turned to him again. "How did it happen that this Sister went to Farside and married into your family?"

Macurdy told him that, too, Hauser recapitulating it for the shaman. When he was done, the shaman gave what seemed to be instructions again. Finally Hauser turned back to Macurdy. "You're to go to Professor Talbott's hut now, get whatever you have there, and come back. A guard will go with you. You'll live here for now, but work for the village, as you've been doing. Only you'll get off early, and I'll teach you the language, and other things you need to know.

"My master's name is Arbel. From time to time he'll test you. And if things go well, especially if you learn to speak Yuultal well enough, he'll teach you things a shaman needs to know. No one else in the village has shown talent enough for him; he has high standards. And there are precedents for slaves being trained as shamans."

Hauser paused, still gazing at Macurdy, who said nothing. "He says he can see why your wife chose you. He says your aura . . ."

"What's an aura?"

Hauser grunted. "It's apparently like a halo, but around the body as well as the head. Maybe stronger around the head, though." He shrugged. "I've never seen one myself. Anyway, each person's is different, and Arbel can tell a lot about you by examining it.

"Better get moving. He's a good boss, but he doesn't put up with standing around when he's given you something to do."

Macurdy returned to Talbott's hut, got his sheepskin jacket and holstered pistol. Talbott was there; his back had gotten worse, and he hadn't been sent out that day. As he rose painfully from the bench, his expression reflected both pleasure and regret. "I knew Charles would tell the shaman about you," he said.

Macurdy shook hands with him. "If I can get permission," he told the old man, "I'll come visit you." But as he said it, it seemed to him this was the last time he'd see Talbott.

"Please do," Talbott said. "It's meant a lot to me to have you here this little while."

Macurdy was given a clean straw-filled bed sack, and slept in the workshop with Hauser. The next morning, Hauser, as interpreter, accompanied him to muster at the slave compound. There Macurdy was given an ax, taken to work by himself in the forest, and put to cutting wood: fence rails, fuelwood, and logs from which planks and roof boards could be split. Whatever was assigned. Hauser told him the local words for the different products, and had him repeat them several times. The overseer or his assistant would stop by to tell him when to return home to the shaman's, and to inspect his work for the day. If his production was inadequate in quantity or quality, he'd be beaten. Meanwhile he would not eat lunch with the other slaves— that would take him away from his own work—but would carry one from the shaman's.

The overseer looked Macurdy over for a minute, then gave him a warning through Hauser. "Don't take liberties with me. It will go ill with you. And if you try to run away, your death will be slow and painful."

From then on, each morning, rain or shine, Macurdy went to the woods with his ax. The overseer or his assistant arrived at two or three o'clock, until, after a few days, he was told to leave on his own when he'd made his day's quota. They'd inspect his work at a time convenient to them. Each afternoon, often while doing another task or project, Hauser drilled him on Yuultal. And also much of the evening, except when Arbel had some test for him, Hauser acting as interpreter.

Two weeks passed before Hauser had a chance to visit Talbott again. He was back sooner than expected, and Macurdy knew why, for Hauser looked distressed.

He asked anyway. "What's the matter?"

"He's not there. The gate guard says he was taken away two weeks ago."

Put down like a wind-broken horse, Macurdy guessed. "It was his back," he said. "I think he was expecting it. He didn't say anything because he didn't want to grieve us."

"I suppose so."

"You meant a lot to him," Macurdy added. "He was proud of you, of what you've done."

He dropped the subject then, to let Hauser deal with his grief himself.

❖   ❖   ❖

Each Six-Day evening a slave girl was brought to the house to spend the night with Arbel. It wasn't always the same one, but she was always good-looking. And whether her demeanor was demure or playful or bold, she never seemed unhappy to find herself there. According to Hauser, Arbel had told him that working with the spirit as he did, a lissome slave girl in his bed once a week kept his body properly grounded in the physical world—a necessity for a healthy shaman. On the other hand, twice a week would be to submit to the physical world; he'd limited himself even as a young man.

"How about you?" Macurdy asked. "Do you ever get any?"

Hauser smiled ruefully. "Four times a year—at each equinox and each solstice. As a reward; work keeps me physically grounded." Again Hauser smiled. "Sometimes I find myself counting the weeks."

Macurdy tried to picture Reverend Fleming, a widower, having a slave girl brought to the parsonage once a week. It was hard to imagine. Folks would be horrified.

Occasionally Macurdy was afflicted with unease at being here while Varia was—wherever she was. But he needed to learn, learn the language well, and enough about the country and the people to travel around without ending up a slave somewhere else, or dead.

Busy as he was, and as tired at bedtime, it was relatively easy not to dwell on the problems. His thoughts of Varia were mainly sweet fantasies.

Spring became summer, then late summer. Meanwhile Macurdy discovered a non-magical talent he hadn't known he had. He already knew he had an excellent memory and learned quickly, but now discovered an unexpected skill at duplicating sounds. With such intensive instruction, not only was he rapidly learning the local language; he was already pronouncing the words nearly as well as Hauser, and Hauser spoke them almost like a local. Now Arbel began to examine Macurdy more deeply, asking most of his questions directly, guiding as much on the responses of the big slave's aura as on his verbal answers.

Arbel's "instruction" lay only partly in teaching. Even more,

it involved questions, the answering of which exposed and peeled off layers of opinions, beliefs, attitudes . . . like peeling an onion, freeing what lay beneath. And gradually, as Arbel worked on him, Macurdy became aware of changes in himself. He'd always tended to be confident. Now he felt stronger, bolder, more self-assured. And his natural charisma was more apparent. Even as a slave, his intrinsic dominance showed, expressed as competence, a comfortable readiness to act, a dominance more over situations than over people.

Gradually he became aware that others were treating him differently. Thus in dealing with Macurdy, even the overseer's assistant was—not actually courteous, but his brusqueness had lost its truculence and threat. Then one morning, Macurdy glanced at Hauser pulling on his breeches, and saw around him a sheath of warm light, mostly blue, but with elusive patterns of other colors. It glowed around him from the hips upward, flaring more widely around his head. Hauser's aura, he realized.

Before going to the woods, he looked in on Arbel, seated at his workbench. The shaman's aura was primarily shamrock green, and started about at his knees. As if he felt Macurdy's gaze, Arbel turned and looked at him with raised eyebrows. And grinned, almost the first smile Macurdy had seen on him; it lasted perhaps three seconds. Then without comment the shaman nodded and turned back to his work.

The rest of the day until quitting time, Macurdy was seeing auras of one sort or another around every living thing, mostly thin and simple, requiring conscious intention to notice. *Varia was right about me,* he told himself. *I'll never doubt her again.*

11
Blue Wing and Maikel

Well before adolescence, Macurdy had learned to use the ax. But in Washington County, the crosscut saw was the main tool for logging, while for cutting fuelwood, the homemade bucksaw was mostly used. The ax was simply used for swamping, notching, limbing, and of course splitting.

Now, working exclusively with it, he found his skills had improved; a given task took less time. Meanwhile, Arbel had peeled away layers of imposed and assumed considerations, and Macurdy no longer felt the need to prove himself, to show how much work he could do in a unit of time.

Thus, as his axman's skills improved, instead of turning out more wood, he commonly took a nap in late morning, allowing his mental clock and hungry stomach to waken him for lunch and to finish his day's work.

One noon, with the leaves showing the first tinges of fall color, he awoke aware of being watched. Getting to his feet, he looked around, and saw no one.

"Up here!" called a voice. "In this tree."

He looked up. At first he thought it was a vulture, but its head was feathered. Its crown was scarlet above the eyes, as if it had tried to become an eagle and gotten the colors wrong, while its strong beak was longish and nearly straight.

"There," it said to him. "You've found me."

Macurdy gawped. "You can talk!" he said.

"Of course I can talk."

Macurdy pondered briefly, wondering if this was another expression of his talent. "Could anyone hear you?"

"Assuming they're not deaf, yes."

Macurdy frowned thoughtfully at his hands, as if looking to them for enlightenment. "Back home," he said, "if I told folks I'd been visiting with a giant crow wearing a red . . ." He stopped, lacking the Yuultal word for "pompadour," and became aware of tittering.

"That was not funny!" the bird snapped. Not it seemed at Macurdy, but at someone else nearby. With the bird's irritated response, the tittering became laughter, and Macurdy looked around for the source. It seemed to come from the base of a walnut tree, but he could see nothing there. Then his hair stood on end. There *was* something there; he could almost see it. *Relax*, Varia had told him. *Relaxing helps turn it on.* And Arbel had said *don't try too hard. Let things come.*

And there it was, looking like a small, tight-furred man, a fuzzy creature naked except for a belt, and slender, wiry. Almost at once the halfling realized his invisibility spell had been seen through, and without an instant's hesitation, sprinted with startling speed to a slender ash sapling, scrambling into its top till his weight bent it, and he could transfer to the lower branch of an oak. There he sat; Macurdy could almost see his body tremble. When he'd climbed, a small knife and bag had been visible on his belt in back.

"So much for magic," the bird called after him. "I'll take wings any time."

The halfling said nothing, simply sat with his face working, somewhat as if palsied, somewhat as if chewing, his eyes glistening black as obsidian. Faster on the ground than a squirrel, Macurdy thought, and not too much slower up the tree.

"Though I'll admit I couldn't see you," the bird added. "I'm surprised this human could."

Macurdy's attention returned to the bird. About as big as a turkey vulture, he decided; far larger than even the biggest crow. It showed an aura much like a human's, when he thought to look. "What sort of bird are you?" he asked. "What breed?"

The bird looked down his beak at Macurdy. "Not a crow, I promise you that."

"Then what?"

"Men and tomttu call us the great ravens. And while the term reflects an inadequacy of concept, for our purposes here it suffices. Keeping in mind that intellectually we are far superior to ravens, which in turn are considerably superior to crows, which are—et cetera."

"Where did you learn to talk so well? You used some big words. I'm not even sure what all of them mean."

"Um. My species tends to be more intelligent; more, let us say, scholarly. Certainly much better informed."

Macurdy stared bemused. "How did you get so smart?"

"He's got a hive mind!" the halfling called; his nerves settled now. "Or more correctly, he's part of a hive mind!"

"Hive mind?"

The bird explained. "My kind has a shared mind. Each of us is an individual, but whatever one of us learns is available to us all. When we need it or care to access it."

Macurdy frowned. He thought he understood, but it was strange.

"For example. Suppose you carried a bow and shot at me. And I saw you do it. All of my people would then avoid you."

"Wouldn't that get confusing? How do you separate in your mind what's happening to you from what's happening to someone else? And somewhere else!"

"That's not difficult; there's always a sense of where and who. And at any rate, I don't even know what my nest mates are doing right now, though I could. But if you'd shot at one of us, we'd all avoid you as dangerous, and know the reason. On the other hand, the others wouldn't know I'd been talking to you unless one of them wondered what I'd done lately that was different."

"And they're all gluttons for knowledge," the halfling put in. "Afraid there's somethin' interestin' goin' on that they're missin'."

The bird nodded. Physically nodded. "True. It's why I associate with him." He gestured toward the halfling with his head. "He's a tomttu, you know. From time to time we great ravens form relationships with individual tomttus. They're veritable mines of lore—facts, stories, and opinions."

Macurdy saw possibilities. "Is that right! I'm new in this

world, and there's a lot I don't know about it that I need to. Maybe you could help me."

"Indeed? Obviously you're no hatchling—excuse me; newborn. What do you mean, you're 'new in this world'?"

"I came through a gate last spring. From Farside."

"Indeed!" This time it was the halfling, the tomttu who spoke. "I've heard of gates to a world called Farside. I've also heard they're dangerous to men and tomttus; that only those of ylvin blood can use them."

Macurdy decided not to say too much. "Well, at least one human's come through safely. Myself."

"Farside." Blue Wing cocked his head. "Interesting. I am Blue Wing, incidentally, and my friend is Maikel. What is your name?"

Macurdy didn't answer at once. What might happen if the Sisterhood learned he'd come through? And where he was. On the other hand, suppose Varia heard. "Macurdy," he said. "Do you know of anyone by that name?"

The bird's gaze seemed to lose focus, as if he scanned the hive mind. "No, no I don't. But then, I've never run into anyone from that mythical country before. What are you doing here?"

Careful now, Macurdy, don't say too much, he warned himself. "I'm a slave. The Ozmen made a slave of me when I came through. So I can't travel around. And there's a lot I'd like to know about this world."

Bird and halfling looked at one another for a long moment, and it was the tomttu who spoke. "We'll trade you knowledge for knowledge. Yuulith for Farside."

"I'll agree to that," the bird seconded. "It's infrequent that *any* of us exchanges thoughts and knowledge with a human. And when it happens, it's usually with one of your immatures, typically female. Your immature females are more—open. They tend to feel more affinity with such as we. And it's rarer yet to have a three-cornered exchange. It should be quite interesting."

"I've a question for you," the tomttu said. "How were you able to see me? The spell I cast should have kept me invisible to you."

"I didn't, at first. I heard you laugh, and looked toward the sound. And there you were."

"Ah. Of course. I shouldn't have laughed. But you likened him to a crow, and I know what he thinks of them. And rightly, in my view, though the crows would disagree. Hmh! And you saw me! Well. Individuals differ, whether man or tomttu—or even the winged folk, in spite of all their hive mind. And you were able to come through a gate, after all. Assumin' you've been truthful with us."

Macurdy shrugged. "You two seem to trust each other. You just need to stretch your trust to include me."

"Ah," said Blue Wing, "but neither of us is human. And the tomttus' experience is that humans are much less reliable."

"Humans and ylver," added the tomttu, "or so the stories have it. But humans are said to be more cruel."

Well, Macurdy, Macurdy thought to himself, *they've got us pegged.*

For nearly two weeks, the three of them met each midday, Macurdy giving up his naps to talk with them. He learned a lot about the country, and about the language, for Blue Wing used big words, and both he and Maikel sometimes used long involved sentences. And both would pause to explain, when they lost his understanding.

The great ravens, Macurdy learned, were a sparse breed, gathering only in their rookeries to raise young. Their sole passion in life was knowledge. As far as Macurdy could learn, they didn't use it for anything in particular. In a sense they *were* like crows, but instead of collecting shiny things or smooth round things, they collected odd bits of knowledge, with no real interest in what use they might be to them.

The tomttu, on the other hand, were essentially farmers and gardeners, and herders of miniature sheep. From time out of mind they'd lived almost entirely in dwarvish kingdoms, where mostly they were safe from human predation. The dwarves, in turn, traded with the tomttu for some of their foodstuffs.

Some tomttu got the wanderlust. Maikel was one. It wasn't so much an urge to see new places, he said, though that was part of it. It was more a desire to be free of the strictures and formalities of Tomttu life, and learn new things. And any tomttu who'd reached puberty could pick a living in the forest from tubers and nuts, snails and slugs and tree frogs, seeds and fleshy roots. Their magic helped them find what they needed. Some such wanderers returned home in winter, this requiring a family willing to feed one who hadn't worked. Otherwise one found a good den for winter, defended it by spells, stored as much food as he could before the weather turned bad, then slept a lot. Maikel was bound for his home in the Diamond Mountains, some thirty miles west. He'd been gone three years, and was ready to settle down.

From Maikel, Macurdy learned about dwarves and tomttus; and from Blue Wing, geography, humans, ylver and the Sisterhood. The viewpoint and evaluations were considerably different than a human's would have been, but they were valuable, particularly the information that the Sisterhood now was lodged far to the east, in the Kingdom of the Dwarves in Silver Mountain. How this came to be, Blue Wing had no idea; his concepts of formal treaties, politics, and even commerce were rudimentary.

Each spoke of other creatures, as well. Macurdy learned there were jaguars, catamounts, wolves and bears in the forests. And rare but savage night-stalking trolls. Rarer yet were the great boars, large as cart ponies. Sixty stone or more, Maikel guessed; probably more. (Blue Wing's notions of weight were vague and useless.) Maikel claimed to weigh about two stone, and judged Macurdy at fifteen, so Macurdy figured a stone would be roughly fifteen pounds.

According to that, a great boar would weigh half a ton They were uncannily clever, the two agreed, and had magic of their own. For men to succeed in killing one was unheard of. If one of the great boars became sufficiently offended by them, it could lay waste a farmstead, killing the livestock, destroying the fences, and rending whoever got in its way.

Or so tradition had it; neither could cite a known instance, not even Blue Wing, with his access to the hive mind, which stretched far back in time. But the potential, they insisted, was there, and must surely have been used at some time or other.

They also agreed there were no females of the species.

Privately, Macurdy considered that myth; otherwise they'd be worse than rare. He'd have suspected the two of pulling his leg, but from Arbel's lessons, he was beginning to read auras as well as see them. And it appeared to him that Blue Wing and Maikel both were honest with him. Blue Wing insisted a great boar had been seen to breed a razorback sow, a very large one, but Maikel was certain it couldn't happen. "What was seen was one eatin' a sow. But breed one? Even if he'd been inclined to it, he'd have squashed her flat."

Macurdy wasn't eager to meet the great cats, or wolves, and certainly not a troll or great boar. To humans, black bears on the other hand seemed benign; tomttu had more cause to fear them.

And there was information on dwarves. "If they have no grudge against you," Maikel said, "and if you're not trespassin', they're no danger to you at all. But if you wrong them, knowingly or not, they're implacable. Implacable! They do be friendly to us though, because we're small, you see, and because we're not given to human treacheries.

"Dwarves consider that they aren't, either. But I must tell you that their greed sometimes gets the better of them. Then they can cheat and lie like a human. Well, not like the worst humans, but badly enough. Still, I'd trust a dwarf before a man. Not before every man—not before yourself—but judgin' the species broadly. They deal fairly with us though, the dwarves. Close but fairly. It's dealin' with men and ylver that brings out the worst in them."

Indeed, dwarves and geography were the subjects that most interested Macurdy. For if the Sisterhood had moved to the Kingdom in Silver Mountain, it seemed to him he'd have to go there.

Then one day, Maikel didn't show up. "The nights are becoming cold," Blue Wing explained, "and he woke up this morning with the decision to continue westward to his people. He asked me to give you his best wishes. As for me—the scavenging is poor around here. The people in Miskmehr keep more sheep, and sheep are rather given to dying without apparent cause."

Then the great bird and Macurdy wished each other well, and Blue Wing flew off northward.

12

Pursued

With the solstice near at hand, the sun rose early. From an outlook, Varia could see its luminosity through thinning clouds, but it failed to warm her. The mare she'd stolen plodded stolidly on, but more and more slowly. When it paused to browse on the young leaves of maple, Varia was scarcely aware of it, she was so sunken in hypothermia from the cold, night-long rain.

At length the mare stopped, to stand quietly on a stretch of bare bedrock almost free of shade. The sun had burned the clouds off, and shone on her wet flanks. Gradually its warmth, trapped by blackened oilcloth, seeped through Varia's torpor, and she slid from the saddle, hobbling to an outcrop to lie in the sun.

She awoke cold on one side from the rock, and warmed on the other by sunshine. Looking around slowly, she saw the mare standing broadside to the warm rays, hide steaming. Wincing, Varia got to her feet, her legs and buttocks solid pain at the effort, sore not from the saddle, but from occasional uphill hiking to rest the horse.

And you're the girl who was ready to walk to Ferny Cove, Varia thought. Barely able to hobble, she went to the horse, aware also now of the blisters she'd gotten, hiking in wet, ill-fitting boots. From a saddlebag she took a broken piece of loaf and the slab of cheese, sat down in the sun on a windfall and began to gnaw. Just the act seemed to warm her. The mare watched her eat—reproachfully she thought. "You and I depend on each other now," she told it. "Be patient and we'll find you some grass pretty soon."

81

For a quarter hour Varia sat gnawing, and soaking up sun, her thoughts slow, her eyes on the mare. *You need a name,* she decided. *You're my best friend now; I can't just call you Horse.* She gave it a minute's thought, then nodded, her chuckle sounding a bit like the Varia of Washington County. "Maude," she said aloud. "I name you Maude." And chuckled again. Maude had been the name of her father-in-law's favorite mare, named in turn for the queen of some place in Europe.

She gnawed and sunned till the mare got restless, then wincing with pain, pulled herself into the saddle and rode slowly on. The ridge dwindled, and they slanted down its north flank to a soggy glade, the grassy headwaters of a brook. There Varia took the bit from Maude's mouth, to let the creature graze more easily. Then hobbled to a sun-heated boulder, large as a roadster, crawled onto it and quickly fell asleep.

It was near noon before she awoke and looked around. Something had wakened her, apparently not a predator, for Maude still grazed placidly. Sitting up, Varia realized what it was: Miles away, someone had found her trail, some tracker, and she'd sensed it. Tomm, it seemed to her. Such psychic incidents were well known to Sisters. She could only wish they were regular, something she could rely on to keep her informed.

Then it struck her that in the cold and rain, the night before, and later in her torpor, she'd forgotten all about casting a net of confusion. She'd remembered at the stable where she'd stolen Maude, but afterward had gone into a stupor from rain, cold, and finally fatigue.

She didn't panic though, or slip into despair. She simply got painfully from the boulder, and painfully approached Maude, who paused in her grazing to look at her. After putting the bit back in the mare's mouth, Varia pulled herself, painfully again, into the saddle, and turned westward out of the gap, working her way up the next slope.

But not before casting a net of confusion over the site.

And now, from eating and napping, she'd recovered energy enough to begin healing her painful muscles.

❖   ❖   ❖

They traveled slowly but more or less steadily the rest of the day, Varia dozing in the saddle from time to time. Steadily, but not without short breaks, when they came to glades with good grass. There she rested Maude and let her graze. The mare seemed not to have stiffened at all. Varia grazed too, on occasional patches of wild strawberries. Speed was important, but survival also depended on endurance.

Meanwhile she took her boots off, tying them to the saddle, riding barefoot to help her blisters heal. And at intervals casting a net of confusion.

The country was more broken now, and she changed direction from time to time, sometimes taking the most favorable way and sometimes not. The idea was to throw off pursuit, for even if she succeeded in confusing Tomm, he could look at the terrain and judge which way seemed best for travel. She had to outguess him, make him wrong.

Once, in the mud at the edge of a creek, she saw tracks that were clearly of jaguar or catamount. But Maude seemed unworried, though the tracks had to have been made since the rain stopped.

Eventually evening came, and again they stopped at a headwaters in a small marshy meadow. Varia left Maude to graze, depending on a bonding spell to keep her from straying, and sheltered beneath another large thick hemlock, plucking away stones and sticks enough to make a place to lie down. To sleep, and hopefully dream of Curtis.

Curtis. She cast an earnest thought: *I'm coming to you, darling! I am! It won't be long!* And wondered if thoughts ever traveled between the worlds.

A second day, and a third, they traveled mostly westward. Only when the terrain required a change in direction did she turn north, from time to time casting her spell. Once she heard wolves, but at a distance, trailing other prey. And once as they traveled a game trail, the mare shied at fresh bear dung, but they passed it by and saw no further sign.

Finally they turned north on a trail too distinct, too unbroken and purposeful not to have been made by humans. It would be faster, and it couldn't hurt to follow it for a while. After a bit evening came, and a tiny patch of meadow at a seep. Again she left Maude free to graze, stowing the saddle and saddle bags beneath a nearby blowdown. The last of the bread and cheese she put in her shift, and climbed the ridge a little way, to shelter under an overhanging ledge she'd noticed. Climbed barefoot, walking carefully among the rocks and sticks.

Before long she slept, eventually to dream that something came shambling upright on two legs, then stopped and peered about while the dream-Varia lay paralyzed with fear. Suddenly Maude screamed, and Varia awoke with a start, rolling to hands and knees, heart pounding in her throat. The scream repeated, and she realized it was no dream. And there was more: a muffled half growl, half roar, that froze her where she crouched. She had no doubt it came from the throat of something whose jaws were clamped on Maude's neck.

She realized she'd drawn her knife, though it would be useless against a bear. The mare didn't scream again, but there were occasional growling grunts, and sounds as of joints being broken. She stayed where she was, crouched beneath her ledge. Dawn, she discovered, had preceded the predator, faint gray light bleeding through the treetops. As it grew, the sounds of feeding stopped. Birds awoke as if in celebration, first a robin, then a wren, then a clamor from many throats. The sun's rays would soon light the higher treetops.

Something was coming up the ridge. Varia's short hair crawled with fear, then terror. A shaggy, hulking, upright form, some eight feet tall and five or six hundred pounds, strode into sight at half a trot, one great hand shielding its eyes. Its belly was grossly distended, not with pregnancy but gorging. Its other hand held a horse's hind leg over one shoulder, like a man might carry a club.

Varia almost missed seeing the small one, perhaps smaller than herself. Unlike its mother, it ran on all fours like an ape, carrying something in its teeth. Varia couldn't see what; brush was in the way. Probably something its mother had torn off for it.

Then they were gone.

She'd always heard that trolls hated daylight. The belief among the Sisters was that their eyes were too sensitive. Folklore had it that they stayed in their dens till twilight, not even coming out on cloudy days. That daylight turned them to stone, though no reasonable person believed that. At any rate trolls were night stalkers; that much was certain.

Still she stayed where she was till the sun was well up. When she went down to the seep, it was shocking how much of the mare had been eaten. *You're going to walk to Ferny Cove after all,* she told herself. *Poor Maude.*

Three ravens had already landed on the carcass, one a different species than the others. Large though the two were, the third was much larger, its high and feathered crown scarlet against black. Pausing in its breakfast, it looked at Varia. "Yours?" it asked. Its voice could have passed for human.

She nodded.

"Sorry. I trust you don't mind excessively. One must eat, you know." And with that, the bird returned to feeding.

Varia didn't answer. She went to where she'd left the saddle. Not only the mare had been attacked. The saddle too had been mauled, gouged by sharp teeth in smaller but still powerful jaws. Her boots had been pulled loose, and one of them torn apart. The other was missing; it might have been what the troll cub carried in its jaws. She would not only walk to Ferny Cove; like it or not, she'd walk barefoot. Certainly she couldn't stay where she was; the trolls' den had to be somewhere near.

A thought occurred to her, and she looked back at the three ravens. "Excuse me," she called softly, and the red-crowned bird looked up. "I'm afraid I'm being followed. By a man."

"Really!"

"He should be a day or two behind. If you meet, he may ask if you've seen me."

"And you want me to say I haven't."

Varia nodded. "Please."

"My name is Everheart. A name given me by a tomttu; we have our own names, unpronounceable to you. And yours?"

"Varia."

"Let me see if I can guess what's happened," the bird said. "You're a Sister, a young girl who's run away from the Cloister. Right? I've heard of such. And your Dynast will have set a tracker after you."

Varia stared.

"You're speechless; obviously I'm right."

"Not entirely. I'm—somewhat more in the Dynast's attention than a young girl would be. I'm forty-three, not some sixteen-year-old to be brought back for correction and counseling. I escaped a—a punishment house, and this time they might kill me."

It seemed to Varia that if the bird had had eyebrows, they'd have arched at that. His aura suggested that he didn't quite believe her. She didn't herself. They'd degrade her, perhaps break her will, even her mind, but they wouldn't deliberately kill her.

"Hmh!" the bird said. "I wish you well in your escape, and I certainly won't betray you." It chuckled. "I've been told that among humans, a gentleman never tells a lady's secrets." Pausing, he cocked his head. "I do have that right, don't I? Who might your tracker be, do you suppose?"

"A man named Tomm."

"Tomm. Tomm is known to us. In fact I know him on sight. We all do I suppose; what one of us knows, the others know, or can if we care to look. It's how, over the centuries, we've learned your language. By sharing, word by word, phrase by phrase."

Varia stared.

"But I must tell you," he went on, "that my silence won't help you much. Tomm has a talent that apparently you're not aware of. No doubt his most important talent. You see, he can question any creature, large or small, about you. Mostly birds, because we see more, and our perceptions are very largely visual, as humans' seem to be. He may not gain much detail from his questions, for the minds of most species handle only simple concepts. But the question, 'have you seen this one?' accompanied by a mental image . . ." Everheart physically shrugged. "The eagles and greater hawks are no more susceptible to his demands than I, for their own reasons, of course, while the vultures and goshawks and falcons?—I doubt they'd hear his thought. They are totally focused on their own affairs.

"Crows, now—crows he may or may not ask. They lie,

inveterately. But if he can recognize when they lie and when
they do not . . . Some of your Sisterhood can do that, I'm told.
And crows can be bribed, if he has something they might covet.
Some shiny gew-gaw. Or a piece of fat; they are fond of fat.
Beyond crows, there are many susceptible species too
unimaginative to lie: sparrows, bluebirds, thrushes, waxwings . . .
And jays, the tattlers of the forest! Very definitely jays!"

The great bird paused to threaten a rival. The lesser raven
drew back too slowly, and there was a moment's squawking
before it rose on flapping wings, to circle in rumpled dignity.
Then Everheart looked at Varia again. "He won't tell either.
His species is proud, like my own, and the eagles and greater
hawks. And stubborn, as you've just seen.

"Meanwhile I recommend that you keep to the deeper woods,
where you'll be hard to see from the air. Avoid meadows and
open ridges. And jays so far as possible, for they tell everything.
Now if you'll excuse me."

He began to peck and tear again at the troll-mangled flesh
of poor Maude's ribs. Varia watched for just a moment, then
turned and hiked off into the forest, stepping carefully with
her bare feet.

Hiking barefoot went better than she'd expected; in avoiding
areas where the forest roof was open, she also avoided the
stonier places. Now she held northward more than westward.
Occasionally, unavoidably, she roused a jay, but they seemed
so territorial, she decided the odds were small that Tomm would
run into one of these particular jays. Crows, on the other hand,
flew widely, but hopefully wouldn't see her in heavy woods.

That day she ate the last of her bread and cheese, and later
stepped hard on a sharp stone, earning a bruise on her right
heel. She slept hungry that night beneath another hemlock.
And in a dream, Curtis Macurdy found her, and held her in
his arms.

In the morning she spelled a grouse to her hand, and after
begging its pardon, wrung its neck. She considered eating it
raw, but couldn't bring herself to. Instead she broke dead
branches, lit them with a pass of her hand, and half roasted

the bird. She ate most of it on the spot—there was little more to it than breast—and stashed the greasy remains in her shift. She also took time to heal her bruised foot sufficiently for swift walking. Then she hiked again.

Toward midday she became aware of magic about her, a spell of invisibility, and saw through it to the source. In the fire-hollowed base of a great-boled golden birch stood a tiny, furry man, a tomttu. She'd seen one in a cage once, when she was a girl traveling with an embassy. This one was larger, perhaps thirty inches tall. Their eyes met, and after a long moment it was the tomttu who broke the silence.

"Good mornin' to you. I didn't realize it was a Sister comin' up the trail, or I wouldn't have cast my spell. I'd but to crawl up my hollow here, and you'd never have seen me." He shook his head. "Betrayed by my own magic! Embarrassin'!" Doffing a non-existent cap, he bowed. "I'm called Elsir."

"Do you live here?"

"Here? My no! 'tis but a place to shelter on the way. I travel, you see, short though my legs are. Like more than a few of us, I've a wanderlust." He paused, cocking his head as Everheart had. "And what are you doin' out here alone, girl? With the hair on your head no more than a copper-red cap. A runaway, I don't doubt. Your people will be worried."

She looked at him and saw a chance for help. "I'm not a girl," she said. "I'm a married woman, stolen from my husband and returning to him. Do you ever cast spells to mislead?"

He laughed. "Perhaps a small one now and then. To lead the troll away when he's near, or the great cats."

"And what of men? I've heard they sometimes capture you for sport, or steal a girl from you."

He scowled. "You're ill-advised to speak of such things to me, if it's favors you want."

"I didn't say it to offend. And as for being stolen and misused by men, I know more than you about that. Can you cast a spell to throw someone off my trail? Something beyond a net of confusion?"

He stared at her for an endless minute, gnawing his lip. Finally he spoke. "You're a Sister, are you not? Who is it you'd have me mislead?"

"A tracker named Tomm."

"I know of him by reputation. It wouldn't work."

"Could you cast a spell that would hide me from birds?"

Again he stared a long moment before he spoke. "Ah! The birds. Yes, I could that." Varia stood unbreathing, while Elsir squatted, thinking, frowning. "But I won't," he said at last. "I dare not meddle in affairs of the Sisters." Then, reading the depth of disappointment in her face, and the underlying desperation, he added: "We're a careful folk, bein' small as we are. And if Tomm sensed my spell, he'd know by its nature that it was one of us cast it. Your Dynast would hear of it then, and she's a vengeful woman."

Varia bowed her head. "Thank you for considering it. Is there any advice you can give me?"

The small man shook his head. "Only to hurry. Travel as fast as you can. The pass north of here is called Laurel Notch; take it and you'll be in the drainage of the Tuliptree River, the East Fork, which is only a brook at first. It will lead you north into the Kingdom of Indrossa. They might hide you there, or send you on and interfere with the tracker. It's possible."

Varia began to walk on then, and he called after her. "I'm sorry, girl. But if I cannot give you a spell, I give you my best wish that you escape them. And the wishes of a tomttu are not without force."

She paused to look back at him. "Thank you," she said softly, then trotted northward on the same trail she'd been following.

Watching her trot out of sight, the tomttu shook his head. *Ah, if only my wishes did have force,* he thought. *But if it's Tomm followin' you, it's little chance you have.*

She camped that night by a spring, and healed her new stone bruises. Her feet were toughening. At daybreak she awoke, and soon after sunup called a dove down, and ate it. Raw doves had become her staple food. Near midday she reached the head of the pass, a rugged cleft in the highest ridge she'd come to. There, though the stones were harsh, she climbed to a ledge to see what she could see. The ridges northward were progressively lower. Beyond them, at the edge of vision, the land looked level, and not dark enough to be forest.

As she looked, she heard cawing, saw crows flying southward, and scrambled to hide as best she could beneath a dogberry bush, enduring its sharp spines for the concealment it gave her. When the crows had passed out of hearing, she climbed down into the notch again and trotted on.

Hungering, she spelled another dove to her, and shortly heard water rattling over rocks. Not long after that she came to a brook, and followed it near enough to keep the sound in her ears.

Her way led almost continuously downhill, and often she trotted. It seemed to her that two more days would bring her to populated country again.

That night she dreamed of Curtis. She'd found him, but he refused to believe it was her. "My Varia is young," he said, "and has beautiful long red hair. Yours is short and gray."

She raised her hands to her face and felt wrinkles, then remembered. Tomm had caught her, and she'd spent five barren brutal years in the Tiger barracks before Sarkia cast her out, broken and aged. She awoke with a cry, and saw dawnlight. And on an old blowdown near her feet, a man, lean and hard.

"Good morning, Sister Varia," he said quietly. "You've been traveling hard. I thought you should finish your sleep."

She raised to an elbow, staring at him, willing that this was still the dream. After a minute he got to his feet. "You're probably hungry for something more than the doves whose bones and skins you've left along the way." Stepping over to her, he reached down for her hand. She shrank from him.

"Come Sister. I'm not a Tiger. I won't harm you."

Her answer was hardly more than a whisper. "What greater harm than to take me back? You'll return me to my death."

"No, not to your death. Sarkia has better plans for you. She told me so when she sent me. You please her, even in rebellion; she likes your strength."

"You don't know what they did to me."

"The Tigers, you mean, I know. And Idri's been sent away, months since, to other tasks elsewhere. Sarkia intends to train you in the duties Idri did for her, as her personal aide."

Idri's duties! At the sight of Tomm, Varia had given up, but to do the work that Idri had done? Her will took new strength. "What has the Sisterhood ever given you?" she asked.

His expression didn't change. "Life," he said. "And the hunt."

The hunt? Yes, that would be it. "Have you ever thought of leaving? There's work anywhere for a man with your abilities. What chains does the Sisterhood have on you?"

He didn't answer at once. Then, "Without the Sisterhood, the ylver will someday conquer the Rude Lands, to command whatever tribute they want. To see the girls and women raped, and punish those who displease them."

It seemed to Varia that he recited, rather than speaking spontaneously. "And what did the Dynast have done to me? I was raped more than any Sister at Ferny Cove, my punishment for displeasing Idri and Sarkia.

"As for the ylver—the Sisterhood can't stop them. It has no great army to hold them off, nor will the tribes and kingdoms gather to Sarkia in support. Consider how helpless they were at Ferny Cove, when an ylvin army came!"

Just for a moment he showed emotion. Fervor. "That is ever in my mind. I was there; the cruelties went beyond evil. But helpless? Sarkia's magic troubled them greatly. We found our way through them by dint of her spells—hers and those she'd trained. Dense fogs arose in broad daylight, spreading over the country, and only the chosen could see through them. While ylvin warriors—even ylvin!—fell asleep on horseback, or at their posts. Else I'd be dead, as your children are."

My children! Would I even have recognized them? "On Farside," she answered, "each mother raises and cherishes her own children, and each child cherishes its mother. Have you ever wished to cherish your mother?"

He shrugged. "It is all the same to me. The Sisterhood is my mother."

"It's not the same to me! I have a husband who has sworn himself to me, and I to him. By our own choice. Idri stole me from him—Idri and a cull named Xader—and brought me back through the Oz Gate. My husband and I love each other; we were happy beyond anything you've known. And if I can, I'll return to him. Together we'll go far from any gate, have children by ones and twos, raise them ourselves, and love them."

She couldn't read the man at all; his aura hardly changed. What must Sarkia have done to him when she'd chosen to train him as a tracker! After a moment he spoke, as impassive as before. "But you can't, you see. Return to him. For I've caught you, and we are going back to the Cloister together. This time you'll like it there."

She stared quietly for a moment, then softly her mind caressed his. "Have you ever had a woman, Tomm? Held one in your arms?"

"I have never wished for one. But if I did, Sarkia would give one to me. You waste your breath, Varia."

"You've never wished for one because Sarkia spelled you as a child. Deprived you of your birthright, as she deprived you of your mother's love. Sarkia is evil, Tomm."

Again the pause before his answer. "If she does evil, it's for a greater good."

"Ah! So now evil is good! And day is night, and hunger a full belly! She's twisted your mind, Tomm, as she did the minds of us all. As the first Dynast did hers. But I lived more than twenty years on Farside, and unlearned much that I'd been taught. I wish I could take you through with me. You'd like my husband, Curtis Macurdy. He is honest and good, and you would have a friend at last. The two of you could farm together, drink coffee and talk together. Go to Decatur, eat 'ice cream' "— she said the words in English— "and see a 'movie.' You could even learn to laugh!"

Tomm stared at her silently for so long, she wondered if he'd answer at all. "You must get up now," he said at last, patiently. "It's time to start back." There was no more expression in his voice than before.

She got to her feet without help. *You won't take me back,* she vowed to herself. *You won't. Somewhere along the way you'll let your guard down, and I'll kill you. With knife or rock, or sharp stick through your eye, I'll kill you. Then I'll walk to Ferny Cove, and once I've gated through, they'll never catch me. Not again.*

13

Cyncaidh

The trail was familiar from the day before, but much slower now. She was drained, physically and emotionally, the urgency was past, and the trail was mostly uphill. In late afternoon they were still short of Laurel Notch.

It was Tomm's responsibility to keep alert, thus she'd let her mind wander. She imagined him dead and her slipping through the gate at Ferny Cove. And finding Curtis: She visualized it happening at the farm in Indiana. He'd be overjoyed. They'd hug and cry and kiss, then run together into the house and make love, and the terrible months in the Tiger barracks would be forgotten.

For now, though, Tomm padded a few strides behind her. He hadn't tied her hands, for which she was grateful. Probably he would when they stopped to sleep. She'd been walking slowly, and so far he hadn't hurried her. He was tired too.

Tall clouds had built and a wind had risen, swooshing the trees overhead, and she considered suggesting they look for shelter. Thinking about that, she missed the sound of the arrow that struck Tomm. Then men were all around. Tomm, a feathered shaft protruding from his chest, tried to stand, and one of them raised his sword to finish him. Varia screamed, and lunged reflexively to stop it, but strong hands grabbed and held her. The blade chopped down, taking Tomm through the back, and she screamed again. Then her knees buckled, but whoever held her, kept her upright.

"You're all right," another said. "You're safe now."

She looked around to see who'd spoken. A tall man . . . No,

a tall ylf, his eyes tilted like hers but blue, his skin fair, his hair raven black. His eyes and coloring and magician's aura all gave him away: an ylf, though he stood before her in the fringed and greasy buckskins of a fur hunter. "We know who he was, and who you are. A tomttu told us. He was afraid for you, the tracker was so close behind."

Safe now? Did he mean it? Hope surged. "Am I free then? Free to go?"

He looked long at her without answering. "Free of him," he said at last. "Free of those you fled from."

"Not truly free then? Just new captors?"

"There are things we need to learn from you."

"I heard how you questioned my Sisters at Ferny Cove." Her words were little more than a hoarse whisper now. "When your army raped sixty of them repeatedly before you killed them. In front of the people there."

"No," he said quietly. "Not the army."

"Who then?" The question was defiant.

His expression was bleak. "The Kormehri. Men and boys of the town. Farmers of the district."

"You lie!"

He shook his head. "General Quaie ordered it. The original plan had been to capture all the Sisters and their children, or as nearly all as might be, and bring them to the Empire. Unharmed so far as possible. But your magic was more powerful than we'd supposed, and most escaped. So those we caught—" He paused, took a deep breath. "Those we caught, Quaie required the local men to rape publicly. Even the dogs that afterward destroyed the victims were war dogs of King Vertorus. They'd been useless against us, against our magic. Now Quaie made his own use of them. The story would spread, Quaie said, and no one in the Rude Lands would ever regard the Sisterhood as they had before. They'd see a Sister and remember them humiliated, raped by a line of men like themselves, their magic broken. Then torn—even eaten—by dogs.

"He didn't even bring one home to question. Said it was needless. Pointless. That the Sisterhood was finished, and the lesson of Ferny Cove was best taught his way."

The ylf's face had twisted as if the words were bitter in his mouth. He stopped, breathed, stabilized. "That was Quaie's reasoning," he went on, "and to some degree it worked as he'd said. But the business was vile, and on our return, the Emperor dismissed him, both from command and from his seat on the council." He shrugged. "And as the story spread, it has harmed us everywhere. As I warned Quaie it would when he gave the orders."

Varia stared. "You were there!"

He nodded. "I was there."

She looked around and saw six others. Except for the leader, they were men. Or no—half-ylver who could pass for men. Six that she could see; there might be others. Her voice became little more than a whisper. "What will you do with me?"

He looked down at her from his six-feet-four, and shook his head. "Not that. Nothing like that, I promise you. But we have to take you with us. To be questioned."

"Take me where?"

"To our own country. The Empire."

Again her tears sprang silently. Truly there could be no more hope.

Tomm's cloak was taken from his pack, and put over Varia with its storm hood up to conceal her telltale Sister's face. Then bronze manacles were put on her wrists, manacles with a twelve-inch chain that allowed some use of her hands. Meanwhile the storm had begun, flashing and booming, but the rain passed in a minute, a spattering of large cold drops with wind and a smell of ozone, to blow off northeastward. Then her captors set her on one of their spare horses and started northward. They would travel by night now, albeit the nights were short in that season.

Varia scarcely noticed. Her mind was numb. On their brief stops, she neither ate nor drank. Finally, as dawn paled, they left the trail, set sentries and cooked. A military camp, for despite their clothing, these were soldiers. One of them led Varia a little distance off, gave her cloth and a pan with water, to use after relieving herself, removed her manacles and left her in privacy. After a bit he reappeared and took her to the others. She accepted food—a thick, honey-sweetened corn meal mush, and cheese—and drank from a cup that was offered. There was more in it than water or brandy—some potion— and she fell quickly asleep.

They rested through the day, ate again as the sun set, and moved on. Before dawn they'd passed the first farms. Meanwhile she'd grown more alert, and begun thinking of escape. To her it was obvious that their leader had set a spell to help them ride unnoticed. Not an invisibility spell—that wasn't practical for a traveling party—but a spell that made them easy to ignore, to pay no attention to. It would hardly cover an uproar though. Perhaps, she thought, she could make an outcry, screaming and struggling, when they passed through some town, or met some large party of travelers.

But the two villages they passed through that night were tiny and fast asleep, too small to waste what would undoubtedly be a single chance. Nor did they pass any travelers. And as if her captors knew her thoughts, the next evening she was gagged before they broke camp. Apologetically it's true, complete with explanation, and not brutally as Idri had gagged her, but still firmly gagged. She glared as the leader tied it.

In camp she was left ungagged and mostly unchained, but somewhat segregated from most of the party. One of the half-ylver had been assigned as her guard and companion. His name was Caerith, and when they camped, he talked to her. By the third day her reserve had softened, and his occasional brief monologs had become limited, intermittent conversations. This had been a reconnaissance party, she learned, sent to explore the territory where reportedly the Sisterhood had relocated. Not that there was any intention to make war, he insisted. For one thing, the new location was in a dwarf kingdom. This had been simply a matter of intelligence-gathering. What they'd do with such intelligence, Caerith didn't know.

After the third day, with the country increasingly peopled, they turned to one of the pack horses and replaced their buckskins with more civilized travel clothing. Oddly, there was even a set which more or less fitted Varia, though she continued to wear Tomm's too-large cloak for concealment.

They continued to travel only by night. Varia knew the pole star, and saw that their road took them more northwestward than north. Ferny Cove was northwesterly. Each time she thought of it, she felt a pang of desperation. Thus, in camp after the fifth day, she went to the leader.

"You're Cyncaidh?" she asked.

His expression was calm but grave, his face not only handsome but aristocratic, though few aristocrats had one like it. "Yes," he said, "I'm the Cyncaidh."

"I lived for more than twenty years on Farside, and have a husband there. Then the Sisterhood stole me from him and brought me back. They kept me in detention at the Cloister, and—used me badly, but I watched for my chance, and ran away. When the tracker caught me, I'd been traveling northwest, working my way toward Ferny Cove, to the gate there. To find my husband again. We can't be many days walk from there now. I want you to let me go."

She saw and felt his gaze, and before she'd well started, a sense of pending refusal tightened her throat, raising the pitch of her voice.

"I'm sorry," he said quietly. "It's not possible. Not now. You have information more valuable to us than you realize. And beyond that, the Kormehri feel that the Sisterhood abandoned them: While Quaie butchered his Kormehri prisoners of war, the Sisterhood used its magic to escape. And—the rape at Ferny Cove had an ugly effect on the Kormehri. It would be terribly dangerous for you to go there. You'd never . . ."

Her shrill anger cut him short. *"Dangerous? Dangerous! I escaped from a Tiger barracks at the Cloister! Got out over the wall, under the noses of sentries! Traveled the wilderness for days, alone! A troll killed my horse, and another ran off with my boots! And you talk to me about danger?"*

"My lady, I cannot release you. Jaguars and catamounts, bears and trolls, are not as terrible as men can be. And . . ."

She screamed and lunged, her unshackled hands raking at his face, his eyes. He caught her wrists, astonished at her violent strength, and held her arms overhead while she screamed and kicked and spat. Caerith grabbed her, wrestled her down squalling and struggling, then wide-eyed, looked up at Cyncaidh. The leader stood white-faced, lines of oozing red scoring his cheeks and forehead.

Kneeling, he opened his kit and took out two pills. "Open her mouth," he said quietly. Caerith pressed hard with his thumbs on the latches of her jaw, forcing her mouth open as he might a cat's. Then Cyncaidh dropped in the pills, far back where she couldn't spit them out, though she tried. They held her down while she strained red-faced, then gradually she went slack. Her pupils dilated further, and her eyelids slid shut.

Cyncaidh nodded, and with Caerith carried her to where she'd spread her cloak and blanket. "That," Cyncaidh said, "is a woman of character and strength. They are fools back there, as well as evil, to have dealt with her so cruelly."

And speaking of cruelty, he asked himself, *what of your own? You intended to steal a Sister if the chance arose, take her away, and wring out her mind for your own purposes, yours and the Emperor's. And then what? Not send her home again; that would never do. You hadn't thought about that, had you?*

Varia spoke to no one the rest of the way to the Big River, not even in camp. Occasionally she wept, but always silently, inconspicuously. And now not only Caerith looked after her, but from a little distance, Cyncaidh as well.

They reached the Big River and the Inderstown ferry docks in the black hour before dawn, to wait for daylight and a ferry crew. The soldiers, with their commander's permission, got down from their horses, and napped or sat talking on the shore. Cyncaidh, however, waited in the saddle. Perhaps, Varia thought, because she did. Her anger had passed, replaced by resignation, but she refused to show anything less than deep offense at her captivity. She was here against her will, a prisoner guilty of nothing—certainly not against these people—and she would not seem reconciled to her captivity.

Varia pulled her mind from her situation, focusing on the Big River. She'd never seen it before. Its Farside equivalent, the Ohio, she knew well from visits to Evansville, and it was large, but the Big River was clearly larger. A meteorologist might have told her that the conformation of the east coast, combined with this world's equivalent of the Bermuda High, the size and circulation of the Southern Sea, and orographic effects of the Great Eastern Mountains, combined to produce high and fairly constant runoffs from its extensive watershed.

On its north side lay the so-called "Marches"—kingdoms not ylvin, but which paid tribute to the ylver's Western Empire, acknowledging its Emperor as their suzerain. She knew little about them, she realized. At the children's school in the Cloister, they taught that the Marches had been conquered in a bloody war which ended with the ylvin boot on their necks. And that the ylver planned the same fate for the Rude Lands. How much of it was true she didn't know. Some of it no doubt.

Finally, with the sun clear of the horizon, a crew arrived. From her horse's back, Varia watched the oarsmen clomp down the wharf and board the ferry, muscular men in short, open, canvas vests, gibing each other, laughing and roughing. Shortly, chains rattled as two of the ferry's crew lowered the end gate, which became a ramp for loading. Led by Caerith, she rode her mount out onto the ferry, hooves clopping on the wooden deck. Then Caerith dismounted and tied her reins to a rail. She watched oarsmen unship their oars, heard commands shouted, saw them lowered, dip, pull, and they moved away from the wharf, a dull drum beat regulating the strokes.

"It's a fine sight, the river," Caerith said.

She looked coldly at him from within her hood. She had nothing against the half-ylf. He was decent and patient with her. But four or five days' westward was Ferny Cove. She didn't doubt it held the dangers Cyncaidh had implied. But neither did she doubt that, with care and stealth, she could be within dashing distance of the gate when next it opened. Now she'd get farther from it every day.

The crossing did not take many minutes. When they were firmly docked, the gate at the shore end was lowered. Then the riders untied their mounts, and Caerith led his horse and Varia's off the craft. Again they waited on the shore, while the half-ylvin soldiers roped the pack string and remounts into an orderly file. When they were ready, Cyncaidh, instead of mounting and giving the order to move out, walked over to his captive and reached up to her.

"Let me help you down, my lady."

For a moment his offer and form of address unsettled her. Then she turned, leaning sideways a bit, and he took her under the arms, lifting her down. "Your wrists, please," he said, and when she'd extended her hands from the cloak, he removed first the manacles, then the gag.

"We're entirely safe here, my men and I. And you."

He turned and walked to his horse. Caerith stepped up to help her mount, but she shook her head. "Thank you, Caerith," she told him, "I can do for myself now," and raising a foot to the stirrup, swung into the saddle.

A moment later, Cyncaidh gave the command, and men, horses, and captive started up the road from the river bank, Varia looking ahead at him with a new unease. Dismounting had been difficult with manacles, and Caerith had usually helped her. But that had been simply a soldier helping a lady from her horse. When Cyncaidh's large hands had lifted her down, it had triggered her heart, speeded her blood. The feeling was one she hadn't wanted; not in this world.

She set her jaw, concentrating on the easy movement of the mare beneath her.

They rode no farther than a livery stable at the north edge of Parnston, for their horses were worn out from long use and no grain. The proprietor brokered a sale with a local breeder, and before noon they had new mounts. Not especially good animals, but adequate, well fed, and rested. Meanwhile, the travelers actually ate breakfast at an inn, and an early lunch. Varia had thought they might lay over a day, but Cyncaidh didn't even give his men time to fall asleep at the table before ordering them back into the saddle.

It threatened to be a long afternoon, not having slept the night before, and in the pleasant warmth, Varia dozed off and on in the saddle. Clearly Cyncaidh's method of changing from night travel to day travel was to ride all day. They were seasoned riders; no one would fall out of the saddle simply because he dozed. And when they did camp, no one would have trouble falling asleep.

The country here was as much open farmland as woods, but even where the road passed through fields, maples, oaks, or tuliptrees shaded it. It was a better road than any she'd seen in the Rude Lands, ditched through low stretches, with a bridge or white oak culvert where it crossed a stream. In the soft stretches, rock and clay had been dumped, covered with gravel and leveled, to prevent miring and rutting.

The towns had no defenses; not even a bailiff's stronghold or a reeve's stockade. Varia hardly noticed. Repeatedly her lids slid shut, her mind drifting dreamward from lack of sleep.

In mid-afternoon, Cyncaidh, who seemed an iron man, took pity on them and stopped at a large crossroads inn. A sign outside proclaimed that the bedding was boiled with every change of users, and each room treated by sorcery to destroy possible vermin. An expensive place then; Cyncaidh's expedition, she decided, must be well financed.

It was early enough that they had a choice of rooms. Cyncaidh's choice, not hers. Off a larger room there was a smaller, without an independent exit. The larger, Cyncaidh would share with Caerith. The smaller was hers, complete with undersized chairs and a low table, clearly intended for children. But the bed was long enough.

She looked at the door—all that would stand between her and Cyncaidh when night came. It had no bolt. She didn't like the twinge of excitement that accompanied the thought. *Don't be silly,* she told herself. *If he was going to try something like that, he'd have done it days ago.*

She looked for some thought to displace it, and escape came to mind; each day now was a day in the wrong direction. She went to the window and peered out thoughtfully. *I could use bedding as a rope, and climb down into the courtyard tonight. Or jump, as far as that's concerned! It's not as far as I dropped from the palisade, escaping the Cloister.*

The problem was, she'd still have to get out of the courtyard. And if she did, then what?

Wait, she told herself, *and see what opportunities time provides. Maybe when they're done questioning you—maybe they'll let you go. Maybe even with a horse, and money to eat with. Cyncaidh seems decent; he might do that.* It seemed to her he would.

Someone knocked—Caerith, with clean traveling clothes

for her, obtained from the innkeeper, who also kept a small store for travelers. Clean clothes and word that the inn provided baths—two of them, actually, one for women. They went downstairs together and crossed the courtyard. The tub she found was scarcely large enough for four or five—women travelers would be few—but she'd have it to herself, with bathing utensils, towels, a small bowl of soap and one of sweet-smelling oil, all neatly arranged along a low bench. The tub was oval, with a ledge to sit on, and its distinctive tiles were surely Cloister made, arriving through who knew what avenues of trade. She fiddled with the water gates. The flow was fast, both the hot and the cool, for this was limestone country, with great flowing springs, and abundant good oak to heat water with. She stripped while it filled, then stepped down into it.

It was the most luxurious bath she'd had since she'd left the old Cloister at Ferny Cove. Her scalp, its hair less than an inch long, she scoured thoroughly under water. The rest of her she scrubbed till her skin was pink, then soaked some more at her leisure, relaxing, watching her toes peek out at her from the water.

When she'd soaked long enough, she toweled off, and tried on the new clothes. They were a reasonable fit, and included a light tunic with a hood that would hide her scalp. She was grateful for that. She left, to find Caerith waiting, still unbathed. For the first time his aura reflected sexual thoughts; perhaps he'd fantasized sharing her bath. It was nothing like the aura of a Xader or Corgan though; more like that of Curtis in adolescence. She discovered she felt a sisterly fondness for the half-ylf.

"When do you get to bathe?" she asked.

He smiled ruefully. "As soon as I deliver you to the Cyncaidh for safekeeping."

She surprised herself by laughing for the first time in more than a year, and they sauntered together across the courtyard, toward the wing they were housed in, Caerith carrying her dirty clothes. "What if your Cyncaidh's still in the bath?" she asked.

He shook his head. "The enlisted men, perhaps. But he'll have been quick so I won't have to wait. He's a rare commander, the Cyncaidh."

She said nothing more. When they got upstairs, Cyncaidh was waiting, scrubbed and in uniform, damnably attractive. She went into her room and found a clean, soft cotton sleeping-shift on the bed. Though it was still afternoon, she changed into it, lay down, and rather quickly slept.

Caerith's knocking drew her reluctantly from sleep. "It's almost time for supper," he called. She dressed and found him uniformed, and they went downstairs together. There were several alcoves off the dining room, and the soldiers, their commander and prisoner, were shown to one of the larger. Their conversations were quiet, perhaps because their commander was seated with them. When Varia had finished, she sat quietly watching him, observing her own response to his attractiveness. *You'll have to live with it, deal with it,* she told herself. *It's physical, that's all. Not love like you feel for Curtis. Just ignore it.*

When most were done, Cyncaidh excused those who wished to leave. Varia waited till Caerith had finished his rhubarb cobbler, then left, the half-ylf a step behind.

"Can we go to the river bank and sit awhile?" she asked.

"Certainly, my lady."

My lady. He sounds like Cyncaidh, she thought. The river passed perhaps a hundred yards from the inn, forty yards wide and of uncertain depth, a thinly milky blue from dissolved limestone. Someone, presumably the town fathers, had put out split-log benches, and they sat on one, the late sun behind them off their right shoulders.

She touched the bronze lozenge on Caerith's collar. "What does this signify?" she asked.

"That I'm a sublieutenant in the imperial army."

"An officer! I'd assumed you're only half ylvin."

He nodded. "That's right, my lady."

"What's it like, being half ylvin?"

He looked at her with dark brown eyes, good-looking in his clean uniform, young in years as well as appearance, his brown hair washed and brushed now. "The Sisters are half ylvin, aren't they?" he countered.

"In our ancestry, rather more than half. But we're a people of our own. We don't live under ylvin domination."

He let that pass, turning instead to her question. "Life as a half ylf? Hmm. There's no simple answer. Too many variables—who your father is, your mother, their ranks . . . It's my father who's full ylvin, a baronet's son who was captain of the governor-general's guard in the Kingdom of Quabak. My mother was the human, a daughter of the regent. It was a minor political marriage, but a happy one."

"So you grew up in the Marches?"

"No. When I was four, my father was transferred to Duinarog, the imperial capital. I grew up within a mile of the imperial palace, wanting to be a soldier."

"And what was that like, growing up in"—she paused over the name, realizing she'd never heard it before, and finding that strange—"in Duinarog?"

He laughed, something he hadn't done in any conversation they'd had till now. "Ask me again when you have a day to spare. Mostly it was good."

"Was there prejudice? Because your mother wasn't ylvin?"

"Sometimes. Children can be cruel. But nothing troublesome. I had good friends."

"And your career?"

He thought about his answer. "I'm unlikely ever to attain high rank, though such things aren't unheard of. But then, few of my cadet class will, though only three of us were half ylvin. You hope for a good commander and serve diligently, and if he notices your service favorably, he'll see to your development and advancement."

"And you were assigned to serve Cyncaidh?"

"Not initially. The Cyncaidh is a general; he commands the 2nd Legion. I served in its 3rd Cohort, under Colonel Lonuaigh. Then I learned of a confidential mission I could apply for." He exposed a smooth forearm. "Except for having little body hair, I hardly look ylvin at all, and I'd had certain training." He shrugged. "Colonel Lonuaigh recommended me."

His aura suggested he'd become uncomfortable with the subject, so she changed it. "I've assumed your commander's name is Cyncaidh," she said. "Yet you refer to him as 'the Cyncaidh,' as if it's his title."

"The Cyncaidh family is one of the noblest in the Empire.

They rule a large domain on the Northern Sea—a sweet water sea bigger than all the Marches combined. Cyncaidhs have been regents, ministers of state, and chief counselors. One was even a pretender to the throne, in the Time of Troubles, though I'm sure the family doesn't boast of it." Sublieutenant Caerith grinned at that, then rearranged his face. "I hope you won't tell him you know."

"Would he be angry with you?"

"He'd be disappointed in me. It would seem I gossiped."

"You still haven't said why you refer to him as 'the Cyncaidh.'"

"It's simply custom. Whoever is head of the family is referred to as 'the Cyncaidh.'"

Varia examined what he'd told her. In Farside terms, it was equivalent to learning that a reconnaissance patrol, a squad, was being led not by a sergeant or lieutenant, but a general— a general who was also governor of New York! And she was his prisoner. "Then why," she asked, and waved vaguely southward, "was he leading this patrol?"

"My lady, I don't know; truly I don't. And if I did, I couldn't talk about it. Nothing against you, you understand; I admire you as much as he does. But it wouldn't be proper."

Admire you as much as he does. The comment introverted her. After a minute Caerith spoke again. "We should go back to the inn now. This conversation has outgrown us."

I'm not sure "outgrown" is the word, she thought as they walked, *but I certainly don't know where it might take us from here.*

The next day they replaced their packhorses, and each day after that made at least twice the distance they had on any day south of the river. They traveled by daylight, no longer had to make and break camp, and the summer solstice was at hand, so the days were long. And happily cool, with skies that held only small and transient clouds. On the third such day, they arrived for a late supper at Fort Ternass, where an imperial garrison was stationed. They'd resupply there, Caerith said, and get fresh horses, ylvin horses. They had, he commented, a long way to travel yet.

❖   ❖   ❖

Before they left the next morning, Cyncaidh brought a young woman to Varia, a girl lightly tanned and rather pretty, with honey-blond hair. "My lady," he said, "this is Hermiss. Her father is a professor, supervisor of the local commons school. I've obtained her services as your traveling companion and lady-in-waiting; it's time to give Lieutenant Caerith other duties. Hermiss has been employed as the companion of Colonel Faimler's daughter, who's at Port Arligh just now, visiting her grandmother. I trust you'll enjoy each other's company."

The move took Varia completely by surprise. She wondered if Caerith had asked his commander to be relieved. Meanwhile Hermiss crossed her hands on her chest and dipped a slight bow. Varia didn't know whether to reply in kind, then decided not to; she was, after all, "your lady." The girl's act was probably the equivalent of the curtsies she'd read about on Farside, and seen in movies. "I'm happy to meet you, Hermiss," she said instead. And thought: *I have absolutely no idea how to relate to you, girl. We may look the same age, but I've got perhaps twenty-five years on you, and twenty times the experience. Our lives have been totally different.*

It struck her then that she'd never before spoken with a woman in this world except Sisters; this girl had a whole area of experience that she didn't. Her smile surprised both Hermiss and Cyncaidh. "I'm sure we'll have some interesting conversations," she added.

Fort Ternass was on another major crossroads, and instead of continuing north, they turned west. The weather turned too, from dry and pleasantly cool, to sodden and cold. At intervals they met thunderstorms, and between storms it still rained, sometimes hard. The countryside seemed abandoned. Most travelers had holed up in inns, and farmers were staying indoors. In the pastures, cattle and horses grazed humpbacked, rain streaming from them.

Cyncaidh's party was the exception; they rode despite the rain, as if they had to be somewhere by a certain time. Which might have been true; no one had confided in Varia. She'd thought of asking Cyncaidh, then decided not to; she felt too ill at ease with the attraction he held for her. She also thought of asking Caerith, but told herself no; if she wasn't willing to ask Cyncaidh, she'd do without knowing.

At least they stayed at inns.

As for the interesting conversations she'd expected with Hermiss—on the road they were too rain-beaten to talk much, and the first two evenings they'd ridden late. The third day started a bit better, with snatches of sunshine in the morning, and they did talk a bit. But after noon, sporadic showers fell, soaking their breeches where their knees peered from their rain capes, the moisture proceeding coldly upward by capillarity to their hips, chilling their spirits as well as their bodies.

As afternoon rounded into evening, a coming storm darkened the sky in the west, like early dusk. The clouds pulsed with lightning, and soon were near enough that their thunder could be heard. Wind had begun to gust and swirl when an inn came into sight at a crossroads ahead. Cyncaidh shouted an order and they began to canter, slowing at the last minute, thudding into the hoof-churned yard. Stable boys ran out through the first skirmishers of rain to help the soldiers with the animals, while Varia and Hermiss slid down and ran inside, to stand panting and red-cheeked in the potroom.

Poorly-lit and steamy with moisture, it was already mostly full of travelers, men. They were the only women, and stares, leers, and randy comments were the order of the moment. The men inside didn't know about the soldiers. A twentyish potboy came over and said loudly, "If you're here to do a little business, you'll owe the house a half share." Then guffawed, smirking around at the men seated there. There were whistles and cat yowls; mugs banged on tables.

Varia would never know why she said what she said next. Perhaps it was a reaction to the smart-mouthed potboy: If he wanted an uproar, so be it. Whatever the reason, she said it loudly: "We'll eat first. Then, if you can let us use a bed . . ." The cat yowls and whistles swelled, and there were shouts of "you can use ours!" followed by laughter.

They sat down at a table, and Varia quickly realized how seriously she'd erred, for several of the bolder men came leering to their table, leaning over them and making propositions.

Hermiss was big-eyed with fright, and Varia, feeling responsible, stood up abruptly.

"You've got us wrong!" She said this loudly too. "We want the bed for sleeping!" That turned most of the yowling to laughter, and for the moment disarmed the more aggressive. Then someone called, "She's playing with you, Barney!" and one of the men grabbed her.

"Just a little kiss to start with," he said, and pushed his stubbly face in hers. She grabbed him rather as she had Xader, though much less strongly. The electric charge she gave him wasn't as strong, either, but he screamed, leaping backward with a force that astonished everyone but Varia, to lay curled on the floor mewling.

"Come on, Hermiss," Varia said, "let's get out of here."

No one got in their way, and outside, they stood under the entryway roof, watching rain pour down. Lightning struck nearby with a tremendous *snap! BLAM!* that shook the porch and almost knocked them down.

A minute later Cyncaidh came loping longlegged through the deluge and stopped near the two girls, grinning like a boy. "We made it just in time! I'm not sure what the possibilities are for lodging though." With his head he gestured toward the stable. "There were barely stalls enough for our saddle mounts. The remounts and pack animals are tied in a shelter without walls." He looked at the two women more closely now, examining their auras, especially Hermiss's. "What's wrong?"

"I said something stupid," Varia told him.

He peered at her a moment, then went in, leaving them outside. Two of the soldiers loped up, also drenched and grinning, nodded to the girls and followed their commander.

"What's going to happen?" Hermiss said timidly.

"Nothing." *I hope.* "Wait here."

Varia went back in, her senses turned high. The air was a mixture of resentment and caution, but gratefully she sensed no impending violence. The man she'd grabbed had made it to hands and knees, to puke out his supper and ale on the plank floor. There wasn't one whistle or cat yowl. She stood behind Cyncaidh, who was waiting to arrange for seating and beds, and murmured: "I'm afraid I caused some trouble."

"I've noticed." His tone was dry, acid.

"I didn't intend to."

"I'll take your word for it."

The innkeeper came out then, and recognizing Cyncaidh as an ylf, nodded deeply, almost a shallow bow. Food, he said, was no problem. But as for rooms . . .

When his troops had gathered at the table, Cyncaid told them they'd bed in the hayloft that evening. *And no doubt pay for it*, Varia thought. She wondered if she was to blame, and decided she probably wasn't; the place was simply full. Then Cyncaidh turned to her and told her a bed of hay was being made for Hermiss and herself in a box stall normally used for storage.

The meal proved barely edible, perhaps as repayment for what the innkeeper considered ylvin troublemaking. The soldiers endured it glumly. The Cyncaidh, by contrast, was grim, not glum. From his aura, Varia surmised that he was irked with her for putting the ylver in a bad light.

The rain still poured thick and cold when they left the building, but as the two girls ran through it, Hermiss laughed in a sort of high glee. She'd eaten little but the bread and cheese, trimming the mold off, and had had a single mug of ale. Varia decided the girl's mood was more an aftereffect of the initial excitement than of drink.

The storm-dimmed daylight had graded through dusk into twilight. Someone, probably a stable boy, had hung a lantern inside the stable's front entrance. A clutter of old single-trees, eveners, pack saddles and the like was piled outside a box stall, cleared from it to make room for the two of them.

A soldier entered the stable carrying a stack of large coarse blankets provided by the innkeeper. He took off the piece of canvas protecting them, then came over and handed a pair to Varia. She looked at them with more than her cat vision, then began to pass her hands over them.

"What are you doing?" Hermiss asked.

"Killing the vermin."

"Really?"

"Certainly."

"What kind of vermin?"

Varia paused, concentrating. "Let's see. There are lice—and fleas. No bedbugs."

Hermiss giggled. "You're fooling."

Varia shrugged and made her final passes, then spread the blankets side by side on the thick hay. The air was pungent, but not unpleasant, with horse urine and manure blending with the smell of hay—clover and timothy. From their cubby she could hear the low easy talking of the half-ylvin soldiers, the sound somehow comforting as they climbed the ladder into the hayloft. *There are worse places than this to be,* she told herself.

Earlier a soldier had brought their oiled leather bags from a horse pack and hung them on harness pegs. She pulled dry clothes from hers and changed into them, draping her wet breeches and socks on the edge of the manger, and her tunic over a horse collar still hanging on its peg. Her wet boots she stood near the stall's entrance. Hermiss followed her example.

Then they lay down on their blankets. Varia willed the girl to be quiet and go to sleep, and lay quiet herself, her eyes closed, waiting for the drumming rain to still her mind, a mind beset by unwanted thoughts. Of Idri. Of Liiset, who'd abandoned her. Of what Tomm had said about Sarkia's plans for her. Of how far they were now from where she wanted to be. Interrupted by the sound of a man running in through the stable door—a man alone—bringing her out of herself. Cyncaidh, she decided. He'd probably been talking with the innkeeper. She closed her eyes again.

"*Were* you fooling about killing vermin?" Hermiss murmured. The question almost made Varia jump; she'd thought the girl was sleeping. Looking at her, she shook her head.

"I really wasn't. Fooling, that is."

Somehow this brought giggles from Hermiss, followed by a question in, for whatever reason, a conspiratorial tone: "What did you do to that man who tried to kiss you? Really do."

"Our term for it is shock fingers. I gave him shock fingers in his crotch."

Hermiss almost burst, trying to control the giggles bubbling out of her. When she'd calmed again, she murmured, "He had it coming."

"True. But I shouldn't have said what I did. Then *he* might not have."

"They were all whistling and saying things before you ever said anything."

"True again. But I still shouldn't have. Especially when they were whistling and yowling like that."

There was a moment's silence. Varia lay back and closed her eyes again.

"What do you think would have happened if you didn't know how to do shock fingers? And the soldiers hadn't come in?"

Varia sighed, answering without opening her eyes. "Nothing. Because I'd have turned around and gone back out as soon as the whistling started."

"Do you think they'd have raped us?"

Hermiss, you're a blockhead, Varia thought, but said nothing. Hermiss interpreted her silence, and this time her words were soft, quiet.

"Were you ever raped, Varia?"

Varia said nothing.

"I wonder what it would be like."

"It's ugly. Painful. You feel like shit." *Time after time. Night after night.*

Silence again for a moment. Then, contritely: "I'm sorry I asked, Varia. I really am."

Varia opened her eyes. Her voice was wooden, a monotone. "It's all right. You're young. Just be careful in a situation like we walked into. Turn around and walk out." *If you can.* Varia discovered her guts were tied in knots.

"Are you young?" Hermiss asked. "I'd forgotten you're like the ylver; that you can look young for a long time. I thought you might be—twenty."

Varia looked at the earnest face on the blanket beside hers, and felt a sudden pang of—something. Loss. "I have daughters about your age," she said. *Had,* she corrected herself.

The face looked troubled again, and this time Varia broke the silence. "Tell me what it's like to be a girl growing up in Ternass."

Hermiss told of school and parties. And about the colonel's daughter, who sounded a bit full of herself but pleasant enough.

And especially about the young men of Ternass, and the ylvin soldiers stationed there. Of flirtations, stories of occasional love affairs and briefly broken hearts. The ylver, Hermiss said, were especially exciting because they were supposed to be better lovers, and being relatively infertile, were less likely to get a girl pregnant. But the imperial army had rules against "slipping it to" local girls, and other rules against marrying them without official sanction, which involved a lot of time and trouble.

She also told about her father. "He knows an awful lot. He's read hundreds of books, some of them ten times, I guess, and thought about them all. He knows a lot about the ylver. Some people at home don't like them very much; some don't like them at all. But my father says ylver are just people with tilty eyes and pointy ears. Some of them can't even do magic, he says. And they don't live forever; they just stay young a long time. He says we're lucky they're here. For every person in the kingdom who died during the war, he says probably three have been saved because we don't fight our neighbors anymore."

Varia didn't reply. She was thinking it would be better if there weren't wars at all.

"What was it like growing up a Sister?" Hermiss prompted.

"Different than you told about. We had duties."

"Like what?"

"Whatever work they trained you for, assigned you to. Making jewelry, all kinds of ceramics, taking care of babies, working in the dining room . . . I was best in the kitchen. I got to be a very good cook."

"Really?" Pause. "Did you, you know—have to make babies?" Hermiss paused, then added, "I've heard . . ." and trailed off.

"After I grew up, I was sent to Farside to marry a man the Sisterhood wanted me to have babies with."

"Farside!?"

"Farside."

"What happened to him?"

Varia began to cry, quietly as usual. Hermiss could hear something though, and peered intently at her in the seepage of lantern light. "Are—you crying, Varia?"

Varia nodded, fighting now to keep silent.

"Oh Varia! I'm so sorry!" Hermiss too began to cry, and put her arms around her. "I shouldn't have asked. I shouldn't. I've been terrible to you!"

The girl tried to cry quietly, too, but began to sob and hiccup, and now it was Varia doing the comforting, hugging her, patting her shoulder. "It's all right, Hermy, it's all right. You couldn't know. You couldn't know."

Hermiss quieted and they let each other go. After a bit, Varia could see the girl's aura smoothen, softening in sleep, but she herself was wide awake now, listening to the rain drum on the roof. "God, Curtis," she whispered drily, "how I wish! How I wish!"

She became aware of movement then, as if someone had been outside the stall and was moving away. Rolling to her knees, she got up and peered out. Cyncaidh was at the hayloft ladder, a hand on a riser. Realizing he'd been seen, he stopped, stood waiting. Varia walked to whispering distance.

"It's all right," she murmured. "The trouble in the potroom got to her, that's all. And the ale. She's fine now. Sleeping."

Cyncaidh stared at her, his eyes dark in the lantern light, and she realized he hadn't just come down to investigate Hermiss's sobbing. His aura was thick with emotions: embarrassment, grief . . . something else.

"You were listening," she said.

He nodded.

"From the beginning."

"From when Hermiss said something about killing vermin. Then she asked what you did when the man tried to kiss you. I'd come down to hear your version of what happened in the potroom, so I stayed where I was and listened. And found out. Then—I stayed and heard the rest of it."

She stared long at Cyncaidh and his aura. "If you're to be my jailer," she said at last, "I suppose it's best you know. And I could never have told you directly."

He nodded, stood silent for a moment. "Good night Varia," he said quietly, and reaching, almost touched her face, then turned and climbed the ladder.

She watched him disappear, heard Caerith's voice question

softly and Cyncaidh's reply. Then she turned and went back to the box stall, settling onto her blanket again.

To stare blankly into the darkness above her, her mind's eye seeing Cyncaidh's aura as it had been by the ladder. *What am I going to do?* she asked herself. *What in hell am I going to do now?* For she realized what another part of Cyncaidh's emotional mix was. She should have seen it sooner, she realized. It had been there all along.

My god, she thought numbly, *he loves me! He's not just attracted to me physically, though that's part of it. And he's not attracted because I'm a pretty woman in a trap. He actually loves me!*

The rain continued to beat. She willed it to beat forever—beat until it washed the world away; that part of it at least. Then shook her head at what seemed weakness. *Just keep us here long enough for me to figure out what to do,* she corrected. *I'll settle for that.*

As if in answer, thunders rumbled, then boomed; another convection cell was moving in. "That's the way," she muttered, and closed her eyes, inviting sleep.

I'm his prisoner, she whispered in her mind, *and he loves me. He'll never help me get back to a gate. Not that he ever said he would. I'll have to get there on my own or not at all.*

14

A Different Land

Varia awoke in the night needing to relieve herself. Rain still drummed on the roof, and she was reluctant to run sixty yards through it to the latrine; her dry clothes would get soaked. She decided instead to duck out the back door, wearing only her rain cape, and use the wide overhang of the shelter where the packhorses were. They wouldn't mind, and it was only seven or eight yards away.

By the time she got back, she had a plan.

She next awoke to Caerith knocking on the outside of the box stall. Rain still fell, but now it only muttered on the shingles, barely audible. Breakfast was far better than supper, and Varia wondered what Cyncaidh had said to the innkeeper, the night before. There was oatmeal without lumps, crisp side pork, cheese, bread and butter and buttermilk. By the time they finished eating, the rain had stopped. Outside, the sun shone through a broad gap in the clouds.

The soldiers were not energetic this morning, but Cyncaidh pushed them, and in half an hour the pack string was loaded, ready for the road again. Varia was ready before them, tight with nerves and purpose, keeping mostly out of sight, not wanting Cyncaidh to note the tension in her aura.

Her plan, such as it was, included only an overall purpose, a general strategy, and a first step. Mostly it was unknowns and assumptions. *When you're desperate enough,* she told herself, *and the alternatives are unacceptable, you grab whatever opportunity you find, and hope something good happens.* The odds, it seemed to her, were at least as good as she'd faced when she'd stepped out the door of the Tiger barracks a few weeks earlier, and that had worked out. More or less. To a degree.

Then Cyncaidh called to fall in and mount up. Varia and Hermiss led their horses from the stable and swung into their saddles, Varia barefoot, her still-wet boots tied to saddle rings—to get them drier, she'd told Hermiss. Cyncaidh, after looking back over the column, shouted another order, and they rode out of the inn's muddy yard.

Until they'd left Fort Ternass, Varia had always been kept in the midst of the mounted men. But since Hermiss had been added to the party, they'd been put behind the remount string, in front of the pack string, with the horse handler the only soldier behind them, back at the very end. Apparently to give them privacy if they wished to talk.

It was Varia who opened the conversation now, telling stories about Washington County and the Macurdies, recounting the funnier things she could remember. Beginning with the time that seven-year-old Curtis had tried to ride a calf and gotten bucked off into a wheelbarrow full of mucky cow manure. He'd run howling and stinking into the house, tracking manure on the linoleum, which enraged his mother. With a grip developed by years of wringing laundry by hand, she'd taken him by the ear to the windmill. It was March, still given to freezing at night, and after stripping him, she'd immersed him in the icy water of the horse tank, which set him howling even louder, then scrubbed him with a gunny sack.

Hermiss' peals of laughter brought a curious glance from Cyncaidh at the head of the column.

Next she told of one of Will's "notions," which struck him during silo filling. For years a neighbor, Deacon Stuart, had pestered Will about his non-attendance at church, hinting at hellfire. Then a skunk had taken residence under Will's barn floor, to make nighttime forays on the hen house, so Will had caught it in a Victor #1 trap. And when the deacon was up in the silo tromping down, Will had thrown the dead skunk into the silo filler. Chopped skunk, along with the content of its scent gland, had shot up the pipe and rained down on the deacon. The silo had been only about five feet short of full, and the overweight deacon, almost overcome by the stink, had clambered over the side and hung by his hands, his feet dangling some twenty feet above the ground. Then, realizing there was little relief in that—the vile smell was as much on him as in the silo—he'd tried to climb back in and couldn't. He'd hung there yelling for help, using language not suited to a deacon, and Will had gone up and rescued him. For two or three years after that, the deacon refused to trade work with Will, but he also stopped badgering him.

That story hadn't worked as well for Hermiss. She knew about corn and skunks, and was familiar with a concept not greatly dissimilar to hellfire, but Varia had had to stop at intervals to explain "deacon" and "Sunday services," "silo" and "ensilage" and "silo filler."

She'd begun telling of a time when Charley, her father-in-law, had been hauling bundles to the corn shredder, when she saw a bridge ahead. Her guts tightened, but she continued the story until she was well out on the bridge planking. Then, with the reins and a mental command, she caused her horse to rear. Behind her, the horse handler shouted a "whoa" to halt his pack string, while Varia, as if fearing she'd be thrown, dismounted. Before anyone was aware of what she intended, she'd vaulted onto the bridge railing and leaped off.

The river was a large one, and swollen now from days and nights of rain. She knew nothing more about it. Not its name, what towns it flowed past, anything. Her assumptions were that it flowed southward to join the Big River; that it flowed fast enough for her purposes; and that there'd be boats tied to the bank here and there, hopefully with oars or a paddle. And that she could swim long enough to come to one of them.

As she plunged beneath the water, she was astonished at how powerful the flow was, how swift. The water of a normally forty-yard-wide river, now storm swollen, with flooding several feet deep on the flood plain, was pouring with a tremendous surge between bridge abutments no more than thirty yards apart. She stayed under water as she'd intended, swimming with the current to put as much distance as possible between herself and the bridge. Her hope was that the soldiers would wait to see her come up before anyone else jumped. By that time, hopefully she'd be far enough away that no one would, that the odds of reaching her would seem too poor. Maybe they'd even fail to see her, and think she'd drowned.

She was neither a skilled nor a strong swimmer, nor experienced at staying under water more than briefly. She stroked as hard she could, feeling increasingly the need for air, and fighting it. Her water-soaked breeches and tunic were like weights, hampering her movements more than she'd expected, while the water was too muddy to see in. She became desperate for breath, and realizing she didn't know how deep she was, fought to the surface, gasping, gulping air.

For just a moment she glanced back. She'd left the bridge farther behind than she'd hoped—perhaps eighty yards, thanks to the tremendous bridge surge—and was almost cut off from view by a curve. Men on horseback lined its railing, but she heard no shouts. Perhaps they hadn't spotted her!

Now she gave her attention to the banks. On the Mustoka River, in Washington County, there'd be rowboats and skiffs now and again, tied or chained to trees along the bank. But this wasn't the Mustoka in any universe, and the water was eight feet above normal. If there were any boats tied there, they'd be swamped. She kept swimming, the current carrying her swiftly. Another hundred yards and she was tiring badly. Some distance ahead and to her left, she saw an oak being swept along, its trunk submerged so that its top resembled a great floating thicket. If she could reach it— But it was traveling nearly as fast as she was. Some distance behind her and near the west shore, she saw a larger tree riding the current, a big silver maple floating higher in the water than the oak, and it seemed to her she could intercept it if she swam hard.

She struck out for it, raising her arms out of the water now in a clumsy crawl stroke, breathing hard. *I'm going to make it!* she thought. But when she'd almost reached it, a submerged branch struck her, snatching her under. She panicked, struggling, swallowed water, somehow pulled free and popped to the surface, strangling and splashing. And went under again, this time because she wasn't swimming anymore but simply flailing. Her natural buoyancy popped her up again, still strangling

on water—and a hand grasped her tunic. Once more she went
under—someone was pulling on her—and twisting, grabbed
whoever it was, pulling him under, too. Then somehow, through
her panic, she realized that she might drown him, might drown
them both, and stopped struggling, letting herself be towed.
Again her head broke the surface.

Through her choking and coughing, she recognized Cyncaidh.
A bank eddy carried them into the floodplain backwater, and
his feet touched bottom. Woofing for air, he towed her heavily
toward the high bank behind it. A few yards farther, he reached
the submerged slope of a natural levee formed by the sediments
and back currents of past floods. Varia felt her own feet touch
then, and the two of them crawled onto its top, to kneel half
out of the water.

Lungs heaving, eyes wide, they stared at each other, tunics
stuck to them, Cyncaidh's hair plastered to his skull. After a
minute he spoke: "God, Varia! What a terrible thing to do!
What a terrible terrible thing to do! Never do anything like
that again!"

Shortly they got to their feet and waded staggering toward
high ground. A few steps took them off the back of the levee,
where they found she could still wade, the water to her armpits.
Soon they were at the high bank, sprawling on its slope,
Cyncaidh still wearing his boots. A voice reached them now.
Above the highbank was a pasture, and a soldier trotted his
horse along its edge, calling for his commander.

"Here!" Cyncaidh shouted hoarsely, then helped Varia to her
feet and up the bank. As they stumbled out of the woods, the
soldier saw them and trotted his horse over. "Thank God,
General!" he said dismounting. Cyncaidh leaned on the horse
for a long moment, clinging to the saddle, while Varia sank to
the ground. Finally he put a foot in the stirrup and raised himself
heavily onto the horse, then beckoned. "Help her," he said. The
half-ylf helped Varia to her feet, then laced his fingers, making
a step for her, and boosted her up behind Cyncaidh.

"I'll follow on foot, sir," he said. "It won't take me long at
all."

"Thank you, Sergeant," Cyncaidh answered heavily, and
nudging the horse with his heels, started for the bridge.

❖   ❖   ❖

No one talked when they got back. Without changing into dry clothes, Cyncaidh and Varia got on their own horses, and when the soldier on foot got back, the column started west again. They didn't stop till they came to a substantial village. At the common, Cyncaidh pulled his party off into its open, parklike woods. A soldier dug his commander's gear bag from a pack, while Hermiss dug out Varia's from another. Then Caerith accompanied the two of them to the nearby chairman's house, recognizable by the pennant on its roof, and knocked at the door. Another soldier had followed, carrying the bags.

Seeing imperial uniforms, the chairman's wife let them in, got towels, and led them to rooms where they could change. When she was dressed again, Varia walked barefoot into the hall, where Cyncaidh waited alone. He put his arms around her, clasping her tightly. "Promise you won't do anything like that again," he whispered, then held her at arms length. "What have I done that you fear me so?"

"Fear you?"

"Enough to try killing yourself."

She shook her head. "I wasn't trying to kill myself."

He gawped. "What, then?"

"I was trying to get back to my husband. I thought I could find a boat. Hoped I could."

He stared, his face slack. His emotion, it seemed to her, was dismay. After a moment he shook his head. "Come," he said tiredly. "There'll be an inn here. The men need to eat."

It didn't rain for several days, and they made good time. Then they turned north again, and a few days later reached the border with the empire itself. Once again the country changed. The main roads all were graveled and ditched now, and frequent mansions showed the existence of a sizeable upper class. With the mansions were compounds, whose cabins could hardly have more than three rooms plus loft, but even they had fruit trees, and small gardens where bean and pea vines climbed frames, while gourd vines climbed the walls.

At the first military post, the quartermaster fitted Varia with a pair of field uniforms. And a female soldier, an ylvin corporal, replaced Hermiss, who'd be sent back to Fort Ternass and the colonel's daughter. Physically, Corporal Keoth could be considered gifted, but personality-wise she was stiff, a stick. She wore her hair in a military bob; its typical ylvin black shone from a good diet and much brushing.

They rested there a day, replaced worn equipment and their whole complement of horses. When the column was ready to leave, Hermiss and Varia embraced. "I don't suppose you'll write to me," Hermiss said.

"Why not?"

"Because—because you're wiser than me, and I'm not ylvin or a Sister or anything."

"I'll write if I can."

"I—hope you'll be happy. You should be. I mean, you ought to be. You deserve to be."

"Everyone deserves to be," Varia answered, then wondered. *Do they, really? Does Idri? Sarkia? Corgan? What would it have taken to make Xader happy? Let him hump every good-looking woman he saw, probably, whether she wanted to or not.*

"I'll write to you, Varia, I promise. And you won't have to write back unless you feel like it."

"Thank you, Hermy. I'll feel like it, but . . ." Varia shrugged. "Who knows what will happen when I get where they're taking me?" She paused, feeling that was a poor note to end their goodbye on. "I'll be glad to get your letters," she finished.

They hugged again. Corporal Keoth stood waiting with a scowl of disapproval. Varia couldn't be sure whether it was for the merely human Hermiss or the evil Sister. *Both,* she decided. She turned, went to her horse, and climbed into the saddle; Cyncaidh gave the command, and the column moved out. As they turned onto the road, Varia looked back. Hermiss still waved, and briefly Varia waved back before looking ahead.

So much for not knowing how to relate, she told herself. And wondered briefly whether she'd ever see either of her remaining children again. Curtis's children. Or know them if she did. Or whether they'd care; they'd probably scorn her for deserting the Sisterhood. Idri would make sure they knew.

Idri. Now she knew who Corporal Keoth reminded her of.

✧　　✧　　✧

Cyncaidh stayed away from her, but she was aware that he watched her now and then, as if to see how she was doing. Keoth wasn't overtly rude, but clearly she disapproved of Varia. Cyncaidh noticed too. After three days, he left the corporal off at a district seat, at the office of the imperial representative, with a written order to have her returned to her base. And again it was Caerith who rode beside Varia.

They traveled till she was tired of riding and inns and an unchanging countryside. Tired even of Caerith, for they'd run out of things they were willing to talk about. But after ten days the country began to change. Forest increased while farmland diminished. From time to time they passed open bogs, often with a small lake in the middle. Lakes were conspicuous in the landscape, and some of the trees were unfamiliar, evergreens of several kinds, some dark and pointed. The golden-barked birches she'd come to know so well in the mountains, returned, joined by much smaller birches whose bark was white as chalk.

After some days of this, with the forest more and more evergreen, they entered a district of large hills ahead. Not mountains, but hills higher than she'd seen since Cyncaidh had brought her out of the Granite Range.

They spent three days crossing them, then came out on level land again, with forests of a pine taller and more graceful than she'd ever seen. And sometimes of other pines, much smaller and with no blue to their greenness, their stands often very dense, with slender trunks and narrow crowns. She wouldn't have thought to find such level land so beautiful. Here too they passed bogs again, moss bogs, Cyncaidh said, though she could see grasses and sedges growing thickly in them, and often knee-high bushes. Even the bogs were aesthetic in their way, though she might not have thought so if the mosquitoes and horse flies and deer flies could have penetrated the spells that she and the others cast against them.

One of the inns they stopped at faced a lovely lake, with a view framed by exceptional pines, thick-boled as old tuliptrees, and even taller. When she'd finished supper, Varia crossed the trail and sat down on a fallen tree to admire the sight. Shortly, Cyncaidh came and sat by her.

"You like this part of the world, I think," he said smiling.

"I do. It's very beautiful."

"It—suits you nicely. I'm glad I could show you to each other."

She smiled back at him. "You're a nice man, Cyncaidh. If I have to be someone's prisoner, I'm fortunate it's you."

He wanted to smile back, and suppressed it. *Guilty conscience*, she thought. It occurred to her then that she might have erred, in the stable in the rain storm, erred in thinking he was taking her north simply because he wanted her. That the interrogation he'd spoken of was only an excuse, that he'd never help her to Ferny Cove after she'd been questioned. Perhaps he would. Perhaps.

Half turning, she faced him. "It's true, you know. You are nice. You've never exercised your advantage over me. You were as gentle as you could have been, back in the Rude Lands, even when I attacked you." She paused, looking back in time. "You provided me with Hermiss when I needed someone like her." Again she paused, this time to laugh. "And rid me of Corporal Keoth without my asking."

She lay her hand on his arm. "You even saved my life."

He stood up, and she stood with him. "I couldn't not have," he said, suddenly flustered. "You—are important to me. Personally. You've known since that night in the stable." He paused. "And you've never exercised your advantage over me, either. You're not the only one who's vulnerable, you know."

Then he turned and strode away, straight-backed but embarrassed, Varia watching him go.

Four days brought them to hills again, high and rocky. The forest here was varied, but with none of the familiar, more southerly trees. The large pines were present in scattered groups, among various smaller evergreens and white-barked birches, and other pale-barked trees whose leaves fluttered prettily in the faintest breeze. As they approached a rock outcrop, she saw a jaguar lying on it, gazing fearlessly at them. As far as she could tell, Cyncaidh cast no protective spell, so she withheld her own.

The cat seemed definitely larger than the jaguars she'd once seen in a menagerie. The horses rolled their eyes and quick-stepped nervously, while their ylvin masters soothed them.

The whole column slowed, watching the animal. When they were past, Varia quickened her horse's pace, pulling up beside Cyncaidh. "It was beautiful," she said. "In the south, I doubt you'd ever see one so close."

He grinned. He'd been smiling more lately; she'd decided he must be getting close to home. "Wait till you see one in winter," he said. "Their coat gets longer, soft and thick, and turns almost white. A pale ice blue, actually, with blue-gray rosettes."

See one in winter? The words triggered anxiety. "How will I come to see one in winter?" she asked.

He hadn't noticed the change in her aura. That required attention, and his was on his thoughts. "We have a place, my family, where we—" He stopped. "You may not have the word for them in the Rude Lands. We fasten long slender boards on our feet, and run on them across the snow. Which up here covers the ground for about half the year."

"They have them on Farside," Varia said. "In my husband's language they're called *skis.*"

His smiled faded. "Well, then," he said, "you know what I mean." He continued with less enthusiasm. "There are several of them there, the Great Cats, and we've developed a sort of mutual trust. We track one or another of them sometimes, to observe them, and sometimes they track us. They neither flee nor offer to attack, though ambush is their favored hunting strategy."

She couldn't tell him she'd love to see one. He might infer an interest in staying. Introverted, she said something vague and dropped back to where Caerith rode. She knew what had killed Cyncaidh's enthusiasm: she'd referred to her husband. While her wonder over the jaguar had died when he'd implied she'd still be with him in the winter. *We need to thrash this out,* she thought. But not yet. She wouldn't be able to stand it if he said she couldn't go back. Or even if he equivocated.

The next afternoon they topped a final ridge that looked across forest to the Great Northern Sea. Cyncaidh stopped, the rest of the party stopping too, and Varia rode up to sit beside him. She liked his grin; it made him look boyish. "That's it," he said pointing. "I've sailed it—including by ice sloop—and skied and skated on it. Everything but swim in it."

"You haven't swum in it?"

He shook his head. "It's too cold. You wouldn't last a minute. Well maybe a minute, but certainly not ten. Probably not five." He pointed northwestward. "My home is off there. Aaerodh Manor. We'll stay in Cyncaidh Harbor tonight, at an inn, and be home about midday tomorrow.

"I love it there. When I speak of home, that's where I mean. That was home even during my twelve years at Duinarog. Though it was about three weeks away by ship, up rivers and across both the Middle and Northern Seas."

The Middle Sea. I never even heard of it before, she thought. *Nor of Duinarog or the Northern Sea, until Caerith mentioned them.* Varia realized again how limited the teaching was at the Cloister. She knew far more about the geography of Farside than about her own world, or even her own continent.

Cyncaidh grinned down at her. "You'll love it too," he said. "It's made for you. It's beautiful."

The inn was a surprise to Varia. When Cyncaidh got down from his horse, a stable boy, a middle-aged human, took the reins grinning. "Good to see you again, Your Excellency," he said. His voice was respectful, but not at all obsequious. Cyncaidh had the man's name ready to his tongue: "It's good to see you, Joleth," he answered. It occurred to Varia then that the inn might be owned by Cyncaidh's family.

It seemed to bustle when they entered. The house staff, mostly ylvin, treated Cyncaidh like royalty. From their auras, they were honestly pleased to see him, and Cyncaidh, in his turn, was friendly—not overly familiar but not at all aloof. The place was almost crowded; the manager told Cyncaidh that a cruise ship had arrived that day.

A small dining room, reserved for special parties, was set up for him and his soldiers. At supper he seated Varia beside him, and the ylvin potboy's treatment of her went almost beyond courtesy, despite her road-worn uniform. In fact, the entire staff was friendly, and seemed to have been expecting her. It introverted her a bit.

While they ate dessert, Cyncaidh leaned toward her. "Stay near me after supper," he murmured.

Afterward the soldiers dispersed, some to sit in a common room for drinks and conversation, while others left to walk around. Apparently none had been in Cyncaidh Harbor before. After speaking briefly with the manager, Cyncaidh took Varia's arm, and together they climbed a flight of interior stairs to a hall, then down it to a large room with a fireplace and upholstered chairs. And a bed, which sent a brief twinge of unease through her.

Her glance moved to the flames dancing in the fireplace, then to the balcony. She walked past Cyncaidh and out onto it. It was flanked by what he'd told her on the trail were spruces, and seemed higher than a second story because the inn was built on a low rocky bluff. Before her lay a bay, with a rocky point on the west that extended well into the lake. *Not a lake,* she told herself. *A sea. A blue, sweet-water sea.* There were docks and a trio of schooners, one of them a long four-master, sleek and clean, painted a strong sky blue. The cruise ship, she supposed.

Cyncaidh stepped out beside her, and their arms touched. She was very conscious of his nearness and size. "Do you find it beautiful?" he asked. He wasn't smiling now, she knew without looking.

He's hung his boyish mood in the closet, she thought. It was a mood she liked, when he showed it, but in her experience it was fragile. She wondered what he'd be serious about this evening. "Very beautiful," she said.

"It seems to me you've been happy these last days."

"I have. More than any time since I was kidnapped and brought back to Yuulith."

As she said it, she remembered the day of her arrival at the new Cloister. She'd bathed, eaten with clone mates, and spent the evening walking and talking with Liiset. It had been a beautiful half day, half a day of blind and foolish optimism.

"I'm glad it pleases you," Cyncaidh said. "I love you, you know."

"I thought perhaps you did." She turned to him, to say more, to tell him that she loved Curtis Macurdy, but his arms slipped around her, and his lips lowered to hers. His kiss was not forceful but gentle, lingering. She was passive, neither returning nor resisting. He stepped back, hands on her arms, his face sober, his aura showing not arousal but love.

"I've wanted to do that—and tell you that—almost since we rescued you. If rescue is the word. And told myself I mustn't; that it wouldn't be fair. Perhaps it isn't now, either, but it seemed necessary that you know."

She stared at him, her fingertips on the lips he'd kissed.

"Tomorrow we'll be at Aaerodh Manor," he went on, "and you'll learn things there. You needed to know this first, know it with certainty." He took a deep breath and half turned, offering his arm. "Let me take you to the steward. You haven't seen your room yet."

He left her with the steward, a robust ylf whose face and aura reflected an even-tempered competence. Instead of assigning a page to guide her, he took her up himself, let her in, then gave her the key and left. The room was a duplicate of the other, with its own balcony facing the lake, and its own fireplace. A fire had been set and lit for her, and her bag lay on a high bench next to the bed. A robe and nightgown hung from a rod. There was a basket on the table, with cheese and bread, and a knife for slicing. A bottle of wine stood beside it.

The sun was low, its light golden on the trees along the water's edge. She stood on the balcony watching it set, saying nothing, almost thinking nothing. Then turned back the covers on her bed, donned the nightgown, and lay down. Thoughts came to her, of being kissed by Cyncaidh, and in them he didn't step away from her, but kept kissing her, murmuring his love while they undressed each other and lay down together.

With a mental jerk, she pushed the images away and stared dismayed at the ceiling. *What are you doing?* she asked herself. And answered that it was only fantasy. *Dangerous fantasy,* she replied. *This man loves you, wants you. Controls you. If you weaken, he'll have you. You'll never get away.*

"Then dream of Curtis," she murmured aloud. "Of sweet Curtis, who was so good, so—innocent." She chuckled. "And had such marvelous staying power."

But this far from Ferny Cove or Oz, to daydream of Curtis was to abrade old wounds. She drank half the wine before she slept.

15

Mariil

They slept in—at least Varia did—had a late breakfast and a later start. Apparently Cyncaidh did not intend to gallop home like an eager schoolboy. They rode through wild and rocky forest for more than three hours when the road—a good road for such wild country—brought them to an extensive opening with farms. Halfway across it stood a building, almost a palace, half seen through shade trees. Cyncaidh pulled aside and turned. "Aaerodh Manor," he said pointing.

His words, his gesture, were for the whole party, but it seemed to Varia he'd addressed mainly her. She was impressed with the size of it, not entirely favorably. To her, a house so large could hardly seem like home. *But it may to him,* she thought. *And I'm not going to live there.*

As they rode on, it held her attention. At least it was handsome, she told herself. Not like the square gray Tudor castles and manors she'd seen pictures of in books, nor the homes of royalty in the Rude Lands. Its designer had been an artist, with a sense of proportion and grace. The walls were white marble, while the roofs were tiled, some green, some red, others blue, their colors saturated. She wondered how often it required cleaning.

Perhaps most interesting, it had no defensive wall, though as they neared it, she could see a tall fence of ornamental black iron pales surrounding the grounds. But the gatehouse, she discovered, had no guards, and the gate was open. They entered, and a graveled lane led them across a green lawn, with flowerbeds, shrubs, and scattered groups of trees. Their approach had been seen, for a major domo met them at the broad steps, a tall, big-framed, uniformed ylf who'd reached the time of decline, his face and figure aging. Nonetheless he shared a strong embrace with the Cyncaidh.

Cyncaidh stepped back. "It's *very* good to see you again, Ahain."

"We've been waiting for the day, Your Excellency."

"How is Mariil?" Cyncaidh spoke with concern.

"Well enough to have visitors, sir. I have no doubt that seeing you"—his glance shifted to Varia then—"and you, my lady, will be better for her than anything else."

"Good," Cyncaidh said. "I'd been afraid. Is she available now?"

"Yes sir. Your messenger arrived last evening before she slept, and her ladyship's been up for some time. She's breakfasted, and waiting for you in her suite I believe."

His mother, Varia thought, *and in her decline, obviously. Why would she be pleased to see me?*

Cyncaidh turned to her. "Varia," he said, "come with me. I want you to meet my wife."

Bewildered, Varia followed him up stairs she was scarcely aware of, and down a hall she hardly saw. He knocked at a door, which opened almost at once. An ylvin nurse let them in, and they followed her onto a deck where a woman sat in the sun, withered and frail on a lounge seat, wrapped in a robe against a breeze that felt balmy to Varia. It seemed to her that Mariil must have been lovely, a decade earlier.

But if her old body was frail, Mariil's spirit showed strong and clear in her aura, which was not depressed by her physical decline. And her ylvin eyes were unclouded; Varia felt thoroughly evaluated by them. "Welcome to Aaerodh Manor," the old woman said. "I'm glad to have you here."

"Thank you. Why?"

The old woman chuckled drily. "Why indeed? I saw strength and endurance in you before you spoke. And the ability to learn, and grow in wisdom. They aren't the same thing, those last two, you know. And I see decency, and an honesty that includes self-honesty. Is that enough for you?"

"Do you see information too? Your husband says he's

interested in knowledge he thinks I have. He may overestimate me. I spent more than twenty years on Farside, and I've only been back about sixteen months, most of it as his prisoner or the Dynast's. It may not take long to learn all I know of the Sisterhood, beyond what I suppose you know already."

"Indeed. That's the least of my interest." She turned to Cyncaidh. "Raien, I have questions to ask you. Before we talk to A'duaill. You'll want lunch first, though, I suppose."

"That's right. I'll come again afterward."

Kissing Mariil's dry lips then, he left with Varia, neither of them saying anything, and took her to a study, where he rang a bell. A half-ylf answered, the second steward, and Cyncaidh told him to guide his guest through the book shelves which covered one wall. "I'll be back for you when lunch is ready," he told her. "I need to be sure my men are properly settled."

Varia watched him leave. *Don't try to figure it out, girl,* she told herself. *There's too much you don't know. Just pay attention. It'll sort out for you.*

After lunch, Varia was taken to Connir A'duaill, who stood as they entered. *The interrogator?,* she wondered. A'duaill looked as young as most ylver—yet didn't, the difference lying in his aura, and in eyes that felt as if they'd seen everything, or near enough. She had no doubt he was a master magician like Sarkia; it fitted both his aura and eyes. Though he could hardly be as old as the Dynast.

The room had no window; that troubled Varia at once. Light came from a skylight shaft and several oil lamps. And the doors were thick; she could scream herself hoarse without anyone hearing.

On the other hand, the appointments were more or less aesthetic, not threatening at all. There were no straps or ties on the table, no whips or tongs or pan of coals, no Xader or Corgan. Besides herself there were only A'duaill and Cyncaidh, and an ylvin scribe with stacked vellum, and a row of sharpened graphite sticks wrapped in paper—effectively pencils.

Musing, she'd hardly heard Cyncaidh's introductions; hadn't even caught the scribe's name. When he'd finished, he looked at A'duaill. "I presume I'm to go now."

"If you please, Your Excellency." A'duaill turned to Varia as if he'd sensed the flash of fear that came despite herself. And said the right thing: "You'll not be harmed, physically or in spirit. That's not something we do here, and in any case we value you for much more than whatever knowledge you may have."

That again. She peered closely at him. "Then why no windows? I could scream myself to death in here without being heard."

"Ah. It's not to keep sounds in, but out. Sounds and more than sounds would hamper what I do here." He turned to Cyncaidh, who hadn't left yet. "Your Excellency."

Cyncaidh nodded to A'duaill, then to Varia, and left. When the door had closed, A'duaill motioned to an upholstered chair across the table from himself. "If you please, my lady." When she was seated, he took the plain wooden chair across from her.

"Why do you call me 'my lady'?" Varia asked.

"It's a matter of status and courtesy. You're the Cyncaidh's guest."

"Why am I his guest? Beyond whatever information you may get from me."

"My lady, much will be made clear to you after this interrogation's over, I'm sure. I hope to complete it this afternoon," he added pointedly. "And when I've questioned you, I promise to receive your questions in turn. Tomorrow, if you'd like. Now, was your lunch adequate?"

She looked curiously at him. "More than adequate."

"Good. And I believe no ale or wine or spirits were served?"

"Nothing stronger than a tea of some sort."

"Fine. Have you relieved yourself since eating?"

"Just before I came here. What . . . ?"

"When we've begun, it's much better if no interruption is necessary. Now. Do you have anything on your mind? Anything pressing?"

She peered at him quizzically. "Right now I want very much to know what you're going to do."

"Good. Let's find out. Start of interrogation." He said the latter as if it were a formal opening.

"First we need to find your memories and open them to

recall. Think of them as being buried. Deeply. Deeply. You'll need to go deeply to see them. Imagine they're so deep, you can only get to them by a deep spiral staircase, going down and down. . . ."

She recognized hypnotism; she used it herself. But she relaxed, letting it happen, letting his voice take her more and more deeply.

In time she woke up groggy, remembering nothing. "Thank you, Varia," A'duaill said, "welcome to the waking world. We did well; you've been very helpful. Now, look around the room and tell me something you like."

I don't remember a thing, she thought. She was—not muzzy, but disoriented. A'duaill repeated himself. "Look around the room and tell me something you like."

She scanned slowly, noticing what was there. "That rug on the wall," she said, gesturing. She hadn't noticed it when she'd sat down; *preoccupied*, she told herself. "It's quite handsome."

"Ah yes," said A'duaill. "Look around and tell me something else you like."

"Hmm! The—carving? Sculpture?" She pointed. "The dwarf on the shelf."

"Either term is appropriate. It's carved soapstone. Tell me something else you like."

She looked and frowned. "In that glass pitcher. Is that ice?"

He laughed. "From our own pond. It's cut each winter and stored in a deep bed of sphagnum moss, in an ice house built of logs. In our northern climate, it lasts from year to year."

Varia frowned. Ice wouldn't last in that pitcher very long. "I didn't notice it before." How long had it been? At least an hour, she decided. Surely that long.

A'duaill smiled. "It wasn't there when you came in. When we finished, I allowed you to rest a few minutes; to 'settle out' as we say, before I brought you back to the present. I had it delivered then. It's a bit after supper, but cook will have something for you. He knows we're done; he sent the ice." He held up a bottle. "Would you like some wine poured over it? There are those who consider that barbaric, but I like it, and the Cyncaidh does too."

After supper!? They'd begun shortly after lunch! She accepted the offer. He poured her only a little, perhaps three ounces. It was as good as Sister-made, she thought, pink and dry, at the edge of sweet. What had he asked? What had she said? The scribe was gone, but presumably he'd written it down, or the gist of it. She doubted anyone could write fast enough to make a verbatim record.

When she'd finished her wine, A'duaill led her to the dining room and left her with the second steward. There she discovered she felt more than hungry. She felt empty! Neither Cyncaidh nor Mariil had eaten with the soldiers; they came in now to eat with her. To the detriment of conversation, she ate like Will after a winter day in the logging woods. And when she finished, felt desperately sleepy, despite having slept, or at least lain unconscious, all afternoon. Something in the wine? A serving girl led her to her room. She was too groggy to bathe. Fifteen minutes after eating, she was in her bed asleep, leaving her clothes for the girl to hang up.

She slept till well after sunup. The first part of the night had not been restful. She'd dreamed strong unpleasant dreams that brought her half awake repeatedly, only to slip back into continuations. The Tiger barracks had been part of it. And a troll, stalking her babies; when she ran to rescue them, the troll turned into Sarkia, who smiled a loving smile and turned her into a frog. Then Cyncaidh had ridden up and cast a spell that turned her not into a woman again, but into a woman-sized frog. He tried several spells, and she grew larger and smaller but remained a frog. Finally he kissed her and said he loved her, and that he'd take her home with him even if she was a frog.

She recalled being reunited with Curtis, too, only to find that the body on top of her was Xader. That time she'd wakened completely, and gotten out of bed shaking. The oil lamp showed her a small wine bottle, but when she'd raised it to her lips, what she swallowed wasn't wine, but something faintly bitter, some medicine. She'd made a face and stumbled back to bed, this time to sleep deeply and unbrokenly.

❖   ❖   ❖

Whatever the drug had been, it left an unpleasant taste. She poured a glass of water and rinsed her mouth, then drank. Her serving girl, an ylf maid named Ardain, came in from the adjoining room.

"Good morning, your ladyship," Ardain said. "I hope you rested well."

Varia assessed how she felt. Neither good nor bad. *A sort of medium gray,* she decided. "Well enough, I guess," she said, and wondered if this girl read auras. Not likely. She also wondered again what A'duaill had learned from her the day before. He'd said he'd answer her questions today. Or no, that wasn't it. He'd said he'd *receive* her questions. *Pin him down,* she told herself.

She bathed, the ylf maid scrubbing her back. What would Liiset say if she could see. She knew what Idri would say, or Sarkia, who as long as Varia could remember, had portrayed the ylver as evil, depraved. She reminded herself then of General Quaie, who'd made the slander convincing. Not that most of the Sisterhood needed convincing; if Sarkia said it, it was so.

I'm well out of all that, she told herself. *The trick now is to get out of here, a much more pleasant prison.*

Clean clothing had been put out for her, including a frock hanging at her dresser set. Ardain suggested she wear it this morning. It was lovely, a pale green; she was surprised that this house had one so suited to her coloring. *If my hair were long,* she told herself, *I might put it on,* then rejected the thought. It wouldn't do to look too pretty, not where Cyncaidh would see, so she dressed in uniform.

She'd expected to eat breakfast with him, and perhaps Mariil. When they weren't there, she told the steward she'd like to see them after breakfast. Mariil, he answered, usually slept through the morning, and the Cyncaidh was out inspecting the property. *That,* Varia told herself, *could take awhile.* "Then I'd like to speak with A'duaill," she said.

"I'll leave your message with his scribe," the steward answered politely, "but just now, he can't be disturbed."

Varia wondered if she was being put off. It smelled that way. She ended up asking a reluctant Ardain to eat with her, clearly not the sort of thing a serving girl was supposed to do. But perhaps she could answer some questions.

"Why am I being treated so well?" Varia asked. "I was brought here a prisoner, you know."

"A prisoner? No ma'am, I didn't know that." Ardain seemed to doubt the claim.

"Why do you *imagine* I'm being treated so well?"

Ardain was uncomfortable now. "The Cyncaidh is a gentleman, and thoughtful, my lady."

He's that, all right, Varia told herself, *but it doesn't answer my question. Besides, Ardain sweetie, you know something you're not telling me.* She tried another angle. "Ahain told me Mariil would be happy to see me, or something to that effect. Why would he say that, do you suppose? She'd never met me."

The ylf maid's discomfort clearly was growing. "I don't know, my lady."

But you suspect, Varia thought, then told herself to leave the girl alone; she'd hardly tell anyway. "Are you from around here?" she asked.

"Yes, my lady, from Salmon Cove. My family fishes. And harvests seals in their season."

"That sounds interesting. How did you come to work here at the manor?"

"My uncle's been with the Cyncaidh's household troops since he was eighteen. He's first sergeant now," she added proudly. "So I got interviewed by Lady Mariil. I've been here since I was fifteen."

"I'll bet they like you; I do. How old are you?"

"Seventeen."

"Suppose you want to get married? Or are those things arranged for you?"

Ardain blushed. "Noble girls get husbands arranged for them sometimes, though they can refuse. For folk like us though, fisher folk or farmers, it's usual to marry a lad who catches your eye." She laughed. "The boy's supposed to ask the girl, but a girl can get him to, if she wants."

"And do the lords ever, um, impose on a girl who works in the house? A lord or his sons?"

Ardain darkened. "Never!" she said.

"I don't mean you, Ardain, or the Cyncaidh. I was thinking about households less well regulated. Less honorable. I'm a stranger in your land, you know."

This mollified the girl somewhat. "I've heard of such, I'll admit," she said, "but it wouldn't happen here. If the Cyncaidh had sons, and they—troubled a serving girl, he'd discipline them severely, I have no doubt."

If the Cyncaidh had sons. "I suppose he would. He's considerate of others." *A noble without sons, whose wife is far beyond child-bearing.* "Thank you for answering my questions, Ardain. I think I'll go to the study now."

Vordan, the second steward, took her, and at her request, showed her the shelf on local and family history, then left her to herself.

Varia ate in the small dining room. Would have eaten alone, if she hadn't again requested Ardain's company. The second steward acquiesced gracefully. Clearly there was no taboo connected with it; it was simply something out of the ordinary. Varia could see the value of not hobnobbing with the help. If the staff was like part of the family, there'd be little privacy, and the distinctions between duties and personal relationships could get badly blurred. But she was a guest, wanting company.

When she and Ardain sat down alone, she asked Vordan when she might talk with the Cyncaidh, or A'duaill, or Lady Mariil. Vordan brought the steward, who promised to get her a more specific answer. He was back before she'd gotten to dessert. The Cyncaidh, he said, was with A'duaill and the Lady Mariil in A'duaill's office, where they'd had lunch as they worked, and would remain till they were finished. She'd be informed at once when they were.

In the study again, Varia did as much thinking as browsing. She'd found nothing about any gate in this part of the world. Were there gates in the empire? If there were, Ylver could safely pass through, at least those with talent. What regulations and policies might they have?

From auras she'd seen in the empire, most ylver had only modest talents, probably because among commoners, breedings weren't arranged. Apparently they weren't among noble families, either, but nobility might originally have been a function of talent. In which case, if nobles married nobles more or less exclusively, most noble children would be born with substantial talent, and no doubt be trained to use it.

Fertility was a problem among the ylver; that was well known to the Sisterhood. Sarulin, the founder and first Dynast, had been ylvin, a sorceror's daughter in the court of a high noble. At least in those days, ylvin nobles sometimes warred on each other, took other ylver captive and made slaves of them. And if the story was true, Sarulin had been such a captive. Beautiful red-haired Sarulin; among the mostly black-haired ylver, she'd been conspicuous. Her captor, who was also red-haired, had raped her—impregnated her at any rate—and the story was that he'd been an exceptional magician.

Sarulin had already decided to escape and start a rebel movement, and with her powers, she'd known almost as soon as it happened that she'd conceived. So she'd undertaken to manipulate the microscopic creature in her uterus to produce a multiple birth, something that had never been tried before, and she'd succeeded. Then she'd run away with her master's discontented son, also very gifted.

Or so the story went, and the truth might well have been something like that.

Varia wondered again what A'duaill's questions had been. Had he learned how fertile her clone was? That among the Sisterhood, multiple births were a learned skill? Had he learned how it was done? Was that why she'd been brought here?

She had her audience with him that afternoon, and didn't ask any of those questions. Perhaps later, but just now . . . Her loyalty to the Sisterhood had been battered since her kidnapping from Farside. But on the other hand, while clearly the ylver were not an evil race, they had their Quaies in high places. Thus she didn't want them learning to do what Sisters routinely did—produce litters.

If A'duaill hadn't learned about this already, to ask would result in another interrogation. Then he'd surely know.

So she asked instead how such interrogations were done.

When the person was deeply enough in trance, he said, they'd answer any question, if it was skillfully put. The trick was to ask the right questions. This he did by reading the aura. A skilled questioner could see and interpret its responses to questions, and use them, along with the answers, to guide further questioning.

"And what will the result be of our session together?" Varia asked. "What is my status here now?"

"My lady, you are still the Cyncaidh's honored guest. Beyond that, you'll have to ask him."

"Honored guest? I'd thought of myself as his well-treated prisoner."

A'duaill seemed honestly pained at that; troubled at least. "I can see why you might think so, my lady. Let me suggest that you speak with Lady Mariil about it. The Cyncaidh is involved for the rest of the day, and I know that Lady Mariil hoped to talk with you after supper, her strength permitting. She's resting just now; sleeping I suspect. The day has taxed her quite severely."

Varia returned to Cyncaidh's study looking forward to the evening. It seemed to her she was getting close to learning what she needed to know. The trick would be to make an ally of Mariil. Perhaps they'd agree to let her go through and bring Curtis back with her. To the empire. If they wanted her as a brood mare, maybe they'd be interested in another unusually fertile blood line—fertile by the standards of ylver and the Sisterhood. She'd promise it, if necessary. But what she and Curtis decided when they were together again might be another matter.

The book she pulled from a shelf was *The Western Empire, from the Reign of Braighn the Red to the Time of Troubles*. She found it fascinating, not least to learn that among this raven-haired people there'd been redheads well before Sarulin and her captor, notably Braighn the First. Who was fascinating, although the ylver he ruled might have used another adjective. If Sarulin was of Braighn's lineage, it would explain her ruthless strength as well as her red hair.

From time to time, Varia encountered something in its pages

that brought her own situation to mind. Affairs and jealousies had played significant roles in ylvin politics then. Probably they still did. And apparently, Cyncaidh wanted, intended, to make her his mistress. Apparently Mariil knew it—apparently the household staff did too—and approved. Certainly the family Cyncaidh would want an heir, preferably male, and preferably of fertile lineage, with demonstrated talent. From what she'd read these last two days, adoption was often resorted to, though historically, adopted sons were less readily accepted in matters of political power.

What would the Cyncaidh and Mariil think of Curtis Macurdy as a sire to adoptive children? Unfortunately, Curtis showed no clear ylvin traits, aside from his untrained talent and minimal body hair. Her tentative optimism of earlier that day looked— unwarranted—given what she'd just read.

Still she'd present the idea, and see what the response was.

She wasn't good company for Ardain at supper. *Being company for Ardain isn't your job*, she reminded herself, then wondered what was. When they'd finished dessert and she still hadn't heard from Mariil, she decided to have a hot bath, and dismissed Ardain for the day. When she'd finished bathing, she dressed in her uniform again, and was sitting on her balcony appreciating the sunset, when someone rapped. The steward this time.

"Lady Varia," he said, "the Lady Mariil would be pleased to have your company in her suite. In twenty minutes, if that's suitable."

Why not now? she asked herself. *As if I haven't waited long enough already*. She shook the thought off irritatedly. *Don't be petty, Varia Macurdy. She gave you the twenty minutes so you could be ready without hurrying*.

"Thank you. Do I go myself, or—?"

"Annith will come for you, if that's all right my lady."

"That'll be fine."

He turned and left. Twenty minutes. Her eyes lit on the dress that had been hung for her that morning; she'd had Ardain leave it out. *That*, she thought. *I'll wear it. Dressed as a soldier, I invite orders. Let her see me as a woman like herself*.

She took off her uniform, then her underclothes, and looked at herself in the mirror. She'd grown up among Sisters where youth seemed almost eternal. But among them, on the onset of decline, a Sister was removed from the community, sent to spend her remaining five to ten years at a retreat "in the south," where no one visited. A practice that grew out of Sarkia's unwillingness to confront the loss of vigor and life, Varia thought wryly. At least the ylver honored their elderly.

As for herself—her critical eyes could find no fault with what she saw. Mother of forty-three, wife of two, and abused repeatedly by a squad of Tigers for how many months. The correct ylvin genes, unhindered by counter-beliefs, healed most wounds short of mutilation or death. *You still look twenty,* she told herself. *Except for the eyes and aura, I suppose, and most don't confront the one or see the other. So here you are, coveted as a brood mare by an ylvin high noble.*

She dressed and looked again. It wasn't a formal gown, but a dinner frock. Still, she'd never had so nice a dress in her life before, not even for her first wedding. She didn't pirouette in it though, just looked. *God,* she thought, *I'm beautiful after all. Truly beautiful, except for that wretched short hair. Curtis, oh Curtis, I wish you could see me in this.*

She felt the damned tears begin to well, and would have changed back into her uniform, except for the knock at her door.

"Come," she said. Mariil's nurse opened it, and Varia left with her, to the east wing and Lady Cyncaidh's suite. Mariil looked up when they entered, and her expression softened visibly when she saw Varia in the frock. She didn't stand, but motioned Varia to a chair in front of hers. "You are truly beautiful," she said softly. "More beautiful than I realized."

"You wanted to talk to me."

Mariil nodded. "To you, with you, about you. I've read the transcript of your interrogation, and there was much personal history in it. You are—even more remarkable than I'd appreciated. Even stronger. Raien had already told me what he knew of you—how he found you after your flight through the wilderness; of your assault on him when he wouldn't free you to find your Curtis; and of your swim. I was impressed. But the things we learned through A'duaill . . ."

"I trust there was more to it than my life history."

"Much more. Much of use to Raien in planning."

"Planning?"

Mariil shook her head. "We could talk about that for days. And will, I hope. Just now I want to talk about you and Raien."

"Your husband."

"My husband. The man I've loved since I first saw him when he was what he looks now to be: a youth in his early twenties." She smiled at Varia then. "I was seventy-two, and quite lovely. At least I thought so, and I'd been hearing it all my life. My first husband was a pleasant and thoughtful man, if a bit careless with the maids, but Raien— And Erig was in decline.

"Raien, it seemed, was as smitten with me as I with him. I was much older, of course, and we knew that barring violence or accident, the time would come . . ." She gestured to herself. "The time would come that has."

Varia kept aloof, as best she could. "And you've produced no heir in those thirty or so years."

"Twenty-nine years last equinox."

"You've had the man you love for twenty-nine years. I had mine for a few weeks."

The reply seemed to shrink Mariil, and for a long moment she didn't answer, then nodded. "But it wouldn't work," she said, "even if you could reach him. Your Dynast knows only that you fled. And where to? To Curtis Macurdy or your death." Again Mariil paused. "Your Dynast is ancient and unrelenting. She doesn't easily give up what she thinks of as hers. She'd send someone after you. Idri perhaps."

The thought jarred Varia. She'd recognized the possibility once, then pushed it away out of sight. Oregon. Suppose they went to Oregon. Could Idri sniff her out so far? Could a tracker?

"Your Dynast still has allies," Mariil was saying. "She'll have sent Idri to Oz, with a strong escort from some friendly king, probably Gurtho of Tekalos. With a request to hold you, if you showed up. But not to Ferny Cove; that would be too dangerous."

Mariil's expression was bleak, grim. "Then Idri would go

through the Oz Gate with three or four guardsmen to hunt you, and if you'd gotten through, you'd be taken, you and your Curtis. Unless he fought. Then he'd be killed."

Unless he fought. And he would. But he wasn't trained to it; and probably they'd catch him with no weapon. Varia felt herself taut, vibrating like a fiddle string.

"The Cyncaidh could take me there," she said. The words tumbled out of her more rapidly than she'd intended. "With a company of soldiers. Let me get Curtis and bring him through. Then we could live here—you could let us have a servant's cottage—and produce sons and daughters for you. You could choose one of them to adopt. Or more than one."

Mariil shook her head slowly. The discussion and emotions had taxed her strength. "It wouldn't work," she said. "Not for the Cyncaidh, and not for you. It was possible for him to slip around in the Rude Lands with a few half-ylver who could pass as locals. But to ride in with a company—they'd hardly come back alive, certainly not from Ferny Cove. Your captured Sisters weren't the only ones savaged there. The fighting was fierce, and Quaie took no prisoners. Vertorus was quartered, and his body thrown to the dogs. His sole surviving son, Keltorus, has sworn his enmity forever, though being an ill-tongued drunkard of a short-lived family, his *forever* might be shorter than he thinks. He's ordered that no Sister be allowed within the borders of Kormehr, and any trespass be referred to him for punishment. I can guess what it would be—death, but not quick."

Frowning, Varia gnawed a lip. "And you want me for a brood mare, for Cyncaidh himself to sire his sons on."

"We want you to be Lady Cyncaidh."

Varia stared. "His wife?"

"His wife. I'm in the process of dying, as you see. And he needs more than heirs. To have a blood heir is desirable, but Raien wants and deserves more than that, believe me."

She paused, seeming to gather strength. "Besides, my dear, he loves you." Again she paused. "I'm an old soul, Varia, with many earlier lifetimes whispering to me. Wisps of wisdom, when I manage to hear and recognize them. And I have no doubt you were born to this. I'll be dead within months. I've been declining for more than seven years now, and am very near the end. The Cyncaidh, on the other hand, is fifty-three, and his line tends to longer lives than most."

She paused, looking piercingly at Varia. "Not that I'm useless yet; certainly not to you. I'm a healer of the spirit, and yours has cruel wounds, not healed, just scarred over." She waved a hand as if impatient with herself. "Back to the issue. Like myself, the Emperor's Chief Counselor has reached his decline, though he may continue in office for another year or three. And the Cyncaidh is likeliest to replace him, for when Paedhrig was Chief Counselor, and Raien his aide, they were haft and blade, two parts of one instrument.

"Our Emperor is eighty-four himself now, and the Diet most often elects the Chief Counselor to the throne, if he's served well. But meanwhile, as Chief Counselor, Raien would start a healing. More than a healing: the spread of trade and learning and peace in the Rude Lands—something made more difficult by that lunatic Quaie. Peace even with the Sisterhood; Sarkia can't live forever. And closer at hand, he'd promote civility within the empire."

Varia shook her head, not disagreeing but overwhelmed— this was too much too fast.

"Meanwhile he's taken no mistress during my decline, though I've suggested it to him. Until he knew you, there was none he wanted." Mariil got laboriously to her feet. "Come, Varia. I'm tired. Even talking tires me these days. And a go-between should take such matters only so far. Let him ask you himself."

As if hypnotized again, Varia stood. "There is something else I must tell you," Mariil said. "Something he cannot and would not. That he is a very good man: kind, considerate, and loving. He is still loving to me. Not in bed of course, bag of bones that I am. Let him remember what I was like in bed in decades past: smooth and supple and full of life." She put her hand on the door handle. "Hmh! I ramble."

Together they walked down the hall to the Cyncaidh's private apartment, and Mariil knocked.

"Come!"

Before she touched the handle, she turned and kissed Varia's cheek, a quick dry touch. "I hope you'll be happy, whatever you decide." Then she opened, turned away, and left Varia standing there alone. The Cyncaidh had gotten to his feet and started to the door. He too had exchanged his uniform for less formal wear.

He stopped in his tracks. "God," he breathed. "Varia, you're beautiful!"

She looked down at herself, then at him.

"Come in! Come in!" he said. She did, and he closed the door behind her. "Mariil's told you what I want?"

"Yes."

"That I want you as my wife, when she's gone? And as my mistress now?"

"The first, yes. The latter she implied."

Reaching, he touched her cheek. "I fell in love with you when I first saw you on that mountain pass, deep inside the Rude Lands."

Varia's voice was quiet, almost emotionless. "There are beautiful ylvin women who'd bring a dowry of wealth and connections."

"I know. Since Mariil's decline became known, a few have courted me, or their fathers or brothers have. But it's you I want to spend my life with. I have no doubt it's our destiny, for I wanted you before I really knew you." He chuckled. "I wanted you when your face and clothes were grimy, and your hair only this long." He indicated half an inch.

Varia failed to smile. "Before you really knew me. Do you know me yet? Really?"

He sobered. "I think I do. I've been on the trail with you. Seen you under stress, seen your aura, and read the transcript of A'duaill's interrogation. And beyond that, there's a knowing that goes deeper than seeing."

"You know I love someone else."

"I do know, and I'm content with it. He must be good, for you to love him."

Good and innocent. But I wonder how Curtis would feel to share me with you. Though I've been overshared already, if not of my own will.

The Cyncaidh put a hand on her waist then, and gently but

firmly drew her close. She did not resist. "It is my wish," he said, "to love you so long as we both shall live."

So long as we both shall live. She'd heard those words before, in English. Had said them. Tears began to flow, silent as always. Cyncaidh kissed first them, then her lips, and she responded the way she'd feared she might.

She did not return to her room that night, nor on any night thereafter.

16

Reflections in a Prenuptial Bed

General Lord Raien Cyncaidh lay on his side, staring motionless at the glowing coals in his fireplace. This far north, a night fire was usual in summer, and rather often, when he was at home, he let watching it lull him to sleep.

Tonight, though, he felt no sleepiness at all, despite more than an hour of love-making. Good love-making, it seemed to him. It had gripped him, lifted him, held him aloft, then spent him. Twice. The first time it hadn't worked for Varia, though it had started well; Curtis Macurdy had gotten in the way. But the second time she'd climaxed despite herself, with urgent movements and sharp cries, her strong clutching fingers digging hard in his back.

Then his joy had turned to dismay, for her climax ended in tears and bitter sobbing. "Curtis," she'd wept, "oh Curtis, I'm sorry. I'm so sorry." Over and over, till she'd run down and slept.

Earlier, when they'd stood in his parlor and kissed, when they'd come into this room and undressed, and gazed at each other, and when he'd caressed her and she'd begun to move beneath his hands, it had promised to be one of the most beautiful, fulfilling nights of his life. And when at last they'd merged in climax, it seemed the promise had been met.

He hadn't imagined it might affect her as it did. He'd thought that once she'd consented, everything would be beautiful. And she did love him; over the weeks, he'd seen it in her aura.

147

But not tonight; tonight there'd been first despair, then yielding, participation, and at length passion. But not love. And afterward—afterward guilt and grief. Obviously, as she saw it, she'd betrayed not only her husband on Farside, but her dreams and her sense of loyalty.

They'd caught her between them, he and Mariil, in a sense had trapped her, then worked on her from both sides. They'd broken her dream of reaching Curtis Macurdy, taken away her hope, then had set himself before her as her only option.

Even Mariil hadn't foreseen the result, he was sure.

After all that had happened to her—imprisonment, fists, knife tips, raped nightly for months—they hadn't imagined that this evening with him, whom she loved, would cause her grief. But in the Tiger barracks, helpless and brutalized, she'd withheld herself in mind and spirit. While tonight she'd *given* herself: body and soul. That was the difference, he had no doubt. It was giving herself that spawned remorse and grief.

He'd rushed things, overridden her uncertainty and scruples, taken advantage of her vulnerability and despair. Perhaps—hopefully—it had been for the best, but . . . He'd back off now, apologize honestly, let her evaluate and adjust. When she felt ready . . .

To a degree they'd lied to her, had exaggerated the hopelessness and danger. In part to keep her from harm, for in fact she could well be killed trying. Given Keltorus' hatred of the Sisterhood, she'd almost surely have been killed, brutally, if she'd continued alone to Ferny Cove. But their primary motive had been to convince her to stay and marry. The odds, he judged, would have been no worse than even—probably better—if he'd sent a squad riding with her to Oz, there to smuggle her to the gate. Volunteers wearing wadmal like tribesmen. He could have. He still could.

But he wasn't going to. Certainly not now.

He turned his attention from his thoughts to the lovely woman sleeping at his back. Listened to her quiet breathing, then carefully turned his head and looked at her. Her aura remained somewhat shrunken, though the colors had cleared a bit, pulsing lightly in dream. Apparently a healing dream. Resilient! She'd had to be to get through this past—what? Sixteen months. Looking at her, he felt love and compassion. And commitment.

In the morning he'd tell Mariil what had happened tonight. No one healed the spirit more skillfully than Mariil, and she admired Varia as much as he.

I love you, Varia, he thought to her, *and I'll make you happy. I swear it. I won't try to make you forget your Curtis, but I'll do all I can to make you happy with me.*

Her aura didn't react to his thought; she was too deep in dream, perhaps of Curtis Macurdy. He wondered what the Farside farmer was doing, after more than a year. How ironic—reasonable but ironic—if the man had settled down on his farm with a new wife. Had he known, really, what a remarkable—what an admirable woman he'd married?

PART 3
The Lion Grows Claws

17

Sword, Spear, and Bow

After work, three days later, Hauser sent Macurdy to Arbel's workshop. Seemingly casual, the shaman stood up when the slave came in. "What is my mood?" he asked.

Macurdy's attention focused. "By your eyes, you seem relaxed. By your aura—you're hiding something. Not unpleasant, but—" Macurdy shrugged.

"Fine. Of course, you've been concealing something from me recently, too. Nothing discreditable, but you've been doing something and not saying anything about it."

"Yes sir. Almost every day recently, I've been visited about noon by a tomttu and a great raven. We've exchanged stories and information about our worlds."

The shaman's eyebrows arched. "Ah! You've been privileged! I've never met a tomttu myself. Nor exchanged as much as a greeting with a great raven; they are highly respected, you know. The popular belief is, they're the spirits of shamans awarded a lifetime of freedom from cares and human limitations. It's said that even goshawks don't molest them." Arbel chuckled. "We shamans tell our people to put meat scraps out when a great raven is in the district. Looking to our own future, you see. Though seemingly they prefer to scavenge for themselves.

"But I believe they're gone now. Right?"

Macurdy nodded. "Maikel left to winter in the Diamond Mountains with his family. Blue Wing went east to sheep country; more scavenging there."

Arbel laughed. "Well. I have news that may or may not please you. Please you, I trust. But first, light my fireplace."

Macurdy went to it, knelt, and with a pass of a hand, caused the kindling to burst into flame.

"Good. And your reading of auras is developing nicely—a rare and useful skill. With use, it should improve without further instruction. Anything else you've noticed?"

"In the way of magic? I saw through the tomttu's invisibility spell. I heard him laugh, and when I looked, there he was."

"Hmh! Very good. You can expect similar surprises from time to time. In many respects you have proven an excellent student, but as a healer . . ."

Macurdy recalled the sick and injured farm animals that Arbel had had him try to heal. In a few there'd been healing or marked improvement, but usually not. And twice he'd been assigned to heal humans—once a severe rash and once a wry neck, examples of things that, according to Arbel, were readily healed by magic. When the patients returned the next day unrelieved, Arbel had taken them into his workshop one at a time, for ten or fifteen minutes each, and banished their conditions then and there.

"It seems clear to me," Arbel continued, "that being a shaman is not your destiny, but neither is the slave crew. So we will try something else and see what happens. You will continue at your present work, living with Charles so that he may continue to help you with our language. You use it well enough now for ordinary purposes, but I see in you—possibilities I cannot identify. So I want you truly fluent. And instead of my working with you in the evenings, you will train with our militia, in the skills of war."

The shaman raised an eyebrow. "I see that pleases you. Good. It was no little trouble to get approval for this; you are, after all, a slave. Sergeant Friisok spoke for you, or I would certainly have failed. It was he who captured you when you came through the world gate. He said you showed presence of mind, toughness, boldness, and measured judgement. And Captain Isherhohm, in turn, values the sergeant's judgement."

Arbel paused, his gaze calm. "Wolf Springs is a proud district. And as we are not satisfied with an ordinary shaman here,

neither are we satisfied with an ordinary militia. Captain
Isherhohm demands diligence and strict obedience, and our
militia is the best of any in Oz, including Oztown itself. But
from your aura, I have no doubt you will excel in this training,
and who knows what good may come of it."

The district militia were infantry, and consisted of three
categories: novices, youths, and veterans. The novices, who
trained four evenings a week, included all able-bodied fourteen-
year-old boys, and worked primarily on weapons skills. Youths
aged fifteen to twenty trained twice a week on weapons skills,
and twice on fighting drills and tactics. Veterans trained only
once a week.

The novices already had four months training when Macurdy
joined them. Emphasis was on the spear and sword, as most
had been practicing with the bow from age four, as play, and
were skilled with it. Among them, Macurdy was a giant in
strength, and the story of how he'd almost killed a guard, the
day he was captured, was already known around the district—
thanks to the man's family, which had asked approval to kill
or at least maim the new slave. But their brother had a
reputation as a sadistic idiot, and good slaves were valuable,
and when the father hinted that he and his sons might take
matters into their own hands, the headman had threatened
floggings and ruinous fines.

As a novice, Macurdy quickly demonstrated excellent
weapons talent. His coordination and quickness to learn were
outstanding. Within weeks he showed more skill than any other
novice with spear and sword. And with the shield, which was
worn slung on the back, and used only in sword drill.

From the beginning he could draw the heaviest bow, and
after only a month, his accuracy approached ordinary for
novices. While he matched almost any of the veterans in the
number of practice arrows shot successfully into a target area
in a given time—timed by a small sand glass. When the target
area was at extreme ranges, he was almost unmatched.

At the end of four weeks, he was promoted to the youth
level. However, on two additional evenings he was required
to continue his weapons training under a hardbitten, partially

disabled sergeant whose usual job was to coach and browbeat those who needed extra sessions.

By late winter—the end of Two-Month—Macurdy showed substantially higher skill with both spear and sword than anyone else at the youth level, and his accuracy with the bow was quite good. As for tactics, he'd already seen improvements that could be made, but diplomatically kept them to himself. His reaction time and concentration became notorious, yet no one showed resentment, for there was no vanity or arrogance in him, only good nature.

Arbel had given Hauser the use of a large, heavy-bladed knife to cut branches of shrubs and trees whose leaves or buds, flowers or inner bark, had medicinal value. At Macurdy's request, Hauser loaned it to him in the evenings, and Macurdy practiced throwing it at a log shed for ten or fifteen minutes in the dark. Always, as Hauser told Arbel, returning it razor sharp. Although the knife was not at all balanced for throwing, Macurdy was soon able to stick it reliably and deeply into an area the size of a man's torso, at distances out to twenty feet.

While at his lunchtime in the forest, he almost always spent a few minutes throwing the axe at some large-boled tree. And like any Ozian woodcutter or Hoosier logger, carried a file and stone to remove nicks and dullness. By winter's end, he could reliably sink this unorthodox weapon deeply into the wood at the height of a man's chest.

He felt good about it all. It wasn't the sort of thing he'd been brought up to, certainly not by his mother. The Macurdies didn't much hold with violence, except in games. Or self defense, and the need was rare, given the Macurdy reputation for size, strength, and quickness.

But this wasn't Washington County.

In fact, he found himself exhilarated by his emerging skills. He had no doubt at all that when summer came, he'd leave Wolf Springs. Run away, travel eastward to the Kingdom of the Silver Mountain, and take Varia away from Idri or whoever had her. He was a warrior now, and if someone tried to stop him, too bad for them.

Once they were back on Farside, there'd be time enough

for peace. Peace and love and children. But first, he told himself, he'd have to bring it about. Earn it.

With the last new moon at hand before the spring equinox, Captain Isherhohm took him aside. "Macurdy," he said (as a slave, it was all the name Macurdy had there), "we're sending you to Oztown. It's where the Chief has his house and farm. He also has a company of Heroes; a hundred, more or less. Only the best from the districts are chosen for it, and Wolf Springs already has more than any other in its ranks."

Macurdy's brows rose. He'd heard the Heroes talked about, but hadn't thought a slave could be chosen. And they were cavalry. Though trained to ride to battle, then dismount and fight, they were also trained to fight in the saddle. This was an opportunity to expand and improve his warrior skills.

"Both Friisok and myself were Heroes in our youth," Isherhohm went on. "You serve for six years, then usually return to your village. Heroes have no other duties than to train, and to serve the chief as his personal troops. You can bring credit to Wolf Springs, and when you return, you'll be a free man. Given a good farm with oxen and good saddle horses, and slave girls to father children on. If you bring home a spear maiden, it'll be a large farm, with slaves enough, you won't have to lift a hand in labor."

He paused. "Captain," Macurdy said, "I thank you. I'm indebted to you for all you've taught me." *And to repay you,* he added silently, *I'm going to run away before the summer's over. Probably make you look bad, and kill the chance of any slave being chosen in the future. But if there's some way I can make it up to you later, I will.*

He couldn't even imagine what that way might be, but his intention was honest. If it was possible, he would.

After a day's ride, Macurdy arrived at Oztown, escorted there by Friisok. There were perhaps twenty Hero candidates loitering outside the split plank building that housed and officed the company's officers: Captain Palkio, the commander; his aide; and the two platoon commanders. The captain tested each candidate, requiring a demonstration of spear forms and sword forms, followed by sparring with one of the Heroes assigned that day for the purpose. Macurdy was passed without hesitation, despite Palkio's eyebrows rising at a slave being sent. It seemed to Macurdy that the Ozmen were pretty sensible about their slaves. Property was property. You took decent care of it, and used it to good advantage.

All but one of the candidates passed. Macurdy was assigned to 2nd Platoon, whose recruits fell in behind their corporal, and marched to the longhouse that would be their home.

18

House of Heroes

When the recruits arrived at the 2nd Platoon long house, the platoon was absent, except for the corporal who'd guided them, and three men who'd helped test them. There Corporal Jeremid talked to them about their new life. They would, he said, become not only the best fighting men in the tribe, but the best in the world. And they had the toughest sergeant in the world; he'd beaten a man to death with his bare fists once, for backflashing him.

In the Rude Lands, most months are divided into four weeks of seven days each, with freedays at the end so that each month begins with the new moon. (Twelve-Month and One-Month are trimmed and patched so that One-Month begins on the New Moon nearest the Winter Solstice. The system lacks elegance, but suits their needs.) On six days of the standard week, the Heroes trained to improve their weapons and tactical skills, and the novices learned horsemanship.

Most Ozian farmers owned no more than a single horse—some plowed with their milk cow—and few new Heroes were satisfactory horsemen. So each morning of their rookie month, the novices were taken out to ride across rough pastures and through forest. At no more than a trot to begin with, later at a canter and eventually a gallop. When they could gallop breakneck through forested hills without losing control, they were ready to hunt.

Jeremid's eyes glistened in the telling. Hunting, he said, was the high point of training. They'd ride behind hounds, pursuing whatever game they put up—fox, wolf, bear, the great

159

and small cats—with the Heroes hurtling after them. Most deaths or cripplings in training were from hunting accidents: a neck or head broken by a low branch, a horse failing to clear a blowdown, even a jaguar brought to bay and charging. Heroes were forbidden to use a bow against large prey, he went on; it was considered cowardly. The spear was the kill weapon, with only one man wielding it.

The training days, he told them, started at sunup and continued till dusk. During the week, drinking was forbidden, except for a large mug of ale served nightly with supper. But after supper on Six-Day, the slave girls were brought in. Slave girls selected for Heroes, good-looking girls who considered it a privilege. So the corporal said. It was a party for the girls as well as the Heroes, and it gave them favored status, sparing them the more disagreeable jobs between parties. And on Six-Day night, there was all a man could drink, spirits as well as ale. Seven-Day was given to recovering.

As the corporal described it, Macurdy decided he'd have to sneak out. He'd be true to Varia in spite of all.

Meanwhile it was One-Day. He had five days to come up with a strategy.

He found it easy, adjusting to a Hero's workday life. You just did it. Riding was the aspect he'd felt concern over. He'd ridden horses all his life, both in the saddle, and bareback on work horses. But back home, riding had pretty much amounted to plodding. Now and then, mainly as adolescents, they'd raced on a road or in a pasture, hopefully when no one's pa or ma or sister was watching, but that was about it. So the notion of galloping headlong through forest and brush was sobering.

All the new trainees were skilled with weapons, though probably few at throwing the ax, or even the knife. (Hauser and Arbel had given him the knife he'd learned on, as a parting gift.) But here they learned additional techniques, with spear, sword, and shield, techniques well beyond those taught to militia. And from the first, the infantry tactics they drilled included tactics more refined than he'd learned before. Thus Macurdy discovered he hadn't been as skilled as he'd thought. On the other hand, the horsemanship training wasn't as hair-raising as he'd expected. Most of the other new Heroes were no more skilled in the saddle than he, and the training was pitched accordingly.

By the end of his first week, he'd improved a lot—and had his strategy for avoiding the Six-Day evening orgy. It was simple enough: Heroes had access to the several Oztown shamans, which gave him somewhere to go. So he told his platoon sergeant his back was seizing up on him. Sergeant Zassfel scowled but gave his approval, and Macurdy left. On the premise that it was best to go to the top, he'd already learned which shaman was regarded as most powerful. When he got there, though, he said nothing about his back. His hope was to be accepted as a student on Six-Day evenings.

He told the shaman an edited version of his history with Arbel, but this man was no Arbel. He was haughty and unimpressed, and sent Macurdy on his way. Bumpkin soldiers and rural shamans were beneath his interest. So Macurdy found a decrepit, abandoned outbuilding not too far from the longhouses, and spent the rest of the night there.

At early dawn he awoke from cold, not for the first time, and went to the 2nd Platoon longhouse. The place buzzed with snoring, and smelled of vomit and rut. By dawnlight and the glow from the fireplaces, he saw the bodies of Heroes and slavegirls, most of them naked, lying singly or more or less entwined on low beds, floor and tables. In some obscure corner, two of them had re-engaged, grunting and moaning, the sound stimulating Macurdy sexually. *Yes*, he thought, *it's a good thing I wasn't here last evening. I'd have never held out*.

Next Six-Day, not having come up with a better strategy, he again used that ancient military complaint, the bad back. Zassfel eyed him skeptically. "Again? If this keeps up, I'm sending you back to the slave crew. Heroes don't have bad backs."

The man's aura reflected irritation and hostility, but not suspicion. "Yes, sergeant. I never had it before, and I'd just as soon never have it again. If this time doesn't take care of it for good, I'll tell you so you can get rid of me."

Zassfel, who was larger than Macurdy, jutted his jaw. "All right. This one time. Jeremid says you're the best of the new men, otherwise I wouldn't put up with it. Now get out of my sight!"

Macurdy got. He tried a different shaman, but the man's aura showed little psionic talent; he might or might not be a competent herbalist. This time Macurdy spent the night in a hayloft, which risked discovery by someone at morning chores but was a lot better sleeping.

Many in the new training class found themselves attracted by Macurdy's charisma. All his life his peers had tended to look up to him, more so since Arbel had freed him of the false modesty imposed by his upbringing. In addition he was older than the other rookies, twenty-six compared to their twenty or twenty-one.

Macurdy, in turn, particularly liked Corporal Jeremid, a third-year Hero from Oztown itself. Jeremid was nearly as tall as he, and if somewhat less powerfully built, was exceptionally athletic. His principle duty was teaching horsemanship to the recruits.

The next Six-Day was the first time the rookies hunted, riding with the veterans, galloping recklessly through woods and brushy bottomlands, while the hounds bayed on the trail of a jaguar. Finally they brought it to bay in a broad-crowned oak, to snarl down from a branch well up in the crown. The hounds circled, necks craned, their trail song become a clamor.

Zassfel looked around. "Macurdy!" he shouted, "take your spear and drive him down out of there."

Even the veterans found the order hard to believe. "Yes sergeant," he called back, mind racing. *Drive him down out of there!* he echoed mentally. *What an ass!* It seemed to him he'd better take his shield, too, so he left it slung on his back. "Gester," he said to one of the others, "hold my spear till I get up in there." Then, while the others watched, he rode to the oak. Leaning his hands on the thick trunk, he stood up on the horse's back, grasped the only branch he could reach, and pulled himself up, then regained his spear from Gester. Sliding it through the back of his sword belt left both hands free, and he began to clamber up through the branches, doing his best not to catch the spear on a branch, or dislodge his shield.

No one spoke, not even Zassfel. *Not even any horseshit advice,* Macurdy told himself grimly. *They don't have any more idea of how to do this than I do.* He stopped about fifteen feet short of the cat, which had been hissing at him the whole way. *So far, so good,* he thought eyeing it, *but if you come for me now, I don't have a prayer.* He withdrew the spear, an awkward job. "One hand for climbing, one for the cat," he muttered. "This is the shits!" Sweating with tension, he climbed one branch higher, paused, and reaching with the spear, poked at the jaguar. Its hiss swelled, and swatting, it cut its paw unexpectedly on the blade, almost knocking the weapon from Macurdy's hand. *Shit!* he thought, *got to get closer.* His heart drummed in his rib cage, but his hands were steady. *One branch more and see what happens.*

The cat began to back out on its branch, flattened to it. *Just what I need: two hundred pounds of spotted cat out on a limb, with me between him and the trunk.* He stopped on a branch about five feet below the cat, stood on it, and edged outward. The cat moved up one, but didn't take the opportunity to move to the trunk again. *Okay,* Macurdy thought, *give me a chance at your belly.* He rested the spear on the branch overhead, like a pool cue on a bridge, ready to stab upward. The cat reached down, slapping in his direction with a broad hook-rimmed paw, slaps so quick he couldn't have counted them, and Macurdy realized even more how overmatched he was. Again his spear darted, stabbed a muscled shoulder, and after squalling, the cat moved in to the trunk, to begin backing down. Hopefully to continue downward, because now it was Macurdy who was out on a limb.

When it got to his branch, it paused. Macurdy jabbed again, the blade slipping past the jaguar's guard, slicing into the muscles of the chest. The cat screeched—the sound freezing Macurdy's heart—partly lost its hold, then recovered. Macurdy had drawn the spear back; now he jabbed again. This time the paw was quicker, striking the spear aside, and now the cat stepped out toward him, inside the spear's reach. Hands almost spasming, Macurdy gripped the branch next to his head, the cat hardly six feet from him, jaws wide, the sound from its throat like the steam hose at the creamery.

He tossed the spear away, drawing cries from the men on the ground, but at such close range, he couldn't use it one-handed. Then, holding the branch above with his right hand, he rolled his left shoulder enough to slide his shield down onto his left arm, shifting it between himself and the cat.

He couldn't crouch—the branch he held for balance was too high—and he could only bend a little. If the cat chose to, it could easily attack his lower legs. But he thrust the shield toward it, and that held the cat's focus. "Haah! Haah!" he shouted. A paw struck the shield before he could see the movement, struck so hard it almost dislodged Macurdy, who nonetheless inched another step forward. "Haah! Haah!" The cat backed away. For a moment it crouched with its hindquarters against the trunk, then with a quick scrabbling began to back down the tree again. When it reached the next to lowest limb, it paused, then launched itself, clearing the men near the tree, landing on last fall's dead leaves.

Its impact and horizontal momentum caused its legs to collapse for just an instant, and two of the hounds were on it before the cat could streak away. It twisted, raked one hound off, then other dogs were at it, and the action, with squalling, yelping and growling, was too swift for Macurdy to follow. A spear drove, taking the cat in the flank, another spear struck, and another, and the dogs swarmed over it, tearing.

Shit, thought Macurdy. *Whatever happened to the rule that only one man wields the spear?* It was just as well though, he told himself; saved wear and tear on the dogs. He reslung his shield until he reached the lower branch, then tossed it to the ground.

On the way back to town, most of the trainees were still exhilarated from the kill. Macurdy, on the other hand, was grim and angry. He'd hunted all his life, perhaps not with great enthusiasm, but it was what men did, and he'd found pleasure in it. But this time—

He sat beside Jeremid at supper. The young corporal was still somewhat excited. "You've got to stay for the party tonight,

Macurdy," he said. "There's not only the slave girls; there'll likely be a spear maiden or two, maybe more. Probably try someone out. A good-looking guy like you, one of them may even take you home with her for the night. Get her pregnant, and you've got a life of ease, making babies with her. With luck she'll even let you hump slave girls on the side." Jeremid laughed. "Especially if she doesn't know about it."

Macurdy had heard about spear maidens. Other nations didn't have them, he'd been told. The daughters of Heroes were trained from girlhood with weapons, the best being honored as spear maidens. They almost always married Heroes. No doubt the practice had been started deliberately to breed up warriors.

Marrying a spear maiden was nothing he wanted to do, but to leave with one, then pretend to get too drunk—

So he waited around, sipping at an ale to pass the time. There was cheering from the doorway, and laughter, male and female. Slave girls came prancing in, wearing nothing but little aprons in front and behind. Thirty or forty poured through the door in a brief flood, dispersing through the room, pairing off, men grabbing them, kissing and pawing. One, a blond with bold breasts, had spied Macurdy's large body and fended off other Heroes to reach him.

"I never saw you before," she said, and grabbing him, kissed him roundly while rubbing against his erection.

Good God! he thought, *talk about brazen!* "Sorry," he said, "I'm waiting for a spear maiden."

"Come on, Muscles, don't be that way. Let's you and me hump, and *then* you can wait for a spear maiden."

His powerful hands gripped her shoulders and removed her, holding her at arm's length. "When she comes in," he said, "I want to be ready and loaded. You're a great looking woman, and there's lots more guys here. You'll get all you want."

She tossed her head, insulted despite the compliments, and turning, walked away, reaching back to flip up her rear apron and expose her buttocks to him. Macurdy sighed. This could be a trying evening. Not a dozen feet away, one of the Heroes already had a slave bent over the table, his buttocks driving. More, though, were drinking and laughing with their girl of the moment, kissing between swigs.

Then he saw another woman enter, broad-shouldered, dressed in decorated calfskin breeches and shirt, wearing a short sword on one hip and a knife on the other. Just inside she paused, scanning the chaos with half a smile. Macurdy waved to her, and she started over. None of the unpaired Heroes grabbed at her, though several spoke as she passed. She answered without looking aside, her focus on Macurdy.

Half a dozen feet away she stopped and looked him over, seeing a man taller than most, lean and hard, with wide heavy shoulders and a strong, good-looking face. Macurdy, on the other hand, saw a woman as tall as an Ozman. Eighteen or twenty years old, he guessed, and long-legged, with shoulders that made her waist look small, and large muscular hands. She had a warrior aura. Her brown hair bordered on blond, and her face, dusted with freckles, suggested straightforward honesty.

She smiled at him before she spoke, and her teeth were strong and even. "I haven't seen you before. Where've you been?"

Suddenly Macurdy felt stupid. He couldn't tell the truth, it seemed to him, yet anything else would sound lame. "Visiting a couple shamans," he said.

"Shamans? On Six-Day evening?"

"When else?"

She cocked a critical eye at him. "My name is Melody."

Melody. With a sword and knife, fully clothed at an orgy. "Mine's Macurdy,"

"Macurdy? Never heard of a name like that. And you've got an accent. Where are you from?"

"I came here from Wolf Springs. Before that—I came from a far place."

"Sit down," she said, and motioned to a long bench built along the south wall. They went to it, and sat side by side. "Wolf Springs sends more than their share of Heroes," she said. "My dad's from Wolf Springs, and got my mother pregnant with me. She was a spear maiden too. Now tell me about this far place."

Without examining the wisdom of it, Macurdy began to talk on the premise that truth is usually safer than lies. "You've heard of the wizard gate there?"

She frowned. "Sure. What about it?"

"I came through it."

"Are you lying to me?"

"Nope. I came through a year ago. Got made a slave, and then the shaman's apprentice, till he found out I didn't have a healing touch. So he had me put in the militia. Now I'm here."

"A slave in the Heroes! I never heard of such a thing. You must be something, to have gotten sent here."

While they'd talked, a grinning Jeremid had come over with a slave girl, one of his hands kneading a breast. "He's a Hero, all right. We got a big jaguar up a tree today, and he climbed up and chased it down! It's true! Better grab him, Melody. He's going to be one of the all-time best!" He led his partner to his sleeping pad then, where she began undressing him. From nearby came the urgent, passionate grunts of some Hero's orgasm.

"This place gets me horny," Melody said, and getting up, sat astride Macurdy's lap, her face in his. "Let's you and I get acquainted. Where's your bed sack?"

"Uh, Melody, I'm married."

"Married!? They don't send married men here."

"Married on the other side. Through the gate."

Both her eyebrows raised. "On the other side doesn't count," she said. "The gate is one way. Guys have tried to go through it, but no one's made it except Sisters. Like swimming against a strong current, and the closer they got, the stronger it got." She put her arms around Macurdy's neck and kissed him, soft and moist, lingering. "The other side's lost to you, Macurdy," she murmured. "While I'm here, and I like you. I want to try you out. Who knows? Maybe I'll marry you."

He reminded himself to breathe. This woman was a lot more enticing, compelling, than the big blond. "I promised her to take no other woman as long as we both shall live."

She stared. "Even when she's somewhere else? Why would you promise such a thing?"

"It's part of the marriage agreement."

Melody frowned. "Crazy! Do the men there actually live up to it?"

"Most of them."

She kissed him again. "Think about it," she said. "Think about us naked on your bed." She got graphic then, describing sound, sight, and feel. Taking a long quavering breath, he put a hand on her shoulder. "Please," he said. "You're making this hard for me."

She laughed. "That's how we want it. The harder, the better."

"I'm not the one for you. Really. I'd like to be, but my wife is on this side too." It occurred to him that he might be saying too much, but he went on. "She got stolen and brought through. That's why I came through. And I love her more than my life. If I ever have a chance, I'll find her."

Melody stood up frowning. "Macurdy, you're a strange one, no doubt about it." She backed away a step. "I'll ask you again sometime. I don't give up easily." She turned then and walked away, his eyes following her to the door. When she reached it, she stopped and looked back, as if to see if he'd changed his mind and followed her. Instead he waved, once. She turned away again and disappeared.

By this time all the slave girls were sexually engaged, Hero haunches bobbing everywhere Macurdy looked. He took a deep quavering breath, walked to the narrow rear exit and left. No one would notice, he felt sure.

Outside, he ran off down the road, through the dusk, determined to run himself exhausted before he came back.

The next morning, Macurdy was lame. He'd alternately run and walked three or four miles the night before, and unaccustomed to it, was sore from buttocks to calves. "What's the matter with you?" the sergeant asked.

All around them were men hung over, or sleeping off exhaustion. "I'm sore," Macurdy answered.

Zassfel scowled. "Someone said you turned Melody down last night, then left. You never screwed anyone at all, did you."

His aura was hostile. To Macurdy's surprise, he found himself feeling better. Hostility was something he could deal with. "You don't know what I did," he said, "or what I can do."

Zassfel's eyes sharpened. "Is that some kind of threat?"

"I don't threaten anyone. Least of all the platoon sergeant."

"Don't play games with me, Macurdy. I can ruin you. Any kind of ruin you can think of."

"Sergeant, I'm the best new man you've got, and by the time the leaves turn, I'll be the best new or old. There's no need to get on me."

Zassfel's face froze in a grimace, and his hand moved as if to the hilt of the sword he wasn't wearing at the moment. "You son of a bitch," he growled softly. "You better be careful. Real careful."

Macurdy nodded pleasantly. Later he'd be astonished that he'd felt no fear, no upset or anger. "Just remember who went up the tree yesterday," he said, "and how it worked out."

Then he walked outside and sat in the sun, to occupy himself with a dream of rescuing Varia.

The week went well enough. Mostly Zassfel ignored him, as if he'd forgotten about it, but whenever his glance passed over Macurdy, Macurdy could literally feel it, and see the anger in the sergeant's aura. Not until Six-Day before supper, though, was anything said. Then Zassfel walked over to him.

"Macurdy," he murmured, "tonight we'll see whether you're a man or a pansy. Don't leave the longhouse unless I say so, or I'll put you on punishment. Bad punishment."

Macurdy nodded without speaking, wishing the uncanny calm of the previous Seven-Day would come back to him. As it was he ate his supper, but his stomach churned.

Afterward the men sat around, waiting for the slave girls, some of them telling what they were going to do. To Macurdy, they sounded like a couple of eighth graders he'd known in the one-room Oak Creek school. Then Zassfel stepped into the middle of the floor and called for quiet.

"Men," he said, "we've got a pansy among us, someone who's been here four weeks now and hasn't humped a single girl, let alone half a dozen a night like a real Hero. So tonight we're going to test him. When the girls come, I'm going to set Maira on him. He turned her down once; she told me so. If he can satisfy her . . ." His pause was met by knowing laughs. "If he can satisfy Maira, we'll keep him around. Otherwise, the slave bastard goes back to the potato field.

"So when the girls come in, nobody grabs one. Nobody."
He looked around. "That includes you, Margli. I'm going to
take Maira to Macurdy, and he's going to hump her on this
table in front of all of us." He grinned at his victim. "We'll
see how he does. The rule is, he has to satisfy her. My bet is,
he won't even be able to get it up."

When Zassfel identified his victim, the laughter stopped.
Macurdy was liked—admired—especially since his climb up
the tree. Now his pulse pounded like a triphammer, while his
guts kept churning. A long few minutes later, the watchers
outside the door began their cheer, answered at a little distance
by female voices.

Macurdy became aware of Jeremid behind him. "Ride her
rough, Macurdy," the corporal whispered. "Really bang her!
It's your only chance; Maira likes it rough. And whisper to
her that you'll sneak out and go to her during the week. Maybe
she'll fake it for you. Usually she humps one guy after another.
Long after everyone's had enough, she's pawing guys in their
sleep, trying to get a rise out of one."

Macurdy heard, but his mind had frozen with determination.
The girls trooped in subdued, aware now of something unusual
pending. The sergeant ordered the men into a large oval around
the central table, while he held Maira by an arm. "Macurdy,"
he said, "drop your pants."

It felt to Macurdy as if his throat was coated with cotton
batting, but surprisingly his voice seemed normal. "No thanks,
Sergeant. You've got no authority to do this."

Zassfel grinned. "Strip him, boys."

Most of the men stood unmoving. The four men Zassfel
had prearranged things with were his closest friends, four of
his own year in the company. They'd stationed themselves close
behind Macurdy, and two of them grabbed him now.

"Zassfel!" Macurdy shouted, "if you're such a Hero, fight me!"

The room fell absolutely silent for a moment. Then Zassfel's
grin grew wider. "Ho ho ho!" he said. "It seems like every
now and then I have to beat someone up. Otherwise people
forget." He waved the crowd back at his end of the oval, then
stripped off his shirt and stepped forward. "All right, Macurdy,
we fight. And when I'm done, we tie what's left of you to the

tree out front, with a sign telling people what you are." He raised his hands; apparently this was to be with fists. "Let's do it."

The four let Macurdy go, ready to pounce if he tried to run. He didn't. He stripped off his own shirt, raised his fists, and stepped to meet Zassfel.

When Mr. Anderson had taught Oak Creek school, he'd brought boxing gloves, and had given the boys lessons with them. He had, he claimed, been the Golden Gloves champion of Indiana. Whether or not he actually had, he'd impressed them with his moves and style, and taught them how to jab, to throw a right cross, a proper hook, an uppercut.

And clearly, Zassfel had never heard of any of them, certainly not the jab. What he did know was the crushing roundhouse swing, grabbing the hair, the use of knee and elbow—all things that Macurdy expected and watched for. Meanwhile Macurdy introduced him to the jab and all the rest of it. Within a minute, Zassfel's mouth and nose were bleeding, one eye was swelling, a cheek was cut, and he was raising himself to a sitting position, purple with rage. "Kosek! Ardonor! Kill the son of a bitch."

They were on Macurdy in an instant, not only Kosek and Ardonor, but the other two, grabbing, slugging. When they were done, they threw him out the front door, to lie semiconscious and bleeding in the dirt street. After a bit he was aware of someone, two someones, helping him to his feet and supporting him an uncertain distance to—somewhere, then letting him down onto a bed.

He recognized a voice: Melody's, and opened the eye that would, enough to see lamplight. "Thanks, Jeremid," she was saying. "I'll take care of him now. Tomorrow I'll tell the captain what happened, and you'll back me on it. He might or might not do something, but what Zassfel did in there didn't fit any law I ever heard of."

"He's legally a slave," Jeremid murmured. "You can do anything to a slave, as long as you don't reduce their value."

Her words were crisp. "He's also a Hero. There are laws about what anyone can do to Heroes."

After a minute, Macurdy felt a wet cloth dabbing at his face, and winced.

"You're awake."

His mouth felt ragged, his lips swollen, and he knew he had teeth missing and broken. He began to answer, then thought better of it and nodded. That was a mistake too. She continued dabbing and wiping, hissing now and then, occasionally swearing. Briefly she plucked pieces of broken teeth from his lips. "We'll fix his ass, Macurdy," she said. "My father was captain in his time. He has influence, and he spoils me. When I tell him—"

She stopped there. It seemed to Macurdy she didn't feel much confidence. He was a slave; it would come down to that. He felt her fingers prod his ribs, his collarbones. The ribs on one side hurt, but not enough that he flinched.

"Open your mouth."

He did.

"The filthy bastards!" He could hear her breathe in and out through her nose, controlling herself. "You'll be all right here," she said. "I'm going to the shaman and get some things."

She left. For a while he drifted in and out of consciousness; then she was back. He could hear her doing things, he didn't know what. Preparing poultices from something the shaman had given her, because now she was placing damp cloths over each eye, on a cheek, on his mouth, crooning as she did so. Then she stroked his forehead with gentle fingers, and left him.

He slept. And sleeping, dreamed of the jaguar. And of Varia, who kept changing into the spear maiden. Sometime in the night he felt hands tug down his breeches, fondle him. Felt himself swell and harden. Felt someone straddle him, insert him, ride him gently . . . And when it was over, felt his good cheek very gently kissed. "I love you, Macurdy." The voice was Melody's, not Varia's. "Don't ask me why. I only talked to you once. Maybe I'm crazy."

Then he drifted into sleep again.

19

Pillow Talk

Pain half wakened him occasionally, and now and then the delicate replacement of a poultice. Gradually he awakened fully, and carefully peeled the poultice off one eye. The swelling seemed mostly gone; his vision through it little restricted. Then he peeled off the other; he could see through it too, though it was still pretty swollen. His mouth, on the other hand . . . Gingerly he touched his split, still-swollen lips, and decided it was best he had no mirror, otherwise he'd be tempted to look at his teeth. His exploring tongue told him all he needed to know about them.

The evening before, and the night, were all there for him; the concussion hadn't been severe enough to block recall. Sitting up, he looked around. Melody dozed on a mat, curled beneath a blanket. He pulled his breeches back up and got out of bed, staggered a bit, then steadied. Found his boots and pulled them on. Before he left, he looked back at Melody. She'd wakened, was resting on an elbow looking at him. On an impulse, he tossed a kiss at her, then left, wondering if she knew the gesture.

He didn't walk to the longhouse, he trotted. The jarring hurt—not his head, but his mouth and ribs. Trotted limping on legs still sore from running on Six-Day night. It was already half light outdoors, but seen from the road, the village could have been deserted. He stopped on the longhouse stoop and peered inside, which was darker than he wanted, but he was in no mood to wait. Besides, even from the door he recognized Ardonor sprawled nearby, naked on a bed not his own.

173

He went to him, grabbed a handful of hair and lifted. Waking, Ardonor squawked in pain and indignation, grabbing at Macurdy's left wrist. Macurdy's right fist hit him on the nose. Cartilage gave, and Macurdy let him fall to the floor, then kicked him heavily in the ribs, once, twice, and felt them give too. Ardonor keened weakly, so he kicked him in the belly.

Then looked around for the others who'd beaten him. He saw Maira sitting astride a Hero, motionless now, frightened. Both had watched. He winked at them, raising a finger to his swollen lips as if saying hush, then spotted his next victim and headed toward him. Belver lay sleeping on his own low bed, snoring coarsely. Crouched above him, Macurdy locked both hands on the man's throat and squeezed, at the same time sitting on him. The snoring stopped and the eyes popped open, to stare in horrified recognition. "I'm back," Macurdy growled, then chuckled deliberately. Belver clawed at his wrists, but Macurdy just squeezed harder. After the body went slack, he got off, grabbed the man's ankles and dragged him from the bed, across the floor and out the door onto the stoop. By that time Belver was recovering consciousness. Macurdy kicked him in the leg. "Stand up."

Belver just stared. Macurdy kicked him in the belly this time, not too hard. "Stand up or I'll burst your gut with the next one." Carefully, fear in his eyes, Belver got unsteadily to his feet, then Macurdy struck him as hard as he could in the mouth. The man flung backward, hit his head on the wall and slid down it like a sack, stunned.

Hoisting him on one shoulder, Macurdy took him back inside and dumped him heavily beside Ardonor. Then he kicked Belver in the ribs, hard, and Ardonor again, before looking around. The naked Maira was trying desperately to waken Zassfel, who wasn't responding. Macurdy ignored them and headed for Kosek's bed. Kosek wasn't in it; he'd rolled off in his sleep. Macurdy knelt astraddle of him, held his head down by the hair, and began clubbing his face with a fist, shouting hoarsely now through broken teeth as he hit him. "When you"—*sock, sock*—"beat on someone"—*sock, sock*—"like this"—*sock, sock*—"you can't get good leverage"—*sock, sock*—"so you've got to use technique." When he stopped, Kosek's eyes were glazed, his face a bloody smear.

By that time a dozen or more men were sitting up or standing, watching. Zassfel was on his feet now, Maira crouching behind him. Macurdy took Kosek's ankles and dragged him toward Ardonor and Belver, pausing however near Zassfel. "Sergeant," Macurdy said, "are you ready to fight again?"

Zassfel already looked pretty well beaten up. "I had enough last night," he answered hoarsely. "Enough to know you're ready for promotion to corporal."

You're not talking too well this morning either, Macurdy thought, and moved in on him. "You told those piles of shit to beat me up. Are you ready to get down on your knees and beg forgiveness?"

Zassfel looked around wildly. "Kill the slave son of a bitch!" he yelled. "That's an order!"

No one moved except Macurdy. He slammed Zassfel right on his swollen, already broken nose, and again the blood flowed. The sergeant fell backward over the crouching Maira, to lie unmoving, tears flowing from the pain. Macurdy kicked him in the ribs then, hard enough to feel them give, leaving the man openmouthed and gasping. That done, he dragged Zassfel and Kosek, one after the other, to where he'd left the first two. There was another around somewhere, but he wasn't sure who. Dieser, probably, but he'd let it go at that.

Instead he went to his bed, buckled on his belt with its Hero-issue saber and Arbel's gift knife, and stuffed his few other personal possessions in his saddle bags. Then he rolled his blanket, slung his bow and quiver, grabbed his spear, and stalked from the building. All eyes followed him, but no one said anything or moved to interfere.

Melody had watched from the road as Macurdy had beaten up Belver, and from the door as he'd beaten Kosek and Zassfel. Now, as he came out, she stared half in awe, half in concern. "Come on," she said, "you've got to get away from here," and tugging on his sleeve, pulled him toward 2nd Platoon's stable. *Melody, I know that much,* he thought. *I'm not totally out of my skull.*

"Hurry," she said. "Saddle up and wait inside. I'll be right back." Then she left running.

Macurdy was cinching down the girth on his horse, when someone came into the stable. His head snapped around. It was Jeremid, also carrying his personal gear. The man said nothing, just grabbed a saddle blanket and began to saddle a horse.

"Saddle two, if you're coming with me," Macurdy said. Jeremid said nothing, working quickly. When each had a mount and spare ready, Macurdy stopped Jeremid inside the door. "We wait here."

"What for?"

"Melody."

Mouth open, Jeremid stared at him. The longhouse was still quiet, but there had to be activity inside. Presumably, Macurdy thought, no one had seen where he'd gone, but if any of them were thinking at all this morning, they'd surely guess. His heartbeats counted down two long minutes before he saw Melody riding toward them, a remount tethered behind. Seeing him, she beckoned. "Now," he said, and leading his mount out the door, swung into the saddle.

Like the two men, Melody had her spear in its saddle boot. Together in the growing light, the three of them trotted their horses eastward out of town, Macurdy's ribs, swollen face, sore haunches feeling every jar. He took the lead, setting the direction, though he knew nothing of the road eastward beyond the first hours' ride.

Eastward. If the others wondered why, they didn't ask.

Their horses were strong and splendidly conditioned. Thus for more than an hour they jogged without a break, then changed mounts and trotted another hour before slowing to a walk. They stayed on the road; to leave it would only slow them. And pursuers would undoubtedly have hounds which could track them easily in the forest. For the first three hours, the land along the road was as much clearings as woods, with a small village in every major opening. Finally they entered low forested hills, and having heard no sign of hounds, dismounted to lead their horses awhile.

In those three hours, no one had spoken, aside from functional suggestions and Macurdy's few orders. For one thing, Macurdy's ruined mouth made talking painful. Melody's and Jeremid's thoughts were mostly on the possibility of capture, and why on Earth they were doing this. Macurdy's were on escape, and on how hard he dared push the horses. He was willing to wear them out, if it resulted in pursuit being abandoned, but he dared not break them down. Because of his size, he'd taken two of the company's larger horses, but even so, he was a heavy burden for them.

When a meadow came into sight ahead, Jeremid said they'd best stop and let the horses graze a bit. Macurdy agreed. They took time to hobble them; there were hobble straps in every set of equipment, and they couldn't risk losing a horse.

Their pursuers would undoubtedly have a pack horse carrying a sack of oats, Jeremid said, which meant their mounts would hold up better. And the White River lay less than an hour's ride ahead, if they kept pushing. There they'd have a choice of either swimming their horses downstream or up, or straight across. Which with luck would confuse and delay pursuit.

So they rested less than twenty minutes. At the White, they swam upstream, even though it was harder on the horses. Then, instead of coming out on the other side, where their tracks would be looked for, they came out on the west bank again, and followed it upstream for several miles, on foot again, leading their horses to rest them. The hope was that their pursuers would overlook the west bank option.

At length they reentered the water, crossing this time. Then Macurdy led off eastward through untracked forest. Until, abruptly, a voice froze them. "Macurdy! Macurdy!"

None of them spoke. Their eyes scanned the woods.

"No no, Macurdy! I'm up here! Blue Wing!"

They looked up in unison to where the great raven sat in a tall, thick-boled walnut tree.

"I saw you crossing the river, and wondered why humans would be riding so far from any road or trail." Blue Wing paused. "Why are you?"

"We're in trouble," Macurdy said, "and we think men might

be following us. Soldiers with hounds. We're trying to leave a trail they won't find."

Blue Wing said nothing to that, and it seemed to Macurdy that the bird comprehended neither his problem nor his strategy. A raven's solution to danger would be flight, he supposed. "I wonder," Macurdy called, "if you'd do me a favor?"

"Ask and find out."

He described the road they'd fled on, and the form that any successful pursuit would take. "I will look and see," Blue Wing said, and with a thrust of legs and wings, lifted into the sky.

They rode on then, not hurrying, for this was old forest, long unburned, and though the hills were mild, the ground had gotten pocked and humped, over the centuries, from the tipped-up roots and mouldering trunks of windthrown trees. Only once did they pause, to shoot and gut a turkey. Three miles farther, they came to a small isolated clearing, more or less level, with a cabin and outbuildings of logs. From a little distance, their roofs looked more or less intact, but saplings were already invading the clearing. There was still abundant grass though, beaten down and grayed by winter's frosts and rains, and tinged green by the new growth beneath it. Macurdy wondered why the place had been abandoned.

By then the sun was low. They rode over to the buildings and dismounted, hobbling the horses and leaving them to graze. Inside the cabin, things had been smashed, and bones were scattered around, the broken skulls human.

"Troll work!" Jeremid breathed the words, sounding spooked. The stock shed had been similarly vandalized. There too bones lay scattered and broken, with skulls of a cow, a calf, a horse.

By the time they'd looked it over, Blue Wing had found them. "No one is following you," he said. "I flew above the river to the road, and then westward quite a distance. With the trees still bare, I couldn't possibly have missed anyone. I saw not more than two riders together, and no hounds at all."

Jeremid looked at Macurdy. "What now?" he asked.

"We camp," Macurdy said. "There's plenty of wood in the woodshed. We'll take turns standing watch and keeping fires going, in case the troll's still around here somewhere. We can picket the horses inside them."

Without anyone actually suggesting it, they made their beds in the hay shed, where there were no bones, fluffing up the hay in the driest corner. The decaying roof wouldn't hold out serious rain, but it would hold heat somewhat, and protect against a shower.

Macurdy selected eight fire sites close outside the cluster of buildings, and they carried a pile of firewood to each. There was a well in front of the cabin, its white oak shoring still intact, and they raised water from it. Blue Wing announced he would sleep on its sweep. Then, in front of the hay shed, Macurdy lit the cook fire with the pass of a hand. Jeremid stared big-eyed.

"Where did you learn to do that?" he asked.

"The shaman at Wolf Springs taught me. He said I had talent, and trained me in the evenings for a while."

"Could you have, uh, set fire to Zassfel this morning?" Jeremid asked.

Macurdy shrugged. "I never thought to try."

As they roasted the turkey, dusk began to settle. Eating wouldn't be easy for his damaged mouth, so Macurdy had taken an iron pot from the cabin and was stewing turkey in it. *Rust stew*, he thought drily as he raked coals around it.

"It's hard to believe no one's chasing us," Jeremid said quietly. "Could the bird be lying?"

Macurdy shook his head. "We're old friends from Wolf Springs."

"I believe him," Melody said. "My father was commander in his time, and a councilman since. We grew up, my brothers and I, being lectured by him. A platoon sergeant can get away with a lot, but what he did last night?" She shook her head, then cut off a slab of half-roasted turkey breast. "Of course, what you did was damned extreme, too, but you were justified."

"Justification's not all I had," Macurdy mumbled. "I had to try getting away without getting chased and caught. So I humiliated him, and pretty much crippled him for a while. That way, one of two things would happen. He might go crazy, and order the men out to get me at all costs—or he might cave in and order nothing. Or maybe he was in too bad a shape to give orders. After that it would depend on the captain, but he wouldn't send men out till after someone took the story to him. Or he might write it off and bust Zassfel."

Inwardly he grunted. *Face it, Macurdy, you wanted to get even. It felt good, beating them up like that.* Whatever; the good feeling was gone now. Heavily he got up and circled the buildings, lighting the watch fires.

Jeremid had volunteered to take the first watch. Now, as dusk thickened, he left with spear and sword. Using mostly his back teeth, Macurdy gnawed briefly on a piece of stewed turkey, his eyes watering from the pain. Eating, he decided, would be more of a problem than he'd feared. After a few minutes, he and Melody went into the shed and made nests in the hay. "It's going to be a cold night, Macurdy," she murmured. "We could keep warmer if we lay close together. The way you lit those fires, you could keep us both warm."

He sighed. "Melody, I'd like to. I really would. But I told you my marriage vows."

She frowned. "I never heard of anything so ridiculous. For a wife, yes, but for a husband?"

"For a husband it should be the same."

"Not for a husband who's a Hero."

"Maybe not, if he's an Ozman. But I'm not a Hero any longer anyway." He paused. "If I was married to you, would you like me to, uh, hump other women?"

That stopped her only for a moment. "I wouldn't care. It's expected. As long as I had you when I wanted you. But you wouldn't, because I'd give you all you could handle.

"Your vow's already broken," she went on. "Last night at my place. You remember; I know you do. You weren't unconscious; you couldn't have been. Even beat up like you were, you were pushing, helping out."

He almost said he couldn't help himself—that he'd been confused from his beating. Then asked himself, *Who do you think you're kidding, Macurdy? You were confused when she put it in, but when you realized, you could have pushed her off.* Instead he nodded. "I remember. I let it happen; it was too good to stop. But that was once. Doing it once doesn't make it all right a second time."

He thought she might get angry, but her mouth didn't tighten and her aura didn't darken. She lay thoughtful a minute. "What's she like, Macurdy? This wife of yours."

He didn't actually think about it, but answered on the premise that he needed confederates, and that she'd need to know sooner or later. "She's a member of the Sisterhood, Melody. She'd run away from them. Then, one day when I wasn't home, they came and stole her. Brought her back to Yuulith. But she had time to write me a note, and put it where I'd find it, so I followed her."

Melody's eyes reflected belief. And concern. "That's where we're going, isn't it," she said. "That's why we're going east instead of some other direction: to get her back."

He nodded.

"What's her name?"

"Varia."

"Varia." She tasted it. "Does she love you?"

"Yep."

"I've heard stories about the Sisters. If they stole her back, you know what kind of life she's leading now. In spite of any vows."

"I don't know."

"They put them with studs, like you do mares, but not just one stud. Different ones hump them till they're pregnant. And when they've weaned their kid, they send the studs around again. And the story is, they like it, like the slave girls do that get taken to the House of Heroes."

His face was swollen and discolored, but she could read the bleakness in it, even in the failing light. "Forget I said that, Macurdy," she murmured. "I was being an asshole, and I'm sorry. You've been a real Hero, not like some of those others. What I said is true, or at least it's what people believe, but—shit!"

She sighed gustily. "I ought to wish I wasn't in love with you, but I am." She raised herself on an elbow, and reaching, caressed his better cheek with her fingertips. "If you change your mind, I'm right here beside you. And I don't think your Varia would be mad at you for humping me."

She turned away, and Macurdy went to sleep thinking that maybe Varia wouldn't be angry, but a vow was a vow. He wondered if Melody would try anything after he went to sleep, and found himself half hoping she would.

He woke to Jeremid's hand tugging his foot—his turn on watch—and got up quietly, his stomach complaining with hunger. Outside the horses looked at him briefly, then returned to grazing. The cook fire was stone cold. Cautiously he touched the pot, then reached into the still-warm water, scooped out a piece of turkey cooked soft by long boiling, and chewed painfully as he walked to the nearest watch fire. They were burning strongly; Jeremid had re-fed them before coming in.

The thin moon had already set, but he guessed it was still somewhat short of midnight; three hours would be about right for his shift, he decided; maybe three and a little bit. Recalling something Mr. Anderson had taught them at school, he found the Big Dipper; it was supposed to circle the North Star once a day. So in three hours, the dipper should go a quarter—no, an eighth of the way around the North Star. Which meant that when the pointer stars got around to—about there—he'd go wake up Melody for her watch.

He stayed on his feet, walking the perimeter to stay awake. Paying only occasional attention to his surroundings—the horses would tell him if anything was prowling. Part of the time he occupied his mind with Varia and Melody. Jeremid was a good-looking young guy; maybe Melody would decide it was him she wanted. At least she might settle for him. *Hell*, he told himself, *they could be humping in the hay right now, for all you know. They're Ozians, and she sounded horny enough.*

A twinge of jealousy surprised and irritated him. Briefly he examined his feelings, and there was no doubt: Varia was his love. Melody was—nice and kind and tough. And crazy to have run off with him; reckless at least. In Oztown she'd been someone important and privileged, and she'd thrown it away, apparently because she wanted to be humped by him, even though he'd already turned her down. *Or could she actually love me?* He examined the possibility to no conclusion.

The watch wore on. Several times he added wood to the fires, twice went back to the cookpot, and occasionally checked the Dipper before deciding his three hours were up and returning to the shed. Crawling, he groped, finding a bare foot that could only be Melody's. It pulled away with a rustling of old hay.

"Macurdy?" she whispered.

"Yes."

She rustled around some more, finding her boots, then got up and went outside to put them on. He felt an urge to follow her, talk with her, learn more about this girl who said she loved him. But his mouth hurt, and besides, it felt dangerous. So instead he found his blanket and settled down, leaving his boots on as before, in case of emergency.

It was daylight and the sun about to rise when Jeremid woke him. "Macurdy," he said, "Melody and I talked last night."

The words brought a pang: *They've decided to pair up, to leave me and go back.* But that made no sense. They could hardly go back now. "She told me about your wife," Jeremid went on. "What does she look like?"

Macurdy frowned. An odd question to be asked on waking. "She's beautiful. Long red hair and green tilty eyes."

"And the people with her? Do you know?"

He's seen her! Macurdy's mind focused. "Another good-looking woman, and a man. The woman's name is Idri; her hair is auburn, and she's got tilty eyes too, only not as green."

"God! That was the name: Idri. The other was Varia. They came into Oztown about a year ago, with a bull of a guard. The chief loaned them an escort, and I was one of them. Your wife was a prisoner."

Macurdy's throat was dry now. "Right. I had to wait a month before the gate opened again and I could follow them."

Melody had come to the door, and stood looking in at them, listening.

"We took them east, across the Great Muddy," Jeremid said. "They got other escorts there, and we came back." He shook his head. "Your wife's the prettiest woman I ever saw. And dangerous! Her guard tried to rape her one night. I don't know what she did, but he screamed the worst scream I ever imagined. I ran over with a torch, and they were both there with their breeches off. Your wife looked at me and said never to try raping a Sister, or I'd end up like him. He was doubled over with his hands in his crotch, hardly able to whimper. Then the other Sister came with a saber and ran him through."

Melody spoke, her voice flat. "Sounds like she's worth saving, Macurdy. Congratulations." Then she turned and walked out of sight.

Jeremid's story shook Macurdy so, it took him several minutes to get up and come out of the shed. Varia had got through that experience seemingly unhurt, and Idri had killed the guy, but what a terrible damned thing to almost happen.

They ate more turkey, then left the rest for Blue Wing. Breaking camp amounted to little more than catching their hobbled horses and saddling them, taking the cookpot and ax they'd found there. The sun was still low when they rode away eastward, shielding their eyes from it with a hand. Here there was a clear trail to follow. After a bit, Blue Wing caught up with them. *I suppose this is interesting to him,* Macurdy thought. *He can share it with the rest of his people.*

Later that morning they hit a rutted cart road, and followed it south to the eastbound road. There they rode well strung out, as if they weren't together; there seemed less chance they'd be remembered or reported that way. Only occasionally did they meet other travelers—farmers and other locals going about their business.

In late afternoon they reached the Great Muddy River, running wide and smooth, but powerful. Both Melody and Jeremid had coins in their purses, and when the next ferry crossed, the three of them were on it.

20

Four Become Seven

During the first three days east of the Great Muddy, they traveled in a kingdom named Miskmehr, land hillier than they were used to, with farms in every significant bottomland. It was a lovely season, the forest canopy washed pale green with opening buds. At a village they bought a cheese and hardtack for basic rations. Their breaks they took in moist roadside woods, eating the wild leeks that grew there till they reeked of them. Macurdy was healing rapidly; his mouth was enough better, he ate what the others ate, though he soaked his hardtack first.

Their road trended more south than east now, and this troubled Macurdy, for his understanding was that the Silver Mountain was east from Oz. But Blue Wing explained that it angled south to strike the Valley Highway, the great road that paralleled the Green River. The highway would take them up the valley all the way to the Great Eastern Mountains, and the dwarvish kingdom named for one of them. No, he had no idea how many days ride they had ahead of them; humans traveled so slowly, he didn't see how they could stand it.

The valley and its margins were kingdoms instead of tribal territories, Blue Wing said, with far more people, towns and villages than the lands they'd seen so far. Its farms were famous for their fertility.

On the fourth day they rode out of the hills into the valley, to the Highway, which was better than any road Macurdy had seen in this world. But the land where the two roads met was

185

nothing to brag about—brushy forest, with half its trees tipped over or broken off by some twister.

Blue Wing, who'd been foraging, was waiting there for them, perched in a swamp white-oak. "Macurdy," he called, then spread his broad wings and hopped off, gliding down to the roadside. "There are men and dwarves just ahead beside the road. They've been fighting each other; there are bodies. It may be dangerous for you there."

"How many men? And dwarves? Alive, that is."

"Numerous. We have trouble with numbers. More men than dwarves though. The dwarves are surrounded."

"How far from here? On which side of the road?"

"You know I don't know your distances!" Blue Wing said, then paused. "If they were shouting, you could probably hear them from here. They're on the south side of the road, but their horses are farther on, on the road itself, with a man guarding them. Another man watches the road in this direction."

"We can bypass them through the woods on the north," Jeremid said. "They'll never know."

Macurdy thought for a moment before answering. "Jeremid, you take the horses off the road and stay with them. Melody, your clothes are harder to notice in the woods. Sneak through the brush on the north side of the road until you see their horses, then stop and keep your eyes open. I'll ride down the road and find out what the situation is. It'd be useful to have dwarves as allies."

He thanked Blue Wing then, and started eastward down the rutted, hoof-packed highway, while Jeremid and Melody disappeared into the forest. He'd ridden perhaps a hundred and fifty yards when a man rose up from behind a fallen tree. His left hand held a bow, and his right a nocked arrow; at twenty yards he could hardly miss. "Stop right there," he called. More loudly than need be, Macurdy thought, unless he wanted his own people to hear him.

Macurdy reined in. "I've been sent to talk to your leader," he said, also loudly.

The man scowled uncertainly, peering at Macurdy's face, still purple and green with bruises. Then a voice called from the woods nearby. "Send him in. I'll listen to him."

Macurdy swung down from his horse, and after tying the reins to a clump of willow, walked into the woods, leaving his spear and bow, but keeping his sword at his waist. The blowdowns were old enough that decay had weakened the branches, allowing many of the trunks to settle to the ground or onto other fallen trees. The heavy opening of the forest roof had allowed the undergrowth to thicken, and saplings had sprung up twenty or more feet high.

A mess, Macurdy thought. *At home these would have been cut up for logs and firewood, except for the elm*. He picked his way around and over blowdowns in the direction the voice had called from, not trying to keep a low target. A man crouched behind a thick elm, bow ready, his gaze shifting from the woods in front of him to the approaching Macurdy, and back again.

"Are you the leader here?" Macurdy asked.

The man looked at him suspiciously. "I am."

"What have you got pinned down in there?" Macurdy called. Loudly enough, he thought, that the dwarves would hear too.

"What business is it of yours?"

"It's my master's business. I act on his orders. He's a magician, and he says it's dwarves you've trapped here."

The bandit ignored the question. "What the hell happened to your face?" he asked. "I never saw anyone beat up so bad."

Macurdy fingered the hard welt on his broken left cheekbone. "I displeased my master."

They were, he decided, being held off by dwarvish marksmanship. The bandits might have an advantage in numbers, but it seemed to him they had some disadvantages, for at least the leader's quiver looked light for a siege, and he carried a longbow. While according to the lore Macurdy had learned from Maikel and Blue Wing, the dwarves' long-range weapon was the crossbow, whose bolts, short and heavy, would be less deflected by undergrowth.

Meanwhile the bandit had turned to face Macurdy, his bowstring half drawn. At ten feet, Macurdy told himself, the arrow could pass through his breastbone and mostly out his back. He ignored it, lowering to a crouch himself, moving in closer with a hand cupped to his mouth, as if for private conversation. But his voice, when he spoke, was loud.

"Excuse me for shouting," he said, "but your men need to hear me, too. My master's not known for his patience, and your lives mean even less to him than mine. He does business with dwarves from time to time, and considers himself a dwarf friend. He orders you to make terms with them."

The man's eyes bulged in angry reaction, then abruptly Macurdy lunged, his left hand chopping sideways, deflecting the bow while his right drew his knife. He backed the bandit against the elm, the man staring not in anger now but fear, for the knife blade was at his belly.

"If you knew my master," Macurdy told him loudly, "you'd understand that I fear him much more than I fear you. Tell your men you're going to make terms. Tell them to be ready to leave when you've got an agreement with the dwarves."

He twitched lightly with the knife, slicing the man's homespun shirt, and the skin beneath it.

"You heard what he said!" the leader shouted.

"Lords of the Mountain!" Macurdy called. "Will you agree not to shoot at these people while they withdraw?"

The answering voice was a deep, accented bass. "Yewr mad if ye think ye can fool us so easily! Ye'd shoot us down in cold blood!"

"What's your name?" Macurdy asked the bandit quietly.

"Slaney."

"Slaney," Macurdy said loudly, "step out here!"

"What?! They'll shoot me!"

"Louder!"

"I said they'd shoot me!"

"I don't think so. But it's a chance you take, being a highwayman, and if you don't step out, I'll spill your guts on the ground right here. I'll count to three: one . . ."

Slaney stepped away from the elm, Macurdy with him, the heavy knife still at the bandit's belly. "We're not highwaymen," the bandit muttered. "But rebels have to eat, and with Gurtho on the throne . . ."

Macurdy's left hand reached, drew Slaney's knife from its sheath and tossed it away. "Hold your bow against the tree."

He did, and Macurdy cut the string. "How many men do you have here?"

"In the woods? Fourteen alive and fit. Three others are dead by those vermin, and two badly hurt."

"Plus two on the road," Macurdy prompted.

The man nodded. "Plus two on the road."

"Tell them to cut their bows with their swords, lay them on a tree and chop them. So I can hear it happen." With a flick of the knife blade, Macurdy made another slit in the man's shirt, another thin red line on his belly. "Tell them!"

Worms writhed in Slaney's face. "You heard what he said," he called. "Chop your bows in two."

Several seconds passed before Macurdy heard the first chop. A moment later he heard a second, then more, though how many had actually struck a bow . . . "Anyone who walks out of here with a whole bow will answer to my master!" he shouted. "With his life!" There were three more chops, then a fourth.

"Lords of the Mountain!" he called, "does that convince you they won't attack if you come out?"

"And what's to prevent *yew* from fillin' us with arrows?"

"Because we're dwarf friends." Macurdy raised his voice to full shout. "My lord! Send the great raven to vouch for us!"

Blue Wing, who'd been circling well above the trees, spiraled down to perch among the upper branches of one. "Lords of the Mountain," the bird called, "these are honorable men! Trust them!"

"Yew!" the dwarf called out, "the man who's taken it on himself to intercede here! What's yer name?"

"Macurdy."

"Macurdy, why don't ye just kill the boogers?"

"My master is a magician and warrior, not a butcher. And these men haven't harmed us."

"What will they pay for our dead and wounded? And our ponies, and the tallfolk groom they killed?"

"Nothing!" Slaney bellowed, then paled chalk-white as Macurdy's knife slit again, this time through skin and shallowly into the muscle beneath it. Blood oozed, flowing down his hairy belly.

"They'll pay the contents of their purses," Macurdy called back, "whatever that may be. And their horses, keeping enough to ride home on, doubling two on a horse."

Macurdy heard the brief bass rumble of dwarves conferring. Then their leader called again. "All right. Have them hold their purses above their heads. We're comin' out with bows at the ready. We'll not shoot if not threatened, but . . ."

"Do you pledge that on the honor of your sons?"

"On the honor of our sons through three generations!"

Long generations, Macurdy thought. According to Maikel, dwarves lived longer than Sisters, though they aged more or less gradually, and seldom had children before age forty.

"Careful now, Slaney," Macurdy called. "If even one of your men plays false, you all die. Yourself first." Then he shouted at full voice again. "My lord, send in someone to collect their purses for the Lords of the Mountain."

Blue Wing flew off with the message, in case Jeremid hadn't heard. It took several minutes for the Ozman to get there. With saber in one hand he made the circle; the purses he stuffed in his shirt mostly felt empty, or near it, and not every man even admitted to one. Eight dwarves came out, two of them limping. They wore mail shirts that seemed too light to stop a sword blow, but by their shimmer, Macurdy suspected they were more than ordinary steel.

The bandits, it turned out, had more dead than they'd realized. With a well-aimed arrow, Melody had killed the bandit who'd first challenged Macurdy, shot him when he'd started in from the road as if to intervene. Then she'd gone on to the horse guard and shot him too. Her marksmanship impressed Macurdy; both her arrows had pierced the victims' hearts. Her casual willingness to kill people also impressed him—shocked him a bit despite how warlike the Ozians were.

It was dwarves with their crossbows who stood guard over the bandits and chose the horses with which they'd be paid—the ten best of nineteen. Two others had been wounded during the original skirmish, and run off. Meanwhile the dwarves searched the bandits for valuables they might have transferred from their purses, and found little. Another visited the dead bandits, collected their bows and swords, and chopped their spears in two.

Slaney stepped over to Macurdy. "The truth between the

two of us," he growled, in a tone not to be heard by his men. "There is no master, right? There's only the three of you."

"Right and wrong," Macurdy lied. "There are seven of us, but I'm the leader and magician. The other four don't want their presence known in this country. Also I am dwarf friend, and couldn't let them die here."

Slaney didn't know what to believe, and said nothing more; his aura was thick with hate. He and his men mounted—two to a horse except for himself—and without looking back, headed east down the highway.

Dwarves do not ride full-sized horses; Macurdy had learned that from Maikel. Their legs are short, they require special saddles, and there's the problem of climbing on and off. They ride ponies specially bred—short of leg and very tame, with a quick-footed gait.

This party had been traveling with two saddle ponies each, plus spares and pack ponies, and enough were left that each survivor had one to ride, with several left over. With tallfolk help, they loaded their goods on compensatory horses, on pack saddles lashed together from stout ash saplings. Their dead, including the tallfolk groom they'd hired, were also loaded across horses. Macurdy wondered aloud if it might not be better to build a pyre and burn them, this being the tallfolk custom in Yuulith. The elder dwarf answered that there'd be no decay, and he'd have strong coffins made at the nearest village where a proper cart could be bought.

That said, he put his hand on each corpse, one after the other, concentrating and muttering, as if preserving them with a spell.

The dwarves didn't look forward to tending a string of horses—they preferred not even to tend their ponies if they could hire some tallfolk to do it—but they seemed not to doubt that they could if they had to.

Their biggest problem was that four of them, venturesome youths by dwarvish standards, wanted to join Macurdy, whom they believed would be doing more bold adventurous things— things they hoped to be part of. This, however, would leave their leader with a party of only four, of whom two had been wounded, though one but slightly. But those who wanted to leave claimed the right to do so. They hadn't been part of the original party; had attached themselves to it because they were also from the Diamond Flues.

Old Kittul Kendersson Great Lode disagreed. He pointed out that as a member of the ruling council, he had the authority to take command in emergencies. On the other hand, young Tossi Pellersson Rich Lode, eldest of the four cousins, claimed the emergency was over. And a tallfolk could be hired at the next village to tend the animals.

Old Kittul was apparently not a typical dwarf. He undertook a compromise, for he saw that the Pellerssons would leave despite him, which could give rise to ill feelings in both clans. And at any rate the younger dwarf's arguments had merit. While Tossi, though young, understood the politics of the Diamond Flues. The upshot was that one of the cousins would leave with Kittul. And Tossi, if he lived long enough, was to personally deliver, to the King In Silver Mountain, a report of the events here. He was also to send one in writing, for the king should be apprised that travel entailed risks in this region.

Tossi's three cousins drew straws—Tossi, as senior, held aloof from the risk—the short straw to ride west with Kittul.

When Kittul's party was in the saddle, he called Macurdy to him. "And yewr people," he said, "and yewrs, Tossi Pellersson." When they'd gathered, Kittul cleared his throat and began.

"Macurdy," he said, "ye haven't told me where yer goin' nor why. But yewr a born commander, both in yer manner and yer thinkin', though ye don't flaunt it. And I have no doubt at all that whatever yer about, it's honorable.

"As for yew, Tossi, I suspect yew and yer wild cousins will find adventures enough to last yer lifetime. Which I hope will be long enough to have children to tell them to."

He looked into the crown of a roadside tree. "And yew, great bird," he called. "Knowledge of yer folk is part of our lore, though it's at second hand from the tomttu. We're too much inside the mountain to know ye first hand. But it's well known that yewr kind has a penchant for doin' that which, from time to time, influences events. Sometimes for good, sometimes not, but always honestly. Yer connection with this man is a favorable omen, and I wish ye well."

He turned in his saddle. "Macurdy, hand me your blade."

Macurdy did, and Kittul lay it across his lap (dwarves ride with their knees high), then sat with his eyes closed for a long minute, head back, beard jutting, his ruler's aura swelling upward like pale, purple-blue flame. Then he took Jeremid's saber, frowned a moment over it, and repeated the performance. And then Melody's. When he was done, he looked long at Macurdy before speaking. "It's a hazardous road you've chosen. That much I know, even if I don't know what it is. Much will happen that none of us can foresee. But what I've done with these will help." He gestured at Macurdy's sword. "There is more to refinin' weapons than just forgin'. And though it's not dwarf made, like theirs"—he gestured toward the cousins— "still it's better now than others made by tallfolk."

With that he tossed his head in a dwarvish farewell, turned his pony, and trotted off westward at the head of his party.

With Blue Wing scouting ahead, Macurdy, Jeremid, Melody, and the three young dwarves rode eastward in the direction of the Silver Mountain, the Sisterhood, and he supposed Varia. Before long they crossed a modest river, and shortly afterward, saw where hooves had left the highway on a narrow, well-worn trail that disappeared northward into the forest. It seemed safe to bet they'd never see Slaney and his crew again.

21

The Inn

Within an hour of leaving the skirmish site, they rode out into cleared farmland, the most Macurdy had seen in this world, with woods only here and there. A couple of miles southward, a dark strip of forest stretched from east to west as far as he could see, with more farmland on the other side. The river woods, he supposed. Northward at the edge of seeing were high hills dark with forest.

As they rode, he questioned the dwarves about the country they'd pass through. Tossi, being the eldest of the three, did most of the answering. This, he said, was the beginning of Tekalos, whose king was Gurtho. The oppressive ruler the bandit chief had mentioned, Macurdy realized.

Occasionally they met traffic, most seeming local. There were numerous tiny hamlets—clusters of farmers' huts and out-buildings—and here and there villages. Near evening they saw a rather large village ahead.

Tossi trotted his pony up beside Macurdy's. "Macurdy!" he said, "there's a decent inn ahead. I suggest we stop for supper, and spend the night."

"Feel free, you and your cousins, Tossi Pellersson," Macurdy answered. "The three of us will eat here, but our money's too short to stay under a roof at night. We'll camp by the road east of town, and meet you in the morning."

"Ye don't understand," Tossi said. "We folk who live in the mountain seldom travel without money. I'll pay for the rooms, and the meal too." Macurdy began to decline, but Tossi cut him short: "Think where I'd be tonight, if it wasn't for yew three. Dead in the woods, likely."

194

"Say yes, Macurdy," Melody broke in. "They probably have a bath house, and ale."

Macurdy agreed. And there was indeed a bath, but only for men. Melody said she'd share, but the innkeeper refused, looking worriedly at Macurdy's discolored face. He had a number of guests, he said, all of them male, and he feared if she bathed with them, there'd be fights, which could result in his being fined for encouraging disorder.

"How does your wife bathe?" Melody asked.

"In summer, in the walled courtyard behind our apartment, in a big tub. Otherwise in her own kitchen. If the lady would care to, you can use the tub in the garden."

Tossi offered to hire their clothes laundered, along with the dwarves', but they had nothing to wear while their clothes were being washed. So before supper, they went to the shop of a clothier, who sewed clothing of several sizes on speculation. Cottons were cheap enough that Melody and Jeremid covered the cost for the three of them. Macurdy had also hoped to buy an old dog from someone, some blind and feeble hound for a copper, to take out of town and shoot for Blue Wing. But the great raven had left when they'd arrived at the inn, so he let it pass.

Supper was better than he'd expected—a beef stew with assorted vegetables not cooked to pieces, and oatmeal mush with honey, cooked somewhat stiff, with bits of dried apples stirred in after cooking. By local standards, he supposed it was quite good. The pot room was well occupied, seemingly as much by locals as travelers, the ale as popular as the food. But their table, in an out-of-the-way corner, they had to themselves for a while, though it had seating for more. Macurdy wondered if his discolored face was the reason—that and his size and brawn. People might take him for a troublemaker. Or was it the dwarves they were leery of?

Later, while they ate, a man came and sat across from Tossi, and when the potboy came over, ordered supper and ale. Macurdy paid little attention to him till the man spoke to Tossi. "Excuse me, sir dwarf lord," he said quietly. "Do you deal in weapons?"

"Some in my clan do. What, specifically, are ye interested in?"

"Swords."

"Indeed? How many? When circumstances permit, I might speak to someone who could discuss the matter with ye while passin' through."

"Ah. How many indeed. It would depend on the price; my friends and I have limited resources. Probably not many."

Macurdy looked the man over. By Arbel's system of evaluating auras, this was a ruler of sorts, someone whom others tended to defer to. He wasn't sure how meaningful that was though; Arbel had said *his* was a "ruler's aura," yet he'd been a slave at the time. Just now, Macurdy decided, the stranger lacked money. He was more wishing than anything else. Although his aura reflected inner power.

The conversation ended with Tossi giving him an estimate. "I can't speak with authority though," he finished, "not bein' in the trade myself." The man thanked him and turned to his supper, and the dwarves left, saying they seldom drank more than a single ale in public. And when Jeremid and Melody had finished a second tankard each, the three refugees from Oz went upstairs to bed.

The dwarves shared one room and the tallfolk another, with a single large bed in each. Jeremid suggested they draw straws to see who slept in the middle, and Melody drew the short. After they'd lain down, she raised herself on one elbow and leaned over Macurdy. He could smell the ale on her breath. "Macurdy," she said, "your mouth looks well enough for kissing now," and lowering her face to his, kissed him sweetly, long and lovingly, while groping him. "Make love to me, Macurdy," she murmured.

"Melody, I can't," he said, moving her hand away. "You know that. And anyway we're not alone."

"Would you if Jeremid weren't here?"

"God, Melody, I'd like to, but it wouldn't be right."

She lay back down exasperated. "I've never in my life heard of anyone so damned difficult," she said.

Jeremid spoke then. "Spear maiden, there's a Hero on the other side of you who'd happily hump you all night long."

"You're not the Hero I want humping me."

He laughed. "Then you're as damned difficult as he is."

"Go to hell, Jeremid."

He laughed again, and after a moment, she did too.

Macurdy didn't. After a bit he went to sleep, but awoke some time later to quiet sounds. He was the only one in bed, and the sounds were of panting and moaning on the floor beside it. He lay without moving, feeling miserable. The sounds speeded and intensified without growing appreciably louder, peaked, then died. A minute later, Macurdy heard Jeremid's whisper: "How'd you like that, spear maiden?"

"You're good, Hero," she whispered back, "you're very good."

"It's here for you whenever you want it." Jeremid's chuckling was a series of soft aspirations. "I'm better than Macurdy'd be, I'll bet."

"Hard to say. His horn is bigger though, that's for sure. He's a real horse."

This time Jeremid didn't chuckle. "How do you know?"

Melody told him of mounting Macurdy on the night he was beaten.

"Then all that stuff about loyalty to his wife . . ."

"He wasn't awake when I slid it in. And even then he didn't start pushing for a while."

Neither spoke for a minute or so, till Jeremid said, "Why did you follow him? Just to get humped by him? I always thought that recklessness of yours would get you in trouble. And he's not even good-looking anymore, with his teeth all broken out."

"I'm in love with him. That's not something you'd understand. Humping's as far as it goes with you."

Jeremid didn't respond. Despite his own state of mind, Macurdy wondered what the Ozman was thinking.

"Why did you follow him?" Melody asked.

"Don't know. I guess—I admire him. He's got more guts than anyone I've ever seen. And he's honest. And smart, damned smart—except when it comes to you." Jeremid chuckled again. "Besides, where he is, interesting things are going to happen."

Their conversation lapsed, and Macurdy wondered if they'd gone to sleep there on the floor. Then one of them began to breathe a little raggedly. "Damn you," Melody whispered, "I said only once."

Again Jeremid chuckled. "Here we are naked, and who knows when we'll have this good a chance again."

After a moment, Melody said, "Just a minute."

Between half closed lids, Macurdy watched her go to her gear. In the dimness, the vague sight of her bare buttocks made the breath stick in his chest. Half a minute later she was back out of sight, on the floor with Jeremid. Before long he could hear them having sex again. His torment lasted considerably longer than the first time, and Melody was harder put to keep her climax quiet.

This time when they'd finished, there was no conversation. They put their cottons back on and came carefully back to bed. It was quite a while before Macurdy slept again.

22

Decorations on a Town Square

On the road next morning, Macurdy did not feel refreshed. His dreams had been restless and troubling, though he couldn't remember them. He had no trouble at all, though, recalling what he'd heard when he'd wakened in the night. He supposed he should feel complimented by the things they'd said about him, while by the standards of Oz, or at least the House of Heroes, their couplings had been unobtrusive, even modest.

These realizations didn't help. He felt—deprived and jealous. Feelings which he realized were totally unjustified. Jeremid wanted Melody as much as he did, and had as much right to. As for Melody and himself—clearly all he needed to do was say yes.

And how had Varia spent last night? he wondered. Being bred by some stud? Enjoying it? She'd been more than enthusiastic when they'd been together. He imagined her groans, her cries almost yelped, her strong fingers digging his back. Whose back now?

While he imagined, Melody trotted her horse up beside his. "Macurdy," she said, "we need to talk. Privately."

He dug heels in his horse's ribs, and they pulled farther ahead of the others. "You woke up last night, didn't you?" she asked.

He nodded without speaking.

"When I got back in bed, your breathing didn't sound like you were sleeping. And this morning—it was pretty obvious."

199

Yeah, he thought, *I suppose it was.*

"What did you hear?" she asked.

"All of it, I guess. The first time, and the second, and the talk in between."

"Macurdy, I love you, you—jackass. And it's damned hard to be around you without having you."

"It's the same with me."

"I suppose it was bad for you, listening to us go at it."

He grunted. "That's not your fault. Not your problem."

"I know it's not. But I don't like having caused you pain. I'd rather cause you pleasure."

"Suppose you get pregnant?"

"I've got lamb bane in my gear."

Lamb bane. Of course. He'd heard of it from Hauser, who collected it in season for Arbel. It didn't keep anyone from getting pregnant, but both sheep and women, if they ate it early enough, miscarried with no trouble. The two of them rode without speaking for several chains. "Look," she said finally. "I can't promise I won't hump with Jeremid again. But I do promise not to do it where you can hear us. Will that help?"

By Oz standards, he realized, that was downright thoughtful. Even sweet. He looked at her earnest face and found himself smiling. Fondly! The realization startled him, left him mentally gawping. *You're in love with her, Macurdy!* he told himself amazed. *You are! You're in love with this girl!* "Sure," he found himself saying. "It'll help a lot. And Melody, I don't want you to feel bad about it; I really don't. Because I love you, too."

She stared at him, surprised, then annoyed. "Macurdy," she said, "you're an exasperating bastard." And pulling aside, fell in a little distance behind him.

Leaving Macurdy wondering what he'd said wrong. But the question was fleeting, giving way to the matter of being in love with two women at once. Truly in love with them. He'd never thought about such a thing before, had grown up accepting that you could only love one at a time. Yet it seemed to him both loves were real. His love for Melody was different than his love for Varia, but it was love, he had no doubt.

The difference that counted, he told himself, was the vow he'd taken. And he'd abide by it in spite of all.

✦   ✦   ✦

The weather had turned nearly summery. Gnats were out, though not a kind that bit. The elms along the road were pale green now, with countless millions of disk-winged seeds, while the new leaves of various species were expanding.

This plain, this Green River Valley, was pleasant to Macurdy's eyes. Tekalos was good farmland. Talbott and Hauser assumed there was a geographical equivalence between Yuulith and Farside, and as closely as Macurdy could figure, if there was a gate here, it would open into Tennessee. Western Tennessee or maybe west-central. From all he'd heard, Tennessee was mostly hills and mountains, and he wondered if it had any area of farmland to compare with this.

In midafternoon, Blue Wing caught up with them. He'd flown back to the site where the bandits had attacked the dwarves, and filled his belly and crop with dead horse meat. Or so he said. But Macurdy was aware that even vultures, with their hooked and powerful beaks, let dead horses and cattle lay longer than that for the hide to soften. It seemed likelier that some dead bandit had been Blue Wing's meal.

The dwarves slowed their progress. Their ponies were slower, and they took breaks long enough to make fire and boil water for sassafras tea. They felt no urgency. And while Macurdy's experience with horses hadn't included long crosscountry trips, he told himself this was probably a more sensible speed anyway. Besides, more than a year had passed since Varia had been kidnapped; what difference would a few days make now? She was no doubt safe enough.

And it seemed to him the dwarves were much more important to him than the time they were costing; they were his passport to the King in Silver Mountain. Meanwhile they were good companions; it was one of them who shot a possum with his crossbow, then carried it along as supper for Blue Wing.

Still, from time to time he felt restless.

Near dusk, the six of them made camp in a pleasant woods, along a river not much more than a creek. It allowed them to bathe again, which they did naked, though the dwarves used a stretch of riverbank screened from the tallfolk by undergrowth. Naked, Melody was prettier than he'd realized, though muscular for a woman. Breaking the spell, he jumped from the cutbank into the river, to conceal his developing erection. The cold water killed it utterly, and he grinned as Melody waded tentatively in, her arms wrapped around herself.

"Shall I splash you?" he called.

"You hadn't better," she answered, then launched herself, gasping as she surfaced. He did splash her then, and she charged him, splashing back. In a moment they were tussling and laughing, their wet bodies twisting against each other.

Abruptly Macurdy let her go and backed away, chagrined, and at the same time pleased with himself. Melody smiled. "That's a good start, Macurdy," she said softly, and reaching, touched his cheek. Then she turned and waded out of the river. Macurdy watched first her departing back, then her buttocks and legs, while his fingers touched his cheek where hers had. Varia had touched him like that.

That evening, fireflies were out by the hundreds in their camp, yellowish glowing lights bobbing and circling in the twilight and dark. Melody went to where Macurdy squatted, and squatted beside him, their arms and shoulders touching as they watched. But only for a little. Then the three tallfolk bedded down near each other, Macurdy feeling as if, for the first time in his life, he had a girl friend. His relationship with Varia had skipped that stage.

The next day brought a thundershower by midmorning, and a prolonged thunderstorm in late afternoon that drove them to cover at a crossroads inn. It wasn't as large as the inn they'd stayed in before, nor as clean, and Macurdy decided this was a good time to exercise the magic Arbel had taught him for killing fleas, lice, and the like.

It seemed to work well; either that or there'd been none to start with. And no one had sex out of sight on the floor, because there was no bed, only three straw-filled sacks unrolled side by side.

About two hours into their ride next morning, Blue Wing's voice called from overhead: "Macurdy! Macurdy!" Macurdy reined in and waited, looking up. The great bird spiraled sharply down and reached for the roadside with long legs.

"What'd you find?"

"There's a town ahead, not far from the highway."

"Aye," said Tossi. "Gormin Town. I recall it. It's a reeve's town, a shire seat, walled with a palisade. There's a better than usual inn at the crossroads nearby."

Macurdy nodded, looking at Blue Wing, waiting.

"The town has an open space near its center," the bird continued. "With poles standing there, and men hanging on them."

"Hanging?"

"By their wrists. Some appear to be dead. Others were just then being fastened up."

"Sounds like a good place to stay away from," Jeremid suggested.

Macurdy spoke as if to himself. "Men hung up from poles." He focused on Blue Wing again. "How many?"

"You know I'm not good with numbers," Blue Wing said a little testily. "You are six, right?"

"That's right."

"At least twice that many, I would guess."

"If we spend a day or two there, what will you do?" Macurdy asked. "I may need you."

"There's a slaughterhouse nearby, with a place where the offal is thrown. They'll very likely put out some choice pieces for me: a head already skinned perhaps, and some organs. And I can keep track of where you are by the dwarves' ponies. There'll hardly be anything else like them there."

"Thanks. Keep an eye on me for a while, if you would. I may have questions."

"As you wish."

The raven took to the air, running and hopping a few strides for his takeoff, as if his crop was full; perhaps he'd already visited the slaughterhouse. Macurdy nudged his horse with his heels. "Gormin Town doesn't sound like a good place to be," Jeremid said.

Macurdy's lips pursed thoughtfully. "To get Varia away from the Sisterhood, it could be useful to have armed men with me. Not to take inside the dwarf kingdom, but standing by."

It was Melody who answered. "What do men hanging in the square have to do with that?"

"I'm not sure. But—why hang men up like that? Are they bandits? Rebels?"

She waited for the rest of it, and when there was no more, rode on frowning. An hour and a half later they came to the inn, at the crossroads a half-mile outside the town's north gate. Macurdy stopped outside the courtyard, and looking up, spotted Blue Wing high overhead. He waved until the bird tilted and started down. Then Macurdy gathered the others close around him. In a minute, Blue Wing arrived to perch on the top rail of a fence beside the road.

"Tossi," Macurdy said, "would you take a room at the inn for Jeremid, Melody and me? But not for you three?"

The dwarf gnarled his brows. "What have ye in mind?"

"I'm not sure. But it may be I'll want you to take a place in town for yourselves."

"In town?"

"Can you make swords?"

"What?!"

"You told Kittul Kendersson you wanted adventure. It might be we'll find some here. If I decide it's the thing to do, would you hire a room at the inn for the three of us?"

"Aye, I would. But as for making swords . . . We could, any of us, but they'd not be of first quality. Better than tallfolk make, but . . . Every dwarf lad is taught to work metals, from gold to iron, but we'd rarely be called on to do it without a master smith at hand to supervise."

"Good enough. Making swords would only be an excuse for hiring a place in town. Let's leave our remounts and pack animals at the stable here and ride in. We won't take rooms yet; I have to see what's going on first."

At the town gates, Macurdy felt the sentries eye his spear, and those of the two Ozians, but didn't stop them. The dwarves, he decided, had been their pass. Inside the stockade, the cobbled main street was wide enough for wagons to pass easily, though buildings overhung it. The six visitors walked their mounts briskly, the quickstepping hooves of the dwarves' ponies a sharp counterpoint to the louder clopping of the horses, and shortly they came to the town square.

It was decorated with the bodies of men dead or dying, or soon to be—fourteen of them, standing or hanging with their wrists lashed overhead, the sun beating on them. Above each was a sign in blood red: REBEL. Two were conspicuously dead, had begun to swell, and flies swarmed on them. Six others were either dead or too weak to stand, hanging on their tethers, their hands swollen and black. Another six stood grimly, their weight on their feet instead of on their wrists. Three guards stood by. Most bypassers avoided looking. A stray dog, in slinking mode, approached one of the dead and sniffed. Spear leveled, one of the guards ran it off.

"Stay here," Macurdy murmured to the others, and dismounting, walked up to a guard. "We're strangers," he said. "From the Kingdom of the Diamond Flues." He gestured toward the posts. "What sort of men are these?"

The guard looked sourly at the posts, then at Macurdy's discolored face, but his speech was civil. "They're from the hills off north," he said. "Part of a rebel band." He wrinkled his nose. "The dead'll be cut down this evening."

Macurdy thanked him and returned to the others, to continue slowly on around the square. Here and there were benches, mostly unoccupied. Macurdy looked over the auras of the few who sat there, and shortly pulled up and dismounted again, walking over to a man who was old by Rude Lands standards, his mouth a sunken, lipless crease.

Sitting down near him, Macurdy spoke quietly. "A hard way to die, on those posts."

The old man said nothing, as if he hadn't heard.

"We're from over west of the Great Muddy, traveling east to the Silver Mountain. Came in to buy some goods, and saw those poor devils hanging by their wrists."

Still nothing.

"Why would men rebel, in a country as fertile as this? Surely there must be plenty to eat."

The toothless mouth seemed hardly to move, but words came from it now, low and monotone. "There are kingdoms where men are pressed down by cruelties and demands. Where the man who swings the scythe may have too little bread to eat, and where he'd best not have a pretty wife or daughter. Or pride."

"Ah. Then why so few rebels?"

"The commons have no generals, no strong and able leaders. Nor weapons, most of them, nor any place to hide."

"And yet those men . . ." Macurdy gestured.

The old man took a slow breath. "They're Kullvordi—hillsmen from off north. Their not-too-distant grandfathers were tribesmen who lived in their own way. Even now they have bows and spears; some even have swords. And forests to hide in, where soldiers hardly dare to go. But if a rebellion grows troublesome, the soldiers burn some farms, drive off their livestock, and kill hostages. And after a bit, the rebellion dies as if it never was, leaving only a few hard men living off what game they can shoot, and by thieving. Until someone gives them away for a purse."

The old man stopped then, and Macurdy asked no more. After a minute he lay a paw on a bent shoulder and squeezed lightly, then got up and left.

The six of them rode back to the inn for the midday meal. Afterward, Macurdy, Melody, and Jeremid took a room with money Tossi provided, then rode northward, killing time with exploration, while Blue Wing flew high, learning the land far more widely than they could.

Meanwhile the dwarves, with their ponies and a pack horse, returned to town to carry out their part of the plan. When they'd finished their business for the day, the youngest of them, Yxhaft Vorelsson Rich Lode, rode back out to the inn, where he sat in the pot room nursing a short mug of ale till the tallfolk got back. After a supper of pot roast and boiled potatoes, they all went to the small room the three tallfolk were to share. Tossi, Yxhaft said, had seen to everything agreed on. As for security—during the day there'd been a single guard in each of the rather widely-spaced watch shelters on the town walls, but it was logical to expect two or more at night, to keep each other awake. He also mapped the whereabouts of the ground-floor apartment Tossi had rented. "If yer uncertain," he finished, "there'll be a small sign by the door, with dwarf runes in charcoal, tellin' those who can read it—and I doubt there's one such in all Gormin Town, except ourselves—that 'here dwell three sons of the Rich Lode Clan.' "

He grinned at Macurdy then, for he was a youth as dwarves go. "It has a cellar hole," he went on, "and its own weed patch in back, with its own privy. We've put the anvil block on the cellar lid, and strewed sand over the floor, as one might to prevent fires startin' from the forge. It's a poor place for smithin', but who'd know except a smith?"

"Oh! And Tossi got a letter of retainer from the reeve, which no doubt we can use, if we need to, as a pass to get through the gate. Should they start keepin' folks in, which I expect they will."

Then Yxhaft left, riding back to town.

According to the innkeeper, the town gates closed at sundown, or on cloudy days when dusk began to thicken. And because of recent disorders, there was a curfew. So when the sun was low, Macurdy, Melody, and Jeremid walked the half-mile to town, chatting and laughing deliberately as they approached the gate. They entered without being questioned, and strolled the perimeter street, still chatting while Macurdy unobtrusively examined the palisade. Each stair-flight up to the archery walk ended at a watch shelter, and even as they walked, a column of guardsmen marched past them, pausing to send three to each shelter, replacing the one on day watch.

"We'll have to figure out some other way," Jeremid said. "We can do the job tomorrow night."

Macurdy shook his head. "Tomorrow night's too late. We need to free them while they're able-bodied."

"Maybe we can use a rope with a hook," Melody suggested. "Throw it onto the archery walk, and climb."

Macurdy nodded, thinking that the odds of success were not good. Maybe Tossi would have some ideas. It wouldn't do, though, to be seen going into the dwarves' apartment, so when twilight came, they sheltered in the shadows of an unpaved alley nearby. Once they heard the hard-booted feet of a street patrol, but didn't see it. After the curfew bell tolled, Macurdy sent Jeremid out; he'd yowl twice like a cat if everything was clear. A minute later they heard the yowls and slipped out of their alley. Jeremid beckoned, and when they got to him, Kittul Kendersson stood with the door ajar. "In! In!" he rumbled softly, then closed it behind them.

The room was lit by the usual lamp—a bowl of oil with a wick on one side. Kittul took them into the room fitted as a smithy, and grinning, waved around. "The reeve provided all of it: forge, anvil, tongs, hammer, quenchin' tank—everything."

They're hungry for dwarf steel here, Macurdy thought. There were coarse sacks of charcoal, too, and from behind them, Kittul took a rope with knots at intervals. At one end was a triple grab hook that he held up chuckling. "Just made it. Thought it might be useful."

"Good. We've been talking about that. And the crossbows?"

"They're in the sleepin' room." Kittul paused. "I've been thinkin' though. 'Tis us should do the shootin'. We're used to crossbows; we'll not miss."

Macurdy shook his head. "I don't doubt you're better marksmen with them," he said. "But if anyone saw, even in the night, they could tell the patrolmen it was dwarves. While with us—in the dark we look like anyone else around here. And if there's a chase, our legs are longer.

"Besides, Jeremid and Melody have used crossbows, and in my world, we use weapons called guns that you aim pretty much the same way."

"Ah. Well," said Kittul thoughtfully, "there's no doubt we'd be recognized, even if just glimpsed. So then. Best ye start while the moon's still up." He led them into the bedroom, and standing on tiptoes, took two crossbows from pegs on the wall, crossbows that were cocked using a stirrup, and a hook on the belt. Macurdy had thought to use one himself, but the belts were too small to buckle around him.

He handed it to Jeremid, saying, "Try it on." Jeremid did. It buckled in the last notch. "You and Melody will do the shooting," Macurdy told him.

They got ready and left, walking to the square via an alley that opened onto it not far from the posts. At the alley's mouth they huddled in darkness, eyes sorting through the moon shadows around the post area.

Macurdy's eyes made out four guards now, one each on the southeast and southwest corners, while two stood conversing quietly within a few feet of one another on the north end, near where the main street hit the square. He wondered how alert they were. Did they think someone might try a rescue? Or was guard just routine, another dull watch?

He led the others back a ways. "Melody," he murmured, "circle 'round and come out the next alley south. Jeremid, circle north, cross the main street where they won't see you; come to the square on the other side. You two will kill the two in back, the corner men." He paused. "Melody, tell me what I said." She did. Then Jeremid repeated the instructions.

"Good. I'll take the two in front. After you've had time to get in position, I'll go out to one of them. I've got no bow, no spear, and no sword, and my knife's around back of my hip, so they shouldn't be too leery of me.

"Keep a close eye on me. I'll pretend I've been drinking, and walk up to him and start talking. Then I'll knife him and jump the other one. That's when you'll shoot your men and reload. Got it?"

They both stared at him. *I know,* he thought. *I can't believe we're doing this either.* They'd discussed the broad features back at the inn, and it had felt spooky enough then, in daylight and safety. "Good," he said. "Go!"

It took them three or four seconds to turn away, leaving Macurdy where he stood. *Come on,* he told himself, *it's for Varia. Let's get going.* He took another alley, moving quickly but quietly, eyes and ears fine-tuned. Asking himself how this could be for Varia, or how it could possibly work. But not wavering.

Shortly he reached the main street. The moon was low and the whole street in shadow, when he turned quietly onto it. He was in mid-block when he heard what had to be a patrol, and pausing, looked backward. They were turning onto his street from a cross street a hundred yards away. With torches.

Hell! he thought. Some of the shops along the street had small marquees over their entrances, perhaps to protect them from slops thrown from windows above. Striding a few quick steps farther, he jumped, grabbed a marquee, and pulled himself up. It took his weight, and he lay as low and flat as he could. If they'd seen him . . .

But the shadows were dark, and the torches had little reach. He shielded his face with his arms. The patrol passed so close below, it seemed to him they should have heard his heart pounding. Passed and continued along the street, hard-soled boots thudding and scuffing on the cobblestones. After half a minute he raised his head enough to see them from behind. Eight or ten, it seemed, fewer than he'd thought. At the square, instead of turning west or east to pass it by, they walked directly to the poles and stopped. Faintly he heard commands being given; seconds later they turned and started back his way. Again he lowered his face, shielding it, and again they passed beneath him, marching back north up the street, turned onto another and were gone.

Changing the guard! he thought. *Gentle Jesus thank you! If I'd been three minutes sooner . . .* He stayed where he was for several minutes, giving Melody and Jeremid more time, then dropped quietly to the cobblestones and moved on. *That was an omen,* he told himself, *a good one!* And tried to believe it.

The square opened before him, the nearer guard about thirty yards away, and he scarcely hesitated, emerging from the shadows, walking unsteadily. It only then occurred to him that they might shout or blow a whistle or something—maybe kill him—because he was breaking the curfew.

The new guards stood about five yards apart, instead of side by side like the previous two. Both pointed their spears at him, ready to thrust long or short. He walked up dangerously close to one of them, pretending drunkenness. "'Scuse me," he said. "I'm lookin' for a frien' I used to have. Name is Lucky. Someone said he was one of these guys." He waved broadly at the pole-bound captives.

Both guards laughed. "Nobody here's called Lucky," one said. "Not anymore."

Macurdy peered as if to penetrate the night, stepping nearer, weaving, and spoke confidentially. "He owes me five coppers.

Did you know that?" Then lowered his voice further. "Are they dead?"

"They cut the dead ones down at sunset, and took them away. These are all alive."

Macurdy leaned. "Lucky," he called hoarsely, "are you there?"

And moved, his left hand closing on the spearshaft, shoving it aside and pulling it past him, drew his knife as he strode into the guard, plunging it under his ribs, in and up and back out, letting the man fall, catching the other with his eyes. The second guard's reaction was slow; he took an uncertain step toward Macurdy, and the heavy knife, thrown hard, struck him in the middle of the chest. With a weak bleat, the man slumped and fell. Macurdy was on him in an instant, ignoring the third and fourth guards, who were Melody's and Jeremid's responsibilities. Gripping a shoulder, he turned the man over and grabbed the knife hilt. It had gone through the breastbone to the hilt and was slippery with blood. He'd probably stepped in blood, too, he realized.

Then Melody's voice hissed at him. "Macurdy! Hurry! A patrol's coming!" He looked around, feeling just an instant's prick of panic, then strode to the nearest rebel and cut the thong that held his arms overhead. The man fell unmoving, and Macurdy realized he'd been dead weight on his bonds. The next was standing, and he freed him. "Stay with her," Macurdy husked to him, and went to a third. He became aware that Melody was also cutting men free. When they were done, six rebels stood. Three others lay still. Without hesitating, Macurdy cut their throats; he couldn't take them, and wouldn't leave them for further torture. Only one gushed blood. The other two had died already.

"Come *on!*" Melody said.

"You take them," Macurdy answered. "My boots are bloody; they'll leave marks. Go!"

He heard a command shouted from near the south end of the square, and ran not north with Melody and the rebels, but west, scuffing his feet in the grass and dirt to wipe off what he could of the blood. Crossing the street, he ducked into an alley, wondering where Jeremid might be. Somewhere off southeast someone was shouting, and he wondered what that was about. Around a corner he stopped, and pulling off his boots, tied them together, slung them over a shoulder, then trotted off barefoot.

The cobblestones were rough-surfaced, and he was limping when the dwarves let him in. The front room was dark, crowded but quiet. Men sat on the floor with cups and bowls, and the place smelled of stew—supper reheated. Melody gripped Macurdy's sleeve and pulled him into the kitchen. "You did it!" she said, and began to unbutton his bloody shirt. "We need to rinse this before the blood sets."

He dropped his boots and stripped it off. Melody immersed it in a small tub, surging it up and down while the water reddened. "The boots too," Macurdy said, looking around for more water. Apparently it had to be carried from some public well.

"I need to get the blood out of your shirt, first."

"Where's Jeremid?" he asked.

"The last I saw, he was running toward the patrol. Probably to draw them off."

Macurdy's face was stiff with tension. He'd hoped to pull this off and get over the wall without an uproar. But now . . . Now the whole damned police force would be out, and any soldiers garrisoned there. The gates were already closed, and the guards in the watch shelters would be wide awake now, alert as hawks. "Where's Tossi?" he asked.

"Right here." The dwarf had come in behind him from the front room.

"Will your cellar hole hold six men?"

"If they don't mind dark and discomfort."

"Anything will be better than what they've just been through. But they'll need air and water."

Tossi frowned. "I can leave the trapdoor open most of the time. If someone bangs on the door, one of us can answer it while another closes the trapdoor and slides the anvil block over top of it." He paused, peering intently at Macurdy. "How long will we be stayin', with the six of them under the floor?"

"I'll try taking one or maybe two out with Melody and me tonight. And Jeremid, if he gets back in time. Police and soldiers will be searching house to house tomorrow—maybe even later tonight—and it'll look suspicious to have tallfolk here, even if they're not the prisoners. But these men need to stay somewhere, until things quiet down or I get them out somehow."

"One or two tonight, you say. The danger's great, I'm sure ye know. It'll be buzzin' like a beehive out there."

"It'll be worse a little later, when the confusion settles and they get organized. Let me trade shirts with someone, to wear while this one dries. Then we'll be on our way."

Ten minutes later, Macurdy was out in the night again, with Melody and a rebel named Verder. Macurdy carried twenty-five feet of slender, knotted rope wrapped around his waist, concealed by a tunic the canny Tossi had bought for the purpose. He carried the grapnel in his hand for lack of a better place. At the first corner, not a hundred feet away, they turned down an alley, moving at an easy jog.

It took a minute for the sound to register on Macurdy, but when it did, he stopped. The night, the town, held a diffuse droning. Melody and Verder were listening, too.

"What is it?" Verder asked.

"People," Melody said in a hushed voice. "People off south."

Then it struck Macurdy. He knew as if he'd been there and heard it happen! Striding to a shutter, he banged on it with the grapnel, shouting: "Have you heard?! The guards were killed in the square, and the prisoners cut free!"

Melody and the rebel stared shocked. "Macurdy!" she hissed. "What—"

"The people you hear," he answered. "They know! It must have been Jeremid. He must have run through the streets yelling what happened, and people are coming out. They don't like their rulers here; that's why there's a curfew. And if enough people come out, it'll keep the street patrols tied up." He turned and trotted off, still shouting, pausing now and then to bang on shutters. Melody and the rebel trotted after him, both of them shouting too. Voices answered from indoors, some questioning, some angry. When the alley opened onto a street, they turned east on it and trotted three more blocks shouting, before they saw five youths run into the street ahead of them from an alley. They were shouting too.

"The guards in the square are killed!" Macurdy yelled again. "The prisoners are freed!" Just ahead was a broken fence enclosing a weedy garden, and abruptly he stopped to yank staves loose from it. The youths watched, uncertain but alert. Melody realized at once what he was up to, and began piling the staves in the middle of the street. Verder helped, and now the youths, catching on, kicked and shoved on the supports of a rickety porch till the roof fell. Macurdy ignited the pile of fence staves, then ran on. They'd gone hardly more than a block before they heard shouts of "Fire! Fire!" behind them.

He shouted no more, nor stopped again till panting, they reached the perimeter street. The half moon was low in the west, but by its pale light, Macurdy could make out guards in and by the watch shelters. The sound of people was growing. To the guards it must seem dangerous, threatening.

"Let's go for it," Macurdy said. "If they see us, they still might stay where they are. If necessary, we'll run across the street again."

"What about the others?" Verder asked.

"I'll lower you two from the wall and go back for them. Melody knows where to take you."

The perimeter street was bare dirt, very wide by Rude Lands standards, about forty feet, but in dense moon shadow all the way to the palisade. Macurdy had opened his tunic while he'd talked, and unwound the rope. Now he dashed across, twirling the grapnel, and flung it up to the archery walk midway between watch shelters. It caught, and he started climbing, wishing the rope was thicker and gave a better grip. Thank God for the knots, he thought. After a moment's pause to look, he pulled himself onto the walk. There was a tug at the rope, and he hauled the rebel up, then repeated the performance with Melody. Still no one seemed to notice them. In another minute he'd lowered first Melody, then Verder down the outside.

Only then did he turn and look over the town. He wasn't the only one who'd set fires, and some hadn't taken care to light them in the middle of the street; south of the square, part of the town was burning. He rehooked the grapnel on the planking and lowered himself to the street, then with a few flips of the rope, dislodged it.

For a moment he considered leaving it there, finding it again
when he came back. But afraid of losing it, he wrapped it around
himself again, buttoned his tunic, and ran back up the street.
It was starting to fill with people, and more porches were
burning.

When he arrived at the dwarves' apartment, Jeremid was
there, grinning excitedly. In a hurried conference, it was decided
the dwarves should leave too. Their ponies were lodged at a
stable on the main street, near the north gate, and it seemed
likely that considering the fires, the gate guards would let them
out. They were dwarves, after all, and had a letter of retainer
from the reeve.

They'd take Jeremid with them, posing as their servant, to
help them handle their personal gear. The smithing gear they'd
leave behind. They'd gotten it on credit anyway, using the reeve's
letter of authorization

Macurdy left with the five remaining rebels, taking alleys
to bypass fires, and in minutes they'd reached the stockade.
It was burning too, though not vigorously; the guards had
abandoned their posts, and fires had been lit in some of the
watch shelters. Moments later, Macurdy and his five charges
were on the outside. Leaving the rope and grapnel hanging,
he led his rebels north past the town.

23

The Rebel Commander

When he'd left the northeast corner of the stockade behind, Macurdy took his little band through a field of some spring-seeded small grain—whether oats or barley, he couldn't tell in the dark. It was heavily loaded with dew that had already soaked his boots.

Well before he reached the road, his rebels were getting strung out, too weak to keep up. "We'll stop here," he said, and at once, three of them sank to the ground despite the cold dew. Southward, the sky above town was ruddied by fires, with here and there flames tall enough to be seen above the town walls. Macurdy felt a certain guilt at his role in the burning. But the townsmen, he told himself, had been ready to rise up, to riot, and the fires had been inevitable.

Rebellion, he told himself, was the easy part. The hard parts would be winning, and replacing their government with something better. But that was up to them. What he needed to do was work this to somehow help him rescue Varia.

Meanwhile he had allies now, or so it seemed. He looked them over. All but one had what Arbel had taught him to recognize as warrior auras. The other had an artisan aura; he'd be good at making things, and maybe at coming up with ideas. "I guess you know my name's Macurdy," Macurdy said. "What are yours?"

They told him, stepping on one another's lines. It turned out they were from two different districts. Three were from north, up the road not many hours' ride; the others were from three day's ride northeast.

"Anyone here injured?" he asked.

They'd all been beaten after their capture, and the two from the northeastern band hadn't eaten for four days, except what the dwarves had fed them. Macurdy realized that he was pretty hungry himself. "All right. We're going north another quarter mile or so. There's an inn there. I'll hide you near it and go see about horses."

One of the rebels spoke then—one of the northeastern group—a rangy, tough-looking man who'd given his name as Wolf. "Where are you from?" he asked. "You don't sound like Tekalos, neither hillsman nor flatlander."

"From off west," Macurdy said, "the other side of the Great Muddy. A country called Oz; I was a soldier there. Two of us were, and the woman's father was a commander. She's one of a caste of warrior women, weapons-trained all her life. She's killed two men since we left there."

"How'd you get mixed up in our trouble?"

Macurdy laughed wryly. "We didn't get along with our troll's spawn of a commander. So one morning about daybreak I tromped the seeds out of him and three of his bully boys. Then we grabbed some horses and took off. Kept ahead of them long enough to cross the Muddy."

Macurdy realized that his story sounded unlikely, but it went with the lingering discoloration of his face, and his missing and broken teeth.

"That doesn't answer my question," Wolf said. "How'd you get mixed up in the troubles here? Why'd you cut us loose?"

"Any king, or count, or reeve who'd hang people up like that, deserves all the enemies he can get. We decided we'd give him six more."

"How'd the dwarves get mixed up in it? I never heard of them mixing in tallfolks' troubles before."

"They're young westerners, feeling their oats."

"Umm."

It was apparent that Wolf still had reservations, but he'd go along for the time being. The rest were probably too grateful, Macurdy decided, and too hungry, to question their rescuer's motives. "Okay," he said. "Let's get moving. We've got to get well away from here before daylight."

They walked slowly, keeping to the grain field to avoid people riding away from town and the fires. His rebels were rural, automatically considerate of growing crops, and stayed in single file to lessen damage. After a bit they crossed the Valley Highway and continued well past the inn, then angled northwest across pasture. Northeastward, Macurdy could make out horses grazing, probably rental animals belonging to the innkeeper. Scattered along the north-south road were spreading trees that would have inhibited dew formation, and he steered toward one of them. When they got there, they found a thin fringe of shrubs and saplings growing along the rail fence, screening the pasture from the road. The rebels sank to the ground.

"I'll leave you here for a while," Macurdy said, "while I see what horses I can scrounge. Wolf, come with me. I'll be back before long." Then he headed toward the inn.

The dwarves had come in just ahead of him. The town gates had been opened, and the last room already let when they'd arrived, so they'd crowded in with Jeremid, Melody, and Verder, in the small room Macurdy had rented earlier.

"I've got the others waiting north up the road," he told them. "They're not in very good shape; haven't been eating, and two were beaten up pretty badly. I'll take them north up the road to the nearest rebel camp, but I need horses for them."

"Simple enough," Jeremid said. Melody was nodding agreement even before he explained. "Just take some from the stable. Saddle what you need and go."

Macurdy shook his head. "There's the stable boy, and whatever guard or guards the innkeeper has there. We'd have to manhandle them; tie and gag them. And the only enemies I want in this country are the king and his henchmen."

Tossi spoke before Jeremid could argue. "As I count them," the dwarf said, "we need only three more. I'll hire them from the innkeeper in the mornin', or buy them if he'll sell."

Macurdy was relieved. He'd decided the dwarves had deep pockets, but hadn't been sure that Tossi would go for another expense like this. Now he gave instructions: He, Melody and the rebels would leave at once. Jeremid and the dwarves would follow at dawn.

Within a few minutes, they were headed north up the road in the moonless dark, Macurdy and Melody on their own horses, the six rebels doubled up on three others. None of them knew where they were going. The men were either from Wollerda's Company, off east, or Dell's Band, which had been broken. There was another band off north, Orthal's Company, but they didn't know where it was. Macurdy grunted. "We'll find it," he said.

It took some four hours to reach forested hills; fifteen or twenty miles, he guessed. By that time there was a hint of dawn in the eastern sky. Half an hour later they left the road at a creek, splashing westward through gray dawn-light, heavy forest on both banks. When they'd gone a hundred yards or so, they left the stream, pushing through a fringe of osier and willow onto dry ground.

"We'll rest here a few hours," Macurdy said. "Tie your horses and get dry wood for warming fires." He and Melody helped, and after they'd piled a stock of branchwood, he built and lit a pair of fires. Then the two of them walked back out to the roadside, carrying the oiled leather rain capes that were part of their saddle gear, and picked their careful way up the slope to an overlook forty or fifty feet above the road.

At the top, Macurdy sat down on leaf mould just within the forest edge. "What do you think?" he asked.

"About what?"

"Anything. Our evening's work. Our rebels. How we're doing."

"Macurdy, you're a magician, and I'm not talking about how you make fires. Things go right for you." She shifted closer to him. "All that excitement made me horny. If you had to separate Jeremid and me tonight, the least you can do is kiss me. The very least."

She held her face toward his, perhaps a foot away. He didn't close the gap. "Melody," he said. "I like sitting here with you, but . . ."

"I know. You're married, with some kind of strange Farside

vow." She sighed. "All right, I won't push it. Who takes the first watch?"

"I will."

"Wake me up if you get too sleepy. I don't want to miss the others." She paused and grinned wickedly. "Especially not Jeremid. I may not be in love with him, but he knows how to please a woman."

Macurdy managed to grin back at her. "So do I. Take my word for it."

"Take your word?" Melody sputtered. "Bastard!" He could tell she wasn't serious though, and as if to prove it, she chuckled, the sound reminding him of Varia. "You know, Macurdy, I loved you from the first, before I knew you well enough to like you. Now I like you, too."

Then she wrapped herself in her rain cape and curled up on the cold ground. When her breathing and aura said she slept, Macurdy put his own cape over her and stood up. He was getting sleepy, and considered doing calisthenics to stay awake and warm, then decided he was too tired. Instead he fingered his gums and broken front teeth. They'd begun to hurt. He'd assumed they'd start to rot in time, but hadn't thought it would be so soon. Presumably they had tooth butchers in this world, but he was willing to bet they were a bloody, painful lot.

He sat down again. They were back barely within the trees; the sun, when it rose, would shine in his face. It ought to be all right to sleep till then. He should have three or four hours before the dwarves arrived.

The sun rose, but by then he'd turned his back to it, as Melody had. An hour later it was Blue Wing's raucous voice that wakened him, from a limb almost directly overhead. "Macurdy! Macurdy!"

He jerked abruptly to a sitting position. "Huh? Oh! Blue Wing!" He turned to Melody; she was sitting up too.

"The dwarves are on their way," the bird said. "Tossi sent me to tell you. Where are the others?"

"In the woods, up the creek a little ways."

"Have you slept?"

"A little bit."

"Humans are strange! Go back to sleep. I'll wake you when they get here."

He didn't need to urge them. They lay down again where they were, backs to the sun, letting it warm them. It didn't much make up for the cold, hard ground, but they quickly fell asleep again.

The next time Blue Wing wakened them, Macurdy could see the dwarves coming, a quarter mile south down the road, Jeremid riding a little ahead as if impatient. Their pack animals trailed behind, along with three new horses. Macurdy waved, getting their attention, then he and Melody scrambled down the side of the ridge and led them to the rebels, who still slept beside cold fires.

While Macurdy and Melody stacked a new fire, Tossi brought out a huge summer sausage, along with some potatoes that weren't too badly sprouted. The activity had wakened most of the rebels, who watched impressed as Macurdy lit the fire. They'd seen him do it the night before, but they'd been half unconscious then; it could have been a dream.

"Are you part ylf?" Wolf asked.

Macurdy laughed. "I used to be a shaman's apprentice. Learned to start fires and kill bugs in the bedding. That's pretty much it."

They seemed comfortable with that.

Now Macurdy raised his face. "Blue Wing!" he shouted. "Blue Wing!" The rebels looked at him as if he'd lost his mind. "Huh! I hope he hasn't flown off out of hearing." Not many seconds later, the great raven landed in a tuliptree, perching on a branch about sixty feet overhead.

"What do you want, Macurdy?"

"We need to find a band of men. Rebels. There'll be quite a few of them, and they'll be armed. Men that may resemble the men we found with the dwarves a few days ago."

Blue Wing didn't say anything for a long moment. "Can you tell me more? What direction? Anything?"

Macurdy looked at Verder. "What can you tell him?"

Verder stared impressed at the big bird. "I suppose they'll

be somewhere north and west of here not many miles. Probably where there's open ground with grass for the horses; a burn maybe, a year or two old. There's likely to be lean-tos and tents."

Blue Wing didn't ask for clarification on "not many miles." Probably, Macurdy thought, he'd taken it to mean not too far away. The great raven launched from the branch, big wings thrusting, lifted through a gap in the forest roof and out of sight.

He was back in half an hour to describe a camp he'd found. "I'll bet that's it," Verder said.

They got on their horses, three of the rebels riding bareback. (The innkeeper had been unwilling to sell any of his saddles; the saddle makers in Gormin Town might have burned out the night before, and he didn't know when he could get more.) Over the next hour the bird guided them west and north, then landed in a tree. "Macurdy!" he called, "it's only a short way farther. Leave the ridge and follow the draw on your right. You'll come to a large grassy area."

"Thanks!" Macurdy called back, then turned to Verder. "They're not going to know us. Could there be any trouble?"

"I don't know why. They ought to welcome volunteers."

Macurdy's eyes scanned down the line of horses and ponies. "String your bows," he said, and waited while the dwarves dismounted to draw their braided wire crossbow cords.

He followed Blue Wing's directions then, and in the draw found a well-used trail. Before long they were challenged. He stopped, and a sentry came out on foot, sidling toward him, bow half drawn. "Who are you?" the man asked. "What are you doing here?"

"We came up to join, if we like the look of things."

Another voice called from out of sight behind a thicket. "Kahl, take them to Orthal. He'll decide what to do with them. And you! Strangers! All of you off your horses! On foot!"

Macurdy looked back. "Do it," he said.

Another, presumably Kahl, rode out on horseback then, and herded the newcomers to a broad meadow. As they crossed it, a heavy-set man sauntered to meet them, a man with considerable fat over thick muscles. Orthal, Macurdy decided.

In one hand he carried a roasted joint of some animal, a deer maybe, or calf. His face, hands, and hairy belly were slick with grease. His aura marked him as a natural ruler, a man born to give orders and be obeyed. It also showed him to be brutal. Most of his command seemed to be loafing, and Macurdy got the sense of people who didn't know what to do next—men without a clear objective or plan or strategy.

"Captain," Kahl said, "these people were coming up the trail. Thurgo told me to bring them to you."

Orthal scowled at the newcomers. "What do you want here?"

"We came to join," Macurdy said.

"Who in the devil's name are you?"

"My name's Macurdy, and these are Jeremid and Melody. We're from Oz. These dwarves are sons of the Rich Lode clan, from the Diamond Flues. These others are rebels from other bands, men we rescued from the reeve in Gormin Town. I don't know all their names."

None of it seemed to register on Orthal, who looked them over slowly, his eyes stopping on Melody for a long moment before returning to Macurdy. Meanwhile, more and more of Orthal's band gathered around, bows nocked or spears in hand. Jeremid kept his own arrow casually directed at Orthal's greasy chest, the bowstring half drawn. Orthal was very aware of it.

"Who do you know here that can speak for you?" Orthal asked.

"Here? No one of yours. But these . . ."

Orthal waved him off. "They don't mean shit to me. I never saw them before."

"I'll tell ye who he is," said Tossi angrily. "He's the one that killed the reeve's guards in the square in Gormin Town. He and those tew. And cut these others down from where they'd been hung up to die in public. And led a public riot against the king, that set the town burnin'."

Most of Orthal's men were staring hard at Macurdy now, unsure whether the claims were true, but feeling a certain awe. Macurdy could sense it.

Orthal grunted. "Huh! Sounds like bullshit to me. What's your name again?"

"Macurdy."

"Macnurley!" His mispronunciation, Macurdy guessed, was deliberate. "I've got foragers out, and they bring news as well as food. If the things this halfling says are true, we'll welcome you. But for now . . . For now you'll have to give up your weapons. And your horses."

Macurdy felt his people tighten. He was also aware that Orthal had reestablished his authority; his men were ready to let their arrows fly, their spears thrust. One of them even stepped in front of his captain as if to shield him. Macurdy looked back. "Do what he says," he ordered. "If we're going to be part of this, we need to take orders." He slipped his sheathed saber from his belt and lay it on the ground; unhappy, the others followed his example with bows and swords. Meanwhile rebels had moved in, taken the reins of the horses and ponies, and were leading them away.

No one but Macurdy paid attention to the heavy knife still behind his hip. They were led to a place in the shade and seated in a cluster, unbound but guarded. After a little, the rebels ate their midday meal, offering their prisoners neither food nor water. Jeremid gave Macurdy dirty looks. Before the meal was over, a sentry rode up. "Captain! There's men coming up the trail from Three Forks. Slaney and his, I think!"

Macurdy swallowed bile.

Other rebels mounted horses and rode off southwest, clearly not in hostile reaction, but to confirm and greet.

"Slaney?" Jeremid murmured. "Isn't he the one . . . ?"

"He's the one," Macurdy murmured back.

"Shit! What do we do now?"

"Wait for our chance. Don't do anything till I tell you."

Six or eight minutes later, Slaney rode into the clearing at the head of about twenty men. Macurdy got to his feet, the rest of his party rising too. As the newcomers rode up, Slaney's glance stopped on him.

"Well! What have we got here?" he said. Reining up, he dismounted and swaggered over. "Looks like you caught yourself some prisoners, Orthal!" He laughed then. "Yes, you surely did."

"You know them?"

"Oh yes. Yes, I know them. I know them real well. This

one especially." He pointed to Macurdy, then actually rubbed his hands together. "I never forget a face, and that one I'd remember in hell."

He told about the affair at the blowndown timber then, his account more or less factual, but incomplete. Finishing with, "He took our horses then, and our loot and weapons, and rode off with it."

"Slaney," Macurdy said, "you're a liar as well as a coward. I left you horses enough to leave on, and what I took, I gave to the dwarves, as blood money for their cousins you killed. Anyone with even half a brain knows better than to start a war with dwarves."

Slaney flushed, and with an oath drew his sword. Macurdy's knife struck him just below the breastbone, and the bandit took one wobbling step before falling on his face. Rebels crowded around Macurdy then, punching and kicking, getting in their own way, until Orthal bellowed to let him be. Probably, Macurdy thought, he had his own ideas for punishment.

Then someone else spoke, Slaney's second-in-command. "Are these the ones Burney told us about when we were riding up? That want to join?"

Orthal took a moment before answering. "That's right. What about it?"

"What their leader said is true: They could have killed us all, or left us afoot. And if they want to join . . . When we stopped at Stoney Creek, Bekker told us recruitment's down to nothing, since Dell's band got massacred."

"That's us!" Verder said. "I was one of Dell's. Some of us were taken alive. Dell and Liskor were hung up on the spot and used for target practice."

Again there was uncertainty on many rebel faces.

"Counting the dwarves, there's twelve of them," someone added. "Enough to be worthwhile."

"Eleven," someone corrected. "The other one's a woman."

"I'm as good as most men in a fight!" Melody answered. "Anyone want to test me? Orthal?"

Orthal laughed. "Oh, I'll test you all right. On your back, after we've executed these filth. Starting with him." He gestured at Macurdy. "Then we'll all test you."

It was Melody, not Macurdy, that Orthal walked up to, as if to grab her. Her right fist caught him flush on the nose, and blood flowed as he stepped backward in surprise. Then, with a roar, he drew his sword.

Macurdy's bellow stopped everything. "NOW WE SEE WHAT KIND OF SPINELESS COWARD ORTHAL IS!" he shouted. "TOO GUTLESS TO GIVE HER A SWORD AND FIGHT HER."

Orthal stared bug-eyed at him for a moment, then gradually relaxed and grinned. "Larny!" he called, "give the bitch your sword."

Some of the rebels laughed. Larny stepped forward, a massive shambling man not much taller than Macurdy but considerably heavier, mostly muscle. "It ain't right, Orthal," Larny said. "It's too big for her. She couldn't hardly lift it, let alone fight with it."

"Will you shut up, Larny! Just give her the damn sword!"

"Just a minute, Larny," Macurdy said, and stepped away from the spears at his back. "Let me see how heavy it is."

Before anyone but Macurdy realized what was happening, Larny handed him the sword, and Macurdy leaped. Orthal never got his own sword up before Larny's heavy blade thrust him through below the ribs. Macurdy wheeled then, sword ready. "What in hell," he shouted, "does a man have to do to join this humping outfit?"

Someone laughed, then someone else, then others, but most stood indecisively, till a voice called from overhead. "Macurdy! Macurdy! Men are coming on your trail!"

"How many?"

"More than ten!"

"Someone go see who they are!" he shouted, and several rebels ran to their horses as if used to taking his orders. They'd barely mounted when a man galloped up from the sentry post in that direction.

"Tarlok's coming! With recruits!"

The rebels seemed glad to turn their attention to this new development. They waited, and within three or four minutes, a dozen men rode into the clearing. Their leader trotted up ahead of the others. "Good news!" he shouted. "There's been excitement in Gormin Town! The reeve strung up a couple dozen of Dell's and Wollerda's guys in the square. Then someone killed the guards and cut the prisoners loose, and the whole town went on a rampage! Burned half of it to the ground! Including the stockade!"

"You see!" Wolf shouted. "I'm one of Wollerda's, and Macurdy's the one that cut us free. After knifing two of the guards himself."

Earlier, the matter of Macurdy and his people had focused the rebels. The arrival of the recruiting party had dispersed that focus. Now Wolf had returned it to Macurdy, in a manner of speaking; people were talking to each other about him, though leaving Macurdy pretty much to himself for the moment. Orthal lay ignored where he'd fallen.

Slaney's second came over to Macurdy. "You really want to join up?" he asked.

Macurdy examined the man's aura. It was the same general type as Arbel's; he was what Arbel called a student. Just now he was a bandit-rebel, and before that probably a farmer-herdsman, but beneath it all he was a student, perhaps of life. His aura seemed basically clean, with a zone suggesting a pragmatic nature. And he'd been Slaney's second, which meant he'd been accepted as capable, but took orders. Saner and smarter than Slaney though, and bigger, stronger-looking. So maybe not very aggressive.

Aggressive enough to make a pitch to Orthal, Macurdy reminded himself, *a pitch to save my neck. That took guts, with Slaney lying dead there.* He grunted. "Do I really want to join up? Not exactly. I want to command this outfit. Turn it into the core of an army that can throw Gurtho down once and for all. And I need someone by me that knows these people: what they want, what they need. What their strong points are, and their weaknesses. You want the job?"

The man didn't answer. Instead he said, "Don't be shy with them. They may not know it, but they're looking for a leader now. They want one. And they might accept a stranger. The right stranger."

They. They. That explained the aural coolness, Macurdy decided. The man was a local, one of the group, but inwardly held a little apart from it. *I believe I'm getting good at this aura analysis,* Macurdy told himself. "Thanks," he said. "Who'll take over if I don't?"

"Probably no one, with Slaney dead. And I expect they'll break up and drift home if someone doesn't take over."

Macurdy nodded. "What's your name? And the guy's name that just came in with recruits?"

"He's Tarlok. I'm Jesker."

"Thanks." Macurdy spotted Tarlok at the center of a large cluster of rebels, and started over. Some of the rebels from Gormin Town were there too; Verned glanced his way and beckoned. The cluster opened on Macurdy's side as if to receive him.

Let's do it, Macurdy told himself, and lengthened his stride.

"You're Macurdy?" Tarlok asked. "The one that killed Orthal?"

"I'm Macurdy. And yeah, I killed Orthal. Partly. Mainly he killed himself, by stupidity, and treating people like shit."

Tarlok's gaze was steady. Analytical. He had a warrior's aura, a fairly clean one. This was a man who'd take responsibility, and give loyalty where it was due.

"A couple of your people know a couple of my recruits," Tarlok said. "They tell us you killed the soldiers guarding them in Gormin Town, then cut them loose. And that you're the one who lit off the uprising there."

"I'm from Oz, me and two others. We each killed guards, but I was the ringleader. Lighting off the uprising was easy. People there were ready; they hate Gurtho as much as you do. All they needed was someone to start something; they took it from there. I'd rather they hadn't burned the town, but it's their town."

"So what do you do next?"

"Let me ask *you* a question. I know what the people in Gormin Town want. They want to get rid of Gurtho. But what do you want? What are you up here for?"

Several men tried to speak then; Macurdy pointed at one. "You," he said. "What are you up here for?"

"Freedom for the tribe! Our grandfathers' grandfathers were free men. Then we lost a war with the flatlanders and had to swear allegiance to the kings of Tekalos. Obey their reeves and pay their taxes."

By this time, most of the rebels had gathered around to listen.

"All right," Macurdy said, "so you want freedom from lowland kings. Just don't replace them with somebody like Orthal, or you'll be as bad off as ever. You, Wolf! Is that what the rebels want where you're from? Freedom?"

"Pretty much. We want to rule ourselves."

"Anyone got something different?"

The only answers were shouts of "No!", or "that's it!"

"Then what were you sitting around for? You ought to be training for war! Learning to fight as a unit! Learning tactics! I came up here today and people were loafing! Did I get here on a holiday or something?"

No one answered.

"The only way to get your freedom is fight for it! And it's not enough just to fight! You've got to win!" He paused. "Now fighting's what I do. Fighting and winning. And I didn't come up here to waste my time. If you want to fight, and win your freedom, I'll organize and train you. Make a fighting force out of you. Lead you if you want. Otherwise I'll take my sword and my friends and go somewhere else. Tell me now."

There were several seconds of silence, long enough for Macurdy to wonder which answer he really preferred. Then Wolf said, "I've already seen him in action. He's smart, he's not afraid of anything—and he's *lucky!*"

Tarlok spoke next. "Orthal turned out to be a loudmouth bully, and Bono and I figured if things didn't get better, someone would cut his throat some night soon and we'd try a different captain. Maybe Macurdy's the man."

A number of voices shouted agreement, but it wasn't general. Jesker had followed Macurdy over; he spoke next. "Slaney'd been saying we needed to do something about Orthal, that as long as Orthal ran things, nothing would happen. Fighting with fists, he was the most dangerous man around, but for thinking? Then Slaney got crosswise with Macurdy over west, and Macurdy made a fool out of him; tricked him out of his boots. I know; I was there. Then here, when Slaney had the advantage of him, sword against knife, Macurdy split his breastbone. Now we hear what he did in Gormin Town last night. If we're not smart enough to make him commander after all that, I'm going home, and to hell with the rest of you! The gods sent him to us as our last chance. If we turn them down, we're finished. We'll deserve whatever happens to us."

Macurdy stood briefly stunned at the speech, and at the voices shouting his name now. Grinning men pushed up to him to shake his hand, and when things had calmed a bit, he raised his own voice. "Tarlok! Jesker! Jeremid! Melody! Tossi! Wolf, you too! I need to talk to you over by the cook tent! We need to get things started here!"

It took awhile. There were sixty-three rebels now, with Tarlok's new recruits, Slaney's band, and the six rebels Macurdy had rescued. None had been soldiers, and in Tekalos there was no militia training. All were good bowmen—many very good—and that was about the limit of their military competence. Most had also brought spears, such as hillsmen take when hunting bear or cat or razorbacks, and could stab a man with them if it came to it. But clashing spears with trained soldiers, they'd be in deep trouble. A few had swords, passed down through the family from tribal days, but almost none were trained with them, beyond the games boys played with sticks.

If competence was a problem, so was supply. With sixty-three mouths to feed, and located back in the wild as they were, foraging would be a problem. The nearest clusters of farms had been heavily drawn on already, and the camp had been there for only about a month, but getting food from farther away presented problems of transport.

Macurdy wondered again if this was a good idea, being here, doing this. To create an army out of a few thousand scattered hillsmen looked virtually impossible. And how was it going to help him rescue Varia anyway?

On the other hand, he reminded himself, he'd been operating on impulse, on intuition, ever since his run-in with Zassfel in the House of Heroes, and he'd succeeded beyond all reason. He'd been operating on "notions," like Will had, but bigger notions, and his had worked out.

Anyway here I am. And this makes more sense, or maybe it does, than just walking into the Sisterhood and telling them I've come to take Varia home.

With Tarlok's and Jesker's advice, he selected two platoon leaders, a sergeant at arms to enforce discipline, and a commissary chief. In the future, foragers would write chits for what they took, payable when Gurtho was thrown down. He named Jeremid his chief of operations, to see that men got trained, and to schedule foraging and other work assignments. Melody would lead the actual training. Tarlok would still be the recruiter, along with Verder, who could tell firsthand stories about Macurdy, but they'd take only two men with them, instead of four or five. One of the older men, a smith himself, would travel around the district visiting smithies, to get production started on spearheads and arrowheads in quantities. Tossi and his cousins would find a suitable smithy and begin to train local smiths in the making of swords.

And Wolf would take Macurdy to visit the rebels in his district. They were a larger, considerably more effective band, and sooner or later coordination would be desirable.

When he'd worked these things out, Macurdy called a muster by shouting, reminding himself to see about getting bugles or trumpets or something. Squads were created, and assigned to platoons. Then, to inspire some enthusiasm for training, he had Jeremid and Melody give an exhibition of skilled spear fighting, first in slow motion, then at full speed, using training spears cut on the spot from saplings. It also prepared the men for taking instructions from Melody. When they were done, two of the dwarves gave an almost dizzying exhibition of swordsmanship, changing any perception of them as amusing halflings.

Macurdy had intended, when it was over, to send the squads out to cut practice spears for themselves. But before he could give the order, he saw three women watching from a little distance, and called them over. They were filthy, their clothes were torn, and their hair was matted with dirt and leaves.

"Who are you?" he asked.

It was the oldest who answered. The younger two were silent, eyes on the ground. "We're captives."

"Captives? Captured from who?"

"From our farms. From our families. A foraging party grabbed us when they came around to take food."

He realized why, but asked anyway. "What did they take you for?"

"They brought us here to hump us."

"Just the three of you? For all these men?"

The woman nodded grimly.

"And your family let them?" He knew the answer to that, too, but it loosened their tongues a little, or rather the older one's.

Their circumstances had differed, one from the other. The oldest was perhaps twenty-five, and married. Her husband had been away. The foraging party raped her on the spot, then tied her and took her with them. The younger two were sisters, fourteen and fifteen. Home alone with their mother, they'd been carried off and raped on the way to camp.

The rebels, standing around waiting for further orders, had listened to the whole exchange. Macurdy turned to them now, face dark with anger. "Those who were on those foraging parties," he ordered, "raise your hands."

Five hands reluctantly went up. "Orthal told us to," said one man.

Macurdy turned to the older woman again. "Is that all of them?"

"Yessir."

"All on one foraging trip?"

"Yessir."

"Which of the rest humped you?"

"Most all of them, I guess. Maybe a few didn't. They humped the young ones the most, I think because they cried. There was someone at them morning, noon, and night."

"Orthal said we could," one of the younger men called.

Macurdy's eyes found him. "What's your name?" he asked. His voice was a dangerous purr; the man paled at it.

"Parl, Captain."

"Parl, step out here." The young man hesitated. "NOW!"

He stepped, and Macurdy, standing close in front of him,

barked a question in his face. "If Orthal told you you could hump your grandmother, would you do it?"

Silence. The commander seemed to swell. "GOD DAMN YOU! I ASKED YOU A QUESTION! WOULD YOU DO IT?"

Parl could barely get the words out. "No sir," he whispered.

"What would you demand of men who'd stolen and raped your daughter?"

"I—I'd want them punished."

"Punished shit! You'd want them killed!"

Parl almost fainted.

Macurdy looked around for Melody, and found her, her mouth a hard line. "Lieutenant Melody, talk with these women and come up with amends and punishments for the foraging party. And what the whole company can do for them before we take these women home again. I'll decide after supper."

Melody and the oldest victim came up with castration, to be followed by staking out over ant hills, naked in the sun. The girls couldn't bring themselves even to talk about it. Macurdy, though, wouldn't go along with such draconian and terminal punishments. The older victim relented before Melody.

He announced the amends the next morning at muster, and the punishments were meted. Each of the three captives was awarded 20 silver teklota or the equivalent, at the cost of every man but the newcomers, which virtually stripped the rebels of money. Some had to borrow from newcomers to pay their share. And remarkably no one grumbled, at least where Macurdy could hear. Beyond that, two conscience-stricken youths—brothers—asked leave to marry the girls, if they'd have them. The girls didn't say yes, but they didn't refuse, either, and Macurdy gave the youths a three-week leave, should the girls and their parents accept the offer. He didn't really care whether they came back or not. The girls, he thought, might need their reassurance more than he did their military service.

As for the foraging crew who'd stolen them, their leader was to receive ten strokes of the rod from each victim, and the other four, five each. The rod being unpeeled hornbeam about half an inch thick. But when it came down to it, the younger girl struck only the leader, twice, then burst into tears, threw away the cane, and ran to hide. Her sister wouldn't touch it. The older woman, though, laid it on with vigor, as if to make up for the unwillingness of the others, and Macurdy allowed her to strike for the younger two.

The results were an ugly bloody mess. Macurdy would let them suffer a day before trying the healing techniques Arbel had taught him.

The two girls were returned to their homes the next day, Jesker and Melody leading the escort to tell the families what had happened to Orthal, who'd ordered the capture, and to the foragers who'd taken them. Macurdy didn't think the girls could bring themselves to talk about it. The escort included the two volunteer bridegrooms, who didn't come back. Melody said they'd been allowed by the parents to stay.

The older woman remained with the company. "After what happened," she told Melody and Macurdy, "my husband would never have me back. And he's prosperous; he'll soon enough have another wife to keep his bed warm and mother our son." For a moment her mouth twisted, not with grief but bitterness, then she shook it off. "My father had no sons, and I was the oldest of three daughters. I'm strong. I worked in the field until I was married, behind the plow and with scythe and ax, rake and spade, pitchfork and pry pole. I never had a doll; I played with the bow. On summer pasture I've slept in the cow shed with a sword to hand, when there were tracks of cat or bear or troll around. I'm a good enough shot, I killed a wolf once, when they threatened the cattle, and another time I sent a catamount running off with an arrow in its flank.

"These"—she gestured at the camp and its men—"took my old life away from me. You can give me a new one now, and a spear and bow, and let me stay as a rebel. Afterward I'll see, if there is an afterward. These others are no more trained for fighting than I am, and women, more than menfolk, feel the curse of Gurtho. Some have even scarred their daughter's face, be she pretty enough that Gurtho's agents might take her away as part of the tax."

With that, Macurdy lost any misgivings about leading these men.

✧   ✧   ✧

After muster, he sorted out the things in Orthal's tent, stacking outside those he didn't want, for others to take. When he'd finished, he sat on a short section of log, elbows on his knees, face in his hands, his energy suddenly gone. Looking back at Washington County with greater appreciation than ever.

24

Wollerda

He'd have gone to bed, but lacked the energy. Felt too tired to spread his blankets—Orthal's blankets—on the pile of dry grass. Then three men came to the tent. One of them, Tarlok, peered in at him.

"Captain?" he said hesitantly.

"What is it, Tarlok?"

"There are things we want to talk to you about, but they can wait if need be."

Macurdy got slowly to his feet, remaining somewhat bent because the roof was low. "No, let's hear them now," he said, and ducked out through the opening. The other two had come into camp with Tarlok. One was an older man who'd kept apart from the others at muster, like a bystander.

"Captain, this is Terel Kithro and this is Arva Bono, old friends of mine." He put a hand on the shoulder of a man about his own age, perhaps thirty. "Bono joined the company when I did. For the last eight, ten years, he's traveled around amongst the settlements, teaching the young to read and write and figure. Knows most everyone. He's been helping me recruit."

Tarlok paused as if ordering his thoughts. "I didn't tell you the entire truth, earlier. Bono and I'd planned to murder Orthal. Last night. Orthal and Slaney and a few others had a reputation for fighting and getting in trouble. Making trouble. Then the reeve came in with his bully boys and killed some people, burned some farms, and drove off livestock. For holding back on taxes, he said. When the word got around, folks were pretty upset, and Orthal and his buddies were naturals to recruit wild or would-be wild young bucks to form up a rebel band." Tarlok shook his head. "We didn't realize what a damned troll he really was. In the long run he was a hindrance for recruiting. Bono and I brought in quite a few men that afterward slipped off and went home—didn't like the way Orthal did things. It was their stories, more than anything else, that hurt recruiting. Looked like he'd turn the whole thing into banditry."

Macurdy interrupted before Tarlok could say more. "I'm worn out, Tarlok. What are you getting at?"

Tarlok nodded. "Right. We brought Kithro back with us because people know and respect him, and because he's a friend of Pavo Wollerda, the captain of Wollerda's company. Of the eastern clans. It's supposed to be a lot bigger than ours, and better organized and trained. And we figured when we had a better leader, maybe the two bands could work together."

"Who did you figure would lead, once Orthal was dead?"

"Well, I sort of planned to, if we couldn't talk Kithro into it. But now you're here, and we're all agreed you'd do a lot better job."

Macurdy grunted. "Kithro, do you think this Wollerda would be interested in working with us?"

"I think so. Otherwise I wouldn't have come up with Tarlok. I'm too old for a rebel. Old and spoiled by comfort."

Kithro's aura was pretty clean. Arbel would call him a warrior, in this case an overage warrior who'd go for his goals by other means than a sword: by focus and intelligence, and maybe other people's swords. "Tell me about Wollerda," Macurdy said.

Wollerda was of a lineage of chiefs, Kithro told him, and that still meant something among the Kullvordi, which was what the hillsfolk called themselves. When Wollerda had been a small boy, the king had been having trouble with the Kullvordi, and because Wollerda's father and grandfather had both been headmen, Wollerda and his mother had been taken to the palace as hostages. Wollerda had grown up there, he and his mother living in a small room in the servants' wing. As a bright, inquisitive child whom adults tended to like, he'd learned a lot about the flatlands, its government, and the royal court. And about the rest of the world, because the palace held a royal library with two or three hundred books, and the old man who looked after it took a liking to him.

When he'd pretty much grown up, he and his mother were let go, but after a few years of farming and herding, he'd returned to the capital, Teklapori, and set up business as a traveling salesman of books and jewelry. He not only traveled all over Tekalos, but east to the Great Eastern Mountains, west to the Great Muddy, and north to the Big River, buying and selling books, and fine jewelry made by the Sisters. He'd even been north of the river, into the Marches of the ylvin empire.

"How do you know so much about him?" Macurdy asked.

"We traveled together now and then," Kithro said. "I used to go from place to place making fine boots. And when you travel together and stay in inns together, you talk a lot. He and I got pretty close. I've made boots for him and his servants—traded them for books."

Macurdy nodded thoughtfully, not as tired as he had been. When his visitors were done, they left. By then the smell of smudge fires filled the camp, mosquitoes being out in force for the first time that spring. He'd killed several on his face and neck already, and decided to try a spell Arbel had taught him—one he hadn't had a chance to use before: creating a repellent field to keep them away. Briefly, as he muttered the formula, his hands moved, weaving something unseen.

It worked; the mosquitoes stayed too far away to hear. As he lay waiting for sleep, Macurdy thought about what Kithro had told him. He'd planned to get together with the commander of the other group anyway; now it seemed he had someone besides Wolf who could vouch for him.

A few hours later he awoke, slapping and scratching. The field had worn off. He wove another and fell asleep again, but the bites he'd already gotten still itched, troubling his dreams.

Macurdy spent another day helping the company get started in its new training mode. To his surprise, Melody was sharing a tent with the woman who'd changed from sex slave to recruit. He somehow found that gratifying; he'd expected her to be sharing one with Jeremid. *Macurdy,* he told himself, *that's a lousy attitude. If she was with Jeremid, they'd both be happy.*

On the next day, leaving Jeremid in charge, he left to meet Wollerda, accompanied by Kithro, Wolf, and Yxhaft Vorelsson Rich Lode. He'd chosen them to make a good impression: Kithro was Wollerda's old friend, and Wolf one of his rebels, and surely he'd respect the dwarves. Recommendations, Macurdy felt, would be important; he was a foreigner with his front teeth missing or broken, and a face that Melody told him still showed the pale green and yellow of old bruises.

A brawler, that's what I look like, he told himself. *Another thug like Orthal.*

The day had dawned to rain, not hard, but steady and cold, and they didn't talk much as they rode. Blue Wing had started out with them, but was seldom in evidence, flying high, and perhaps from time to time, far. Occasionally checking on their whereabouts though, Macurdy hoped, for the new leaves were almost full-flushed now. Men riding in forest would be harder to spot from the air without a good idea of where to look.

They rode north awhile, then stopped at a small village where Kithro spoke to several older men, opinion leaders instead of potential recruits, telling them about Macurdy's Company. One called a son in, a well-built lad who Macurdy guessed at seventeen. Yes the boy was interested. He'd have joined up sooner, except his father disapproved of Orthal.

"Who do you know that can take us to the Saw Pit Road?" Kithro asked.

"I can," the youth answered. "I've ridden and hunted all through these hills with my friends. We know every creek and trail."

"That far east?"

"Sure. We hit it last fall, after a troll raided a farm over above Berol's Run. A bunch of us spent more than a week hunting him."

"Did you get him?"

"Nah. Struck his tracks a couple times though, his or some other's the same size. Seems like he was just traveling through, instead of moving in. Maybe went on east to the Granite Range. It's really wild over there; no farms at all."

Kithro nodded to Macurdy. "Well, then," Macurdy said, "if you want to join us, get your rain cape and bow, and wrap something to eat. Your first job is to guide us to the Saw Pit Road."

The lad scrambled. In ten minutes he was saddling his horse. Then they set out more or less eastward through rugged hills, picking their way along trails some of which were little better than game trails. Here and there, a tree had been blazed with esoteric marks that meant something to the hillsmen, but nothing at all to Macurdy. Twice the boy swore and they backtracked a ways, but they had no real difficulty. It occurred to Macurdy that he himself had only a vague notion of how to find his way back, if it came to that.

The rain stopped late the first afternoon, so they didn't have to camp in it.

Soon after sunup on the third day, they reached the Saw Pit Road, an actual road with the tracks of wagons and carts. Kithro said it crossed over into the Big River drainage to the north, but they turned south. Now it was Wolf who took the lead. By late morning, the creek beside the road had grown considerably, and the draw it cut had become a narrow valley, with clustered farms. At one of these they left the road, riding eastward on a wide, well-beaten trail. Blue Wing came down then, calling to Macurdy, and they stopped to wait. There were men ahead, he said, "waiting with bows, in a place where many trees have been cut down."

Wolf nodded. "The commander had trees felled to block the woods," he said. "Any king's men can only come in on the trail. Men will stop us when we come to it, and ask questions, but there'll be other men watching us before we ever reach the woods."

They rode on. Shortly the trail left the cleared land, entering another forested draw. After a quarter mile, they saw abatises ahead, one on either side of the trail, presumably extending to the steep slopes that flanked the draw.

Macurdy had never seen or heard of an abatis before. Many trees had been chopped down, to lie on top of or diagonally across one another, their tops pointing more or less westward toward possible intruders. No one could ride through them. Even walking would be impossible, he told himself, for anything much bigger than a weasel. Anyone riding through the draw would have to keep to the trail, which could be defended by a handful of spearmen backed by archery.

When they reached the abatises, two men stepped out from behind trees; one of them ordered the travelers to halt. He talked with Wolf, whom he recognized, and got Kithro's name, then sent the second man trotting on foot up the road. A minute or so later, Macurdy could hear the dull thud of hooves ahead, galloping off eastward.

Half an hour later, a dozen well-armed men arrived on horseback, to escort and more or less enclose Macurdy's party. Six in front and six behind, herding them farther down the trail. *They're organized all right,* Macurdy thought, *and trained, by the way they do things.*

Less than a mile farther on the draw widened, and they entered an oblong basin. Three or four hundred acres had been cleared for pasture, some of it planted now to corn and potatoes, the rest a drill field. The grassy look of the surrounding woods told of livestock pasturing there, too. The rebel camp was at the near end, eight longhouses, and more under construction. Wollerda occupied an old log cabin, which served as both headquarters and living quarters.

The commander himself stood in front of it, waiting for them, and as they approached, Macurdy recognized him— the man who'd eaten with them once at an inn, and asked Tossi about dwarf swords. He was medium-sized and maybe forty years old, Macurdy guessed, and fit-looking, though not as physically hard as the escort he'd sent.

Wollerda recognized him, too, but it was Kithro he gave his attention too, pumping his hand as the two exchanged good-natured queries and comments. Now Kithro half turned, looking at Macurdy. "Pavo," he said, "I've brought someone I think you'll be glad to meet: Curtis Macurdy. He's taken over Orthal's band. We call it Macurdy's Company now."

Macurdy and Wollerda stepped up to one another and shook hands, Wollerda examining him. "Macurdy and I have run into one another before," he said to Kithro, then spoke to Macurdy. "How did you get rid of Orthal? From what I've heard, he wasn't someone who'd step down."

"He didn't. We rode into his camp to volunteer, and he decided he didn't trust us, so he made us prisoners."

Wollerda's eyebrows twitched. "And then?"

"Then I killed him, and his men made me their commander."

Wollerda cocked an eye. "Well. Best we go inside and sit down." He beckoned them into his headquarters, and seated them on split-log benches. "Now," he said, "there's got to be a lot of that story you didn't tell."

Macurdy shrugged. "It gets complicated."

"Excuse me, sir." It was Wolf who interrupted. "You might recall me; I was one of Minska's platoon. I've been with Macurdy since he cut me free from a hanging post in Gormin Town, and I guess I saw all of it."

Wollerda examined the hard-bitten rebel. "You're the one they call Wolf," he said. "Suppose you tell me what Macurdy left out."

Exaggerating only a little, Wolf told the whole story, beginning with the hanging posts. He included the campfires started with a gesture, Blue Wing, the slaying of Slaney, the tricking of Orthal, and the freeing of the captive women, ending with the organizing of the company and its training. "And we're giving chits to farmers when we commandeer food," he finished. "Good for payment when we've thrown down Gurtho."

Wollerda had seemed to enjoy the story. Briefly he grinned, a wry grin. "Well, that gives them another reason to want Gurtho gone. Now. You said '*we're* giving chits.' Does that mean you're staying with Macurdy instead of me?"

Wolf didn't flinch. "Sir, you trained me hard. Now Macurdy needs men to train his people, and it seems like I'd be of most use to him just now."

"Umm. So you would. Well, I leave it to you." He turned to Macurdy then, quizzically. "You sound like one of the heroes in the old folk tales. Did you ever kill a dragon?"

"Never even saw one."

"When I saw you before, I ignored you. Your face was more discolored then. I took you to be a large, rough young man who'd been hired by the lords in the mountain to tend their beasts and baggage. Someone who drank and got into brawls." He paused. "*Do* you drink and get into brawls?"

Macurdy grinned. "Water's my style, and buttermilk. And I generally try to stay out of fights, but sometimes—sometimes that's not so easy." He'd almost said *sometimes in this world*, and wondered if Wollerda would have made anything of it.

Wollerda turned to Yxhaft Vorelsson. "How did you lords in the mountain come to associate with this unusual tallfolk?"

The dwarf grunted. "That's a story to match the others ye've heard here," he said, and proceeded to tell what had happened at the fallen timbers, including the release of Slaney and his men.

"It still seems out of character for lords in the mountain to mix in tallfolk affairs."

"Aye. I can't imagine it of folk in the Silver Mountain. But we're westerners from the Diamond Flues."

"Hmm." Wollerda turned to Macurdy again, looking at him long enough to have made some men nervous. "I suppose I should show you some of our training," he said at last, then snapped his fingers as if remembering something. "After I've had you all fed! You and myself. Sometimes I forget to eat when I'm interested in something."

Lunch was a stew of potatoes, turnips, beef and carrots, and round hard loaves of bread they cut chunks from with their knives. Bread! Macurdy was impressed: Wollerda's commissary was obviously better than his. He made a mental note to learn more about it. Another broken tooth came out as he ate. His gums and teeth hurt from one side to the other, top and bottom, even the back teeth, which hadn't seemed damaged. It wasn't too bad yet, but he shuddered to think what it might be like in a month or a week. After they'd eaten, they witnessed the training of new recruits and of more experienced men. Macurdy couldn't help but appreciate the well-trained Ozian militia back at Wolf Springs, and wondered how good Gurtho's army was.

After supper he asked Wollerda about the Teklan army. It was made up of several levels, Wollerda told him. The best was the king's personal cohort, close to six hundred cavalry, whose training was sometimes a disaster to farmers whose fields they trampled in their exercises. Fortunately they trained mostly on their own reservation. Their pay and upkeep was a significant burden on the people, but they were the best troops in the kingdom; some of the best in all the Rude Lands. In addition, each of the six counties had a standing force of two mounted infantry companies—an even greater burden on the people. Each county had at least four shires—as many as six—each administered by a reeve with a platoon of fifty-five mounted infantry. Plus a reserve platoon, called on mainly at tax time. All told, Wollerda said, the king could call out more than forty-five hundred soldiers.

Most of the population were peasants, who fell into several categories. The highest was prosperous enough to hire help, or to contract with sharecroppers. The second class owned their own land and farmed it with the labor of their family. The third was sharecroppers, and below them day laborers who found paying work as they could.

The Kullvordi had a slightly different situation. One thing remained of their previous independence: they had no bailiffs. Local headmen, whom they elected themselves, presided over day-to-day life, but could be overruled and dismissed by the reeves, who also set and collected the taxes.

"And there you have it," Wollerda finished. "Our obstacles and our opportunities. We've got to work out ways to make use of the one and get around the other. What you did in Gormin Town showed me more potential in the flatlanders than I'd realized they had." He got to his feet. "Come ride with me," he said. "Just the two of us."

"All right," Macurdy said, and got to his feet. The invitation hadn't been casual; the commander wanted privacy. Wollerda saddled his own horse; he was not a leader who demanded to be waited on, though he might if his army grew enough to seriously tax his time. Unaccompanied by aides, they rode out of camp in the beginnings of dusk.

"There are things about you," Wollerda said, "that don't add up. First, you claim to come from Oz. I've never been in Oz, but I've known a few Ozmen in my travels. And you? You're different from any of them."

"All men are different."

"In details. But every people has its own ways, its own beliefs and viewpoints. Ozmen tend to be impulsive and more or less warlike. You fit there. But some of the things you've done . . ." Wollerda shook his head. "It's hard to imagine an Ozman undertaking what you did in Gormin Town. Or intervening at such risk in a fight between bandits and dwarves. And not keeping the horses?" He shook his head in rejection.

"Hmh! Interesting."

"Why did you do those things? What drives you?"

"I guess I'm an adventurous soul."

Wollerda grunted. "It goes beyond that."

Macurdy said nothing for a while, not consciously thinking about it, feeling the roll and shift of the horse beneath him as it walked, the animal's smell, the sound of tree frogs in the evening. And the hum and bite of mosquitoes. He wove a repellent field as he rode.

Finally he spoke. "If I told you, you'd think I was lying. Or crazy."

There was a short lag before Wollerda replied. "I can't commit myself to an ally whose motives I can't even guess."

Macurdy reined in his horse. "Are you telling me you'll turn down my help if I can't explain why I'm doing this?"

Wollerda eyed him calmly. "My friend, I admire what you've done—I'm even in awe of it—and I appreciate the guts and strength and ability it took. I wish you success in your efforts against Gurtho, and I'll move to take advantage of them. But unless I know more about you—why you've involved yourself— I can't exchange plans with you. Let alone operate under one plan, as the two hands of one body."

For a long moment, Macurdy sat his horse without speaking, reexamining Wollerda's aura. It told him this man could be stubborn, but offered no clue on what to do about it.

"I've been wronged and abused myself," Macurdy said, "been made a slave, and beaten, and my wife stolen from me. It's easy for me to see things from a Kullvordi point of view."

He felt Wollerda's eyes examining, and recalled something that Arbel had said once in passing: That some people saw auras without realizing it, even learned to read them a bit without being aware of it. Was Wollerda reading his?

"There's more to it than that," Wollerda said. "The heart of it is something else."

Macurdy, looking for what else he might say, decided to try the truth. "All right," he said, "I'll trust you. I'm from Farside.

I was a farmer there, and married a beautiful woman with red hair—and tilty green eyes." He paused, letting Wollerda absorb the words, examine them, realize their significance. He also watched Wollerda's aura, thinking to learn more about the indicators of disbelief, and maybe indignation. Instead he saw a flash of realization. "After a while," he went on, "she told me about Yuulith, and the gates, and the Sisterhood. Then one day, people from the Sisterhood found us and stole her. Took her through the Oz Gate. I followed them, but I had to wait a month before it opened again.

"Then I went through; that's when I was made a slave. And then a shaman's apprentice, because I had the talent. But not for healing, it turned out, so they made a militiaman out of me, and then a soldier in their Company of Heroes.

"I intend to get Varia back. My wife. Commanding an armed force is a beginning." He shrugged. "Sounds impossible, but I've made a start."

Wollerda's lips had pursed as if to whistle or blow. Now he frowned. "All of that! But your goal has nothing to do with ours—with the aspirations of the Kullvordi."

Macurdy's answer was not quick. He chose his words. "A hundred armed men won't get Varia back," he said. "A thousand won't. Dishonesty won't. But position might. Elevation. Meanwhile I was raised to honor my responsibilities, to be loyal and respect the loyalty of others. When I accepted command of Orthal's Company, I committed myself to them. At least as much as they did to me."

Wollerda turned thoughtful a moment, then a smile quirked his lips, and he grunted. "The Sisterhood! Hmh! Would you like to know who sits on the throne next to Gurtho? He's got a new queen; a Sister. Something new in the world—the Dynast marrying Sisters to kings. They say she's quite beautiful."

By noon the next day, the two commanders had agreed in principle and writing on the coordination of military actions. Blue Wing agreed to be the courier between them; he was experiencing things his tribe would take great interest in. And after lunch, Macurdy and his party started back to his own company.

PART 4
Strange
Alliances

25

Embassy

Entering it for the first time, the capital of Tekalos made a drab impression on Liiset, nor did the raw freezing wind of Three-Month help. Teklapori was large, as towns went in the Rude Lands, with main streets less narrow than some, but it lacked aesthetics. In the section they'd just entered, the buildings, built one against another, were two-storied, of wattle daubed with clay, and its whitewash was grimed with dust and soot. Daub repairs formed dirty brownish patches, small and large, unwhitewashed; its thatched roofs were gray from weather and mold. Outlying sections had included buildings made of lumber, bricks, or squared stone, some with tiled or shingled roofs, but wattle and thatch prevailed there too. Regardless, the smell was of slops: human and cooking wastes, primarily. On Farside, she told herself, Evansville's worse slum didn't begin to smell as bad.

She could have bypassed the town and ridden directly to the palace, a mile outside it, but she'd arranged it this way. She wanted people—lots of people—to see them and be impressed.

And she was in charge! Given the purpose of the mission, Idri had at least to seem subordinate, and at any rate wasn't entirely back in Sarkia's good graces. But the two of them worked well together, and had discussed this project thoroughly in advance. For some unknown reason, Idri had always liked her, different though they were. While Idri's abrasiveness, troublesome to many Sisters, seldom bothered Liiset. When it did, she told Idri, and Idri handled it reasonably. Liiset credited their compatibility to some close past-life friendship.

Sad, she thought, that Idri hated Varia so. Varia in a Tiger barracks! What a cruel situation! Hopefully she'd get pregnant soon and be out of there.

The street was lined with spectators, out to see the fabled Sisters. She wouldn't disappoint them. Even her guard section was marvelously outfitted, its tailored uniforms black, its polished, silver helmets and cuirasses blinking in the late winter sunlight. Its horses, individually handsome, were beautifully matched, their coats glossy black, with white blazes and socks.

In the past, the travel costumes worn by Sister diplomats had been elegant but subdued, and typically the Sisters had numbered three. This time . . . As the Dynast's special envoy, she wore a silver coronet that sparkled with jewels—diamonds and zircons—and her thoroughly brushed red hair was plaited with gold threads. Her riding breeches and tunic were shamrock satin, reinforced with kidskin where practicality required. The cape that protected her from the chill pre-equinoctial wind was of rich and glossy fur, nearly black: *Martes pennanti*, the pekan, from the Eastern Empire of the ylver. It had reached the Sisterhood via the lords in the mountain, who traded freely with ylvin merchants. Idri's clothing was similar, but her tunic and breeches were glossy blue and her cape merely mink, while the jewels in her coronet were less precious. Each had two attendants of her own clone, similarly dressed but uncrowned, their capes of bulkier, less expensive furs. All six rode matched, red-gold geldings, glossy with good grain and much brushing, these too with nearly identical socks and blazes.

She didn't doubt that Sarkia's new foreign policy would work as intended. It had its drawbacks, compared to the old: There were more commitments, not all of them fully compatible. But it would soon rebuild the Sisterhood's status and influence.

Meanwhile they'd enjoy the more agreeable aspects of the mission. She chuckled. *Especially Idri*, she told herself. Idri's role was perfect for her.

Gurtho had seen Sisters twice before, when his father was king and he'd been a child, once at age six or eight, and again at eleven or twelve. The first pair had seemed to him very beautiful, the other pair merely good looking. Which kind would these be?

We'll soon see, he thought. Six of them! To his casual half-comment, half-question, the evening before, their courier had answered that they were "quite beautiful," a generality that only fueled his imagination.

Meanwhile he was edgy. He'd heard about the rape at Ferny Cove, had been excited by it. He'd also heard Sisters described as untouchable, and wondered if he'd dare. Certainly their influence had been reduced, and their army as well.

But what of their magicks? What revenge might they take if he molested one of them? True there were those who said their powers were trivial, but others swore they were deadly. And what the ylver could get away with, and what he could get away with, might be very different.

He knew what his father would say, had heard it more than once: "Never decide with your testicles, boy. That's what brains are for. Base your decisions on the power and money they'll bring. Power and money! Always! With power and money, you can buy whatever you want, including beautiful women. And property, when you're tired of it, can be sold or traded, or given as political gifts. Or killed, if it suits you."

Gurtho had taken the advice to heart. An actual wife was necessary to provide an undisputed heir. Which he now had, along with younger backups, in case the first died or proved unsuitable. But he'd bought his bride, rather than marry politically or in passion. To satisfy his gluttony for women—beyond ladies of the court—there were tax girls. Those he got pregnant he had killed. The others, when he tired of them, he sold, perhaps after loaning them to one of his officers as a sign of the Royal Favor.

Word of the embassy's arrival was brought by the captain of the envoy's guard, ushered in by Rogell, the palace chief of protocol. The envoy, the captain said, was tired from her ride. At her request, the embassy had been shown to its apartments, where they would bathe and nap and have their hair dressed before supper (which the envoy hoped she and her deputy might eat with His Majesty).

She could have paid her respects first, Gurtho thought. *Well. At supper then.* He ordered Rogell to take word to the steward that supper was to be private—the Dynast's envoy, her deputy, and His Majesty. A formal reception would be scheduled for a later date, with appropriate guests.

At supper, Gurtho was hard-pressed not to stare. Briefly he was disconcerted that they looked so young, but the envoy's self-possession soon dispelled that. Their beauty was not so easily recovered from, and Idri, he had no doubt, was the most *desirable* woman he'd ever seen. Even her name he found seductive, and spoke it in his mind. Idri!

Still, he ate essentially as he might have. Their small talk went well enough, and neither woman was aloof, nor even reserved. When they'd finished dessert, it was the envoy who brought up business. "The Dynast is interested in establishing a permanent embassy here," she said.

"Indeed?" He wondered if Idri might be named ambassadrix.

"She's never placed a permanent embassy before, except with the King in Silver Mountain. Now she's considering placing several. Yours first perhaps. After all, Tekalos is one of the larger kingdoms, and you are one of the most powerful kings."

"And we love your countryside," Idri put in. "I for one would not object at all to being located here. I can imagine how lovely it will be when the buds burst, and wildflowers line the roadsides."

Gurtho's pulse quickened. "Indeed! We already have flowers in bloom around the palace."

"We saw them," Liiset said, "daffodils and tulips, mostly," then returned the talk to business. "The Dynast is also interested in the possibility of alliance. If you think you may be, we should discuss it."

"Indeed! I might well be interested," Gurtho said. "How long will you remain?"

"A week. The Dynast has one misgiving. She likes her allies strong, and clearly, Gurtho and Tekalos are that, but it's a strength impaired by internal discord. Your Kullvordi hillsmen revolt in almost every generation."

Gurtho frowned. What had that to do with anything? "True,"

he said, "but we never allow it to become a threat. Just this month, at my orders, the reeves whose shires include the hill districts sent soldiers in and burned the farmsteads of some tax cheats, making examples of their families. Now the hillsmen most inclined to rebellion will rise up, showing us who they are so we can destroy them."

"Ah. And are these Kullvordi good fighters?"

He shrugged. "Not good enough. We always win. Easily."

"What would they be like if you could recruit them for your own army, and train them properly?"

"They'd never join my army. I doubt that as many as a dozen have in my own and my father's time combined. And those who did were lazy and insubordinate."

The envoy nodded. "Of course. If they had no loyalty to their own people, they'd hardly be loyal to someone else."

"Exactly!" said Gurtho, misunderstanding.

It was Idri who spoke next. "You're a strong ruler. We appreciate strong men."

"Yes. Well, one must be, in my position." He turned to the butler and snapped his fingers. "More wine, Elwar," he said. "Whatever best follows the pastries."

Bowing, the butler left the room, and Gurtho returned his attention to the Sisters. "How do two such lovely women pass the time when they aren't doing the duties of envoys?"

"Our duties occupy more of our time than you might think," Liiset answered. "For example, before coming here, we read a great deal about your kingdom."

"Indeed? I wasn't aware that a great deal had been written about it. I trust it was complimentary. Was I mentioned?"

"Complimentary enough that we've looked forward to being here. And yes, you were mentioned in the more recent writings."

"Who writes these things?"

"Travelers. Visitors. Merchants."

"Hmh." Gurtho wasn't sure he was pleased.

"We also play," Idri added.

"Play? At what?"

"Among other things," Liiset said, "Idri plays the lap harp." She turned to Idri. "Would you like to play for the king, my dear?"

Idri looked demurely at Gurtho, then at her hands in her lap, and smiled. "It would gladden me to give pleasure to such a king as Gurtho."

"Well then," Liiset said, and for a long moment seemed to ponder in silence. Gurtho waited. "Have you ever heard our music of spring?" she said at last. "We favor it in this season. Much of it was written for ensembles, but even more for solo instruments. Including the lap harp."

"I'll send for an instrument," Gurtho said.

"She has her own; I've called for it already."

"You have?"

"Through the mind. Many of us can speak through the mind to those we're most closely related to. One of my aides should be here momentarily." Briefly they sat talking; then an outer guard entered.

"Your Majesty! A young woman wishes to give something to her lady," the man said awkwardly. The "young woman" looked so much like the envoy, Gurtho felt sure they were twins. She delivered to Idri a lap harp hardly twenty inches high.

Idri tuned the instrument while the others watched, then began to play, with skill if not inspiration, the music alternating between bright, dark, and serene. Soon, though, Gurtho became restless, and seeing this, Liiset yawned delicately. "Excuse me," she said, "but I haven't entirely recovered from our long ride. I'm afraid I must retire."

"Already, dear Sister?" Idri asked. "His Majesty seems bright-eyed, and as far as I'm concerned, I can play the night away."

Gurtho's pulse quickened. "Indeed," he said, "don't take her away so soon. Let her play some more. I can understand your being tired, and certainly won't be offended if you leave us. But as for me—her playing enchants me more than you might imagine."

"Well . . ." Liiset looked questioningly at Idri, then seemed to have her answer. "If you wish. Idri and I planned to sleep late tomorrow anyway. Very well, my dear."

Somewhat to the king's surprise, the envoy stood and bowed, rather as a man would, showing cleavage that made the breath stick in his throat. "I wish Your Majesty a most pleasant night," she said, and left.

Alone with the enchanting Idri! He could hardly believe his good fortune. Meanwhile she began to play something sensuous, exotic.

"Are there words to it?" Gurtho asked.

She smiled. "It's a love song, supposedly by an ylvin emperor to his favorite concubine." She began to sing, the lyrics subdued but passionate, suggestive, exciting Gurtho.

"I wish you might play for me alone," he said earnestly when she'd finished.

"But I am."

"I mean, without these." He gestured at his guards.

"Well then, tell them to leave."

He stood, giving his order to their sergeant. In a minute they were gone. "Now that we're alone," Gurtho said, "this room seems too large. There is another, more intimate . . ." He gestured toward a door near a back corner.

She stood demurely, the small harp under one arm. Gurtho took her other arm, leading her gently, his heart thuttering. The smaller room had a luxurious couch, mirrors with expensive, nearly true surfaces, large pillows distributed here and there, and several upholstered settees. He hoped it wouldn't alarm her; it was the setting for occasional small orgies staged for special friends. Leading her to a settee, he seated her near the middle and sat down beside her, his left knee touching her right.

"Let me sit by you," he said, "and feel your sweet warmth as you play."

"Of course, Your Majesty." She put her fingers on his arm. "If I seem a little breathless . . . I've never before been alone with a king."

"Ah, and I'm not just any king," he murmured.

"I knew it," she whispered, "when I first laid eyes on you. You are a—king among kings, a—man among men."

He found his hands reaching, his arms slipping round her, his mouth moving to hers. They kissed.

"Oh, Your Majesty," she breathed, and they kissed again; his tongue caressed her lips, and they opened to him. He felt her hand rest on his thigh, and he fumbled at her vestlike girdle. She undid the laces and guided his hand inside it to her left breast, round, firm, hard-nippled. Her own hand slid up his thigh to his cod-piece. For half a minute they fondled one another, kissing, then he could wait no longer, for he was king, and accustomed not to courtship or seduction, but to having, taking. Dropping to his knees before the settee, he began to reach up her skirt, pawing amongst a confusion of petticoats, till she stayed his arm. "Your Highness," she murmured, "it's not necessary to muss my clothing. We need only remove it, mine and yours."

Gurtho often thought of himself as inexhaustible. It was, his father had told him once, a family trait. But even so . . . Lying back for the moment, he wondered fleetingly if he'd been bewitched. No, he told himself, this had not been sorcery. Not unless thighs and buttocks, fingers, tongue and lips, were the instruments of magic. *I never imagined a woman like her,* he thought. And had an insight of his own, something rare as summer snow: *It's as if she knows what I'm feeling, and what to do next!* Now that, he told himself, would be most worthwhile magic.

She purred in his ear. "Your Majesty seems tired."

He grunted. "Even a satyr must rest now and then. Briefly. Long enough to let the sweat dry a bit."

Her laughter was low and throaty. "Dry? We needn't wait for that," she said, and swinging astride his thighs, began to lick the sweat from his hairy chest.

26

Collecting Taxes

Macurdy turned in the saddle, glancing back at the Big Dipper wheeling inexorably through its nightly course, and remembered that night shift by the watchfires, at the abandoned squatter's farm in Oz. How long ago? Less than three months; it seemed longer. He'd been a runaway slave with just three friends backing him, one of them a bird that might weigh fifteen pounds. Now he was Captain Macurdy, with his own little army: some two hundred seventy rebel fighting men.

He grunted inwardly. *Or would-be fighting men.* Tonight he'd find out how good fifty of the more advanced were, how much they'd learned.

He didn't try to set the pace himself. As a Hero, he'd come to be a skilled rider, but he still lacked a sure feel for how hard and long one could push a good horse. So he'd appointed Tarlok route leader. Just now the man rode in front of him, with a pair of scouts out of sight ahead.

He scanned around, seeing the countryside by the light of a newly risen moon a bit less than half full. Dogs barked from sleeping farms, but farm dogs barked at everything that moved—cats, possums, skunks . . . No one's sleep would be seriously disturbed unless the tone became excited.

He expected to return a different way; a way with fewer hills to cross, easier for the pack string, which by then would be heavily loaded. And more importantly, a way that would lead their pursuit into Wollerda's ambush, for the purpose of this raid went beyond plunder.

Macurdy had planned the mission as carefully as he could,

257

given his limitations of time and information, and still felt uncomfortable about it. His Kullvordi officers, on the other hand, were enthused. As he'd explained his thinking to them, they'd reacted as if he was a genius to have thought all those things through.

His basic problem was that he questioned whether his force was ready for something like this. Though he'd gone out of his way not to show it, because one of the pluses was their generally high level of confidence: They had the idea that any hillsman was worth three soldiers and six bailiff's men.

Despite his misgivings, here he was, his timing dictated by opportunity and need. To feed his growing company was a constant problem. Also, some sort of successful fighting action was necessary to keep up morale; to keep recruits coming in; and to prevent excessive desertions, because so far, many of his volunteers had shown limited tolerance for training in the absence of fighting. It was also desirable, though not yet urgent, to show Wollerda and his men that Macurdy's Company was capable of effective action.

And finally to suggest to the flatlanders that the king was in real trouble this time.

The opportunity was the timing of tax collection in the flatlands, and what it might mean to the problem of feeding his rebels. They ate no more as fighting men than they would at home, but at home they ate their own food—food they'd either helped to raise, or bought and paid for. But here . . . Chits or not, most of the farmers they took food from considered themselves more or less plundered.

Then someone had mentioned that the flatlanders were about finished with their wheat harvest, and maybe they ought to raid them.

Macurdy's lips had drawn into a thoughtful pucker. To plunder flatland farmers would kill the hope of rural support there, but he saw another way. He'd already heard how, in the flatlands, the bailiffs' tax squads went out with hired wagons and drovers within a few days after harvest, collecting the tax grain and tax cattle. And presumably as soon as that was done, the farmers would begin carting to market whatever surplus they had, beyond household needs and seed, and no doubt a reserve.

No, he'd announced, *we're not going to plunder the farmers. We'll plunder the bailiffs instead.* Which meant they'd be robbing the king, which would please the farmers (he hoped), and gain the rebels their passive approval at least. While plundering the concentrations in a bailiff's grain bins should be a lot handier than going from farm to farm. And perhaps safer, because they could strike, load up, and get back to the forest far more quickly.

Even his own staff, who were quite willing to plunder flatland farmers, saw the logic of it.

They'd been ready to do it cold. In fact, their concept of planning in general troubled Macurdy. Their attitude was *no problem. We'll just go do it.* Then he'd point out problems, and they'd say *oh yes,* and listen while he asked questions, paid attention to their answers, and came up with handlings, or what he hoped were handlings.

He had no doubt his Kullvordi were resourceful. The unforeseeable things that would inevitably come up, they'd probably handle better than most would. That was pretty much the way the hillsmen lived life. But the more things you foresaw and prepared for in advance, it seemed to him, the easier it would be to handle the rest of it.

Anyway they'd listened; even been impressed and enthused. Partly because he was going to let them fight at last, but even more because they had confidence in him, in his leadership. More confidence than he did. Not that he denigrated what he'd accomplished, from that decisive morning at the House of Heroes, to the confrontations with Slaney and Orthal. And in building and training his company since then. But to him, the challenges ahead seemed much greater. While to his rebels—he'd performed what they considered miracles, and they assumed he'd continue to.

He looked around at the platoon riding quietly through the night. Only occasionally had he heard a murmured exchange or comment. Beyond that was only the soft plod of hooves on dirt and the squeak of leather; they were doing a good job of keeping route security. He could sense no extreme tension, and he'd come to appreciate how sensitive he'd grown to other people's unexpressed emotions, since Varia and Arbel had worked with him. *These guys are a lot more interested in fighting than Slaney's men were at the fallen timber,* he told himself. *Even with the cover of forest hours behind us, and a fight ahead that not all of us may live through.*

Two well-hated bailiffs had been targeted, whose plundering and humiliation would please the flatlander peasants—bailiffs whose strongholds could be reached in something under a night's ride from forest, on trails and roads where their travel would raise no alarm. One was well west, a long ride through wild and forested hills. The reeve in that shire was why Three Forks had been fertile recruiting ground, a reeve who'd selected bailiffs as harsh and arrogant as himself. Macurdy had assigned Jeremid to lead that raid; as a third-year Hero, Jeremid was by far his most competent officer. The other bailiwick chosen was a lot nearer, but the ride through open lowlands was longer and seemed more dangerous. That was the one he was riding to now.

In his mind, Macurdy began to review again what he knew about the bailiff's stronghold. For whatever royal reason, bailiffs weren't allowed a stockade. What they generally had, or so he'd been assured, was a fence not much taller than he was— a miniature palisade of stout locust stakes set in the ground, with stout oak posts every six feet or so—presumably white oak so they wouldn't rot. The whole thing was tied together with a growth of thorny rose vines so no one could climb it. There'd be a padlocked wagon gate in front. He hadn't seen padlocks in this world, but he imagined them as large and heavy. Next to it would be an access gate just wide enough to lead a horse through, barred on the inside, and guarded. Inside were large fierce dogs. This bothered Macurdy more than guards, though his men didn't seem concerned.

For the life of him, he couldn't think of anything he hadn't considered, but he kept reviewing doggedly. The biggest unknown at the village, it seemed to him, was how many men the bailiff would have on hand. Bailiffs were allowed eight armsmen on their permanent payroll, but in tax time they hired as many as thirty toughs from other bailiwicks to help collect the taxes. Would they be hanging around guarding the loot? His people seemed semiconfident they wouldn't, but the possibility troubled Macurdy.

Still, it seemed to him likely that he'd get the loot and out of the village without serious losses. Then, instead of backtracking, they'd turn east. There was supposed to be an east-west road just north of the village, that would get them to the North Fork Road before midmorning. By that time the reeve would have been notified, and have his company on its way from his castle on the river west of Gormin Town. They'd be twice his number, better trained, better armed, and on fresher horses. Of course, by the time they caught him, their horses wouldn't be so fresh, but his own men would have been in the saddle, or working or fighting, since dusk the evening before, and their horses wouldn't have much run left in them.

The North Fork Road roughly paralleled the North Fork of the Calder River, with its stringer of woods. About an hour before you reached extensive forest, the East Fork flowed out of the hills to join the North. There, Wollerda was to be waiting with two hundred men, to jump the reeve's company from behind when it had passed. Then Macurdy's platoon was to turn and hit it from the front. Between his force and Wollerda's, they'd outnumber the reeve's more than two to one.

Macurdy couldn't afford much delay at the village. If the reeve caught them before they'd passed the junction with the East Fork, they were in serious trouble. They'd have to abandon the loot, try to reach the forest and scatter. His people said not to worry, it wouldn't happen that way, and he'd nodded as if he accepted their assurance, but . . .

And finally, how well would his men perform? Would they hold ranks? Fight well? Would *he* make good decisions?

On top of it all, his mouth hurt where new teeth were pushing through. Now he knew why teething babies fussed. New teeth! Weird, at his age. Apparently it was a side effect of Varia's magic to keep him young.

Macurdy could hear the village dogs almost as soon as he saw the village, their distant barking less insistent than that of the farm dogs they'd passed. *Bark bark*, pause. *Bark bark bark*, longer pause. Like Morse code, he thought. Houses hunkered darkly in the moonlight, with here and there something taller—barns and stables he supposed. Somewhere in there was the bailiff's stronghold.

His lips stretched tight over his grin. He felt better now, as if the immediacy of action was clearing away his nervousness. Quickening his horse, he caught up with Tarlok. "Keep it to a walk," he said, loudly enough for the men to hear. "They won't react so quickly."

At four hundred yards the village dogs became aware of them, and the barking spread quickly, gaining energy. Another wagon road crossed the one they were on; they'd take it eastward when they left. Meanwhile their present road took them into and almost through the village before they came to the stronghold, its fence looking solid and formidable in the darkness. The barking from inside was deep and raging, a sort of staccato roar that made him twitch.

His men knew their assignments and needed no orders. One group turned off on the near side, another rode past and turned off at the farther corner, each group with a packhorse carrying a ladder for laying against the fence, a ladder broad and strong enough for three men to cross abreast. Macurdy and the rest stopped in front of the gate and waited. If there'd been an outside guard, he'd disappeared. Meanwhile what were the inside guards doing? Their dogs were just inside the gate, barking like something out of hell. The whole village had to be awake by now, he thought, and for the first time wondered what would happen if the villagers sided with the bailiff. Traditionally, flatlanders and hillsmen had been hostile to each other, feelings dating from ancient wrongs occasionally renewed. The bailiff, on the other hand, was a present and continuing evil. But . . .

Then someone inside whistled shrilly, a signal to those outside, and the dogs raced away from the gates, still raging. There were shouts from several points, and very close by, a man screamed. The barking thinned as dogs were killed. The access gate opened, and one of Macurdy's men looked out.

Macurdy trotted in with another group, and stumbled over a body; a gate guard, he supposed. He wondered if his people had taken any prisoners, as he'd instructed, or if they'd simply killed everyone they didn't know. There seemed not to have been any serious resistance. His attention went first to the wagon gate—a double gate, its two halves meeting in the center. They were barred—that was no surprise—but they were also fastened inside by a heavy, padlocked chain through two large eyebolts. And they needed them open, to get the packhorses back out when they'd been loaded.

"Slide the bar out!" he shouted. "Use it as a battering ram!" One of his men tugged on Macurdy's arm. "Captain! They had a bunch of tax girls shut up in a shed. What do you want done with them?"

He followed the man. The girls, four of them, had been brought outside. Macurdy judged their ages as being from twelve to perhaps seventeen. Even by moonlight they looked terrified. Two, seemingly the younger, were crying, their voices keening. He spoke to the one he judged oldest: "Tell them no one's going to hurt them. Tell them I'm going to send you all home."

Someone else came to him, to announce that the bailiff was dead. "And Captain, we found a little casket in the house, full of coins—silver and gold!"

"Good. Tie it shut and load it on a packhorse."

Someone came to tell him that the battering ram wasn't doing the job. They'd also tried using the ironwood pry poles Macurdy had had them bring along, to pry the gates up off the hinge pins, but the pin ends had been hammered, and the hinges wouldn't come off. Macurdy raised his head. "Someone bring an ax to the gate!" he bellowed, "and a torch. Right away!", and jogged to where the men had laid down their ram.

A sizeable crowd was gathering outside. Tarlock was talking to them. *Damn!* Macurdy thought. *If we don't get this gate open right now, we're going to look like a bunch of clowns to these people.*

"Captain! There's a guy here's got something he says is important."

"Have him wait! Where the hell is that ax?" As he asked it, a man ran up with one and handed it to him. Macurdy stepped up to the wagon gate, eyed the U-shaped padlock bolt, wound up and hit it as hard as he could. The body of the lock fell to the ground. He grabbed the chain, hanging loose now, and pulled it out of the eyebolts, then four of his men shoved the gate open.

The person with the important information was a boy of about fifteen years. He'd seen someone come out of his father's horse shed, leading his father's best horse, a man wearing the helmet of a bailiff's armsman. He'd mounted and ridden quietly south, headed out of town.

The outside guard, Macurdy suspected, on his way to notify the reeve.

The next man who wanted to talk to him was the village spokesman, the man voted by the villagers to represent them with the bailiff. He was agonizing over the tax girls. When Macurdy said he was sending them home, the spokesman blinked with surprise, then shook his head. "The reeve has already been sent an inventory. He will come here and take them back; hunt them down if he must." The man looked worriedly into Macurdy's face. "It's best if you can take them to a safe place."

For just a moment the two men traded gazes. *Shit!* Macurdy thought, *things must be bad here, if he's putting his trust in us.* "All right," he said, "but two of them are children. Bring me a woman of the village, a strong one who can ride well, to look after them. And tell your people why we took them."

He turned away from the spokesman and went to check on the loading of the packhorses, to make sure they weren't overburdened. They'd have to keep up with the saddle mounts. But the spokesman, he became aware, was following him anxiously. "Excuse me, Captain," he said. "Did you know the reeve has stationed his company at a farm on the Great Road? They are more centrally located there, and also much nearer to us. If they arrive before you leave . . ."

"*Tarlok!*" Macurdy bellowed, and the man came running. Briefly they talked, and given this new information, Macurdy decided they had little or no chance of making it via the North Fork Road. They'd have to go back the way they'd come, and as quickly as they could. He sent one of his best riders, a youth who might have weighed 120 pounds, on the bailiff's best horse, to find Wollerda and let him know the trap was aborted.

Hurriedly they then finished loading the pack horses with two bags each of wheat. The tax girls and the woman who'd tend them were helped onto five of the bailiff's horses. Another townsman had told him there were tax cattle in a paddock just outside town, and Macurdy sent men to get them. The guards there had fled too, it turned out.

When they rode north out of the village, they had not only the pack string, but the tax girls, and three village youths who insisted they wanted to join the rebel band. And eight of the tax cattle. The rest had scattered, and there was no time to round them up.

When he rode away from town at the head of his column, Macurdy already could see faint dawnlight along the eastern horizon. Before long he could see a mile or more. No one seemed sleepy, and from time to time they trotted their horses. The sun rose, and began its daily trip. They passed farmers on the road or at chores, or in the fields—men and women who stared worriedly at them, and kept out of their way. Meadow larks challenged each other in liquid notes, while marsh hawks soared over the hay fields, watching for rodents. Gradually the morning warmed, but remained less than hot; the humidity was low and the breeze pleasant. It would be easy, Macurdy told himself, to think the danger was over, if there'd been any in the first place. And maybe it was over, but that seemed unlikely.

After a bit, Blue Wing found him. "Macurdy! Macurdy!" he cawed, and Macurdy, pulling off the rutted, hoof-packed road, waited while the column passed. Waited for what he was sure was bad news. A rail fence bordered the road there, and with uplifted wings, the great raven braked to land on it. Carrying on a conversation in flight was difficult.

"You are not where you told me you'd be!" he said accusingly.

"I found out things I hadn't known. The North Fork Road's too dangerous. We'd have been caught."

"They're coming! Many more of them than you! And they're riding faster! You'd better hurry!"

"Thanks. We'll go as fast as we dare, but we don't dare wear the horses out." *And the pack string may start to gallop, and the cattle. That'll use them up fast.*

The cattle, Macurdy decided, were the most dispensable, but he'd keep them as long as he could. "How close have they gotten? Have they forded the creek with the brushy banks?"

Blue Wing looked at him exasperated. "Most of the creeks around here have brushy banks."

"The creek with brush that comes up to the road. The next to last creek we crossed between here and the village."

"I'll see." The bird flexed its legs, and launched itself with a whoosh! whoosh! of powerful wing strokes. Then Macurdy urged his big gelding into a canter, to catch the head of the column again.

The great raven was back before many minutes, and Macurdy and Tarlok pulled off the road while the column passed. Their pursuers had crossed the creek, Blue Wing said, were well past it. Tarlok shook his head. "We won't reach the forest before they catch us. Not unless we leave the pack string behind, and the cattle. And if we do that, they'll say they beat us—that we quit. That we're scared of them. And the story will spread."

"Right." *And it'll kill the optimism people have been feeling. Especially these guys.* He turned to Blue Wing again. "There are two places ahead where we rode through woods last night, after we left the forest, but I couldn't see well enough to know what it's like there. Go take a look for me."

Again the great raven left, then returned. Blue Wing always described things differently than a human would, but it seemed to Macurdy there were opportunities in those woods.

He chose one squad and told them what he had in mind for them. The country here was higher, sloping generally southward, and where the woods farther south were mostly in scattered small blocks, here they were irregular, oriented on irregularities in the terrain. It was midmorning when Macurdy came to a broad shallow draw, with a creek running through it flanked by woods. By that time Blue Wing had swooped low a couple of times to urge speed; their pursuit was getting close. Looking back, Macurdy could see a dust cloud: the reeve's men. No doubt they were trotting their horses by intervals.

He and Tarlok kicked their own animals to a brief downhill canter, leading the column into the draw. When they were well into the trees, Macurdy and the squad he'd chosen drew up. Tarlok pulled off too, and called for the others to halt.

"Captain," he said quietly, "do you figure on staying here with them?"

"Yep."

"Best you leave me with them. Lose you, and the whole company will melt away like maple sugar in the rain. But lose me and folks will hardly notice."

"I'd notice."

Tarlok ignored the reply. "By now, everyone knows what you've done. You get yourself killed, and people from Gormin Town to Three Forks to the Saw Pit Valley will lose heart. While most of them never heard of me." Tarlok turned to the others and called out. "Men! Anyone here think the captain lacks guts?"

The chorus of noes was emphatic; there was even laughter, as if the thought was ridiculous. Tarlok nodded, satisfied. "Captain," he said, still loudly, "you don't need to stay here because it's more dangerous. What you need to do is ride on with the column, for the same damn reason."

The man sat easy in the saddle, eyeing his commander. Macurdy nodded, and without answering verbally, nudged his horse with his heels, passing the halted rebels to the head of the column. There he paused just long enough to call out, "All but Rensey's squad—move out!"

They rode. At the break of the draw, Macurdy paused. The road had shrunk to little more than a broad, well-beaten trail, though there still were cart ruts. Looking back toward the head of the dust train, he could see the leaders of the pursuit column. After the last of his drovers had passed, urging the cattle with voices and staffs, he turned his back on Tarlok and the chosen squad. For the first time really aware of how these men looked at him.

It was a burden he hadn't recognized before. It seemed to him now that he owed them at least as much as he owed Varia and himself.

When Blue Wing came back, Macurdy rested the column briefly while he took the bird's report. The reeve's company was on its way again, continuing the pursuit. Yes, some of the ambush squad had gotten out alive, riding upstream; four of them, he thought. (He could handle the smaller numbers well enough.) Some others had probably sneaked away on foot. The reeve's company had lost more. Blue Wing concentrated, then guessed that "ten or more" horses or men had fallen.

More important than that, his pursuers had lost time. The picture Macurdy put together was that the initial flight of arrows had felled several. And instead of driving through, the soldiers had fallen back and discussed it; apparently they had little stomach for casualties. Finally they'd sent their own flights of arrows toward the ambush, but from long range, skewering dirt and trees. Meanwhile they'd sent out strong detachments to enter the woods above and below the ambush, and flank it.

Then the reeve's main force had charged again, and experienced no further archery until almost to the woods, when more men and horses went down at point-blank range. The rest rode into the woods and dismounted, presumably to kill or run off whoever had been shooting at them, instead of doing what they should: riding on through, continuing their pursuit. In fact, no one continued up the road until the flanking parties arrived.

It seemed to Macurdy that whoever led them suffered from an acute case of stupidity, losing track of the objective.

Aloft again, Blue Wing spied their pursuers coming harder than before, closing the gap. "All right," Macurdy said to him, "we'll hit them again at the next wooded draw. Go tell Wollerda what's happened. You'll probably get to him before the courier I sent on horseback."

According to Blue Wing's earlier report, the next woods was a broader band, also following a stream, and as Macurdy visualized it, not more than two or three miles ahead. Now, as he rode, he shouted his plan to his men, then let them pass and repeated himself to the packers and drovers.

All of them pushed their tired horses a little harder. This next stand, Macurdy told himself grimly, would be their last chance. If even a dozen soldiers kept going and caught up with the pack animals, the raid would turn into a fiasco that could wound the rebellion badly, perhaps fatally. Even reaching the forest didn't guarantee safety, if the reeve's commander was willing to follow. Then another thought came to him, easing his grimness. *They won't know there aren't some of us still with the pack train. If we down enough of them, they'll turn around and go back, especially if they lack the stomach for casualties.*

The second broad draw, when they came to it, was wooded clear across the bottom and on both slopes. He trotted his horse down into it, then sent the packers, drovers, and noncombatants on up the road. The rest of his men he scattered along the road by threes behind cover, their horses tethered farther back in the woods. He was depending on their pursuers being little smarter than before. Though they should have learned one lesson—to drive on through, or try to.

When he reached the far slope, he had only six men left to post, and it occurred to him he should have saved more for the upslope, when the soldiers' horses would have slowed. And the last six included the three lowlander youths. Unordered, they'd stayed instead of continuing with the train. He wondered if they had any skill with their bows. He'd heard that flatlanders were forbidden to have weapons, which meant they'd had little practice. But at point-blank range . . . He placed them behind a locust thicket where the road started uphill out of the draw, then led his last three rebels upslope to the north edge of the woods, where he positioned them and himself out of sight, ready in the saddle, spears locked beneath their arms.

Now we wait, he thought, and promptly began to worry. He'd told his men to shoot horses instead of riders; particularly on the run, horses would be a lot easier to hit, and the soldiers probably wore mail byrnies. And if a horse went down in the thundering column, its rider was likely to be disabled anyway. But how many of his rebels would do it? These hillsmen valued horses, treating them well for the most part. And how well could they shoot, through gaps in the trees and undergrowth at galloping horses? Of course, the horses might not be galloping. He'd assumed the enemy commander would speed his column up through the woods, like running the gantlet, and by starting the gallop downhill on the far side, it wouldn't be so taxing. By the time they approached him, of course, they'd have slowed. It would kill horses already tired, to gallop uphill.

Minutes passed, then he heard the rumble of hooves. Coming down the far side of the draw at a gallop, he supposed. There was no shouting from either soldiers or rebels. In his mind he pictured falling horses, other horses falling over them, while others veered past.

Still the sound approached. He edged out far enough to peer down the edge of the road, and saw the foremost horsemen starting uphill, now at a slow trot. "Not yet," he cautioned. "Not yet . . . Not yet . . . *NOW!*"

The four of them spurred out onto the road and charged downhill. The soldiers' spears were in their saddle boots, out of action, for this was something they hadn't imagined. The foremost tried to swing aside, but there was no room for maneuver, no shoulder to the road; just packed dirt, then trees. And others were pressing from behind; they piled up instantly.

The shock of his spear striking a soldier nearly unseated Macurdy, and as his own horse braked staggering, he swung out of the saddle. He and his three rebels drew their heavy sabers, and hacking and hewing, attacked those horses and riders trying to get past the pileup. Then the soldiers began to dismount, sabers in hand, and he found himself bellowing *"Break off! Break off!"*

Then tried to break off himself, but a thick-waisted armsman pressed him, red-faced with rage, and he had to kill the man to disengage. It took several long seconds. Then he ran. After a minute, realizing he wasn't pursued, he slowed to a rapid stumbling walk, panting from exertion and excitement, to continue upstream among the trees. Wondering whether or not the reeve's soldiers had caught the packstring and cattle.

One of his rebels came along on horseback and pulled Macurdy up behind him. After a bit they rode out of the woods, and stopping, dismounted to let the horse rest awhile and graze. Then they continued on foot, leading the animal. More mounted men joined them, jubilant over the fight, and Macurdy allowed himself to feel a little optimistic.

Two hours later they were in unbroken forest; by evening

they'd reached camp. The packstring was already there, and the cattle and tax girls. Everyone cheered Macurdy, acting as if he was some kind of genius. Melody kissed him soundly, while rebels grinned.

And Blue Wing was there, with news. He'd reached Wollerda before the mounted courier, and Wollerda, instead of going home, had led his company westward across the North Fork Road, pushing their horses in a forced march on country lanes, still determined to engage the reeve's company. Blue Wing had served as scout.

After Macurdy's second ambush, the soldiers had turned back. They traveled slowly, partly because of their wounded, and partly because some were riding two on a horse. Wollerda jumped them at a draw south of the first ambush site. Numerous soldiers were killed there, and most who fled were caught. Prisoners were disarmed, and their horses and boots taken. They trudged south barefoot, carrying the news.

It took two more days for all of Macurdy's survivors to straggle in, some of them wounded. All but eleven of the original fifty-two made it, and Tarlok was unscratched. The flatland teenagers weren't among them.

Meanwhile a messenger arrived from Jeremid. He hadn't been pursued, and was on his way with grain, twenty-three head of cattle, and several flatlander volunteers. He expected to bring more recruits from Three Forks. The only fighting had been brief, at the bailiff's stronghold; none of Jeremid's men had been killed, and only three wounded.

Macurdy sent a detail south with pack horses to strip the dead armsmen of byrnies and weapons.

Rebel morale was out the roof. Even their worrywart commander was feeling pretty good.

27

Of Truth and Lies

One of the nicest things Macurdy returned to was Melody. She didn't try to take him to bed, just ate breakfast and supper with him, teasing him hardly at all. She seemed reconciled to his marriage vow, though why she remained interested, he didn't understand. Meanwhile she had a women's tent set up to accommodate the tax girls and their guardian, as well as herself and Loro, the ex-captive from the Orthal days.

Three days after Jeremid returned, Macurdy sent him with a full company to hit the reeve's stronghold. The guesstimate was that fewer than twenty of the reeve's company would have returned from their pursuit of Macurdy and his raiders. His fort would be thinly defended, unless he'd been reinforced. Not the usual stockade, its walls were stone, twenty feet high.

Jeremid had known what to use for opening the gate; he just hadn't expected to find one so handy. Scarcely two hundred yards from the fort was an inn, its taproom catering to armsmen. A new stable was being built for it, and there, waiting to be raised, was the forty-foot roofbeam. Now he wouldn't have to tear down someone's roof to get his battering ram.

It took him less than half an hour to have an A-frame made from other timber at the site, meanwhile sending a platoon around behind the fort with bows and scaling ladders. These then threatened an attack on the rear, holding defenders there, while construction laborers and stable horses, protected by byrnie-clad Kullvordi shieldmen, dragged first the A-frame, then the ram to the fortress gate.

It took a bit to set things up, and despite the shieldmen there were casualties, but within half an hour the gate had given way. The fort's defenders—fifteen escapees from Wollerda's massacre, plus a dozen household guards—surrendered promptly.

Jeremid didn't send all his men inside. Four galloped off toward Gormin Town, two miles east, to the tent camp outside its partially burned palisade wall. Less than an hour later, a mob was forming outside the fort, shouting that they wanted the reeve turned over to them.

Meanwhile Jeremid's men had commandeered the thirty horses in the reeve's stable, and across their backs put rope slings. Then they loaded most of them with tax grain brought in from the bailiwicks—two heavy sacks of wheat, and two of the much lighter oats per horse. A few, instead of being loaded with grain, would carry all the weapons his men could find.

At that they could load only a relatively small portion of the grain stored there. Then a long line of grinning townsmen was let inside, and the rest of the grain began disappearing out the gates on their shoulders.

The reeve and his chief deputy were turned over to a local "committee of justice." The A-frame was already being converted to a gallows, and briefly the committee discussed whether to "merely" hang them there, or to flog them and then hang them. Meanwhile Jeremid had a newly named "rebel X" slashed in the forehead of each captured soldier, with the warning that any of them recaptured in Gurtho's service would definitely be executed. His advice was to leave the country till the rebellion was over, to avoid being forced back into service.

Jeremid had arrived none too soon, a captive told them. A count's platoon was expected the next day, with a wagon train to haul the tax grain to Teklapori.

After the raid on the bailiffs' strongholds, Kithro had begun operating a rational supply system for the rebel force, assessing the hillsmen a lighter equivalent of the royal tax, which he pointed out was no longer being collected, a tax which would be used to secure and support their own freedom.

Meanwhile, problems of logistics and space had worsened. The camp was well-located for security, but with the growth of Macurdy's Company, it had too little pasture for its horses and cattle. And with more and more recruits, supplying them over rough trails by packhorse was becoming impossible. So they moved to a much more accessible area, taking over public pasture accessible by wagons from the North Fork Road.

There crews were detailed daily to build longhouses: cutting, dragging, and fitting logs, splitting out roof planks and shakes, and building mud and stick fireplaces. The hillsmen were handy and cheerful at almost every sort of work, and morale remained strong. Partly because they were busy, partly because they could see so much progress, and partly because they had no doubt that with Macurdy's leadership, this rebellion was going to succeed.

Gurtho, and not "the flatlanders," had become the focus. Macurdy continually made a point of their common cause, Gurtho being hated by both. As for what they might do when Gurtho had been thrown down, time would tell.

Meanwhile, Gurtho had embarked on a campaign to gain the affection of the Teklan commons, throwing a large and costly party in every town and major village to celebrate the eleventh anniversary of his coronation. It might have worked to a degree, if people hadn't had to sit through a speech, ill written and mostly ill read, on the virtues of King Gurtho and the dangers of the Kullvordi. If the virtues of Gurtho had been left out, it might have worked to a degree. As it was, both peasants and townsfolk failed to cheer it. What they cheered were the whole roast oxen, the bushels of roasted early corn, and the barrels of beer. Local musicians were paid to play, and people danced till they dropped from beer or exhaustion, or found a partner to have sex with in the shadows.

And of course, none of the counts, reeves, or bailiffs told Gurtho that the speech had failed, for Gurtho himself had written it, and he was highly sensitive to criticism. He'd had Idri read it in advance, for her opinion, and had she been honest with him, it might have been repaired. But she'd praised it. For Sarkia's ambassadrix sent two couriers a week to the Cloister, and received two. And the Dynast had quietly changed her position regarding the existing king of Tekalos.

✧   ✧   ✧

Eight-Month was well underway, and the rebel ranks grew daily. One day after lunch, Macurdy, Kithro, Melody and Jesker began to go over the table of organization together. Wollerda had a raid in mind, a lot bigger than anything they'd done before, that required cooperation from Macurdy's Force. As yet, though, Macurdy had no units larger than companies— 108 officers and men each, following the Ozian system. All in all he had 736 officers and men, as of the day before, but in his opinion, fewer than half had had enough training to be sent into battle, with many of those being only marginally ready.

So they sat sweating in Eight-Month's humidity and heat, cooking up a short cohort that could be brought to full strength later.

They were hardly well started when a courier galloped up. "Major!" he called as his feet hit the ground. (Macurdy had promoted himself with the growth of his command.) "There's two women want to see you! Out by the main road! They're Sisterhood. Got three guards with them, Sisterhood guards I think; their uniforms aren't Teklan."

"Did they name themselves?"

"No sir."

Macurdy's lips thinned. Not Idri, he guessed; not Gurtho's queen. She'd know better. One of her people then. "Tell them I'll meet one of them beneath the oak on the road in. Just one of them. The rest wait where they are."

"Yessir. Oh, and the boss of them—so pretty I couldn't believe it—she's got a tomttu riding up behind her with his arms around her waist. What I wouldn't do to be in his place!"

Flustered by Macurdy's hard stare, the man remounted and rode away. It took the conference about ten minutes more to agree on principles and begin assembling, on paper, a cohort of four companies: three of spearmen and one of bowmen (though all would carry bows and quivers); bowmen required less training. Then Macurdy, leaving the others to finish the job, started for the paddock. Aware that Melody was following, he stopped and turned. He could see the concern on her face and in her aura.

"Do you think one of them is your wife?" she asked.

He shook his head. "She'd have identified herself."

"Is there—any danger that one of them will spell you?"

"They can't. If they try, they're dead meat. Varia told me once that spells aren't worth much against other magicians. Between her work with me, and Arbel's, there's no danger of it."

Melody's expression didn't change. "I'll come with you. With a squad."

His grim face softened, smiled. Reaching, he touched her face. "I'll go alone," he said, then continued to the paddock to catch and saddle his horse.

As he left, her hand went to the cheek he'd touched. But he hadn't changed her will. She commandeered a squad of men and followed him. Not disobeying his order, she told herself. They'd follow only to the far edge of the woods and watch from there, ready to leave when he turned back. But if there was trouble . . .

Alone except for the tomttu, whom she'd moved around in front of her saddle, Liiset watched Macurdy ride toward her. She hadn't seen him since he was a gangling fourteen-year-old. Even at two hundred feet she could see the change in him, not only in his hard bulk—that was the least of it—but in the way he sat, the way he held his head. And as he neared, his steady gaze and the strength of his aura.

I wonder if Varia ever even imagined him like this, she thought. She could see why men gathered to him and followed his orders. Briefly she wondered if he'd think she was Varia.

He answered that when he halted his horse, fifteen feet from her. "Who are you?" he said. "What do you want here?"

She answered in English. "I'm an envoy from the Dynast, come to speak with you. You're looking well, Curtis."

He said nothing to that, nor did he look surprised. He simply sat waiting.

"Varia would be proud of you if she knew. A year and a half ago you were a farmer on Farside, knowing nothing about Yuulith. Not our language, our ways, our weapons—not even our existence. Now you lead an army here."

He answered in Yuultal. "Why did you come to me?"

"To offer you vengeance."

"Vengeance? I could make a good start on that right now," he said, and half drew his sword.

"Vengeance on the wrong target gives no lasting satisfaction. And if I let you, would you cut me down? I'm not only Varia's clone sister, I'm her favorite, her best friend."

He reseated his sword. "You're Liiset then."

She nodded. "I'm Liiset."

"So who am I supposed to take my vengeance on?"

"The ylver. Those guilty of the rape at Ferny Cove; she told you about that. And most particularly on an ylf named Cyncaidh."

"On the ylver? Idri's the one who stole Varia from me. If she was here, I'd show you vengeance."

Liiset had no doubt he meant it. *Sweet innocent Curtis has changed*, she told herself. *Idri's impulsiveness at work. Well, no doubt it's for the best. Sarkia seems pleased, and she doesn't make many mistakes. Though if she could see him now* . . . "I appreciate your feelings," Liiset said, "but you'd have a hard time killing her if she were here. She has considerable powers."

"Bullshit. If she was here, she'd be fly bait. I guarantee it." He paused. "What's this Kincaid to me?"

"There is much you don't know yet. Much you couldn't know." She put her hand on the tomttu's shoulder. "Curtis," she said, "this is Elsir. Elsir, tell Commander Macurdy what you know of my sister."

The tomttu didn't read auras; he simply saw them and got an overall impression, discerning little of their detail. This man it seemed to him, was dangerous. "My lord, she knocked at my door in the forest, limpin', and with a pack on her back. It was the start of dusk, and I'd just built a fire in my fireplace. I'd have asked her in, but she'd have had to squeeze through the door on hands and knees, and couldn't have been comfortable inside anyway.

"So I asked what I could do for her, and she told me she'd run away from her Sisters, hopin' to reach a gate and go back to her Curtis. To you. She asked if I knew of any dangers ahead, and if I could spare her somethin' to eat.

"I told her I knew of no dangers that she didn't; there always bein' dangers in the wilderness. And that I'd be glad to spare her a loaf, and a small mess of greens. Not enough for a tallfolk, but all I had."

He shrugged his small shoulders. "She lay down to rest on the grass then, and I'd just come back out with the loaf—when there they were, a dozen ylvin devils trottin' up the path! Soldiers on a spyin' mission, I have no doubt. Had they been ordinary humans, they'd never have seen my hut, nor your Varia lyin' by it, for I'd protected it with a spell. She'd fallen asleep, and when I opened my mouth, their leader broke my spell with a wave of his hand, the same leavin' me paralyzed and without speech. It wasn't till one of them raised her by the hair that she wakened."

He feigned a shudder. "They questioned her, strikin' her repeatedly, and—did other things to her. And when they were done, all of them, they tied her weepin' and bleedin' across one of their horses, and rode away laughin'. But before they left, I heard the others call their leader Cyncaidh."

Macurdy's tight lips writhed, and Elsir thought his small heart would stop. "Myself they left where I lay," he went on, "and I don't mind tellin' you I was frightened half to death. Any fox that came along, let alone wolf or catamount, could have had me for supper! But about midnight the paralysis wore off, and I managed to crawl inside and bolt my door.

"The next day, another Sister came along, on horseback with a guardsman, and I told them what I'd seen."

Liiset spoke then. "That was Berit, another of our clone. She'd been tracking Varia, and turned back at once. Then Sarkia sent a master of concealment and tracking to follow the ylver's trail, north to the Big River and beyond. He followed them through the Marches and into the empire itself. And far to the north, to Cyncaidh's palace by the Northern Sea.

"He took his life in his hands then, and allowed himself to be seen. After weaving a spell to resemble an ylf, a spell adequate to fool the common ylver. If one of the more powerful had seen him though . . .

"He'd ask one of them an innocent question or two, then ask someone else a question based on what he'd learned from the first. Repeating this a few times, he learned how she'd fared: Cyncaidh had made Varia his slave and concubine, holding her up to public mockery."

Macurdy's aura had thickened and darkened with anger. And there was more which Liiset couldn't read. "They're evil, Curtis," she finished. "And that's where your vengeance belongs: on the ylver and Cyncaidh."

His voice was husky when he answered. "And why not on your Sisterhood as well? It was you who stole her. Took her away by force, otherwise none of this would have happened. I've talked with an Ozman who said her hands were chained when she arrived. And Idri's man tried to rape her."

Liiset took his hard stare easily, though clearly he knew more than Sarkia or any of them had realized. "That's true," she said. "And Idri herself killed him for it. But Idri acted on her own in stealing Varia. And Sarkia punished her for it, saying that Varia owed us nothing, that if anything, we owed her. But Curtis, the ylver killed so many of the children and babies, at Ferny Cove . . . We needed her. That's the truth that Idri acted on."

Macurdy had studied Liiset while she spoke, seeing more than she thought, and his intensity had eased. "If this Kincaid lives by the Northern Sea, what is this vengeance you offer?"

"We talked King Gurtho into offering peace and autonomy to the Kullvordi, if they'll join his army. He's concerned about you, afraid you might defeat him."

"What's that got to do with vengeance on the ylver? By spring, Gurtho will be finished anyway."

"It's not just your vengeance we're interested in. The vengeance *we* want is for Ferny Cove, and that requires a large and powerful army. The crudest tribal chief would not have committed on us the brutalities they did, not on such a scale, and they savaged the Kormehri almost as terribly, earning fear and disgust through all the Rude Lands.

"We've put embassies now in every kingdom but Kormehr, from the Eastern Mountains to the Great Muddy, and from here to the Big River. As Gurtho's general, you and Sarkia can put together a powerful army between now and next spring. With you as general, for somehow you've become a skilled and inspiring commander."

Macurdy looked thoughtful instead of angry. "And how far do you expect me to lead it? Not to the Northern Sea."

"It will be enough if you take it through the Marches and into the empire. The Marches are ready to kick free their ylvin shackles. At best they'll join with us. At the very worst they'll take no part on either side.

"Simply to march into the empire itself will redeem our honor and be vengeance enough. Into the empire far enough that our allies can loot ylvin manors and take their wealth home with them. And by then the ylver's slaves may rise up. If they do, who knows how far we may go. If not—" Liiset shrugged. "The emperor will be glad to negotiate, and we'll demand Varia back. He'll give her to us, too. Then she'll be free to go back with you to Farside, or you can live here together, with far more wealth and power than you could ever have there."

His gaze penetrated, then switched unexpectedly to the tomttu. "Elsir, where was she captured?"

"Why—near the head of Tuliptree Creek, on the Laurel Notch Trail. But that's far off east of here, in the Dales at the east end of the Granite Range."

Macurdy held the tomttu's eyes a moment longer, then returned his gaze to Liiset. "I'll think about it for a week or so," he said. "Send one of your guards as a courier then."

Without another word he turned his back on her, nudging his horse into an easy trot. Liiset and Elsir watched him ride away, and from his perch in front of her, the tomttu spoke quietly. "Ah, lady, it's an evil thing we've done, lyin' to him like that."

"It's not lying, Elsir, if it helps someone grasp a larger truth."

The small face turned to her's. "A lie's a lie, whatever the intention." He turned again and watched Macurdy disappear into the forest. "And he knows I lied."

"No, he was suspicious to begin with, but by the time I was done, he was convinced in spite of himself. And if it's any consolation, consider that we gave you no choice."

"There's always a choice, lady. Even if the choice is death."

"That was no choice for you, Elsir. Macurdy is no friend of yours. You never saw him before."

"And may I never see him again, for I have greatly wronged

him." He looked up at Liiset again. "I believe my people know more about the ylver than yours do. There are good and bad among them, but they've been much less evil to my people than humans have. Cyncaidh would not have made me do what your Dynast has."

Liiset was touched by the tomttu's courage in speaking as he had, and laid a light hand on his shoulder. "Believe me," she said quietly, "the Dynast's spy did follow her, all the way north. And her captor's name is Cyncaidh. It was necessary that you lie a little." *While I told only the truth, the truth according to Sarkia, who lies when it suits her.*

She helped Elsir move behind her, his long fingers clutching. When he was settled, she turned her horse and started back toward the North Fork Road. Macurdy had left with some intention in his mind, something that presumably would take a week, and she wondered what it was.

28

Truth

Macurdy unsaddled his mount at the paddock, and told the herd boss he wanted five strong horses readied for himself and one other by midafternoon, two with pack saddles; and oats for twelve days. He glanced upward in irritation as he spoke, for rain clouds were moving in. Then he strode to his headquarters tent, where one of his runners, a fourteen-year-old, jumped to his feet.

"Find Captain Tarlok. Tell him I need to see him right away."

"Yessir!" the boy said, and took off at a trot. Macurdy fiddled briefly with supply records, occupying himself until Tarlok appeared. "Is there anyone in camp who knows the trails to the Granite Range, and the Dales?" Macurdy asked. "I need a guide, on a mission only I can do. For information."

Tarlok frowned. "How long will you be gone?"

"Until I've learned what I need to know; it could be a dozen days or more. I'm leaving Jeremid in charge."

Tarlok nodded. "Blue Wing could probably guide you."

"He's needed here to scout or courier for Jeremid."

"Well then, there's a lad named Fengal in my company, as good in the woods as any you'll find. He's only eighteen, but grew up wild. His mother is Indrossan, from someplace called Hemlock Cove. She died two years ago, and his dad came back to North Fork, bringing the lad with him."

"Good. Have him sent here, with his horse, bedroll, and saddlebags."

Tarlok nodded and got to his feet.

"Another thing," Macurdy said, and told him to expect a

courier from the Sisters. He was to lodge and treat the man as a semi-prisoner, treat him well but not allow him to talk with people. "I'm accepting him as a courier, not a spy," Macurdy finished.

Tarlok acknowledged and left. Then Macurdy sent another runner to find Captain Melody and send her to his tent. His third runner he gave instructions that Fengal, when he got there, was to wait.

He was packing his saddlebags and bedroll when Melody arrived, her tunic rain-spotted. "What is it?" she asked.

"I'm going on a trip, with just a guide, and someone needs to know what I'm doing and why." He paused. "The Sister I talked to told me where Varia is. Supposedly. Where she is and how she is."

Melody nodded soberly.

"But I'm not sure how much of it I believe. She had a tomttu with her, to tell me part of the story, and both of them were lying part of the time."

"Lying? How do you know?"

"When Arbel worked with me, I learned to see what he calls auras, like a cloud of colored light around a person. I can see yours right now. And with practice, if you see them clearly and you're paying attention, you can tell when someone's lying."

Melody stared at him. "She told me Varia was captured by an ylf named Kincaid, and taken north into the empire—way north, to the Northern Sea. That part she believes, but the rest she's not sure of. The tomttu said he saw her capture, and they both know that's a lie, but at least he saw her."

He paused. "First I'm going to where the tomttu said it happened. Maybe I can learn something. Then—I'll do whatever comes next."

"What about us? Your army?"

"I'm leaving Jeremid in charge. He's as good as I am." He chuckled then, getting up. "In some ways, anyhow."

She didn't smile. "When are you going?"

"As soon as I've talked to Jeremid. Half an hour."

She stepped forward, hugged him hard and kissed his mouth, then stood back and looked at him. "Come back to us, Macurdy," she said. "Come back to me, anyway."

He didn't chuckle now. "I will," he said. "I promise." And wondered again why she felt the way she did.

When Macurdy got back to his headquarters tent, Fengal was waiting. He was a lean youth of middle height, with a look of wiry strength; overall he made a good impression. Macurdy told him what he needed him for, while a courier went to get Jeremid, who arrived inside of five minutes. Macurdy told him he was leaving, going on a mission that only he could carry out, that would probably influence what they did next. And that the Sisterhood wanted an alliance—that a courier would arrive from them in a week or so. Tarlok would take care of the man.

Then he and Fengal went to the cook tent for cooking gear and rations, and rode out of camp in another sprinkle of rain.

For five long days they rode eastward, ignoring stealth, Macurdy picking up bits of woodscraft from Fengal. The days and nights were showery, with occasional brief hard rains, yet they made only a minimal camp at night, sleeping where dusk found them, spreading their oiled tarp over a quick frame of saplings. They left their cooking gear unused, their only fire at day's end, to dry or semi-dry their clothes, though they did bake potatoes in the embers. They were up at dawn with the thrushes and wrens, and ate in the saddle: jerky and hard bread, their jaw muscles aching from it, and cold baked potatoes. And occasional wild apples, worm-tunneled but edible, for on the old burns where they stopped to graze their horses, there sometimes were apple trees. Macurdy wondered how they'd come there.

Finally they came to what Fengal said was the Laurel Notch Trail, used much by wildlife and seldom by man or horse. They turned off on it, northward now instead of east. Beside it, in a small wet meadow, they found horse bones gnawed and scattered; by a troll, Fengal said. Macurdy wondered what had become of the rider. As they continued north, he felt a growing tension, an excitement. He felt more alert, it seemed to him, than he'd ever been before.

Now he watched for a tomttu hut; any spell of invisibility

or protection should have dissipated, but if it not, Macurdy had no doubt he'd see through it. They crossed through Laurel Notch, and some time later passed a spring, the headwaters of the Tuliptree. Still no hut. He wasn't surprised. According to Maikel, tomttu didn't settle in the wilderness. They only traveled, or at most sojourned in it.

What he did find were human bones, the thigh bones long. A tall man then. They weren't splintered and sucked dry by a troll, nor scored by the teeth of wolf or bear or some large cat. Its bones had been cleaned by smaller teeth, weaker jaws, beaks and worms and bacteria.

Its chest had been cleaved by something long and sharp, seemingly a sword.

He hadn't found it by the path. He'd felt an impulse to leave the trail, to snoop behind a laurel thicket not far away. Whoever had killed this man had dragged him there out of sight.

"Not all that old," Fengal said, his voice subdued. "Old bones weather gray. These are still pretty white."

Macurdy knelt, picked the skull up, looked into the empty eye sockets—and began to tingle. Abruptly disorientation struck him, then momentary confusion followed by an instant of blankness. Yet he didn't lose consciousness, just his sense of identity and time, looking through eyes not his own, as if he were someone else. It seemed he was striding uphill, breathing deeply, less alert than usual. Sensing nothing peculiar, nothing dangerous. Then a bowstring twanged, and there was a sudden, shocking impact, a horrible penetration that drove the strength from him, and he fell to his knees, staring down at a feathered shaft protruding from below his breastbone. Ambush! He was aware of men in buckskins, with swords, and strove to rise again. Felt a smashing blow cleave his rib cage, then looked down at his body from a viewpoint perhaps ten feet above it.

But only for a moment. For instead of being absorbed with the reality of his death, his attention went to the action around him. Besides the cluster of men, there was his captive—filthy and with her hair stubble-short—staring at his broken body, her mouth round with shock. One of the ambushers held her from behind, gripping her shoulders, keeping her from falling.

Until the sword struck, there'd been sound—hoarse

breathing, feet on earth, the bustle of movement. Then it nearly stopped, silent as stone, the action below him in ultra-slow motion, speeding gradually, until there was sound again, slow and hollow. "You're all right, you're safe now," one of them said to the woman. The man who held her upright. "We know who he was, and who you are. A tomttu told us. He was anxious for you. Your tracker had been only hours behind."

During that short speech, the speed normalized and the sound became natural, as if his mind had adjusted to a new input channel. Now, while still experiencing the murdered man's perceptions, he was aware of his own identity as Macurdy, heard and watched the sequence that followed, heard the tall ylf tell of Ferny Cove, saw the woman set on horseback. Saw them ride away, out of sight. There'd been no questioning, no blows, no rape, no harshness.

Became aware of someone shaking his shoulder, and for a moment saw nothing, then awoke to present time, lying on soggy forest mould among the bones. It was Fengal who knelt beside him. "Major! Major! Are you all right?"

Macurdy groaned, pushed himself to hands and knees and got up, his speech slurred. "Yeah, I'm all right. I—saw the whole thing: what happened here, what the dead man saw. It's what I came for. Now I know what I need to know."

The youth stared at him in awe, not doubting. He knew his commander was a magician, had seen him light fires. They went to the sound of water over stones, dug dry punk from inside a hollow tree, built a fire, and for the first time used their griddle, making corn cakes.

Macurdy remained preoccupied, as if still assimilating what he'd learned. When they'd eaten, instead of starting back to Laurel Notch, they lay down to nap. His last conscious thought was to wonder where Varia was, and what she was doing.

29

Sea Gate

Cyncaidh and Varia had stayed up late the night before, bundled warmly on a balcony, holding hands while she watched her first aurora, a marvelous play of lights shimmering and pulsing not just in the north but over the entire bowl of sky. Then they'd slept late by their standards, and busied themselves for a time while the sun climbed the sky, he entering various records into a ledger, while she read more imperial history.

By late morning the temperature was perhaps 75 degrees Farenheit, almost hot for late summer on the Northern Sea, and they'd left the manor on foot, hiking a graveled path that led through half a mile of forest to the shore. Cyncaidh wore moccasin-like step-ins, soft, bleached-linen trousers, a low-crowned, untrimmed hat of straw, and a jacket-like shirt with sleeves only to the elbows. Varia wore a short kilt over knit tights, and a knit top with long sleeves. Held by the beauty of the morning, neither of them said much as they walked.

A gap opened in the forest, widening as they approached the beach, broadening the view ahead. The sky held not a cloud, and the air only a light breeze. The dry haze of autumn was three or four weeks in the future, and the air was crystalline, showing the icy water sapphire-blue to the horizon. Well offshore, a string of rocky islets angled northeastward across the view, providing perspective and composition.

They had no escort. Cyncaidh himself carried the basket that, besides a picnic, held jackets in case the wind picked up. A servant had preceded them by half an hour, with blankets, oars and sail. He'd installed the sail, seated the spar, then left by another path, to avoid imposing on their privacy.

The small cove was sheltered on the northwest by a low spine of basalt, the ghost of some ancient volcanic dike, ground down, rounded and smoothed by glacial ice. By contrast with its near blackness, the dry beach sand was surprisingly white, and audible as they crossed it to the small dock where a fourteen-foot skiff was tied. There was a minute of verbal exchange, cheerful and mostly purposeful. Then Varia crouched in the bow with a short boat hook, while Cyncaidh pushed off from the dock and manned the oars, leaning into them and pulling out into the smooth-surfaced cove.

She put down the hook and watched him row, noting the sinews in his long forearms, his lean athletic lines. It was a body that little by little, these weeks, she'd learned to appreciate and love. It differed from Curtis's, as their personalities differed. Both men were muscular, though their lines and proportions were not at all alike. Both were strong-willed, too, but not bullheaded—considerate, able to give way—and both were sweet and loving. But Raien was—not wiser but more intellectual, and in bed a smoother, more skilled lover. Curtis relied more on his reactions. Of course he was nearly thirty years younger, but the difference was more basic than that.

Her life, she told herself, had been rich after all, in gifts as well as trials.

It occurred to her she'd been comparing the two men, the loves of her life, something that would still have been impossible, unthinkable, just four weeks earlier. The changes in her viewpoint and emotions still sometimes surprised her. They'd been sneaking up on her over the gentling, strengthening weeks of intermittent sessions with Mariil, sessions that healed both mind and spirit. And she'd discovered she could think of both men without guilt or any other discomfort. Or compulsive assignment of precedence. Each loved her, and she loved both of them.

But Curtis was in another world. He'd hardly fit in this one.

Not that healing was complete, it might never be, but it seemed to her it had gone far enough that she could face whatever she needed to face, without being overwhelmed or experiencing great grief. And Mariil had seemed to thrive on helping, as if she too was getting a new lease on life. The techniques she used, certain others also knew, A'duaill for one, and increasingly herself, with Mariil her teacher. But Mariil, Varia recognized, had the greater healing talent. It was a healing not imposed like surgery, but internal, replete with tears and laughter, the realizations and decisions her own, though guided and facilitated by Mariil's insights, skilled questions and instructions.

Commonly the effects weren't noticed until, the next day or week, Varia realized that certain responses had changed, that this and that reaction and attitude were different than they had been. And in the process of opening and cleaning out old mental lesions, more than the effects of abuse were dealt with: old learning and conditioning were also exposed. Some of which she cancelled or modified, and some she reaffirmed within her newly evolving world view.

Under the gentle pressure of sun and sea breeze, her eyes had closed. Now she became aware that the skiff's movement had smoothed, and she opened them again. Cyncaidh had stowed the oars and raised the sail, and lost in her thoughts, she hadn't noticed. He sat grinning in the stern with the tiller under his arm, while the breeze bellied the linen. The cove was behind them; his eyes were on her. She smiled back at him. He could be boyish too, a boyishness different than Curtis's.

Cyncaidh watched her eyes close again. Lovely, lovely eyes, he told himself, in a lovely face relaxed and lightly tanned. Looking at her, he felt strong, strong and able. And lucky.

He loved her tan. It was a rare ylf that tanned. Among them, protection from sunburning was a subtler function of ylvin physiology. Which could be overloaded, thus the ylvin fondness for hats and body covering against prolonged exposure. He loved her legs, too, admired them, preferred them bare; their clean lines and smooth muscularity excited him sexually. And he loved her slender waist; her back, well-muscled instead of bony; her easy flexibility. The strength that still surprised him when her passion released it, and the dance exercises that Sisters were taught, to maintain their endurance and beauty. She did them daily now, elaborating on them, she told him; said she intended to make an art form of them.

Dancing she excited him, and relaxed she soothed him. As now. He wondered what she was thinking behind her closed lids, and hoped it was of him.

Varia opened her eyes from time to time, to see Raien in the stern, and the shore falling farther behind. With a following breeze and little draft, they moved briskly.

This was the third time he'd had taken her boating. The first two trips had been overnighters, exploring the coast first westward, then eastward. Bypassing fishing hamlets, they'd skirted wild beaches, snooped cliffs, and explored the lower reaches of streams, Raien unstepping the spar and using the oars when necessary. She'd loved the places he'd shown her; some looked as if no one had been there before. They'd poled up one rocky gorge which in spring, he said, was a raven rookery, loud with the croaking of the large black birds, hundreds of them, their nest trees clinging to rocky walls, where fledglings gripped the branches determined never to let go despite the noisy urgings of their elders.

Sometimes she'd rowed. At first her request had surprised him, but he'd overridden his cultural conditioning and let her take the oars. More than once, she'd told him, she'd rowed Will's rented boat on the Mustoka River, while Will worked the water with his casting rod, for bass. Raien had frowned, and she'd asked him why. He'd been trying to visualize it, he'd said. Trying to visualize Will, and Varia's marriage to him. He had less difficulty, he told her, visualizing her life with Curtis, though he wasn't at all sure his images were realistic.

It seemed to her she handled the complications of her past more easily than Raien did.

With the following breeze, sailing was simple, and Cyncaidh's attention remained largely on Varia. Her lovely eyes opened only for seconds at a time. Her aura, he noted, was almost as calm as if she slept; whatever she was thinking was pleasant but unexciting. Shortly they drew even with the nearer islets, and he angled toward the one they'd picnic on. Most were mere skerries, bare black rocks overswept by waves in the heavier storms. Three, however, had developed shallow soils and a bit of vegetation, while the largest had not only scrubby aspens and birches, but a small stand of black spruce, complete with nesting birds that fed on bearberry and bilberry, and the seeds of other dwarf shrubs that grew there.

"Here comes our picnic ground," he said, and opening her eyes, Varia turned to see. He lowered his sail and manned the oars as they coasted in, letting the tiller trail, pulling up beside a natural dock he knew, a finger of dark basalt. The bow slid gently onto shiny black shingle rock, and Varia, stepping onto the natural dock beside her, pulled the bow farther up, grounding it securely. Someone in the past had driven a steel picket into a crack, and Raien tied up to it, then took the picnic basket ashore, putting it down higher on the narrow beach, where he spread their blankets on the sand.

"It's a little early for lunch, don't you think?" Varia asked.

He grinned down at her from his six-feet-four. "I thought we might do other things. Here where we have both privacy and sunshine."

She grinned back, put her arms around him and raised her face. "What did you have in mind, your lordship?"

He began to show her, his hands in the back of her tights while they kissed. After a minute they lowered to their knees, then lay down, dallying and petting, and before long made slow love in the sunshine. Afterward they had their lunch: coarse bread, apple butter, cheese, and a flask of beer cooled in the shallows. When they'd eaten, he led her into the shade of the spruce grove, and spread the blankets on feather moss. There they made love again, then dressed and napped, and afterward sat in the beached skiff to finish the contents of the basket.

He pointed northeast, out at the farther islets. "You can see the farthest two from here," he said.

The non sequitur remark sharpened her awareness. His aura reflected watchfulness, a certain tension; he had something to tell her, and wasn't sure how she'd take it. Puzzled, she looked where he pointed.

"Out there is the Sea Gate."

"Sea Gate?"

"There's a gate there, presumably to Farside. I thought you should know."

Frowning, she stared at him, not yet angry.

"It's called the Sea Gate because it opens over the water between the last two skerries. And it's different in other respects. The other gates I've heard of open when the moon is full, at midnight or high noon. This one opens irregularly during periods of northern lights, and apparently stays open for hours at a time. Perhaps days sometimes.

"Long ago, one of my great-great-uncles went through in a boat to see what was on the other side. He planned to see, then return at once, and several boats waited for him. Only his boat came back, overturned but intact. Twice since then volunteers have gone through, and not even their boats were seen again."

He paused, looking at her. Her expression had turned thoughtful. "I thought we might go out there," he said. "After last night it may be stirring. We can feel it if it is. Would you like to?"

She answered only after a long moment's lag. "Has anything ever come through from the other side? Besides your great uncle's boat?"

"Not that we know of. Nothing seen floating, no bodies or anything unusual washed up on the beach."

She couldn't correlate the geography of the two worlds well, but it seemed to her that Lake Superior might be on the other side, and told him so. He nodded thoughtfully. "If it is, it's probably cold, like the sea here. And if the arrival there is rough, rough enough to overturn you . . ."

"I've gone through both ways," she said. "Coming through to this side is the most violent, but going through the other way, you never know what position you'll arrive in. Hardly ever on your feet."

"I've read the same sort of thing. Do you want to sail out there? Close enough to feel if anything is happening?"

Again she frowned thoughtfully. "I suppose we should. I don't know what we'll accomplish—nothing, probably—but . . ."

He nodded, and after they'd stowed their things in the skiff, she got into the stern. He untied the painter, lifted the bow free of the shingle rock and pushed off, Varia holding the tiller. Then he raised the sail and sat down by her in the stern. Approaching the gate site, they felt nothing unusual, and after circling it, turned to tack their way shoreward, slowly, for the skiff had little draft, and only skeg and rudder to bite the water.

On their way back to the cove, a slender ship passed them, a Sea Swallow swift and graceful, its mast unseated, driven by long oars. The colors of an imperial courier fluttered at the stern. When the couple reached the manor, the courier met them, giving Cyncaidh a sealed envelope, while a troubled Ahain hovered unnoticed in the background. Slitting the envelope, Cyncaidh read the message, then turned to Varia. "Lochran has died. The Chief Counselor. Unexpectedly. The Emperor wants me to come at once, with the courier."

Ahain interrupted. "Your lordship!"

Cyncaidh turned, noticing him now. "Yes?"

"Lady Cyncaidh lost consciousness this morning after you left. Lord A'duaill says it's a stroke. He doesn't think she'll live out the day."

Cyncaidh's jaw clenched, and he turned to the courier. "I'll stay till my wife can either travel or has died. Meanwhile I'll have preparations begun."

"As you say, Lord Cyncaidh."

"Meanwhile I'll look in on her, and discuss her condition with Lord A'duaill, my wizard and healer. You and I can talk further after supper." He turned to Varia, who stood white-faced, her knuckles between her teeth, not at the unexpected move but at the report of Mariil's stroke. "Lady Varia, perhaps you'd care to come with me."

She nodded. "Of course, your lordship."

They went together to the second floor, to the east wing, and went in. Mariil was still unconscious. They'd been there only minutes when her spirit aura flickered out. She was dead.

30

Confrontation

The ride back from Laurel Notch had been like a vacation. It had even been sunny, with only two showers, hard but not prolonged. Macurdy talked more with Fengal as they rode, and learned more from him. It seemed to him the youth had been born a woodsman, that at eighteen he knew and understood more about the forest than many who'd spent a lifetime in it. So they'd been gone a full eleven days when they arrived back.

Liiset's courier had arrived, but Macurdy made no immediate use of him because the joint operation with Wollerda's force was almost ready. Jeremid briefed him on it, and two days later they rode out at the head of four companies of eager hillsmen.

Macurdy wondered at their easy willingness to face an armed enemy. Some had seen friends die on the tax raid; a few had been wounded themselves. Jeremid commanded; he was more familiar with the situation and plan. Macurdy went along because he felt he should, and to inspire the men, who seemed to think he was invincible.

The town they rode toward was the seat of the county which included the western hills, and for that reason, the count who ruled it had been reinforced with a company each from four other counties. Jeremid had learned this from spies. And the castle had been warned of the rebel approach; Jeremid and Wollerda had seen to that. Now if the count would cooperate . . .

He did, sending out all but his fortress company to meet and destroy Macurdy's rebels.

294

Meeting this much larger force, Jeremid ordered a retreat, which then seemed to lose order and turn into a rout. The count's force pursued them, until the soldiers, more or less strung out, cantered past a river forest. There Wollerda's 1st Cohort had concealed itself the night before, and charging out, had confused and disorganized the soldiers. At the same time, Macurdy's rebels had turned on their pursuers.

The soldiers had fought without enthusiasm and at a severe tactical disadvantage. Rather sooner than the rebel commanders had expected, royalist trumpeters had signalled surrender. The rebels had disarmed the soldiers then (they'd drilled even that), taking byrnies and shields, swords and spears, bows and quivers. And hundreds of horses, on some of which they loaded the loot.

In Kellum, the county seat, well-led teams looted the homes of officials, taking coins, silver, jewelry, scented wax candles and other valuable goods easy to convert to cash to help pay the costs of the growing rebel army. Beyond that, looting was forbidden, a forbiddance assisted by limited opportunity. This caused grumbling, but nothing serious, for Macurdy, Wollerda, and their officers lived among their men and pretty much as their men, commonly eating with them, the same food in the same portions.

The count had refused to surrender his castle, and Wollerda and Macurdy left it unassaulted. It was much more formidable than the reeve's had been. Wollerda's and Macurdy's strategy, at this stage of the rebellion, was to demonstrate without question their military effectiveness, enhance their supply situation, and bleed and demoralize the royal army. In all of which they'd succeeded.

What they hadn't done yet was force the king to commit his personal cohort. They weren't ready for that—not outside the hills—and they knew it. It was why they hadn't challenged the count who ruled the eastern hills: He was much nearer Teklapori.

Meanwhile they held the initiative, and their morale was stronger than ever, despite casualties. Their training had been much briefer, and most rebels lacked byrnies, yet in open combat they'd beaten the count's soldiers, who supposedly were superior to those the reeves could field. The advantage had been rebel spirit and vigor, and better leadership.

It was after his return to camp that Macurdy sent Liiset's courier with a written message to her, expecting a quick response. The first half dozen days of waiting were no problem; after all, he'd made her wait. Meanwhile no further offensive actions were planned. Morale no longer needed them, and it was time to prepare for what seemed a certain royal response, either diplomatic through the Sisterhood, or military—a concerted offensive to destroy the more accessible Kullvordi villages and crush the spirit of rebellion. Macurdy and Wollerda had a strategy to meet that too, one that called for preparations, as many as they had time for. Time that negotiations could help provide.

Jeremid had already designed a shield neither Ozian nor Teklan, that could be made rapidly. Rebel losses would have been substantially less if they'd had them before and been trained to use them. Macurdy and Kithro had developed a system for their manufacture. Kithro contracted with a range of providers: woodsmen who felled large shagbark hickories and cut them into roughly three-foot-long sections. Carpenters who split planks from them, and trimmed and planed them to the proper dimensions and weight; tanners who produced leather from bull hides, cutting it to size and shape; and smiths who made iron bands to strengthen them, and iron bosses and hooks to make them dangerous.

Among the hillsmen, tanners were the glue makers, too. They'd made the glue to glue pieces of hickory together, because suitable single-piece shields were tricky to make, and gluing would often be necessary. Bull hides would then be stretched over them, shrunken into place and hardened. Finally iron cross bands would be riveted on, and bosses and hooks added. And when squads got their shields, they'd begin a simple shield-training regimen borrowed from the militia at Wolf Springs.

Payment for shields, as for much else, would be in captured silver, army horses, and if need be, chits.

✧   ✧   ✧

After the sixth day, though, the continued lack of response from Liiset began to gnaw on Macurdy's mind. What was the holdup? He'd gotten the impression they were eager. Did they plan a surprise? Treachery? Something to give them leverage?

Meanwhile, on Macurdy's fourth day back from the Dales, Kithro had come to his tent, where he sat talking with Melody and Jeremid after supper. "Fengal's been telling an interesting story," Kithro said.

"Oh? What's that?"

"The story of what you found over below Laurel Notch: a set of human bones. He said you dropped to your knees, looked into the eyes of the skull, yelped a cry, and fell on your face in some kind of trance."

"I can't vouch for the yelp, but the rest sounds about right."

"He says you lay there for quite a while, babbling like someone in their sleep. Talking in other people's voices about ylver and Ferny Cove and other things that meant nothing to him. And woke up mumbling about having seen everything that happened there."

"Huh! I never thought he'd talk about it. I'm disappointed in him."

Kithro shook his head. "A boy like that, seeing and hearing what he did, couldn't be expected to keep his mouth shut. And he's done you a favor—done us all a favor—because the story's spread all through camp."

Kithro paused. "My people used to have shamans. Till Gurtho's great-grandfather executed most of them; them and their progenies. Claimed they'd been a source of agitation. After the slaughter, the people lost faith in shamanism and the favor of God. There's a few villages still have someone who calls himself a shaman, but their magic doesn't amount to much. For healing, we depend mostly on old women with a few simple spells and a knowledge of herbs.

"Then you came around and made fire with a wave of the hand, and grew new teeth. Now there's this story of Fengal's. The men have gotten excited about it. They consider you a shaman warrior for sure, now. A shaman of power."

He looked meaningfully at Macurdy. "I thought you ought to know," he said, then left, the others watching him go.

"Hmh!" Melody looked accusingly at Macurdy. "You didn't tell me any of that." She turned to Jeremid. "Did he tell you?"

"Nope." He raised an eyebrow at Macurdy. "How about it?"

Macurdy grunted. "I guess I should," he said, and began.

On the eleventh day, he had an answer that explained the delay: Sarkia had come to Tekalos, was at the palace with a company of guardsmen and one of Tigers. She wanted to meet with him outside Gormin Town, at the junction of the North Fork Road and the Valley Highway, in four days.

The message arrived in midafternoon. Haltingly he read it to himself, and again after supper to Melody sitting across from him, and Jeremid at his elbow.

"Sarkia," Melody said when he'd finished. Her face was very serious. "She's supposed to be the greatest sorcerer in the world. Don't go, Macurdy."

"Do you think she'll put a spell on me? Catch my soul in a bottle? Scramble my brain?"

She peered at him unhappily. His expression was calm, matter of fact. "She'll try something," she answered.

He remembered how easily Varia had influenced him, that night in Indiana. But it hadn't been sorcery that got him in bed with her, though it *had* gotten him to her house. And he'd been an innocent then, ignorant, a psychic virgin. Yet even so, in the morning he'd had second thoughts about marriage, objections she'd had to answer.

"I've got the talent," he said, "and I've had some training. She can't make me do what I don't want to." *And there's a lot at stake here for me. There's no other way I can hope to get Varia back. None at all.*

"These Tigers," Jeremid said. "Are they as good as I've heard, do you suppose?"

Macurdy shrugged. "I guess that depends on how good you've heard. Varia mentioned them once; she thought they were the best. Savage, highly skilled, and stronger than other men. And they won't be tentative like the people we've been fighting."

Jeremid gestured at the paper lying on the table. "Why do you suppose Sarkia mentioned them in her message?"

"I can only guess. Maybe she wants to scare me. Added to Gurtho's cohort, just a company of Tigers could make a big difference. Even without Gurtho's cohort, a company of guards and one of Tigers makes it too dangerous to take a cohort south to capture her. Not that I would."

"They could be to keep us from rescuing you, if she takes you prisoner," Melody said.

"True. But it doesn't feel like anything to worry about."

"You're going to go regardless of what we think," Melody said. "Are you going to take a bodyguard? Besides the escort who'll ride down there with you? Someone who'll be beside you during the meeting?"

Macurdy grinned at her. "Who have you got in mind?"

She grinned back ruefully. "Me."

"If I was going to take someone, it would be you." *And let them think maybe I have a new love. Let them feel they have to offer more. But if something does go wrong . . .*

"But you're not taking anyone."

"Right."

"What about Wollerda?" Jeremid asked.

"That's the next big question." Macurdy plucked a sheet of paper from a small stack, then reached for his inkwell. "I want you to write a message to him, for me to sign."

Blue Wing carried the message and brought back Wollerda's answer: Macurdy could meet with Sarkia but make no final commitment. If he failed to return, Wollerda would accept Jeremid as Macurdy's successor. If Macurdy's Force elected someone other than Jeremid as their new commander, Wollerda was not committed to work with him, although he'd consider it.

Usually Macurdy slept well, and the night before leaving was no exception. The officer of the guard wakened him at the first light of dawn, and he got up feeling exhilarated. He and his escort of ten men were in the saddle and on their way before sunup. Despite the unknowns, Macurdy's sense of strength and confidence grew as he rode. He wasn't euphoric or ecstatic, just alert and confident, sure of himself. This would work out.

The state persisted through the morning.

Near midday, in the distance, he could see the inn at the crossroads. He'd assumed that Sarkia intended to sit down with him there, but almost as soon as he made out the inn, he saw what looked to be a tent, a large pavilion erected on the other side of the North Fork Road. Shortly a dozen men were riding northward toward him at a brisk trot, and after closing the distance somewhat, he halted his escort to wait. The reception party stopped a hundred feet away, sitting its horses in precise ranks. Two of its members rode the rest of the way at a sedate walk. Macurdy had no doubt that they were Sarkia's rather than Gurtho's. Mounted on beautifully matched black horses, they wore black uniforms with polished cuirasses and helmets that, from where he sat, looked to be silver. The two who came to meet him wore clusters of long scarlet ribbons from their helmet peaks.

"You are Commander Macurdy?" one of them asked. He showed no hauteur, despite the rebels' rough clothes and casual ranks, nor did his aura show anything like scorn.

"That's right."

"If you are prepared to meet now with the Dynast, I am instructed to conduct you to her. A meal is being prepared for her and yourself. Your men will eat with us if you wish, or they can eat apart."

"Where do I meet her? In the tent?"

"In the pavilion. Correct."

"My men will eat at the inn. I'm ready to meet the Dynast, the sooner the better."

The guard officer nodded. "Follow me, please." Macurdy turned, called an order, and his men fell in behind the guardsmen while their commander rode beside his guide.

The pavilion, as he neared it, impressed him. Its vivid red, white, and gold roof and wall panels were brighter than he'd have thought possible. (He'd heard that among other things, the Sisterhood made expensive dyes.) Segments of the walls had been rolled up for ventilation. As he drew even with the inn, Macurdy gave another order and his men turned off, riding to the stable beside it. His air of confidence was so strong, so clean, that none of them faltered in leaving their shaman/commander unguarded. He turned the other way and followed his guide to the pavilion, where he dismounted, handing over his horse to a guardsman-orderly.

At the entrance, the leader of his escort reported to a Sister that this was Commander Macurdy. The woman disappeared inside, and two minutes later another came to meet him. For just a moment he thought she was Idri, whom he'd seen but once. But neither aura nor eyes fitted what he knew of her. An Idri look-alike, he realized, as Liiset looked like Varia.

"Commander Macurdy," she said, "the Dynast will see you now."

"Will she? I'm here at her invitation, and I've had a long ride. I need something to drink first, and take a crap."

The woman's aura hardly reacted to his deliberate crudity. "Drink and lunch are both served in the Dynast's room," she answered. "Oran will show you to the guards' latrine."

Macurdy didn't really need to go. He'd been establishing his independence. Following Oran into the latrine, he released the little water he'd accumulated. There were washbasins on a trestle table, bars of white soap, and pitchers of water. On a fresh bar, the name "IVORY" was stamped. From Farside then, probably brought from Ferny Cove.

When Oran returned him to the entrance, the woman still waited. "I don't know your name," he said.

"I am Lariin," she answered.

"Lariin. Right. I'm ready."

He went inside with her, feeling primed but at ease, and found himself in a corridor walled with golden yellow cloth. Its ceiling was much lower than the roof, to help keep the pavilion from overheating in the sun, he supposed. At the corridor's end he found the Dynast in what he decided was a reception room, rather than her living quarters. Its furnishings seemed too fine for even such a tent as this: a handsome table, waxed and burnished, with inlaid squares of some pale wood, paler than white oak, alternating with what he recognized as black walnut: a mosaic of old ivory and rich dark brown. There were matched, upholstered chairs as well, and a small buffet. The room was open to the west, the direction of the breeze.

Three women got to their feet as he entered. Liiset. And Idri; that was a surprise. And what could only be the Dynast herself, looking physically no older than the others, though there could be no doubt she was. And somehow it seemed to him he had little to fear from her.

Her gaze was inscrutable, her aura calm. "So you are Curtis Macurdy," she said.

"I am. And you're Sarkia. And that ugly bitch on your right is Idri." He turned his eyes to Varia's kidnapper. "If I'd known back in Evansville what kind of vicious sow you are, I'd have wrung your humping neck and stuffed you down a privy."

His gaze shifted to Sarkia. "Just so we understand each other."

Idri flushed, her aura flaring dark with anger. Sarkia was coolly amused. "It seems I needn't worry that you won't speak your mind; Varia did an outstanding job of selecting her second husband. Had I been consulted, I'd have left her on Farside, with the understanding that she provide us with litters by you. There'd have been no difficulty in leaving one of each to gladden your personal lives there.

"But I can hardly condemn Idri, for if she hadn't stolen Varia from you, I'd never have had this opportunity. You are even more—far more attractive to me as a leader and general than as the sire of children. Although my Sisters would be more than happy to provide you with company, if you'd like. I'm sure you'd find any of them quite accomplished in bed. And Liiset is much like Varia; she could warm your nights nicely until you get your wife back." The Dynast eyed him appraisingly. "No? Perhaps Idri then. You could consider it revenge of a sort, and she's notoriously good in bed."

Sarkia's face and voice were pleasant and matter-of-fact. Even her aura showed no particular emotion. But beneath it all she was cold. *She could pet a kitten*, he told himself, *then throw it in with the hounds to see if they'd kill it*.

"That's not the kind of vengeance I had in mind," he answered, then turned the conversation to business. "Liiset told me you want an alliance. Between you and Gurtho and the rebels, with me as your general. The fact that I'm here now tells you I'm interested. But I owe my rebels more than just fighting. What they want is their independence, and I won't accept less for them."

"What would your Kullvordi think of playing a special role in the kingdom of Tekalos, with you as its king? And Varia your queen. I have no doubt you can produce worthy heirs, and your hillsmen could provide your royal guard; indeed the core of your army."

Macurdy's eyes were steady. He didn't trust the Dynast yet, even on a provisional level. "You sketch a nice picture," he said. "Where would the Sisterhood fit in it?"

"We want the opportunity to produce and nurture a new race, free of the empire's threat. For that, we need all the realms from the Green River Valley to the Big River united in an alliance. And for any such alliance to persist and be truly strong, the kings must be strong and able, ruling without constant serious injustices, and the rebellions, and wars between kingdoms, that grow out of those injustices."

"And Gurtho?"

"Gurtho has helped bring us you. It seems that was his function. His talents are few and his weaknesses a liability. Once we have an alliance, we will dispose of him."

Macurdy nodded. *She's cold as ice,* he thought. What he said next took them both by surprise. "You mentioned vengeance and Idri. Have her killed now, in front of me, and we'll talk alliance."

Sarkia's face froze, shocked ugly. "I will not!" she hissed. "There are limits!"

Ah! Even to your self-control. "Limits? Good! That's what I needed to know. All right, let's look at the military and political possibilities. If the prospects seem reasonable, we can discuss how to go about things."

They met for three days. Idri was always present, her hatred of Macurdy suppressed and controlled but always there, showing in her aura. Perhaps, he thought, Sarkia didn't trust her to be with Gurtho in her present frame of mind.

Each evening Macurdy returned to the inn and his escort, and dictated a summary message for Wollerda. One of his guards wrote it; Macurdy could read Yuultal, laboriously, but its spellings were phonetically somewhat obsolete, and his own quite nonstandard.

In the morning, Blue Wing carried it to Wollerda. And each evening, Blue Wing brought Wollerda's answer. Wollerda was leery of the Sisterhood, but as long as the discussions were exploratory and no commitments were made . . . What he'd like was an agreement that removed Gurtho without more killing, or a minimum of it, but invading the empire he considered out of the question. It was altogether too strong for that.

On the other hand, Wollerda considered a defensive alliance among the kingdoms very desirable. And while negotiations were in progress, the rebel armies were growing, arming, and training.

31

Dialog

There was a quicker route between the two rebel bases than the long rugged way through forested hills. And with their improved military position, and the abeyance of hostilities, the commanders now took that route from opposite ends, to meet at a tiny, out-of-the-way flatlander village. At what passed for an inn, but was more of a local tap house with a single room for occasional travelers. Macurdy hired it, and he and Wollerda sat across a table from each other, Wollerda's aide at one end taking notes, and a pitcher of sassafras tea at the other. Two companies of fighting men lounged outside, and guards were stationed at the door.

"Invade the empire!?" Wollerda asked. "She's crazy. It's larger than all the southern kingdoms combined, has a lot more people, and it's far better organized. Each of its dukedoms—there's probably fifteen or twenty—has an army maybe as large as Gurtho's; better trained anyway. Then the emperor has the Throne Army, probably five times as large, and there are garrisons in the Marches."

He peered intently at Macurdy. "And you said?"

"I agreed to talk to you about it. What I want to do now is look at all the factors. What about the Marches? The empire conquered them and holds them down, and I suppose it taxes them. What if they revolt when we march in?"

"Unlikely."

"Why unlikely?"

"I suppose Sarkia thinks they will."

Macurdy nodded.

"Sarkia believes what she wants to. I've only been in two of the March kingdoms, but that's two more than she has, I have no doubt. And they were conquered, true enough, but oppressed? Under imperial hegemony, they've grown richer, their conditions of life are improved, they rule themselves better, and they no longer fight each other. There are probably resentments, maybe some with good cause, but the people I did business with— merchants and prosperous farmers—like things the way they are. I expect the rest don't feel too differently.

Macurdy pursed his lips. "What armies do they have?"

"The March kingdoms? Militias. Of volunteers. My impression is, they don't take it seriously. They know, even if Sarkia doesn't, that the empire will protect them. So they don't consider themselves threatened."

"What about the ylvin garrisons?"

"What I've read is, one fort in each March kingdom, with a cavalry cohort stationed there."

"And how ready do you suppose the empire is for war?"

"Hmm. Probably not very. But it could get ready fast enough, if it felt threatened."

Wollerda peered intently at Macurdy. "You've said this is desirable because it would unite the southern lands. And it is desirable, even if it's temporary, because once it's been done, it'll be easier to do again. So I'm in favor of union in the form of alliance, if the terms are right. It can discourage the empire from another attack, perhaps more ambitious than the last one. But to actually invade it?" He shook his head.

Macurdy sipped tea. "Suppose we didn't reach the empire itself." Taking a thick rectangle of folded linen from his tunic, he spread it on the table between them, a map of the empire and the Marches, that Kithro had gotten him. "Suppose we only got to here," he said pointing.

Wollerda examined it critically. There were two tiers of kingdoms in the Marches. The southernmost were the so-called Outer Marches, its kingdoms bordering the Big River. North of them were the Inner Marches, bordering on the empire. Macurdy rested a large fingertip on the northern tier. "If we only got that far before our momentum was blunted, it would still cause a hell of an uproar."

Wollerda looked at him thoughtfully. Macurdy went on. "If, with Sarkia's help, we brought in all the kingdoms along the Green River between the Eastern Mountains and the Muddy, and all those between the Big River and the Middle Mountains . . ."

Wollerda shook his head. "Not enough. The emperor could bring a bigger army against us. Bigger and better."

"How quickly? Would the Throne Army be bigger than ours? Or would he have to wait until the ducal armies arrived? And how long would that take?"

Wollerda shook his head disapprovingly. Macurdy continued. "They'll hear about us getting ready, but how seriously will they take us? According to Sarkia, the kingdoms south of the Big River have never united to do anything."

His gaze was intent now. "Imagine the dukes meeting with the emperor in Duinarog." He pointed at the ylvin capital, on the river between the Middle and Imperial Seas. "Might it run about like this? 'Mr. Emperor, the Marches have their militias. Let them fight the southerners; it's their land and their responsibility. And if they can't manage, you've got enough soldiers yourself; that's what we pay taxes for. Besides, those Rude Landers will never get across the Big River. They'll be fighting each other before that.' " Macurdy looked quizzically at Wollerda. "Like you said, it's a big empire, and most of those dukes would have a long way to march, or ride. Hauling weeks of supplies with them, supplies they probably don't keep on hand in the first place. Supplies it would take awhile to round up. And think of the expense!

"When—if—we actually cross the river, then they might start taking us seriously. But meanwhile we ought to go through those militias like corn through a goose." *Or will we? Suppose they turn out to be like the Ozian militias!* "The imperial garrisons might give us a bad time, but they're isolated cohorts, one here and one there. The emperor would probably get the Throne Army moving pretty quickly, but even they'd have a long way to come, unless he'd already moved them south."

His finger moved across the Inner Marches. "We ought to get this far, anyway," he added, pointing to a town labelled Ternass, on the main route between the Big River and Duinarog.

North of Ternass was a zone well marked with symbols for marshes or swamps. A major road was shown crossing it, but God knew what it was like. "Far enough to shake things up in the empire, not to mention the Marches. Far enough they might negotiate in good faith to get rid of us, but not far enough to get caught with those swamps at our back."

Wollerda sat with his chin in one hand, lips pursed. "Possibly. Or the dukes might be right. It's hard to imagine getting allied forces to operate as an army."

"In that case," Macurdy answered, "we wouldn't invade." He changed tack then. "How solid is the empire? Sarkia says the dukes fight each other sometimes."

"They have in the past. But I don't think there's been any fighting between dukes during the fifteen years of Paedhrig's rule. Or before it for quite a while."

"But some pretty serious political fighting?"

"I don't really know. Historically there've been rivalries, bickering, political factions, and grudges between dukedoms. And the factions have internal squabbles. But I have no doubt at all they'd unite solidly against invasion.

"Furthermore, it could result in a counter-invasion that could ruin us here: the Quaie Incursion five-fold. It might even result in conquest, with the Marches expanded south to the Middle Mountains."

Macurdy frowned thoughtfully. "Suppose we say our strike northward is a punishment for—what did you call it?—the Quaie Incursion. Especially for Ferny Cove. That seems to be something the ylver have strong disagreements about. It got Quaie fired from the army and kicked off the Imperial Council."

Wollerda stared. "How do you know? Is that something Sarkia told you?"

Macurdy shook his head. "I made a trip, awhile back. To the headwaters of the Tuliptree River, to check out a story the Dynast's ambassadrix told me, and another one told me by a tomttu she had with her. I couldn't be sure what was lies and what was truth, so I went to look. That's where I found out about Quaie, whom I'd never heard of before. And what happened to him for what he did."

Wollerda's frown was back. "How could you learn things like that on the headwaters of the Tuliptree?"

Again Macurdy sat briefly silent. "I guess I'd better start from the beginning," he said, then told Wollerda what the tomttu had said about Varia's capture, and what Liiset claimed had happened afterward. And about his trip to the Tuliptree and what had happened there, to him and to the tracker who'd been bringing Varia back to the Sisterhood. And finally what he'd heard the ylvin commander, Kincaid, say.

"And there's no way I could have imagined it. I didn't know enough."

Wollerda wasn't just frowning now. He frowned thoughtfully. "Cyncaidh. There is a Cyncaidh, an important noble. That's all I know about him. But it's hard to imagine an ylvin aristocrat in buckskins, scouting through the Granite Range."

He paused. "And you want this invasion just to get your wife back, right? Have you thought of the blood it'll cost?"

Macurdy nodded soberly. "But if there weren't any Varia, and never had been—if I'd been born in these hills and was in this rebellion for only the reasons you are—it would still look like something to think about seriously. Knowing what I know now. It's all of a piece with an alliance that could make the southern lands stronger. And richer.

"Look at it like this. If you were king of Tekalos . . ."

"It's you the Sisterhood wants as king," Wollerda countered.

"I'd rather you have the job than me, and I don't think it makes any real difference to Sarkia. It was just part of her pitch to win me over. She doesn't read me—understand me— as well as she thinks; probably there are things she refuses to look at, possibilities she can't admit to herself. And if you were king of Tekalos, the country would be a whole lot better off, because you're a lot smarter than Gurtho, and you're not greedy, and you look at people a lot differently than he does.

"Whatever may be wrong with Sarkia, she wants the southern lands strong and prosperous, so she can have peace to breed up the Sisterhood the way she wants. Which might not be all that bad. She's marrying the kings to Sisters, to strengthen the alliance and ensure the royal successions."

Wollerda studied Macurdy. *He's more than a fighting man*

and magician, he told himself, *and more than shrewd. He's deeper than I imagined. And a child of fate, by the look of it. And the Dynast just might have some good intentions after all.*

"But the only way to form an alliance," Macurdy was saying, "is to give it a reason that seems real and strong—compelling—to a bunch of kings and chiefs that don't usually look much beyond their own borders and the next tax collection. An invasion across the Big River might be what it takes. An invasion to teach the empire never to attack southward again. And I suppose we'll have to allow looting. That might even get the tribes to join us. If we could get Oz to send a cohort or two . . .

"We could set it up so assigned companies do the looting. One or two trains of plunder wagons from each kingdom and tribe under a central command, so they don't get into butchering, raping, and burning. We need to avoid the kind of hatreds that Quaie cooked up.

"And because we'll make a big point, with our own people and those north of the river, that this is all to punish the ylver for the Quaie Incursion and the Rape at Ferny Cove. Put the blame on Quaie. Then if someone in the empire beats the drum for invading south again, those against it can point to the grief the Quaie Incursion brought them."

Wollerda shook his head, not in refusal but in the first stage of capitulation. "You've got it all figured out, haven't you?"

Macurdy shook his head. "I didn't 'figure it out,' exactly. That's just how it seems to me."

"You'll need to get every kingdom and tribe included in the alliance," Wollerda said. "Especially those between the Middle Mountains and the Big River, and they tend to be friendly to the March kingdoms. Enough to trade with them."

Macurdy nodded. "Getting their support will be the Dynast's job. She has embassies in every royal court except in Kormehr. And even if she can't talk enough of them into an invasion, she can probably tie them into a defense alliance."

"A defense alliance won't get your wife back."

"True. But it'll be worthwhile for the kingdoms and tribes. And maybe—maybe I could be the ambassador from the

Alliance to the emperor, and get her back that way. Maybe the emperor would make Kincaid let her go."

Wollerda stared. "Macurdy, you're . . ." He groped. "You're a man of faith. All right. I'll go along with further negotiations and see what you come up with. It scares me—makes my hair stand up—but it's a powerful opportunity, and we didn't get this far by being timid.

"Besides, remarkable things happen around you. You even grew new teeth! The Great God himself seems to be with you."

They sent a man down for ale, the first Macurdy had ever had, just a swallow, making a face at the taste. Wollerda agreed to an alliance, Macurdy negotiating for both of them. But Wollerda would need to approve. Macurdy would sign as military co-commander, while Wollerda would sign as co-commander and chief of the Kullvordi.

They shook hands on it, then Wollerda stepped back with a grin, his first of the day. "And now, Macurdy, I've got a gift for you."

Macurdy frowned. "I hadn't realized. I didn't bring one for you."

Wollerda laughed. "I knew you'd say that; you don't know everything about us yet. We have a custom that one doesn't reciprocate a gift; it's an insult to the giver. If you want to give something in return, it'll need to be after a decent interval. A few months, at least." He beckoned. "Come with me." Together they left the inn and walked to the paddock, where Wollerda climbed over the fence and started toward a tall powerful gelding with almost a stallion's neck. It watched him approach without trying to avoid him, though it tossed its head as if to run, or maybe turn and kick. Wollerda spoke as he approached it, took the halter with a hand and led the animal to the fence, where Macurdy watched.

"What do you think of him?"

Macurdy was ill at ease, suspecting but not entirely sure. "A fine horse. Spirited. Big and strong, good hocks to hold up in the hills—and looks like he could run. And big-barreled; lots of endurance."

"He's a stag, actually," Wollerda said. "I didn't cut him till he was two and a half. I was going to ride him as a stallion, to raise my standing with my neighbors, but he was too unruly."

Looking at Macurdy, the animal jerked its head, but Wollerda held him in, speaking soothingly. "He's fine now, broken with an easy hand by a Kormehri magician. From near Ferny Cove, actually, before bad things happened there. Anyway he's yours. If you're ever chased, he won't collapse under you." Wollerda chuckled. "Actually he's more a gift to the horse you've been riding; the poor beast's getting swaybacked carrying you."

Macurdy climbed easily over the paddock fence, and stood for a moment feeling mentally for the horse's mind. *Okay, old timer,* he thought to it, *you and I are partners from now on.* He reached out, took the halter with his right hand and stroked the long silky nose with his left. The animal's eyes neither rolled nor threatened.

"Does he have a name?"

"Whatever you want to call him. I call him Champion."

"I had an uncle on Farside two stones heavier than I am, and he had a saddle horse that carried him with no trouble at all. Not as nice an animal as this, but big and powerful. Had a strain of Belgian in him—back home that's the heaviest draft breed—but a gait smooth as silk. And a really good disposition; my brother and I used to lead him to the fence and climb onto him from it, and he never minded a bit. Carried us wherever we wanted, together or separately. Uncle Will named him Hog. In our language, of course. Said he was strong as one." Macurdy cocked an eyebrow. "I told Frank that when I grew up, I'd have a horse like Hog, but until now I never did. You wouldn't feel insulted if I named him that, would you?"

Wollerda laughed again. "I won't. I don't know about him."

Macurdy looked the horse in the eye. "How about it? All right if I call you Hog?"

The animal snorted.

"He's telling you it's the kind of name a flatland farmer might give him," Wollerda said, "but it's all right with him as long as you treat him well."

Macurdy nodded. "I grew up a farmer, and I'll always have shit on my boots. So. Hog it is." He let go the halter and slapped the horse on the shoulder. It turned and trotted across the paddock to a rack of hay, then looked back at the two men.

"He's telling us something about relative importances," Wollerda said.

"Is it all right to thank you?" Macurdy asked. He felt closer to Wollerda than he'd ever expected to, and it was less the fact of the gift than what he'd learned about him in the giving: the man's ease and humor.

"Of course," Wollerda said. "It's the proper thing to do."

"Well then." Macurdy reached out, and gripping Wollerda's hand, shook it heartily. "Thanks a lot. I've got a feeling that Hog and I are going to get along really well."

They climbed back over the paddock fence, Macurdy first, to round up their men. As Wollerda watched him go, he flexed his right hand, then felt it tentatively with his left, and wondered if Macurdy had any idea how strong he was.

When they were ready to leave, Macurdy asked another question. "Kithro told me the Kullvordi had shamans in the old days. Is that right?"

"Yes, they had shamans. Why do you ask?"

"After I got back from the Tuliptree, my guide told folks what happened there—what he knew of it. And of course, they already knew I start fires with magic, and that my teeth are growing back. Now they talk about me as a shaman/warrior."

"I'm not surprised. What are you getting at?"

"You don't happen to have a shaman in your ancestry, do you?"

The question introverted Wollerda for a moment. "My great grandfather was the last chief of the eastern Kullvordi," he answered, "and his mother was the daughter of the greatest shaman they'd ever had. But the blood was lost by the time I came along, or thinned beyond all virtue." He cocked an eyebrow. "Why do you ask?"

Macurdy shrugged. "Till Varia worked with me," he said, "I didn't know I had the talent. And even a little helps."

Wollerda grunted. "You'll have to be shaman enough for both of us," he said. "I've never shown the slightest talent."

Then grinning, he put out his hand. They shook and parted,

Wollerda thinking he should say something to Macurdy about his handshakes. The man would injure someone, someday.

On his ride back to camp, the afternoon felt more like mid-October than early September, lacking only haze and the smell of autumn leaves. As he rode, Macurdy mulled over things he hadn't adequately considered before. Most particularly Sarkia's policy of marrying kings to Sisters. With any luck at all, Wollerda would replace Gurtho, and Wollerda was eligible, a widower.

Varia had said it was difficult to spell most people against their will, if they suspected what you were up to. It was also difficult, she'd said, to get someone to do something strongly against their principles, even when they'd been spelled.

It seemed to him that Pavo Wollerda was not someone who'd be spelled easily, but if he married a Sister, could Sarkia manipulate him through her?

Varia had said that the person with significant talent was hard to spell without willing cooperation; if their talent had been trained, it was pretty much impossible. He'd asked her then why she'd been able to spell him, that first night. Her reply was, she hadn't. His will, his self determination, had been unimpaired. She'd gone to him leaving her body behind, and even though he'd been untrained, his talent had helped him see her spirit, or actually the image it projected. And because he knew her so well, instead of being frightened, and rejecting her, he'd accepted. Later, when she'd spelled him to help his training—spells not so different from hypnosis—she'd had his cooperation.

So. Say Wollerda married Liiset. Beautiful intelligent Liiset, who could no doubt turn on the sex appeal. Turn it on and back it up. How much could she influence Wollerda to do things against his own interest, and that of the Kullvordi or Tekalos?

A man was always being influenced by people around him: wife, friends—enemies as far as that was concerned. The real question was, if Wollerda married Liiset or some other Sister, would she be able to spell him? Wollerda's aura said he had significant talent, but it was untrained. And like himself at first, resisted it.

He decided that when he got back to his tent, he'd take a quill, inkwell, and paper, and reconstruct, as best as he could, what Varia and Arbel had done to free and train his talent. Maybe he could free up Wollerda's, maybe even to the point of seeing auras clearly and consciously.

32

Coronation

Once she had a covert agreement with them, Macurdy and Wollerda were astonished at how quickly Sarkia moved—quickly if not subtly.

But if her moves were quick, they'd been well prepared. Gurtho assumed he had a representative at the negotiations—Queen Idri. He'd already signed a secret alliance with the Sisterhood, and had appointed her his representative at what he considered three-cornered negotiations between himself, the Sisterhood, and the rebels. His understanding was that the Sisterhood would use his authority, and their influence and presumed sorceries, to get an agreement that would end the rebellion. An agreement giving the Kullvordi virtual autonomy.

Then, when when the time came to name and dedicate the triplets Idri was pregnant with, he'd proclaim and supply a day and night of festivities throughout Tekalos. He already had the brewing underway. Idri was to provide a poison with which to decimate the Kullvordi during the feasting, a delayed action poison undetectable in ale. The night of death would be followed by quickly hunting down any rebel officers surviving.

Meanwhile, as negotiations proceeded, he found an opportunity to have his existing sons and daughter meet with an unfortunate boating accident in which all three died, along with their mother. Whom Gurtho had divorced and set aside but not allowed to leave, because she was also his boughten property, his slave. This quadruple murder, he considered, removed all complications to the succession.

On the day after the cremation of his children and ex-wife, however, Gurtho was found dead, poisoned. And because his queen-widow was away negotiating, there'd be problems in blaming her. She hurried home the next day, took the throne as regent, and turned management over to the Chief Minister, whom she'd earlier seduced. Then, before returning to the negotiations, she had Gurtho's valet poisoned. With his body was what seemed to be a suicide letter, in which he confessed to having poisoned his master out of love for the drowned ex-queen.

The Council had intended to appoint their own regent. Their legal basis was weak, but that wasn't why they held back. They'd gotten to the palace before Idri, only to find her guard and Tiger companies in command. They then called on the commander of the royal cohort to take action, but he declined to act. And not simply out of caution; the queen had already seduced him thoroughly.

The Council had little choice but to accept her regency. Perhaps things would turn out all right.

The formal agreement with the rebels, signed by Idri as Queen Regent of Tekalos, and by Generals Wollerda and Macurdy for the eastern and western Kullvordi, had five main parts: (1) The hostilities were declared over. (2) The Kullvordi were granted tribal autonomy within the kingdom of Tekalos— with Pavo Wollerda as King. (3) Four Estates were now recognized, with their rights and property guaranteed. They were: the nobility; the yeomanry; the merchants and artisans; and the free laborers. (4) The Royal Council, known now as the Royal Assembly, was enlarged to include delegates from the new Estates. And (5), formulas and limits were established for taxation, with the exception of special war taxes.

The nobility wasn't thrilled with it, nor were the merchants, as previously theirs had been the only Estates with legal standing. But on the other hand, the rebellion and domestic uprisings were ended, and the future offered possible prosperity.

At the signing ceremony, in the Great Square of Teklapori, the honor guard consisted of a company of the royal cohort, and one from Wollerda's 1st Cohort, while in the saddle nearby sat a company of the Kullvordi 2nd Light Cavalry, known previously as Macurdy's Rebels. The Queen Regent's guard and Tiger companies were discreetly absent.

Macurdy wore well-fitting hillsmen's clothes of the best quality wadmal. They were much the same as flatland peasants wore, with the addition of leather sewn on the seat and the inside of thighs and knees to protect the breeches from wear while riding. Wore them as the openly stated symbol of the victory of both peoples.

That same afternoon, in a more elaborate and ornate ceremony, Queen Idri gracefully placed the crown of Tekalos on the head of Pavo Wollerda, who then spoke about a prosperous future. Afterward the newly enfranchised yeomen, artisans, and free laborers paraded cheering through the streets.

That evening the people drank the new king's beer, ate his beef and corn, and danced and caroused through the night. This time cheering the king himself, though no doubt some felt skeptical. The last Macurdy saw of Melody and Jeremid, about midnight, they were headed together for the palace where each had a room. He had no doubt they'd share one of them, and allowed himself to wish wistfully that it was he who was hurrying off with her. He ended up drinking whiskey, and caught himself very nearly going to bed with a merchant's pretty and ambitious daughter.

He awoke next morning with his first hangover, mild but unpleasant, which along with his near seduction, he considered a lesson on drinking.

The next day, Sarkia left for the Cloister with her Tigers and guardsmen, taking Idri with her. And a copy of a previously drafted treaty of alliance that had been signed by King Pavo that morning as his first official act. Liiset stayed at Teklapori as Sarkia's ambassadrix. Macurdy had no doubt she'd been ordered to seduce Wollerda and become his bride, and said as much to the new king. Who grinned as if that was all right with him.

Macurdy was scheduled to leave Teklapori on a special mission for the Alliance, but earlier he'd had several evenings to work on activating his friend's latent psionic talent. The question, he told himself, was what, if anything, he'd accomplished.

❖   ❖   ❖

Meanwhile, he, Wollerda and Liiset had sat down together one evening and designed new uniforms for the army. It would take time of course, to provide them. Officers would have theirs first, from the top down, and the uniforms of noncoms and men were already relatively simple and practical. The officers' looked rather like that of the commander of Sarkia's guard company, with the addition of the "Teklan Bear" on shoulder patches, the bear being the symbol of Teklan royalty and the kingdom. Also, for generals, the new dress uniform included a silver-plated cuirass and helmet, decorated and polished.

A week after Wollerda's crowning, a company of the 2nd Light Cavalry, wearing new uniforms, rode off westward down the Valley Highway, with General Macurdy and Majors Jeremid and Melody. Macurdy bore credentials from both Wollerda and the Dynast, as their joint envoy to the courts of Miskmehr and Kormehr, and to the Chief of Oz, authorizing him to negotiate an agreement of alliance with each of them.

It was the first mission in what would be the busiest fall, winter, and spring of Macurdy's life.

33

An Introspective Morning at the Zoo

The Emperor's Animal Park had a foot of wet granular snow on the ground, but the morning was calm and sunny, and before noon already somewhat above freezing. A trickle of citizens strolled through the gate, many of them couples with one or more children hopping ahead.

One couple entered the park hand in hand. The woman was more warmly dressed than most, to humor her husband; with her talent, she'd have been comfortable with no coat at all. But she was pregnant, and he'd never been a father before.

Besides, she'd reasoned, *it's best not to draw attention.* Her husband had serious enemies, and among all of Duinarog's nearly sixty thousand people, there'd hardly be a hundred redheads other than herself. So she wore a fur cap well down over her ears.

There was no map on display, nor any directional signs. One simply walked the path until the large loop was completed; then you'd seen it all. But Cyncaidh had been there before, and knew what he wanted to show her first, so he turned left; that would take them first past animals of other regions. Briefly they stood watching the small herd of pronghorn, Cyncaidh telling her briefly about them, for he'd read the Animal Park booklet years earlier, and as a boy, other books on animals, and had excellent recall. Varia found the pronghorns uninteresting. It seemed to her that running, they'd be beautiful, but here they simply stood in the sun chewing their cuds, their auras reflecting placid contentment.

Beyond the pronghorns were wapiti. The bulls had shed their antlers, but a cast-off pair had been mounted on a post, their spread approaching five feet. She thought she'd like to see wapiti in the wild someday, but didn't expect to. Next they came to the plains bison, with Cyncaidh describing the hunting tactics of the nomads. They sounded to Varia rather like descriptions she'd read of the Plains Indians on Farside. How marvelous it would be, she thought, to ride with them.

Next were the much larger long-horned bison. This was an animal of the near-arctic, with its broad mosaic of tundra, stunted forest, and bogs. These animals truly impressed her. One old bull had horns as wide as a man's outspread arms, and at the hump it stood as tall as Raien. She guessed its weight at two tons—more than Will's team of big Belgians, the gelding and mare combined. According to Raien, these animals didn't form great herds, but wandered in bands of two or three dozen, grazing on grasses and sedges, browsing the low shrubs. She wondered how they'd been brought here. As calves, she decided.

She also wondered what could possibly prey on them—and then found out, for they came next to the lions. She'd seen lions before, the African *Panthera leo*, when she and Will visited the zoo in Indianapolis. And clearly these *were* lions, though their winter fur—white tinged faintly with pink—was thicker than the African, and the males wore ruffs instead of manes. She hadn't imagined lions existing on this continent. And *what* lions!, the males much larger than the African. The Cloister school hadn't mentioned lions of any sort, while on Farside, the long-extinct American lion, *Panthera atrox*, she'd never heard of.

Probably the Cloister's teachers hadn't known of lions, she told herself. But surely someone there had known of Duinarog, and the Northern, Middle, and Imperial Seas, yet they hadn't been mentioned either. At the Cloister, the world virtually ended at the Big River. The Marches, and the Western and Eastern Empires which lay north of them, were spoken of only in political terms. It occurred to her that Sarkia didn't want her people to know wonder or feel curiosity, and certainly not to be honestly informed. Everything was seen in terms of her own explanations, ambitions, and hatreds.

The dire wolves were next, conspicuously larger than timber wolves, and more strongly built. They hunted the plains bison, Raien told her. After the dire wolves they saw tundra caribou, and shaggy musk oxen no larger than ponies. Next were animals from nearer climes. Moose: tall, gangling, and nearly black. She'd seen them wild near Aaerodh Manor; they'd looked better there. In the next enclosure were timber wolves, looking lazy and bored, which was hardly surprising. She liked them better than she had the dire wolves; they seemed less—less dire.

And ah! Northern jaguars, particularly beautiful in their winter coats. Physically they were much less impressive than the lions—two hundred pounds she guessed, three at most—but regal, even here in the zoo. It was partly their auras. She smiled at Raien, whom she knew had a special love for these cats. And wished they were still at Aaerodh Manor, where she would have learned to run on skis, and they'd have gone stalking together. How fulfilling it would be to see these wonderful ice-blue creatures crossing a frozen lake, or padding along some moose trail in a cedar swamp. Now the odds seemed poor that she ever would. They planned to go back for a few weeks each summer, circumstances permitting, but she didn't expect to live there year-round, ever. For being the Emperor's Chief Counselor meant he'd probably be chosen Emperor when Paedrigh declined.

Raien didn't covet the throne for itself, but for what he could do as Emperor: Continue and perhaps even complete the reforms and other projects he and Paedrigh had plotted and planned, back when Paedrigh had been Chief Counselor, and Raien his military adviser. Notably the end of ducal armies large enough to threaten the imperial peace; the end of slavery; and the beginnings of peace with the rest of the continent.

All to be accomplished in the face of factionalized and discordant politics, as reflected in the Imperial Council.

Braighn IV had reformed the slave laws, and Paedrigh had modified them further, but slaves were still subject to abuses, particularly the girls and women. Abuses that degraded the abusers as well, Raien had told her—nobles and gentry who took advantage of their position, and justified it by insisting that slaves had no souls.

There was a faction, an important political party, based on the concept that the ylver had a natural right to rule and dominate "humans," whom they looked at as an only quasi-sapient species. The same party upheld fiercely the rights of slaveholders, though many slaves were descended from ylvin prisoners of ducal wars long past. Almost always they were conspicuously only part ylvin. It had become awkward to justify ylvin slaves, thus they'd been deliberately crossbred with human slaves. The more they looked like ordinary humans, the easier it was to rationalize their slavery.

Raien had pointed out what the books she'd read had slighted—that there were few if any ylver without some non-ylvin ancestry. To speak of half-ylver was a simplification. A half-ylf was someone who had enough human ancestry—especially recent human ancestry—that it showed plainly. The race of ylver, he said, was a blend, with a preponderance of ylvin ancestry.

Legend had it there'd been mixing even before the ylver came here across the Eastern Ocean. For example, red hair among ylver was supposed to be a sign of ancient mixing with the mythical *Voitusotar*, who were said to live in a land of fog and ice and sorcery. Mothers and nurses still sometimes told children the Voitusotar would get them if they weren't good, though such threats were frowned on these days. Interestingly, red hair tended generally to be admired, perhaps because the Voitusotar had been feared. Though that admiration didn't extend to those of the Sisterhood.

While Varia had let her mind wander, they'd passed the lesser cats—bobcat and lynx—the foxes, and the gracefully tireless mustelines. Raien, aware of her preoccupation, had discontinued his monologues on wildlife. Finally the loop took them past paddocks with farm animals, which after twenty years of farm life, hardly excited Varia. At the end they each put a gold piece in the donations box, and she squeezed her husband's hand affectionately. He was more than just an idealist with intelligence, talent, will and political power. He was a good and decent person.

And he'd be an excellent father, as he was a husband and lover.

PART 5
War

34

Invasion

There was still enough twilight that Melody could see the camps spread around her, the armies of five kingdoms and one tribe, their cookfires dying, their tents low shadowed humps. No doubt some of their men were already asleep.

They'd get little enough of it this night.

Late Five-Month had advantages and disadvantages for invasion. Grazing was good, and they had the whole summer ahead of them, if need be. On the other hand, the season was subject to thunderstorms, and the nights were short. And tonight they had much to do between nightfall and dawn, especially between nightfall and moonrise.

She recognized the Indrossan command tent by the torches lashed to spears thrust in the ground beside its entrance. And as she approached, by its being guarded. She dismounted in front of it, handed the reins to her orderly, and loud and clear, identified herself to the guards as Marshal Macurdy's aide, then told them to take her to their commander.

And waited. Despite her position, and her bright new colonel's insignia, they stared back insolently, showing no sign of obeying. So she drew her saber, and before either man realized what she had in mind, held its point to the belly of the nearest.

"You son of a bitch! Did you hear what I said? How do you want it? Quick and bloody, here and now? Or at a rope's end tomorrow, pulled up to strangle from a branch after a drumhead court?"

The man backed away into the entrance, and she followed, keeping her blade at his belly while her aide, a Kullvordi, followed with his own saber, covering her back. When she was inside, she shouted the Indrossan general's name. "Eldersov! I have orders for you from Marshal Macurdy!"

It wasn't entirely dark inside. She could see a short corridor through the tent, with rooms on each side set off by curtains. Lamplight filtered through two of them, and a hand brushed one aside. "General!" the guard squawked. "She drew her sword on me and forced her way in!"

"You miserable get of a troll and a sow!" Melody snapped, "An insult to me is an insult to the marshal!" Her glance shifted to the general. "I'm Marshal Macurdy's aide. I stopped at the entrance, showed them my baton of authority, and told them I had orders to deliver to you from the marshal. They stood there and sneered."

His grunt dripped scorn. "You're a woman. We don't take orders from women here."

"They're not my orders, they're Marshal Macurdy's. Do you refuse them? When I carry a message from the marshal, I speak with his voice."

"We take no one's orders from a woman."

Abruptly her sword tip moved from the guard to the general. "You just signed your death warrant, general. Unless you reconsider." Even while she said it, she knew he wouldn't, which it seemed to her was just as well. Otherwise he'd be a source of trouble and danger throughout the campaign. "No? Where's your second in command?"

Another curtain had been pushed aside; now a man stepped out. "I'm Colonel Lidsok."

"Colonel, you are now in command of the Indrossan Army. General Eldersov is under arrest. I'm taking him to the marshal's headquarters for trial."

With his curtain open, enough light shone into the corridor that the colonel could see the woman's teeth. Lidsok hesitated, unsure. Her wrist twitched and the sword tip bit, not deeply, slicing Eldersov's skin. "Sergeant at arms!" he shrieked, "arrest these intruders!"

Shit! she thought, and thrust hard with her sword, her wrist half turning. *What lousy timing.* For just a moment, Eldersov stared down at his belly while his life's blood poured from his severed aorta into his abdominal cavity. Then his knees buckled, and he pitched forward dead, Melody stepping aside. While she'd talked, another man had emerged from a room toward the rear, saber in fist. The sergeant at arms, she decided, and ignored him. "Colonel," she said, "do you reject Marshal Macurdy's orders?"

Again Lidsok hesitated, more from not knowing how to address this bloody madwoman than anything else. Ma'am? Sir? He settled on rank. "No, Colonel," he said. "I do not reject them."

"Did you hear Eldersov refuse Marshal Macurdy's orders? And order the marshal's aide arrested?"

"Yes, Colonel. I heard him do both those things."

"Good. I suggest you tell your sergeant at arms to drag the carrion out of here and have it tied across a horse. I'll stop on my way back to the marshal's headquarters, and take it with me. Eldersov's no loss. If a general refuses his commander's orders, particularly in war, God knows how much disaster and death he'll bring on people, his and his allies. Now, let's get down to business. You'll be crossing the river tonight, and I've got orders for four more armies to deliver within the hour."

Lidsok looked at the sergeant at arms. "You heard the marshal's aide. Drag the body out."

Reluctantly the sergeant at arms sheathed his saber, came over to his late general, took him under the arms, and began dragging him toward the tent's back entrance. Melody became aware that the guard she'd followed in still stood there.

She spoke softly, enunciating. "Do you have a post, soldier?" she asked.

He looked to his colonel, then back at Melody. "Uh, yessir."

"Good. Return to it. And keep your mouth shut. I've got a good memory for faces."

The man sidled away, then turned out through the entrance.

"Colonel, I presume you know your loading area and boats?"

"Yes, Colonel. I'm our embarkation commander."

"Good. Have your troops strike and pack their tents as drilled, and leave them. In two hours—two hours—your army will be on the shore, ready to go. Their gear will follow in the morning. Any problem with that? Tell me if there is."

"None whatever, Colonel. And Colonel?"

"Yes?"

"In my view, General Eldersov was not fit to command, and most of his officers feel the same. But he was a crony of the king's; trouble may grow from this."

"Thank you, Colonel. At your first opportunity you'll write to your king, telling him just what happened here. That's an order, in the interest of the alliance. Perhaps his new wife will help him see reason."

With her aide she left the tent then, mounted her horse and rode away in the twilight, leaving two awed guards staring after her.

Terel Kithro—Major Kithro—was the "crossing marshal," responsible for coordinating the embarkation of the various armies. Not the easiest of jobs. Significant mental lapses among key officers could cause chaos.

The moon wouldn't rise till after midnight, and the Milky Way produced light enough to see only vaguely his immediate surroundings. Torches and bonfires had been forbidden along the river, and loud talk, because sound carries well over water, and the enemy was less than a mile away on the other shore.

But each embarkation commander, and each cohort commander was marked by a loose white cap or wrapping over whatever helmet or other headgear he had on. Also, Kithro had a head for details, quick intelligence, and a responsive memory. He walked briskly along the shore, knowing every motley concentration of small boats, and the cohorts and companies assigned to them. He stopped to speak briefly with each senior commander.

Each cohort commander would ride its lead boat, and Kithro reminded each of them that the bridgehead commander, in the first boat of all, might elect to change course while crossing. The cohort flotillas needed to follow each other closely enough that they would see and duplicate any course change, upstream or down. The bridgehead commander, General Jeremid, had already told them this, not an hour earlier, but it was well to repeat it.

There were compelling reasons that only cohort commanders

were being told, and in a murmur. Venders of various sorts had been mixing with the soldiers as the camp filled up, and surely there'd been spies among them. Thus the crossing plan involved one deceit underlying another, and even now, only four men knew all of it, Kithro one of them. As things progressed, of course, the enemy commander would figure it out, more or less, but the later, the better.

Earlier, Kithro had seen a fire lit on a small hill upstream a bit, probably some spy's signal, though what the ylvin commander made of it, there was no telling. A spy was unlikely to have a boat available to take word to him, unless he'd managed to stash one in a shed somewhere. But even so, he'd have to launch it above or below the fleet.

Presumably the ylvin general already knew that three more armies were still enroute a day or two away, marching and riding toward the staging area. And hopefully hadn't expected a crossing until all the southern armies were on hand.

Along the south shore, all but the smallest boats had been commandeered for many miles in both directions, including its southern tributaries. Raiders had snatched barges and ferries even from the north shore, to help transport the cavalry. The miscellaneous smaller boats would carry infantry.

Kithro passed the last of the small boats, and came to the wharves along which the barges now were tied, packed tightly with horses and warriors—the Kormehri cavalry cohort. The Kormehri were the only troops with whom Kithro felt uncomfortable. Their peculiar sense of honor had turned bitter and cruel after the terrible events at Ferny Cove, and their smoldering vengefulness gave off a stink of violence. Meanwhile they waited grimly for the bridgehead commander to lead off.

Jeremid and two companies of Kullvordi cavalry would cross on ferries. As Kithro came up to them, he saw that they too had already loaded, as crowded as the Kormehri. Jeremid would be waiting, no doubt impatiently, for word that things were ready.

Jeremid's ferry was the farthest downstream, tied stern-on to the wharf in a sort of slip, and held against the current by a bow line. On her stern, two raised platforms flanked the ramp, one for the steersman, one for the bosun. Jeremid, on the bosun's platform, watched Kithro clomp up the ramp onto the boat. Its oarsmen half sat on tall seats, oars upright.

He could feel Jeremid's glower, and imagined the nervous stress he felt. "Everything's fine," Kithro murmured. "Pull out whenever you want; just let me off first. Us old crocks are too brittle for fighting."

It had been the right thing to say; he could feel Jeremid lighten, and heard him chuckle. "All right, old crock, get off and we'll get started. I'll see you after the war."

Let us hope, Kithro told himself. When he was on the wharf, the bosun and his helper raised the loading ramp with a windlass, the rattling of its well-greased chain a signal. A moment later he heard Jeremid speak quietly to the bosun, who called softly, "Oars in the water and give her slack." Kithro saw the oars lower, felt the wharf bumped by the stern. The dockers cast off the lines. Quietly the bosun grunted "stroke"; there'd be no drum beat to regulate the rowing tonight. The oarsmen pulled and the boat drew away, sluggishly as if dragging bottom. Meanwhile a courier, who'd been waiting for an hour, nudged his horse's barrel and trotted away toward camp, to inform Macurdy that the crossing had begun.

Now too, Kithro knew, a sleek, carvel-built river cutter would be pulling out, Jesker in command, with five similar cutters following closely. Each held Kullvordi brawlers, men selected for their fighting attitudes, three of them bending strong backs to the oars, while a half dozen more sat with spears and axes. Those in Jesker's boat were to cut loose any craft tied at the landing site, freeing the docks for the troop carriers. The men in the other cutters would defend the axmen and their work, and hold the wharves if need be.

Kithro watched the second ferry pull away from the next dock upstream, and beyond that another, and another. First the ferries, then the barges moved out into the current, disappearing into the night. When the last barge pulled out, the small boats would follow.

But not with all the men; there weren't nearly enough boats for that. The rest stood in ranks in camp. In a few minutes, Macurdy's courier would reach headquarters, and Macurdy

would speed march the remaining troops five miles downstream
to the Inderstown docks—another part of his fabric of deceit.

Jeremid's gaze was not ahead toward the unseen north shore,
but back toward the south shore. When it was only a vaguely
darker darkness, he began to count slowly. At thirty, he spoke
to the bosun. "Turn downstream and hold course near the
middle, until I tell you otherwise. I don't want us seen from
either shore." *Not that some cat-eyed ylf can't see us if he's
watching. But it can make him uncertain; make him stop and
puzzle.*

The bosun had been prepared for a change in course, but
this? "Yes, General," he answered, and ordered the steersman,
who pulled hard on the steering oar, turning them sharply left.
The oarsmen continued to dip and pull their long oars, despite
the break in the bosun's soft and rhythmic chant of "Stroke."
With the current, they were making good speed. Upstream
there was no light yet from the moonrise to come, and
downstream Jeremid still couldn't see the guide torches that
should have been lit at dusk. Had better have been, or this
operation could run into serious trouble. Though if it came
down to it, they'd make it work somehow.

Briefly he turned his attention to what he thought of as the
troop deck. Between the oarsmen's narrow halfdecks, with their
low protective railings, the cargo deck was packed with horses,
each with its rider standing by its head, one hand gripping
the bridle while the other stroked the animal's long nose, or
its neck. The horses were another source of possible trouble
when they docked.

Shortly Jeremid saw a row of torches ahead on the south
shore, and spoke to the bosun. "Steer for the Parnston docks.
The rest of the army is marching to Inderstown; they'll cross
to Parnston from there." The order drew an "ah" of
understanding, and the bosun ordered the steersman, who
pushed on the steering oar, angling them right. By starlight,
Jeremid could make out the next two ferries following, could
even hear a low voice calling an order on the nearest—nearer
than he liked.

The north shore became more distinct, until at about sixty

yards, the bosun gave another order and the steersman turned parallel to it. A minute later, Jeremid made out the Parnston barge docks ahead. Now if Jesker had done his job . . . He had: the barge and ferry docks were clear. The bosun gave more orders, sharply now. The steersman turned them sharply. Oars were raised or backed water, and for long seconds Jeremid forgot to breathe. The oars dipped again, stroked once, then backed strongly; the ferry dragged bottom slightly, and bumped the wharf just enough to throw Jeremid against the bosun's rail. Men jumped onto the wharf with lines, while the portside oarsmen dug blades into the muddy bottom, holding the ferry in place till the lines were secured. Then the bosun ordered the forward ramp lowered.

Several horses had fallen when the ferry bumped the wharf, but they all got up again; there'd been no broken legs. Jeremid was the first to lead his gelding up the ramp, at the same time aware of shouts and swearing from other ferries docking without benefit of longshoremen. He scowled; what he didn't need was wrecks, horses with broken legs, or boats colliding, perhaps dumping their troops into the current.

Ashore, his men stood by their horses. Jesker's advance landing party stood watching; if it had been in a fight, there was no sign of it. They should have a beacon fire ready for lighting. "Jesker!" Jeremid called.

"Here, sir!"

"Light it off!"

"Yes, sir!"

If Macurdy were here, the Ozman thought, *he'd have it in flames with a gesture.* He looked downstream. It was the barges and the crazy Kormehri that he needed to see to now.

Subcolonel Caill Cearnigh was thoroughly at home in the saddle. He'd been a horseman since childhood, and had passed the midpoint of the century he expected to live. As for riding by night—while his night vision wasn't the best, it was a lot better than any of the Rude Landers', he had no doubt. Though the advantage was less with the cupped, newly risen moon throwing its light across the land.

Whoever the southern commander was, he'd shown himself

both clever, and capable of complex staging and coordination. But simple arithmetic made it clear that the numbers the man could have landed so soon, half-trained humans that they were, couldn't begin to hold a landing zone against ylvin cavalry. Certainly not without trenches, ramparts, and troll brambles, and they'd had no time even to begin making them.

Cearnigh had elected to lead his seven companies down the road that paralleled the river. It was quicker and safer, for nearer the river, the land was public pastures. Which had rail fences along jurisdictional lines, and woodchuck and gopher holes a horse could break a leg in.

At their easy trot, his companies should be there in another quarter hour. And then . . . He knew the terrain around Parnston. The southerners had probably taken positions along the wooded west bank of the Sweet Gum River, but it was neither broad nor deep, and the banks were low.

"Colonel!" It was his sergeant major. "Do you hear them?"

Cearnigh shook off his musings, and listening, heard a faint rumble of hoofbeats.

"It sounds as if they've sent out cavalry, Colonel."

Where in hell were they? The sound wasn't from up the road. Ahead and to the left, that was it, cut off from view by a low rounding of land. And not far away.

"They must hear us, Colonel, if we hear them." The sergeant major sounded concerned.

Cearnigh had overlooked that. "Obviously, Sergeant," he said, and called an order to his trumpeter. The instrument's crystal notes brought the column to a halt. Another order turned the westward-bound column into three ranks facing south. The next sent them off the road, rank by rank, again at an easy trot, shields raised, spears at the ready. They'd gone only a short way when the southern cavalry topped the rise about three hundred yards ahead. A single weird cry, a warbling epiglottal shrilling uncanny in the night, triggered a wild clamor, and the invaders spurred their mounts to a canter, charging downhill at the ylver.

For just a moment, Cearnigh felt dismay tinged with panic. Then he barked a command. Trumpets belled, and his troopers spurred their horses, but even on such a mild slope, they had no momentum when the barbarians crashed into them. A smashing blow pierced Cearnigh's shield, wrenched his arm and drove him from the saddle. Somehow he got to his feet without being trampled, aware that the arm was useless, the shoulder dislocated or separated. As he drew his saber, a riderless horse knocked him down. He felt an instant of shock as a forehoof came down on his belly, then a hind hoof crushed his rib cage.

The trumpeter saw his colonel unseated, then the ranks passed through each other, and somehow he was still in his saddle, untouched by any enemy. As a trumpeter, his only weapon was his saber. He lacked even a shield, and as soon as they'd passed through, the enemy wheeled, this time closing with drawn steel. The wild war cry had ceased, replaced by shouts of "FERNY COVE! FERNY COVE!" The air was thick with them, and with impacts, grunts, inarticulate cries, the screams of horses. An enemy singled him out and struck at him. He took the blow on his saber, a blow of more force than he would have imagined, almost paralyzing his arm. Then they'd passed again.

Two things occurred to him at once: The cohort must flee— it was that or be butchered—and no one was in charge. With his left hand he raised his trumpet, and unordered blew retreat, then spurred his horse back toward the road.

But there was no safety in flight. Shouts of "FERNY COVE! FERNY COVE!" pursued him closely. Something—a horse's shoulder—struck his mount from behind, throwing it off stride, and he turned to his left to see the horse that had done it, its rider's face a glimpsed grimace. Then someone on the other side struck his thigh with a saber. He felt and heard his own scream, then the ground slammed him, and he bounced and rolled. For a moment, perhaps a minute, he lay stunned. At least a minute, for when he regained his wits somewhat, the sound of hooves was gone.

And he hadn't been trampled! He reached, felt his bloody thigh. The man who'd struck him had been right handed, had had to swivel in the saddle as he'd passed, and the blow had lacked force. Even so, he couldn't stand, but lay shocked, mentally and physically.

What manner of enemy were these, so full of rage and deadly purpose? Shouting "Ferny Cove" as they rode in pursuit. Who had looked at him with such hatred? Kormehri, obviously.

Colonel Morghild inspected his smashed camp, his shattered companies. As force commander, he'd sent two companies of his own cohort along with Cearnigh's. Holding back three, along with the militia cohorts. Then the Rude Landers had come, and most of the militia had scattered without fighting. His own men had fought of course, fought and fallen. And the enemy, after trampling the camp, had whirled back westward.

Fragments of Cearnigh's companies had ridden, walked, or been helped back to camp, some still straggling in after sunup. Altogether, of more than 1,100 imperial officers and men, 362 were known to be fit for duty, and 334 others reported wounded and unfit. Which left some 400 killed or missing. Morale too had been smashed, would take time to rebuild.

As far as the militia was concerned, if he had his way, they could stay wherever they'd scattered to. But having one's way wasn't part of military service, so he would round them up, all that he could, eat the ass out of their officers, and see what could be made of them.

As for the Rude Landers, they'd been ferrying men across since midnight. Apparently they had no intention of fortifying their landing zone; attack was their strategy.

And "Ferny Cove!" their rallying cry. Their attackers had almost surely been Kormehri. Quaie's atrocities against the Sisterhood had received most of the publicity, perhaps properly so, but it was well known that Quaie had slaughtered the Kormehri companies he'd overrun, taking no prisoners and butchering the wounded.

And now, Morghild told himself, *we have our reward. Too bad Quaie isn't here so they can pin it on him in person, with a Kormehri saber.*

35

Duinarog

The jingling persisted, plucking at a corner of his dream until his wife laid a hand on his shoulder. "Raien," she said, "Talrie's ringing."

The Cyncaidh pushed himself upright, groaning. The angle of sunlight through the gap in the curtains told him it wasn't nearly seven yet; why would Talrie be waking him this early? He swung his legs out of bed. "What is it?" he called.

"Your lordship, I have an urgent message for you from the palace. You're wanted there for an eight o'clock meeting. The courier is in the foyer, awaiting your acknowledgement."

Cyncaidh grunted, and turned to his wife. "I hope this doesn't mean what it might," he muttered, then raised his voice again. "Just a moment."

At the door, his steward handed him an envelope, its wax seal pressed with the emperor's signet. "Thank you, Talrie," he said, and went to his dressing table, where his penknife lay in its sheath. Slitting the envelope, he withdrew the paper folded inside, scanned it, then turned soberly to where Talrie stood discreetly outside the door. "Tell the courier I'll be there in good time," he called, "and have our horses ready by seven."

Varia had already disappeared into her bathroom. Cyncaidh went to his, and instead of drawing a bath, knelt in his tub, drew a pitcher of cold water, and poured it over his head, sputtering and gasping. Then he drew warm water, and washed. Shaving wasn't necessary. It was a rare ylf who grew facial hair below the eyebrows; they were likelier to be hairless entirely.

When both had dressed, they went together to their private dining nook overlooking the Imperial River, and the splendid park below their bluff. The morning was cool, and the broad balcony doors only slightly ajar, just enough to let in birdsong from the trees below. Morning sunlight slanted through the numerous panes, and Talrie had adjusted a shade wing so it wouldn't shine in her ladyship's eyes.

While waiting for their omelettes and toast, they sipped the almost obligatory sassafras tea with honey. Varia reread the short message, then looked up, frowning.

"What can she possibly hope to accomplish? I'd assumed the alliance was a ploy, a step in some long-term plan for political union. But to actually invade?" She shook her head. "Perhaps Ferny Cove pushed her over the edge."

"Perhaps it started as a ploy," Cyncaidh suggested, "and got out of control. At any rate she's playing into my hands. And Quaie's as well."

Quaie. The Rude Lands alliance had already increased his influence. The man frightened her. The only time she'd met him, at a palace banquet, his eyes had done more than undress her. If she ever fell into his hands, it seemed to her her fate would be worse than the captured Sisters' at Ferny Cove; he'd keep her alive longer. For she was not only one of what he referred to in his circulars as "Sarkia's brood of witches"; she was Cyncaidh's wife.

Don't think like that! she told herself sharply. *It's not the sort of situation to create in your subjective world. It might start solidifying!*

Quaie's hatreds were extravagant and beyond understanding. He scorned humans; seemingly hated any of them not subject to ylvin authority. But most conspicuously he hated Sisters; they were his most cherished hatred, particularly since Ferny Cove. And he hated anyone who opposed him, notably her husband. Like most hatreds, Quaie's were no doubt rooted in fear, though of what, even A'duaill hadn't discerned.

In a sense, he seemed to disdain even the talent that marked his own race. A large majority of ylver lit fires without tinder or flint, protected themselves from insects by weaving repellent fields, speeded their own healing. Like strength, intelligence and beauty, talent varied between individuals; that was understood. But some, a small percentage, disapproved of or distrusted those whose talent went beyond their own. Which included most who ruled. These disapprovers weren't a political faction, but they saw in Quaie a kindred soul, and supported him.

Varia wondered what A'duaill might find if he were free to interrogate Quaie as he had her the summer before.

Her reverie was interrupted by a serving girl with their cart, and she became aware that her husband had been watching her. He smiled ruefully. "Perhaps I shouldn't have mentioned Quaie," he said, and spread jam on a toasted muffin.

She smiled back, also ruefully. "It's odd," she said, "to think of you two having any common ground at all. I suppose Murdoth will be there this morning."

"He's sure to be."

"He's as bad as Quaie."

Cyncaidh chuckled. "Not really. But he's often thorny where Quaie would be oily."

Varia made a face. "Oily and venomous."

As she spread her toast, she deliberately turned her thoughts to Curtis. He'd no doubt left Illinois for Washington County, where his life would be ruled largely by weather and the other straightforward realities of farming. She'd cleared him for the long ylvin youth. What ill effects might that have on him now, without her? He'd probably remarry, then watch his wife and children age. No doubt he'd have to leave them eventually. Washington County had no place for a man forever twenty-five years old.

If it hadn't been for Idri . . . If it hadn't been for Idri, she wouldn't be here with Raien.

• Cyncaidh didn't break in on her reveries again that morning. By her face as much as her aura, it was best to leave her with them.

The emperor's council room had one large oval table, around which sat the council's dozen members, none of whom looked older than twenty-five, though at least one or two besides the Emperor had passed eighty. There were also two recording secretaries armed with piles of slender graphite crayons, and two consultants, one of them Varia, for her knowledge of the Sisterhood.

The other was a Captain Docheri from Morghild's command, who'd worn out a series of post horses in four eighteen-hour days of hard riding, to report. Since arriving last night, he'd slept seven hours, then been wakened gray-faced and groggy, to wash, dress, and eat before the meeting.

Cyncaidh read the report aloud to the Council. It was sobering, though it had less information than he'd expected. The southern commander's strategy was described—the unexpectedly early crossing, the landing at Parnston instead of Curryville, and the forced march of units to Inderstown to complete the crossing more quickly. It also described the smashing foray of the Kormehri cavalry, identified with certainty by their uniforms and by questioning wounded prisoners. And by their war cry, "Ferny Cove."

Varia's gaze switched to Lord Murdoth. He'd reddened angrily, his aura darkening and thickening. As if the Kormehri had somehow wronged Quaie by hating him for his barbarities.

The number of imperial casualties were given, but those of the March militia cohorts were only estimated, their troops having scattered badly.

Docheri then gave an oral report, and when he'd finished, the emperor asked the first question: "How," he wondered, "did we so drastically underestimate the southern alliance?"

In a sense the question was rhetorical. The evaluations had been made in that room, by himself and this council. But Docheri answered. "Your Majesty, we had no idea that the allies would work so well together. Or coordinate at all; there was no precedent for it. Actually the alliance seemed somewhat of a joke, though neither Colonel Morghild nor Colonel Cearnigh treated it as one. But obviously its commander is an unexpectedly skilled leader and military planner."

Murdoth snorted, his glance touching Varia on its way to the emperor. "The Sisterhood's to blame," he said. "They've married sorceresses to every ruler south of the river." He paused, glaring again at Varia as if adding mentally *and one north of it*. Then went on, "And controls them like marionettes;

I have no doubt that if the light were right, you could see the strings."

The speaker of the majority Empire Party, spoke next. "If it weren't for our ill-advised expedition to Kormehr, and the outrages at Ferny Cove, none of this would have . . ."

Murdoth interrupted angrily. "That vile Dynast has lived for more than two centuries, and has dreamed of our destruction the whole time. She—"

The emperor's light gavel struck the bell in front of him, its brittle clang cutting Murdoth off sharply. "Lord Murdoth, we have rules of courtesy here. Do not interrupt again." His gaze went to Varia. "Lady Cyncaidh, do you have any comments on the role of the Sisterhood in this?"

"Speculative comments, Your Majesty. The Dynast has always been strongly prejudiced against Your Empire, and taught us to fear and loathe it. But the Rape at Ferny Cove seems clearly to have changed her approach. Previously she'd had a treaty only with the Kormehri, and that only for the use of an area of land, and the protection of the Sisterhood within its boundaries. While giving the Kormehri unique rights in marketing the Sisterhood's products."

"May we suppose that the military commander is one of her people? Perhaps the commander of her guard forces?"

"It seems quite possible, Your Majesty."

At this, Captain Docheri raised his hand.

"Yes, Captain?"

"We know a bit about the commander's identity, Your Majesty. His name is Makurdi. He's said to be an Ozman, who somehow came to Tekalos and led a rebellion that overthrew the king there."

Macurdy! At the name, Cyncaidh's glance went to Varia, just for a moment. Her bright green gaze had snapped to the captain like a compass needle to a lump of magnetite.

"An Ozman," the emperor said thoughtfully. "The Ozmen have a considerable military reputation."

He turned the discussion to how they might respond to the invasion. After consulting briefly during a break, the Empire Party, with its plurality in both the Council and the biennial Great Parliament, kept as close as it could to its isolationist

tradition. Its position was that the militias and garrisons should
carry the burden of defense, the March taking the major
responsibility. The Throne Army should not be involved; the
invaders couldn't possibly fight their way to the border of the
empire. However, to reassure the Marches, a senior crown
officer, perhaps Lord Cyncaidh, should coordinate the defense.

The A'conal Party—in these days the center party—went a
long step further. Lord Finntagh was its official spokesman
in the Council, to support the fiction of the Emperor's neutrality.
Finntagh recommended that the 1st Imperial Legion be sent
south to the Elmintoss military reservation, ready to enter the
Inner Marches if the invaders reached them.

Predictably, Murdoth proposed that the ducal armies be
imperialized, and march south with the Throne Army, to crush
the invaders utterly so they could never come back.

When he'd sat down, Cyncaidh stood. "Who," he asked, "do
you propose should lead that army?"

Murdoth glared, and after a moment answered, "If the
decision was mine, I'd name General Quaie."

"And what disposition would you make of enemy prisoners?"

Murdoth's glare intensified, his face threatening to swell
like a balloon. "I'd hold a slave sale," he said.

Cyncaidh nodded. "Would they be safe to keep around as
slaves? In large numbers?"

"There'd be no large numbers."

"Ah. I suppose not, with Lord Quaie in command. And what
would you recommend he do with his army, when he reached
the Big River?"

Murdoth turned to the Emperor. "Your Majesty, I object
to your chief counselor's insults!"

"Your objection is noted, but I fail to see an insult. Please
answer. I'm interested."

Murdoth took a steadying breath. "He should do with it—
whatever Your Majesty wishes."

"Thank you, Lord Murdoth. Lord Cyncaidh, what was your
motive in asking?"

"General Quaie might be tempted to cross the river on his
own determination, to punish the Rude Lands for their
invasion."

Murdoth broke in. "General Quaie might very properly wish to. As I would. But he'd never make such a move without Your Majesty's authorization."

"Indeed he wouldn't. Because if I were to imperialize the ducal armies, which I would only do if my own forces were insufficient, I would not appoint General Quaie to their command. He is a skilled and proven military leader, but I have learned not to trust his judgement in victory." He paused, looking around the table. "Well. Gentlemen, I will not make any firm decisions without knowing more than we do now. Which we certainly will, quite soon. And while there are other matters we could discuss, there are none that can't wait. I am going to conclude this meeting."

He turned to Cyncaidh. "Chief Counselor, do you have any last words?"

"Only that I'd like to question Captain Docheri on details that may cast light on southern strengths and limitations."

"As you wish. Gentlemen, we'll meet here again tomorrow at nine. We may well have further information on the war by then; perhaps the invaders' initial success will have been reversed. Meanwhile, good day."

Chair legs scraped, feet shuffled, and the Council left. The Emperor watched the last of them out, then nodded Cyncaidh and the captain into his adjacent chamber, an intent Varia following. When they were seated, the emperor looked musingly at her before speaking. "Lady Cyncaidh, you seem to have heard something in Captain Docheri's testimony that I missed; something that seemingly your husband also caught. Something to do with the southern commander. Perhaps we should clear that up before questioning the captain on other matters."

"Thank you, Your Majesty. You are most considerate." She turned to Docheri. "Makurdi. It's certainly a strange name. Is it his given or his surname?"

"Your ladyship, that brings us to a somewhat less believable part of the story. He's said to be an escaped Ozian slave. And if that's true, he has no formal surname."

She gnawed a lip. "A slave. What brought an Ozian slave to Tekalos?"

"The stories our sources told are at second hand, or third

or fourth, which makes them more difficult to accept. Some of them seem—quite fanciful. The important part is what we know for certain: he is formidable."

"Nonetheless, the stories may reflect elements of truth. And the Merchants Guild may be able to refer my husband to men who were in Tekalos during the rebellion or since. The more he knows, the better able he'll be to question them. I want you to tell us everything you've heard of this Makurdi, regardless of how unlikely it seems."

"Well, my lady," Docheri said, "the story is that although a slave, this Makurdi had somehow married one of the Sisterhood. And she'd been stolen from him, and he'd run away from his master to find her." The captain paused, as if to see if she'd had enough. She nodded him on. "Then somehow, with the help of dwarves he'd rescued from bandits—" the captain paused again, shrugging, as if to say that should give them some idea of how far-fetched the stories were "—with the help of dwarves, he freed a number of rebels held prisoner in the king's very courtyard, standing off and killing a number of king's men single-handedly while they escaped. Then, supposedly, he got away and fled into the mountains, where he met a great boar and ensorceled it to carry him on its back. That's another thing: he's said to be a magician. He then gathered together an army of Kullvordi." Docheri shrugged. "Supposedly his lieutenant is a beautiful Ozian spear maiden who followed him out of love, but he's spurned her because he cannot love any woman but his lost wife, who'd cast a spell on him."

He spread his hands apologetically. "And that seems to be all of it. Oh! Except that he has two rows of teeth, all the way around!" The captain showed his own in an almost smile.

The emperor had watched Docheri's aura for any sign that he was making it up, in whole or in part. Seemingly he was being entirely honest.

Cyncaidh wasn't surprised that Varia had turned pale. Especially at the last part—that Macurdy couldn't love any woman but his lost wife.

"Your Majesty," he said, "my wife has been ill-disposed. With your leave, I'd like to take her home. Perhaps you'll consent to see me later today."

The Emperor nodded. "By all means, Lord Cyncaidh. I'll discuss this with you promptly after lunch." He turned to Varia. "Lady Cyncaidh, I trust you'll feel better after resting."

He and the captain watched them leave, Docheri puzzled. The Cyncaidh hadn't asked one question.

She knows this Makurdi, Paedhrig told himself. *Knows him personally. If he weren't an Ozman, I'd think they'd been lovers. Well. Raien will enlighten me later. Meanwhile I'd best see that the captain doesn't wonder too much.*

He looked at Docheri. "A highly intelligent woman, Lady Cyncaidh. Also fearless. And highly talented, an adept. I suspect Lord Cyncaidh has gotten her pregnant again; women can be strange in early pregnancy.

"Whatever. Let's you and I explore those military questions."

36

Marching North

The road was a major one, graveled, wide enough for wagons to pass without risk of miring on the shoulders, and in many stretches ditched. Macurdy sat Hog in the bogus shelter of a roadside sugar maple, watching a plunder column pass. A thick soft rain fell almost too quietly to hear, had fallen for hours, and the maple dripped as copiously as the lead-gray clouds. Most of the wagons were covered, their canvas canopies streaming water like the flanks of the teams that pulled them, and the slickers of their Ozian drivers and helpers.

It was a short column; Macurdy counted nine wagons. A Kormehri plunder column had passed an hour earlier with twenty-three. This country was richer than he'd expected—much richer than Tekalos or even Indrossa—but even so, only a town could provide that much valuable plunder. More often, single wagons passed, with the take of some country manor.

He'd been out of touch with the lead cohorts, except through couriers. He'd spent two days seeing to the crossing of the rest of his army. There hadn't been a lot of fighting. After the crushing defeat of the imperial and militia cohorts at the river, more than three days and forty miles ago, the only real resistance had been outside Amotville, and that had been smashed decisively by Ozian cavalry and infantry, supported by archers of several affinities. The imperial garrison, its horses and men disorganized and decimated by heavy archery, had fought hard but briefly, and been overrun. Its militia auxiliaries had already panicked and scattered.

The Ozians too had adopted the Kormehri shout of "Ferny

347

Cove! Ferny Cove!" It had little significance for them, but they liked it, and bellowed it as if they came from there. And at Amotville they'd butchered imperials as freely as the Kormehri had on the night of the crossing. On the other hand, militia men who'd thrown down their weapons had been disarmed, stripped of their valuable byrnies, then freed. A policy Macurdy had propounded beginning with his early instructions to training commanders, and reiterated at every opportunity. And intended to enforce when he could.

When the plunder column had passed, Macurdy rode on, Melody with him. Other officers followed, with couriers and a platoon of Kullvordi guards. Shortly they caught and passed a cohort of Teklan infantry, mud-splashed to the knees. The soldiers recognized their commander, and his oversized horse whose name delighted them. Cheering, they waved as he rode by, some shouting "Macurdy!" and others "Hog!"

He passed through a richly mixed woods along a stream— beech and basswood, tuliptree, ash and elm, assorted maples and oaks—and out the other side. Where he saw and smelled the charred remains of a manor house, a few slicker-clad civilians poking through the rubble. Torched by a plunder company, he supposed; combat units would have had to break ranks to do it. He turned to one of the officers with him. "Bekker, ride over to those people and see if they can tell you who torched that place. Maybe they noticed the emblem on their guidon. And find out whether there were any other atrocities. Even if they don't have any information, they'll know we give a damn."

"Yessir, Marshal!" the man said, and turning his horse away, trotted toward the destruction.

Melody watched him ride off, then pulled her horse close beside her commander's. "Don't let that kind of crap get to you, Macurdy," she murmured. "It's been happening since man discovered war, and it'll keep on till he undiscovers it, if he ever does. At least you don't order it, like Quaie. If you just make it less, you can be proud."

He nodded. At Amotville, where the wounded had filled commandeered buildings, his spear maiden had been subdued by the sight and sounds. It would get worse, he knew, and told himself this wasn't just to get Varia back. Like the Great War in Europe, back on Farside, this was the war to end wars.

The problem was believing it.

The rain stopped not long after noon. The sky cleared, and by evening the ground had dried somewhat. The advance units were only a few miles ahead now; he'd catch up with them in the morning. Meanwhile reports were coming in by courier: Three Teklan companies had ridden westward, and near a place called Herrinsville had scattered a militia cohort marching east, killing "a considerable number." The Indrossan cavalry cohort had ridden eastward and chased some militia cavalry across the Travertine River. There they'd raided a hay barn and got the rain-wet bridge to burn by piling and lighting hay beneath both ends and on its planking.

It seemed unlikely to Macurdy that his army's undefended corridor would become dangerous till imperial cavalry arrived from kingdoms to the east and west. Meanwhile he'd lose no sleep over it; the principal victims would likely be plunder columns. If he had to fight his way back out, *then* he'd lose sleep, though he had a plan for that, too. But the idea was to fight northward, get a treaty, and make arrangements for Varia's return, then march out peacefully.

He also received reports of a small village ravaged, with rapes and murders. And a Kullvordi company had found a plunder detachment raping the women on an estate near the road. The Kullvordi commander had arrested the sergeant and corporal of each squad and had them flogged in front of their victims, then hanged their sublieutenant and platoon sergeant from a tree by the road, their ranks conspicuous on their tunics. Each wore a crude sign reading *rapist*. The rest of the detachment he'd led off with their wagons and loot, to rejoin their own company.

Macurdy wished he'd thought to have medals struck; he could have decorated the Teklan commander. Meanwhile he'd gotten the man's name; with luck he could reward him later.

As the army continued north, the militias fought more often, though not effectively. No more imperials were seen, and someone suggested they'd abandoned the Marches, but it seemed to Macurdy that somewhere ahead they were gathering in force. Perhaps waiting for reinforcements from the north.

He rode near the front of his army now, Jeremid his operations officer. Melody was his chief of staff. One evening as they examined captured maps, an entry guard announced four Sisters. Macurdy had them shown in. Sarkia had assigned him forty of them, her most skilled magicians, she'd said. Mostly they kept inconspicuous, aided by some light spell. And by their clothing; they didn't wear the usual robes, but guardsmen's green field uniforms cut small. They had their own guard platoon, Tigers instead of ordinary guards.

The Sisters who entered his tent looked like a set of clones, and no doubt were. Their leader's name was Omara. "Marshal Macurdy," she said quietly, "are you displeased with us?"

"Displeased? No. Why?"

"You haven't called on us to help."

"Yes I have, at Big Springs. Your healing skills saved a number of lives there."

"That is not what I meant. You have not let us help you defeat enemy forces."

"We haven't needed that kind of help."

"We could have made a difference in some encounters, even though you won them easily. A mist or confusion at the right time could have saved you casualties."

Actually he'd thought of it, but didn't say so. "Sooner or later," he answered, "we'll meet an ylvin army, and if they use sorcery against us, I'll likely free you to do whatever you think will work."

She'd gazed steadily at him while they talked, no doubt observing his aura as he had hers. "Thank you, Marshal Macurdy," she said without nodding.

All four turned then without farewell, and he watched them leave. There were more than enough factors to complicate things, it seemed to him. He preferred to leave sorcery out of it, if he could.

37

Ternass

The early morning sunlight shimmered on Macurdy's armor—the opalescent, dwarf-made byrnie and helmet Tossi Pellersson had given him, the winter past, before going off to the Silver Mountain. From his belt hung the heavy Hero's saber he'd fled Oz with, strengthened by Kittul Kendersson's dwarvish spell, and freshly honed. While Hog, he had no doubt, was the best warhorse in the army; the best to carry him at any rate.

Behind him on a slightly higher hillock, the three covens of Sisters watched, Omara their director, ready to counter any ylvin spells they detected. He'd ordered her not to initiate an exchange of magicks, and she'd said she wouldn't. Her aura showed she meant it. Sisters, he supposed, were good at obeying orders, if they accepted the authority giving them.

Off to his right, the final companies were taking their positions, and a few yards away, Jeremid sat scowling in his saddle. The Ozman didn't like Macurdy's decision to take a personal part in the fighting. "What in hell will we do if someone kills you?" he'd demanded privately. "You don't realize how important you are to this army; if we lose you, the heart'll go out of it. Going out there to cross swords with some ylf is the most stupid thing you can do!"

Macurdy hadn't argued. Basically it was true; his death here would be a disaster. But he also knew that for whatever reason, he had to take an active personal role in the fighting. Had to lay his life on the line, as he required so many others to do. He'd told this to Jeremid, and the young Ozman had simply snorted.

Now the commander stood in his stirrups, staring north across young oats at the large Imperial force he faced. Its formation was defensive, inviting his attack, prepared to chew him up. Judging by their banners, there were four cohorts of imperial infantry alone, and massed in front of them, at least four cohorts of militia: crossbowmen protected from cavalry assault by ranks of pikemen. All of them—pikemen and crossbowmen as well as the imperial infantry—wore byrnies, and swords if it came to that kind of fight. As Macurdy intended it would.

On the enemy's right flank, imperial cavalry sat their horses, four cohorts of them as well, no doubt well trained, and all wearing byrnies. But the cavalry weren't his main concern. Not yet. Very likely the ylvin commander would hold them back until some opportunity or emergency called for them.

He wiped sweat, and wondered how good the enemy's endurance was. His own men were tough, had trained hard all winter and spring, then the infantry had hiked from wherever they lived to Kellerton or Inderstown, generally hundreds of miles. And after that, 130 miles from Parnston to Ternass. Of course, they weren't as well fed as he'd have liked; militias and civilians both had been hauling off or hiding a lot of the edibles in advance. But neither were they famished.

He studied the militia pikemen. He'd assumed something about them, an assumption based on a single observation. Their long, ungainly, simple-headed pikes were intended to stop cavalry, and that required mainly bravery and discipline. To use them against infantry, on the other hand, required considerable skill. He assumed they lacked that skill, and the confidence that would go with it.

His forces had run into pikemen just once, outside a town called Big Springs. A broad stone bridge crossed the river there, and some militia had taken a stand to defend it. Two companies of crossbowmen lined the far bank, while the bridge itself was plugged with pikemen to keep the southern cavalry from crossing. The Kormehri had charged anyway, in the teeth of deadly crossbow fire, expecting the pikemen to break and run, as militias always had. But these hadn't, and scores of Kormehri had gone down, horses and men, between the bristling pikes in front of them and the press of the oncoming ranks behind.

Even so the fanatical Kormehri had won. A single platoon of them had dismounted, swords in hand, and the pikemen had dropped their long cumbersome pikes to draw their own blades. The Kormehri platoon, greatly outnumbered, had attacked them on foot like wolves assaulting sheep, and the pikemen, previously so firm, panicked and broke, running from the bridge, even jumping armor-weighted into the river. Then Kormehri platoons still on horseback had overrun them, howling and killing; it was once when militiamen had not been allowed to surrender.

Even so, the crossbows and pikes had taken a heavy toll. When it was over, the Kormehri cavalry cohort, already short since that wild first night, reported only 264 officers and men fit for action, hardly fifty percent of those who'd crossed the river.

Actually the militias had fought harder the past two days. Not well, not even doggedly, but they'd stood and fought. He'd questioned prisoners, and they'd told him that the Emperor's own army was on its way south under General Cyncaidh. They no longer felt abandoned.

The army he looked at now could hardly be the Throne Army; it wasn't big enough. Mostly these would be garrison cohorts that had withdrawn ahead of him, plus others gathered from east and west and north, with their militia auxiliaries. Macurdy squinted at the sun glinting on distant pikeheads, helmets, and mail. From beneath his own steel cap a trickle of sweat overflowed an eyebrow, but except to swipe at it with a wrist, he ignored it. *So far,* he told himself, *we've had a cakewalk, beating up on frightened militias, and on badly outnumbered imperials who didn't realize what they were up against. Here we'll learn how good we really are.*

He could, of course, have waited another day. The rest of his troops would be there by then. And the enemy seemed content to wait. But Macurdy already had the advantage of numbers, and who knew how many imperial cohorts might arrive tomorrow, or even that afternoon.

Grimly he turned to his bugler. "As planned," he said. "Mounted archers out by companies." All his cavalry were mounted archers as needed, but certain units had been assigned the role for this battle. The bugler blew, company buglers responding. Three Teklan cavalry companies trotted out in single file, briskly and without spears, not *toward* the enemy so much as across the front of its massed infantry. The imperial commander held back his cavalry, unsure what this peculiar move might mean, what might happen next. The course of the southern cavalry took them within seventy yards of the pikemen, within range of the militia crossbows. But the militiamen only gawped, their commander unsure what this meant. Again a bugle blared, and riding parallel to the enemy's front, the Teklan horsemen began to shoot, irregular flights of arrows hissing into the ranks of crouching pikemen, and the massed crossbowmen behind them. At this, the crossbowmen released their heavy bolts, and when a horseman was hit by one, whether he wore a captured byrnie or not, he fell dead or terribly wounded.

More horses than men were struck, though they went down less often. But cantering horses and their riders were poor targets at that range. The longbowmen continued to ride and shoot, circling back in a broad oval and out again. Macurdy watched, held by the sight, excited instead of horrified, his right fist jerking repeatedly with a short hooking motion. The intensity of crossbow fire had greatly lessened, due partly to casualties, but mainly to the time it took overwrought militia crossbowmen to crank their weapons, then load them if they remembered to. Now Macurdy gave another order; the bugles called the horsemen back, and sent open ranks of infantry out with longbows, jogging slowly enough not to get winded. More than a few fell to bolts before getting the order to shoot, but not till the first rank had come to about seventy yards did they stop, draw their bowstrings, and let their arrows fly. The second rank did the same, at slightly longer range, and the third and fourth, each man shooting not just once, but sending arrow after arrow—four, five, six—in the time a crossbowman took to crank his bow and shoot once.

More longbowmen jogged out then, in columns through the ranks already shooting. The columns split, spreading to form new ranks, adding to the flights of feathered death, while the crossbow fire thinned even more. Then Macurdy sent columns without bows, seven-foot stabbing spears in their fists, roaring "FERNY COVE! FERNY COVE!" at first, then simply roaring. Their ranks fragmented by casualties, the pikemen were at a disadvantage against skilled spearmen. Some dropped their unwieldy fourteen-foot pikes and big-eyed, drew their swords, further thinning the pike wall. Here and there, hearts frozen, some turned, stumbling over men behind who'd fallen to the archery, but most fought, or tried to. The roaring was pierced by screams, and after a brief minute the entire militia began to come apart, the crossbowmen dropping their bows and running, struggling and threading their way through the ylvin ranks behind them.

Only then did the ylvin commander send out two cohorts of cavalry in broad ranks, ostensibly to smash the southern infantry, though he knew the southern cavalry would intercept him. Now Macurdy, riding Hog, led out his mounted Kullvordi 2nd Cohort, strengthened by the remaining two Teklan companies. Their formation was slightly different than the ylvin—the Hero formation, densely compact, a tight shallow vee. They trotted slowly, deliberately across the battlefield, each horse almost touching the flanks of those to either side, their riders leg behind leg, shields braced, long spears gripped firmly beneath an arm. At about a hundred yards, Macurdy raised his shield overhead, a signal, and his buglers blew the charge. The whole formation broke into a canter at almost the same instant as the imperial cavalry.

They crashed together, and it was the Kullvordi and Teklar, with their more compact formation, who drove through, horses stumbling over fallen horses, trampling fallen men. Then spears were dropped, sabers drawn, and the melee truly begun.

Back across the oat field, Jeremid watched, prepared to react to any further ylvin cavalry move. He had three cohorts of cavalry available, plus the three companies of mounted Teklar with bows. Meanwhile more ranks of southern foot troops jogged across the trampled oats to engage the ylvin infantry.

Macurdy's heavy Ozian saber slashed and thrust as if it had some dervish spirit of its own. His shield was heavier than the others, its steel bands broader and thicker, and it seemed always where it needed to be.

The ylver by and large were better swordsmen, but with ranks broken by the charge, they fought mostly as individuals. Macurdy dominated wherever he was, and with two picked sergeants, went where most needed. After a few minutes, the ylver began an organized disengagement, back to the small hill from which they'd ridden. Macurdy looked around for his bugler and couldn't find him, so he shouted his order, other voices repeating it: "To base! To base!" Company buglers heard and blew it, and as they started back toward the rise they'd ridden from, squads and platoons began re-forming on their guidons, while a bugler worked his way toward his marshal, to serve him.

Almost at once they saw another cavalry battle, a cohort from each army. Macurdy bellowed "Engage!", and spurred Hog into a brisk trot. The nearest bugler heard and blew. Some of the cohort took a moment to realize the situation and respond, but within seconds they all were headed at a trot for the other fight, still reforming units. Some of the ylver heard them coming. An ylvin trumpet called, and ylvin troopers, those who could, disengaged and retreated; others fought and died. At the same time, Jeremid and the ylvin commander both threw their remaining cohorts toward each other in an orderly charge.

For an indeterminate time Macurdy fought, while men and ylver fell. Twice he saved his new bugler without being consciously aware of it. A saber struck his dwarf-made byrnie hard, and once a blow on his helmet blurred his vision, making his mouth taste of blood.

Finally the last ylvin cohort disengaged, and mostly his men let them go, for they too were exhausted. Hoarsely he called an order to his bugler. The man blew, and the cohort, all the cohorts, trotted their horses back to the hillock, again re-forming as they rode, for it was drilled into them. They were too spent to feel exhilarated.

Macurdy was one of the last to leave, looking toward the site of the infantry battle as he rode. It too was over, had been for a while. His infantry had substantially outnumbered the ylvin and militia infantry to begin with, and when the militia broke, it left the ylver at a severe disadvantage, despite their byrnies and training. After heavy slugging, they'd withdrawn, leaving their dead and wounded to the badly reduced southerners.

Macurdy found Jeremid back before him; the Ozman had ridden out with the last cohort committed, and was grinning ear to ear, his byrnie splashed with blood not his own. "You look like a butcher, Macurdy!" he called in greeting.

Macurdy looked down and found himself bloodier than Jeremid. "Get me something white!" he shouted.

"White?"

"I want to parley with the imperial commander."

"Something white!" someone called. "Get the marshal something white!" The call spread through the cohorts, but no one came forth with anything white. Macurdy trotted his horse back onto the battlefield, where leaning far down, he snatched a fallen spear on the trot, and put his helmet on its point. Holding it high, he trotted Hog toward the little hill.

The ylver commander watched him come, making no move to meet him. At fifty yards, Macurdy stopped. "A truce!" he shouted. "A truce!"

The ylvin general rode out then, his youthful face grim. At twenty yards he too stopped.

"To what end?"

"To do what we can for the wounded!"

For a long moment the ylf stared. "Have you surgeons?"

"And Sisters; healers. I suppose you have your own."

The ylf nodded. "A truce then. Till when?"

Macurdy's face worked. *From now on,* he thought. *Forever.* "Until sunrise tomorrow."

"A truce till sunrise. Agreed." The ylvin general trotted back to his staff, and Macurdy turned toward his. Partway there, he could hear ylvin trumpets, presumably signalling the truce, for the general's aura had shown no sign of treachery. The southern army had no bugle call for a truce, so when he reached his own men, Macurdy sent couriers to inform the cohorts.

And one to bring the Sisters. They trotted their horses to him, their Tiger platoon riding straight-backed and expressionless behind them. Macurdy sent them out to where hundreds on hundreds—thousands!—of dead and wounded strewed the ground, then looked around and spoke to Jeremid. "Where's Melody?"

The Ozman's face fell. "Shit!" he said, scanning around. "I told her to stay here! That she was in charge till I got back!"

"I'll find her," Macurdy said. "Get litter bearers organized; what we've got aren't nearly enough. And commandeer buildings in Ternass for the wounded."

Then he ordered a courier to follow him, and rode out to the last place they'd fought. If Melody was alive, that was probably where she'd be. He went to her like a needle to a magnet, found her sprawled across a dead horse, still and bloody as a corpse. From thirty feet distant, he wanted to die, for he could see no aura. When he reached her, he swung from his saddle. There was an aura after all, thin and dull. Her face was ash pale, her splash of freckles a contrast and alarm. Simply removing her badly dented helmet strengthened her aura. He raised her a bit, and with the courier's help, pulled off her byrnie. Seemingly the blood was not her own, for there was no visible wound.

"Bring a litter," he ordered, then watched the courier mount and canter off.

When she'd been taken away, Macurdy looked around. His impulse was to take one end of a makeshift litter and help carry, but there were many who could do that. His job was to be in charge. Not that he was much good at it just then; Jeremid gave the orders. Much of the time, Macurdy sat silent and motionless in the saddle, watching litter bearers; carters stripping byrnies from the dead and gathering weapons; and after a bit, crews of surrendered militiamen and his own troops hauling and stacking wood and straw for funeral pyres.

Near noon, he rode to the house where Melody had been taken, one of numerous filled with wounded. As chief of staff, and assumed to be their commander's lover, she'd been put in a small room by herself. He found her there in bed, conscious but groggy, head aching. She didn't remember the battle at all; didn't even remember getting up that morning. Macurdy kissed her forehead and told her she'd be all right. Meanwhile she was to stay in bed; that was an order.

Sisters moved through the houses, touching, murmuring chants. He assigned a surly-faced Ozian corporal to stay outside Melody's door, with orders that no Sister was to have access to her. He couldn't have said why.

Meanwhile the enemy had ridden away northward, their wounded in a train of crowded wagons. The base they left behind, Fort Ternass, wasn't much of a fort. Far too small for so large an army, its walls might keep out vagrants, but they'd be little obstacle to a military assault. As soon as it had been vacated, Jeremid had a Miskmehri infantry cohort occupy it.

The ylvin departure drew Macurdy out of his numbness, and he sent an order for his senior staff to meet with him. While he waited, he unrolled a captured imperial military map. Just a few miles north, it showed a broad stretch of country liberally marked with wetland symbols. The road continued north through it. Six miles to both east and west, other roads crossed it; eight or ten miles beyond them, the wetland symbols disappeared.

Macurdy stood silent a few moments, thinking. The army they'd fought that day would no doubt join forces with the Throne Army riding south. An army by itself too large for him to deal with, reportedly a full legion of cavalry and another of mounted infantry. Under its General Cyncaidh, his wife's captor, who when he was at home, no doubt took her to his bed at night.

He shook the thought off, and wished Blue Wing was with him. But the great raven had left near winter's end, for his tribe's rookery in the Great Eastern Mountains. It wouldn't do to take sides in such a war. And he'd never had a mate, he told Macurdy, never raised nestlings. It seemed time.

When Macurdy's staff had gathered, they quieted on their own. "Somewhere north of the marshes," Macurdy said, "there's an ylvin army riding south, and the people we fought this morning will be joining it. We don't know when they'll get here." He looked at his operations officer. "Jeremid, what are the swamps like ahead?"

"The only patrol that's back so far followed the road to the other side and came straight back. It's five or six miles across, mostly cattail marsh, with creeks and open pools. Impossible to cross, even on foot. But the road? You'd have to see it to believe it. It's not only ditched; it's got a raised bed of rock, packed with dirt and topped with gravel."

Macurdy examined the map again. If he continued north with his army, they'd face a much larger ylvin army, with the marshes between themselves and escape, and only the road to funnel out on. And with the likelihood of more ylvin cohorts hitting them from east and west later. While if they stayed where they were, holding the marsh roads, the ylver could bypass the marshes. It might take them a couple of days.

He could, of course, turn around in the morning and head south, leaving rear guards to block the roads, giving the rest of the army a start. It was doubtful the imperials would catch them north of the Big River. Not in force.

For a moment that seemed to be the answer: Get south of the Big River with his army. Then he remembered his purpose—why he was there. South of the river wouldn't get Varia back, nor put him in position to bargain with the emperor. Anxiety flooded. *And say we arrive at the river a day ahead of the ylver: What then? There's no fleet of boats waiting. We'll be trapped! They'll capture thousands. First they'll murder the prisoners and wounded, then they'll cross the river and rape the Rude Lands.* Anxiety became despair. *You've deluded yourself,* he thought, *and Wollerda, and everyone else who trusted you. There was never any prospect of a treaty. Your blind determination to get Varia back has already killed thousands, and thousands more will die before it's over.*

Then abruptly, snarling, another part of him rose up. *Bullshit, Macurdy. Make things happen!*

"Jeremid! I want a platoon from the 2nd, ready at sunup in presentable uniforms. And couriers, and an Alliance flag, and a flag of truce. They'll ride north with me. Pick up the pikes the militia dropped today, and arm some companies with them. Make sure they know how to use them. Assign two companies of infantry and one of cavalry to plug each of the roads."

Jeremid nodded, steady as a rock. "Right."

"Round up wagons. Start the wounded south as soon as they can travel. Commandeer all the civilian wagons you need. And the plunder wagons; we've sent enough plunder down the road. And send couriers to Kithro—separately, in case they run into trouble. Get them started right away and tell them to push it. Tell Kithro we'll be wanting boats again soon.

"I'll ride north to find the enemy commander. The only real ylvin army we've met so far, we've thrashed. It's time to parley, while we're winners."

He scanned the rest of his staff. "Any comments or questions?"

All except Jeremid looked very sober, but only one spoke: "You'll be a long way from help, Marshal. Suppose they don't respect your flag of truce?"

"I heard several days ago that their commander is General Cyncaidh. And I know a little about him. He's said to be an honorable man; certainly he's not another Quaie."

He waited, and when no one else spoke, dismissed them.

After the staff meeting, Macurdy visited the wounded again. Melody was sleeping, and he didn't disturb her. Her aura was much stronger.

The army had brought "surgeons" with it—sawbones actually—one per cohort, and shamans and other healers of greater or lesser talent and skill. But judging by auras, the men in buildings assigned to ministration by Sisters were in notably better condition. Macurdy went to the officer in charge, an Indrossan, and took him aside.

"Major, are you aware that I'm a magician?"

"It is general knowledge, Marshal Macurdy." The Indrossan was grave-faced.

"Have you noticed any difference between the wounded treated by the Sisters, and the rest of them?"

"No sir."

He may have some skills, Macurdy told himself, *but not much talent.* "They're doing a lot better," he said. "Their auras show it."

The major said nothing, but his aura showed disbelief, whether of auras or the Sisters' better results wasn't apparent.

"I'm going to have them minister to the rest of the men."

The man looked stricken. "I— Marshal, Sisters can't be trusted!"

Macurdy laid a large hand on the major's shoulder. "You've had a hard day. When did you eat last?"

"I had an orderly bring me bread and meat at noon."

"Get something to eat, and walk around outdoors. Don't come back till tomorrow. That's an order."

The major looked near tears.

"You know about orders. Eat something and walk around camp. Look at something besides broken bodies. Have a drink, then get some sleep." He put a hand on the major's back, herding him along, and they left the building together.

It was Omara herself whom he took to see Melody. She'd tried before to see her, she told him, but a soldier had kept her out. "At your orders, Marshal. You distrust me. Why?"

"It's nothing personal," he said, and opened the door. Omara went to the bed and looked at the sleeping spear maiden for a long moment, *examining her aura,* he thought. "She doesn't need me," she told him. "By this time tomorrow she'll be largely recovered, though she should rest at least another day."

She looked at him coolly. "You are an enigma, Macurdy, a talented enigma."

"Enigma. That's a word I haven't met. But distrust now . . . I suppose Sarkia told you my experience with the Sisterhood. I like and respect you, Omara, but you'll excuse me if I have the colonel's guard refuse you entrance to this room except when I'm with you."

"Marshal, I have enough to do without troubling someone who doesn't need me."

They left Melody then, Omara going on to visit other patients. Macurdy paused outside Melody's door, talking with the man on guard, then left for supper. *Sarkia never believed you'd get Varia back,* he told himself, *regardless of what she said. And you're the most powerful leader in the Rude Lands; she'd love to marry you to a Sister. If she thought Melody might stand in the way, or maybe even if Omara thought so . . .*

He'd taken off his hillsman boots and was washing his socks when his Kullvordi orderly looked in. "Marshal, sir! Major Tarlok wants to see you! Says it's urgent!"

Tarlok was peering in over the man's shoulder. "What is it, Tarlok?"

"A bunch of Kormehri grabbed some local women. They were carrying them to their camp. I thought you should know."

Macurdy swore and pulled on his boots, not taking time for socks.

"You want me to get a company or two, in case there's trouble?"

"No. If I showed up with a bunch of men, there'd be trouble for sure. But you can come with me if you'd like."

He tied the laces around his ankles, belted on his saber, and left the tent at a trot, Tarlok with him. Both were unaccustomed to running, and Macurdy slowed before they got there so he wouldn't arrive gasping for breath. It was twilight, nearly dark, but he knew where in the Kormehri camp to go by the cheering, and found a crowd gathered on a company muster ground. He couldn't see what was going on—the circle was several men deep, most without their breeches—but he pushed through, Tarlok with him. A fire had been built in the middle for light. More than a dozen women and girls had been stripped, forced to hands and knees, and their wrists tied to stakes. All of them were occupied. He didn't hesitate, but strode to the nearest man, grabbed him by the hair and jerked him backward. The crowd went still, all but the man he'd interrupted, who scrambled to his feet swearing vividly. To find a saber tip at his solar plexus.

"YOU SON OF A BITCH!" Macurdy bellowed, and abruptly, with a backhanded wrist movement, slapped the side of the man's face with the flat of his blade. The man stepped back, hand to cheek, aware now whom he faced, and that he'd been only a turn of the wrist from death. The other rapists had dismounted and backed away, staring with varying degrees of anger and fear. Macurdy and Tarlok strode around the circle cutting ropes, freeing the women.

Macurdy straightened and looked around. "Where are their clothes?"

The company commander stepped into the circle then. He wore no breeches, but his sword was in his hand. "This is my company!" he shouted. "What goes on here is none of your business!"

The place was doubly still now. Macurdy walked slowly toward him. "Do you challenge me, you dog turd?"

The Kormehri took half a step backward before he realized what he was doing, then with an oath, rushed at Macurdy. Their blades met violently—and the Kormehri's snapped. Macurdy thrust him through and let him fall.

The crowd remained quiet as Quakers. "What company is this?" Macurdy shouted.

"Barlin's Company," someone answered.

"Barlin's Company fall in!" he ordered.

Most of the men moved as if to form ranks. But not all, and a sergeant drew his sword. "You might kill one of us, you Ozian pig," he shouted, "but you can't—"

He stopped in midsentence. Macurdy said nothing, simply stalked toward him, drilling him with his eyes—and just off the tip of his saber was a ball of white fire the size of an egg. The man stared at it transfixed, and screamed when Macurdy thrust him through.

"Barlin's Company, *fall in!*" Macurdy repeated, and this time there was a general scramble to obey. "Major Tarlok," he called, "help the women find their clothes."

Most of the men stood in ranks now, but a few, perhaps a dozen, were slipping away into the darkness. "*Stop where you are!*"

Most stopped, though several fled.

"Where were you men going?"

"Back to our company, Marshal," one called apologetically. "We're not Barlin's, sir. We just came to see what was going on."

Yeah, and have a turn at it. "All right," he called. "Just remember what you saw and heard." He turned his attention back to Barlin's Company, a company short by at least a third, no doubt from the morning's battle . . . and felt his anger die. "Do you know why I killed your captain?" he asked. "And your sergeant?" His voice, though loud, was almost conversational. Suddenly it boomed. "BECAUSE THEY DEFIED ME. DEFIED MY ORDERS! Now let me remind you: I gave orders that there is to be no raping. Your captain and your sergeant defied those orders. Now they're dead! Sent to Hell!"

His eyes found Tarlok again. And the women, now with their torn and trampled clothing clutched to them. "Major, take these women to the Sisters. Tell Omara what happened; tell her to do something for them. And get them some clothes; Barlin's Company will pay for them."

He turned to the men in ranks. "Company, 'ten*tion!* Right *face!* Forward *march!*" Calling cadence, he marched them out of the firelight, through the night to the battlefield, most of them barefoot and without pants. On the bloody killing ground, he double-timed them back and forth, controlling them from a central position, for he'd become so much a horseman, he'd done no serious walking for months, let alone running. While they were infantry, their legs tough, their lungs like bellows. After about twenty minutes he marched them back, but before he dismissed them, he asked who'd been second in command.

A tall, rawboned man spoke up. "I was, sir."

"What's your name?"

"Arliss, lieutenant, 2nd Kormehri Infantry, sir."

"Lieutenant, you are now a captain, and company commander. Congratulations on a first class company. But remember . . ." Abruptly his voice raised to a roar. "NO RAPING! AND NO MURDERING CIVILIANS! I don't want to send any more of you to Hell." He paused. "I'm turning them over to you now, Captain. Take up a collection for the women, tonight. Every man *will* give something. Something valuable, whatever he has."

With that, he turned and strode out of the firelight.

From the Kormehri bivouac area, he went back to look in on Melody again. She'd been awake, or on the verge of it, because when he stepped in, her head turned, eyes open. "Hello, Macurdy," she murmured. "Where have you been?"

"Here, a few times. The last two you were asleep, and the first time you didn't know where you were or what had happened."

"Want to feel my lump?"

"Sure." He knelt, and his fingers touched her head. "Pretty good one."

She chuckled weakly.

"How's your headache?"

"Not bad. But when I got up to use my bucket, a little while ago, I was pretty dizzy."

"I had a Sister look at you. She said you'll be a lot better tomorrow, but you need to stay in bed a day or two more."

She looked thoughtful for a moment. "You know what's really good for someone in my condition?"

"I'm afraid to ask."

"Remember what I did for you after you got beaten up so badly?"

He nodded.

"If you'd do something like that for me . . ."

He bent and kissed her cheek. "Not now."

"When, then?"

"Sometime. Soon. If we get through this war alive."

"Do you mean it?"

Again he nodded.

"Will you marry me?" she asked.

He felt his head going up and down as if it had a will of its own.

"Kiss me," she said. "On the mouth. To make it real."

He did, softly, sweetly.

"I feel stronger already, Macurdy."

He stood up. "Go back to sleep, spear maiden."

Obediently she closed her eyes, and turning, he padded quietly from the room. Feeling like a wooden man, wondering how he could possibly have said what he had.

38

Lord Quaie

Cyncaidh rode erect but relaxed at the head of his staff, on a smooth-gaited stallion that would not have tolerated an ordinary rider. In front of him, the Emperor's elite 1st Cavalry Cohort filled the road almost to the top of the next rise. Two complete legions followed, twenty cohorts of cavalry and mounted infantry with their supply trains, a great cumbersome dragon extending for miles, its serpentine body integrated by well-drilled protocol and couriers on horseback.

He sniffed, and smiled ruefully. A morning like this should smell of wildflowers and meadow grass, but already the odors of horse urine and trampled manure dominated. At the rear of the column, the road would be nearly mired with it. If the breeze would just swing round to the east or west, instead of holding from the south . . . From the south. He wondered how yesterday's battlefield smelled, after a day of sunshine, warmth, and flies. Mearigher's casualty report, delivered by courier the day before had been bad enough, but to actually see the remnant of Mearigher's army with its hospital train this morning had been powerfully sobering.

It truly was astonishing that an effective southern army had been assembled from so many different nations. And by a farmer from Farside, with no previous experience of war or leadership in this lifetime.

A marsh hawk caught Cyncaidh's eye, soaring low over the meadow beside the road, single-minded, oblivious to the army. It slowed, and with blurred wingstrokes hovered a moment, then dropped into the tangle of grass and forbs, to fly up with a rodent in its claws. Nature too had its violence, he reminded himself, but seemingly little more than needed to eat and raise young. Only men and ylver fertilized their fields with blood from time to time. Their great challenge, laid on them by God, was to change, he had no doubt. Change, and lose their bloodiness; change by dint of growing wisdom. Meanwhile one did the best one could, dealing with the world as it was.

Ahead, a courier rode toward him against the direction of march, cantering his horse briskly along the road's edge. The rider, a sublieutenant, kept his pace almost until he'd reached Cyncaidh, then stopped, saluted, and turned his horse to ride alongside the general. "Sir!" he said. "The point's met a small force of southerners ahead, under a flag of truce. With a man who says he's Marshal Makurdi."

"Aha!" The voice was Quaie's, calling from behind him. "You'll have him in your hands, Cyncaidh! Don't waste the opportunity!"

The admonition irritated the commander, and half turning in the saddle, he glanced back. Disregarding his aura, the seventy-year-old Rapist of Ferny Cove looked like a handsome youth: tall, slender, impeccably tailored, and utterly hairless, with refined features. But his eyes invariably showed contempt, while the mouth was inclined to mock or smirk. Quaie had been against Paedhrig's orders to negotiate if possible, and had been taking it out on his chief counselor. *May you be reborn as a maggot in your own carcass!* Cyncaidh thought.

As commander, Cyncaidh could always stomp on him, but politically it would be unwise. Better to let the war erode his influence, already shrunken by Ferny Cove.

He glanced at Varia on his right. Her aura had receded and paled at the report, but only a little. "What's the ground like ahead?" he asked the sublieutenant.

"Much the same as here, General."

He sent the man cantering back up to the route leader with orders to stop for an indefinite break, then sent similar orders to the other cohorts. And thought his apologies to the farmers whose crops would be trampled by his camping army. "I'll have the headquarters tent set up," he told his staff. "We'll see what this Macurdy has to say. If he's come to negotiate, we may spend a day or two here."

He ignored Quaie's remark: "Why set up the tent? A sharpened stake in the hot sun would be more appropriate."

The tent was up before the southern commander arrived. If necessary he'd have had Macurdy delayed to get it done. It would seriously jeopardize negotiations if the man saw Varia. As it was, she could listen from behind the linen wall while watching through the spy hole, and he'd consult with her during breaks.

The large staff room had panels rolled up on two sides for ventilation, and Cyncaidh and his general staff lounged around a trestle table with a top of intricate parquetry. He wondered what Curtis Macurdy would think of it, or if he'd notice. Outside, a horse cantered up and stopped; a moment later the sublieutenant stepped inside and saluted.

"He's almost here, General."

Cyncaidh got to his feet, his staff following suit, Quaie sneering something about the disgrace of fawning on a criminal like that. *You're our expert on disgrace,* Cyncaidh thought, and led them outside. From there he could see the southern commander, a big man with big shoulders, on a big horse. With no spear maiden by him, nor any aide at all. His platoon was being guided to the pastured grove set aside to shelter them from the sun, leaving him alone with his ylvin escort. No doubt his men were less than happy with that, Cyncaidh told himself.

Macurdy dismounted, his movements easy, casually athletic. He wore neither byrnie nor helmet. His hair was short-bobbed, the color of wet sand, and as he neared, his eyes showed hazel. His hands, Cyncaidh thought, might be the largest he'd seen. His aura showed more than power and honesty; there was also what Cyncaidh read as purpose and logic, care and concern.

And inborn dominance. The ylver didn't have a specific classification of personality types, as expressed in auras, but he recognized the aura of a man born to command, and the strong aural fullness of one who did. He stopped in front of Cyncaidh. "My name is Macurdy," he said. "I'm the commander of the southern alliance."

Cyncaidh nodded gravely. "I am General Cyncaidh." He gestured at the tent. "Step inside and we'll talk."

They went in together, Cyncaidh's staff following. An orderly held a chair for Macurdy, as instructed. It would give Varia a view of him in profile, while avoiding any chance that he'd see an eye behind the spy hole. When everyone was seated, Cyncaidh asked, "Why have you come to us, Commander?"

"There were two things," Macurdy said, "that I was supposed to do on this campaign. One was to punish the empire for laying waste to Kormehr, and for the Rape at Ferny Cove. The other was to get a treaty of peace to last forever, with a pledge of trade without tariffs, and an exchange of ambassadors. I've been told you're the emperor's chief counselor; I came to talk terms."

Quaie snorted derisively, drawing annoyed glances from the rest of the staff and a sharp look from Cyncaidh.

"You understand," Cyncaidh said, "that my authority is limited. Any terms we might work out will be tentative, pending the emperor's signature. Who on your side needs to sign?"

"Just me. My authority's good."

In the name of all those kings and chiefs?! Even with the Dynast behind the man, Cyncaidh was surprised. And momentarily uncomfortable with it. It greatly expedited matters, but it felt— almost indecent for things to be so simple. "Are you hungry, Commander?" he asked. "Perhaps you'd like lunch first."

"I ate in the saddle."

"Then I suggest we begin an exploratory discussion now."

"Good. I'm ready."

One might almost be hopeful, Cyncaidh told himself. *No arrogance, no posturing, no petty jockeying.* He gestured at the men around the table. "While the authority here is mine, Commander, these lords may have questions or suggestions, or information to contribute, and they will witness any tentative agreement we may come to. On my left are Lord General A'raiel, Lord General Quaie . . ."

At Quaie's name, Macurdy got so abruptly to his feet, he knocked over his folding chair, freezing the others where they sat. "You expect me to sit down with the Butcher of Kormehr? The Rapist of Ferny Cove?" He hawked, and spat on the floor.

Quaie sent his own chair toppling backward then, hand on his saber hilt. Macurdy, in response, reached for his.

For just an instant Cyncaidh was dismayed, then realized that neither man's aura showed rage. Macurdy's showed what might be satisfaction, Quaie's restrained glee. Cyncaidh understood Quaie's motivation: the man was famous as a fencer, a master of the saber.

"My lords!" he said sharply, "control yourselves!"

Each man stopped short of drawing his weapon.

"This peasant has insulted me in words and act," Quaie answered coldly, then turned his glare to Macurdy. "I challenge you to duel."

Cyncaidh was prepared to veto this; he had the authority, and the political repercussions of frustrating Quaie's bloody intention were far more acceptable than those of Macurdy's death. And surely Quaie would win. "My lords—" he began firmly, but Macurdy overrode the words.

"Among civilized people," Macurdy said, "if one challenges, the other chooses the weapon. Are you civilized, Quaie?"

Cyncaidh held back then. Macurdy had something in mind. Best to wait, see what this meant, and step in later if need be.

Quaie was taken aback for only a moment, for he was an expert at spear fencing too, and no other alternative occurred to him. He smiled mockingly. "By all means, human. I've been training and dueling for more years than you've lived. Choose as you wish."

Macurdy held up his large hands, thick palmed, the fingers hooked. "Hands," he said calmly. "We'll fight with bare hands."

Cyncaidh expected Quaie to refuse. Wrestling was popular among ylver in pre-adolescence, but not later, while fist fighting was considered uncouth, suited only to slaves. And Macurdy was clearly far stronger than Quaie. So the ylf lord's answer bewildered Cyncaidh. "Perfect! Perfect!" Qauie said. "Hands it will be!"

"My lords," Cyncaidh said firmly, "I cannot allow this."

It was Macurdy, not Quaie, who foiled him. "Chief Counselor," he said, "if you disallow this, I'll ride back to my army today."

Quaie smirked. "Indeed, Lord General, let the boy take

his punishment. He will learn from it." Then he turned and walked out the door, Macurdy close behind. And for almost the first time since adolescence, Cyncaidh had no notion of what to do in a situation. He simply followed them into the sunshine, his staff dumbfounded at his heels.

"And how," said Quaie, "do we decide the victor? Shall we fight till one of us cannot continue? Or surrenders? I do owe you the option of quitting, I suppose."

"We fight till one is dead," Macurdy answered.

"Ah. To the death then." Quaie removed his tunic and undershirt, Macurdy following suit. Then they faced off, Quaie tall, slender and sinewy, Macurdy nearly as tall and strongly muscled. Cyncaidh had no idea what Quaie had in mind. His fists weren't even clenched; his hands were poised half open.

"Tell me when you're ready," Quaie said.

"I'm ready."

Quaie stepped forward, at the same time ducking, and his left hand darted toward Macurdy. Macurdy's right fist drove in a compact, hooking arc, striking Quaie hard on the side of the face, smashing him backward. For a long moment the ylf sat stunned and blinking on the ground, blood trickling from a gash on one cheekbone. Even before he got to his feet, the cheek had begun to darken and swell, as if the bone was broken. And the smirk was gone; Cyncaidh saw fear and rage in Quaie's aura now.

"Always look up, Quaie," Macurdy said mildly.

When Quaie got up, Macurdy moved in again. A hammer fist shot out, striking Quaie on the nose, and once more the ylf went down hard, blood flowing freely.

"That's called a left jab. The one before was a right hook."

Quaie stayed down seconds longer this time, gathering his wits and resolution, then rolled to hands and knees as if to get up. But instead, as he began to rise, he lunged at Macurdy's legs. Macurdy started to step backward, but Quaie grabbed his left knee with both hands—and Macurdy roared with pain, flinging backward and landing on his buttocks.

Now it was Quaie who stood. Shock fingers! Clearly his talent went well beyond the ylvin norm, regardless of his public attitude. And to interfere now, after the humiliation and injuries he'd suffered, would bring severe censure, Cyncaidh realized, even from the many who disliked Quaie. The Emperor would have no choice but to dismiss him, not only as chief counselor, but from the Council and military command.

Blood flowing from his nose, Quaie began to circle Macurdy. "You see," he said, "the hands are good for more than striking blows." Macurdy swiveled on his tailbone as if to kick out in defense. Quaie feinted a grab, drew a kick by Macurdy's right foot, and snatched it. Again Macurdy roared with pain, rocking backward.

Quaie let him go and began circling again. Macurdy, pale and twitching, had trouble pivoting now. Quaie could easily have gone for his temples, where the shock would have killed, but he preferred to gloat first. "I've heard that shock fingers applied to the genitals shrivel them forever. When I've paralyzed you, Commander, I'll try it."

Cyncaidh took a single step toward Quaie; shock fingers couldn't harm him, prepared as he was, and he couldn't let this continue, regardless of the consequences to himself. But he moved too late. Macurdy, still dazed, had raised a hand toward Quaie—and from it a fist-sized ball of glowing plasma appeared! For just an instant it floated there, then shot out to strike the ylf in the midriff. Quaie shrieked and flung backward, his abdomen a gaping, steaming, messy hole, to lie bulge-eyed, conspicuously, bonelessly dead. The onlookers stood stunned, slack-jawed.

More than Cyncaidh and his staff had witnessed the fight and its uncanny finish. Various soldiers, though keeping their distance, had paused in their activities to watch and listen more or less covertly. Now they stood frozen, mouths open. Cyncaidh, suddenly aware of them, shouted, "Soldiers! If you have things to do, get about them! If you don't, I'll see you're given some!"

They scurried like rabbits.

"Sergeant Glinnoch! Get a litter! Have General Quaie taken to the surgeon!" *Who can declare him officially dead.* "Captain Flion! Pass the order that we'll camp here tonight!"

Then he himself stepped to Macurdy, who sat staring at the ruined corpse. "Are you able to stand, Commander?"

Macurdy pulled his attention from what had been Quaie. "Not without help," he husked. "My legs are weak as noodles."

Cyncaidh had a second litter brought, and Macurdy, quaking now with aftershock, was lain on a pallet beneath a shady tree, and an ylvin healer sent for. Then Cyncaidh seated his staff as a committee of evidence, to draft a statement they all agreed on, describing Quaie's death and how it happened. They'd all witnessed it, and there were no disagreements on what had been said or done. They also agreed on the legality of the duel, that it was Quaie who'd issued the challenge and been first to use magic, and that when Macurdy had seemed helpless, Quaie had said he was going to mutilate him.

On the other hand, Quaie had issued his challenge only after Macurdy had called him the Rapist of Ferny Cove, and had emphasized his scorn by spitting on the ground.

Given the unanimity of the general staff, Quaie's aide, who'd also been sworn in as part of the committee, could hardly avoid signing a statement of witnessed evidence. But he added a complaint that Macurdy's tone, in speaking to Quaie, had been insulting in the extreme. Cyncaidh then added a rejoinder, pointing out that considering the extremity of Quaie's actions in Kormehr, and the intensity of southern feelings, Macurdy's having spat only on the ground could be regarded as an exercise in restraint.

Actually, Quaie had been called the Rapist of Ferny Cove by more than a few of his peers, some of them publicly. There'd be a fuss, and some long-lasting bitterness, but by persons who already hated both himself and the Emperor. Certainly the situation would be far less serious than he'd anticipated during the fight.

When the committee of evidence had completed and signed their statement, the scribe took it to another room to write copies, before the original was sent off to Duinarog. Then Macurdy was brought in, on his feet now, supported by two ylvin soldiers. After a lunch eaten at the conference table, they began discussing the basic features of a peace agreement. Cyncaidh had felt optimistic, but hadn't expected it to go as smoothly as it did. He and Macurdy had similar ideas of what was desirable and just.

They didn't break for supper, but ate again at the conference table, still discussing. Finally Cyncaidh suggested they stop for the evening. His scribe could organize their discussion as a draft agreement for review in the morning. It seemed to him probable that never in the history of the empire had a major agreement, nor many minor agreements, been worked out to mutual satisfaction so quickly.

"Fine," Macurdy said. "But before we sleep, there's something you and I need to talk about, unrelated to the treaty. A personal ambition I have."

Cyncaidh frowned. "Very well, Commander. I'll have our horses saddled and we can take a ride." He turned to his general staff. "Gentlemen, you are dismissed. We'll meet again after breakfast."

The two commanders watched the others file out. Then Cyncaidh turned to the couriers and door guards. "You too," he said. "All but you, Alhnar. I want you to have our horses saddled and brought to us." When they were gone, he spoke to Macurdy in an undertone little louder than a whisper. "We have a few minutes to wait. What is this all about, Commander? Not the details, but the major matter."

Macurdy too spoke in a murmur. "I'm a married man, general. My wife, who was a Sister, was stolen from me, and after a time passed into ylvin hands. Your hands personally: I'm told she's your slave now, or has been, and I want her back. But if your staff knew, someone might say you'd given in on points of the agreement because of it. And I don't want anything to threaten that. Too many have died for it."

Cyncaidh stared for a long moment while Macurdy waited. Finally, in a normal voice, he said, "Excuse me, Commander. Let me call my wife; she may be able to advise us. Varia, would you come out please? We'd like you to take a ride with us."

Varia! It was Macurdy's turn to stare, open-mouthed. The curtain moved at the rear of the room, and Varia stepped out. He felt as if his windpipe had locked; his throat hurt from the constriction. She was more beautiful than he'd recalled. "I'll need to change into riding clothes first," she said, not meeting Macurdy's eyes. Then she disappeared again.

❖   ❖   ❖

She didn't reappear till Cyncaidh called that her horse was there. Then the three of them left the tent, mounted, and rode to the road, all without speaking. A slender moon hung low in the west, while in the east, the first stars climbed the darkening sky. It was Macurdy who spoke first, in American, his voice thick. "Are you really married to him?"

She answered in Yuultal. "Yes. In this world."

A confusion of thoughts flooded his mind, but no words came to him. It was Cyncaidh who spoke. "Let me tell you what might be difficult for her to say." As they rode, Cyncaidh résuméd briefly how he'd found her. Of her assault on him when he refused to take her to Ferny Cove, or let her go alone. Chuckling as he finished. "If ylver scarred as men do, I'd still bear the marks on my face."

He went on from there: how she'd learned of his love, and nearly drowned trying to escape. And how he and Mariil had teamed up to overcome her resistance. "You might well hold a deep grudge against me, Curtis Macurdy. For if I'd determined to, it's quite possible I could have gotten her safely to the Oz Gate. But if she'd gotten back to Farside, she wouldn't have found you, because you were here. It's only because we did what we did that you've met again."

Macurdy didn't answer, simply turned his gaze to her and found her watching him. "I can get our children back for us," he said. "It's part of my agreement with Sarkia."

By moonlight, her eyes gleamed with tears. "Oh Curtis, so much has happened. So much has changed! I've changed, a lot, and you even more. And Raien and I have a baby, a beautiful child. And what he told you isn't all there is to tell. I knew early on that I loved him, and couldn't face it. Couldn't face what it meant."

"Do you want to be with him then, instead of me?"

She turned her eyes ahead, not answering for a bit, and when she spoke, she still didn't answer. Instead she told in a low monotone of her trip to the gate and the Cloister, not omitting Xader's harassments and death. Of her year there, the Tiger barracks, the rapes, her escape and recapture.

"I know some of it, a little," Macurdy said. And told her what he'd learned from Jeremid about Xader's death. Told her briefly of Liiset's lies, and the tomttu's. And what the skull had shown him, the skull that had to be Tomm's.

She was staring at him now. "I could see you had talent," she said, "but even after I'd explored it, I didn't imagine how strong it was. What you did to Quaie today—I've never heard of anything like that.

"We were innocents when we married. Our dream of farming in Illinois couldn't work now, Curtis.

"And Raien has a dream too, one I've come to share. The same dream you worked on today at the conference table: of a peace held in place by treaty and trade and embassies. But the agreement's only a first step; none of us will see the dream complete in this lifetime. Imperial government needs to become more rational, its politics more ethical, our people wiser. That's another part of our dream, Raien's and mine."

Again they rode a bit without speaking, and again it was Macurdy who broke the silence, still in a monotone. "Do you love me, Varia?"

"I'll always love you, Curtis. You were my first love, and it changed me more than you can imagine. It showed me what love is, and that I could love. And later it made me strong."

Her cat eyes searched him in the night, so much less dark to her than to him. "I'll always love you, but—I've changed. My dream has changed."

It was Cyncaidh who broke the next silence. "We've heard tales of the amazing General Macurdy. That you ride a wild boar; that you have two rows of teeth—that an Ozian spear maiden loves you, and you've refused her."

Macurdy laughed, a laugh amused but without joy. "I got my front teeth all broken or knocked out back in Oz, and new ones grew in. A whole new set, all nice and straight. They even pushed out the good ones I already had. I never had sprouted wisdom teeth before; I guess that tells you something." He turned to Varia. "I guess it took, when you spelled me to not get old. I guess that's how I grew them. And there is a spear maiden; you're not the only one who knows about loving two at a time." He paused. "You don't suppose you could do for her what you did for me, do you? Give her long youth?"

Varia's teeth gnawed her lower lip thoughtfully. "If she has the necessary ylvin genes. The blood. But that's very unlikely, for someone from Oz. Where is she now?"

"In camp, in the hospital. Someone put a big dent in her helmet, in the battle. She'll be all right though."

"If you can bring her here to me—"

While the two of them discussed the possibilities, Cyncaidh rode quietly, thinking. The commander of the southern army still showed a little of the farmboy Varia had told him about. Had described to him at length, till she'd become comfortable with her memories. He'd come to feel he knew Curtis Macurdy.

Actually he hadn't, and neither had Varia. Or no, that wasn't right: she'd known him as he had been. Then, held to the fire, instead of flaring and dying, or softening, or going brittle, he'd tempered, strengthened, grown into something uncanny, a man who still hadn't learned how powerful he was.

Varia's voice drew him from his reverie. "Raien," she said, "I want to go back with Curtis tomorrow to visit his spear maiden, with a guard platoon to bring me home. I'll only be gone a day."

For just a moment Cyncaidh felt misgiving, but it faded. He—he and A'duaill and Mariil—had come to know her as deeply as you could know anyone, and there was no dishonesty in her. She would come back. And if somehow she changed her mind, what right would he have to complain?

She'd come back though. As she sat in the saddle looking at him, her love assured him of it.

They started back to camp, and Cyncaidh's thoughts reached ahead to Duinarog. Paedhrig would sign, beyond a doubt, and the agreement with the Rude Lands would be law. Then they'd have to weather the resulting storm. The Expansion Party would be enraged at the agreement, but with Quaie dead there'd be a period, no doubt all too brief, of confusion, probably indecision, and perhaps even conflict within its ranks. Then someone would establish leadership and attempt to drum up public outrage at a treaty without vengeance, made when the smoke of funeral pyres had hardly dissipated.

They'd deal with it, though, he and Paedrigh. If it got bad enough, he'd resign as chief counselor, claiming family reasons, and Paedhrig could appoint Gavriel, a smoother politician. It might be just as well. It might be time for a healer in the Chief Counselor's office. Then, after a time, Paedhrig might appoint him Minister of Southern Affairs.

He smiled to himself. He could stand being dismissed. He'd take Varia back to Aaerodh Manor, and they'd spend a year exploring. Do the coast and islands in his sloop, the rivers by canoe and the forests on skis.

That night Macurdy lay awake thinking. Last night he'd told Melody he'd marry her, and had wondered how he could have said it. Now he'd learned that Varia was married to someone else. Yesterday it had seemed he'd been a fool to imagine this invasion producing anything but disaster and death, and tonight he had an agreement, or seemed to.

It wasn't, he thought, as if things had been preordained. More like, if he just kept doing what seemed right, more good than bad would come of it.

And what about all the dead. What of them?

What indeed? Everyone died sooner or later. Even Sarkia would. And people here believed that after a period in something like purgatory, reviewing what they'd done in life and suffering for their misdeeds, they'd be reborn, until finally they were fit for heaven. It sounded more just than what he'd learned in the Oak Creek Presbyterian Church, though Reverend Fleming wouldn't much approve of it.

He went to sleep on that.

PART 6
Melody

39

Korens Manor

The next day, riding south with their escorts, Varia and Curtis talked at length, speaking American for privacy. She learned much about his odyssey, and he gained a much better picture of the empire.

Not that they talked continuously. The day was clear but breezy, and cool for Six-Month—ideal for riding and enjoying the countryside—and there were moments of looking about, soaking up perceptions. Once, far overhead, an eagle screamed, and for a time, seven vultures, black as crows, sailed in silent, effortless circles. While the marsh, when they reached it, drew the eyes. It stretched beyond the edge of vision—expanses of cattails, black pools sheened with limonite, and here and there patches of ten-foot reeds, or islands of brush and trees. Creeks the color of tea passed with imperceptible currents beneath stone bridges, while along their narrow back channels, muskrat lodges humped like miniature beaver dens.

For Varia there were moments of reflection. Curtis had just told her of Arbel and his system of training, which obviously had had powerful effects. Yet he was still Curtis, Curtis transformed, much more powerful and charismatic now. Curtis minus much of the imprinting laid on him by family, church, and community, that had prepared him for life in Washington County. Before she'd slept, the night before, Raien had murmured, in reflections of his own, "We met a true lion today, Varia, the Lion of Farside. And discovered a friend."

The Lion of Farside. The metaphor had its attraction, but

Curtis wasn't normally ferocious, certainly not cold-blooded. Deadly perhaps, and powerful, but not cold-blooded.

When they left the marsh behind, Varia was telling him of the irrepressible Hermiss, who lived at Ternass, and the stories she'd told her of life on Farside.

"Hmh! I wonder if she made the connection between your Macurdy and the marshal of the southern army."

"I doubt it. I don't think I mentioned your last name; to me you've always been Curtis, and Will was Will. Sisters and ylver are like most Rude Landers about names: mostly we use just one, however many you have."

The road topped a low hill, and now Varia could see, ahead and to her left, large ovals of ashes. Soldiers raked them, finding and piling bones, while prisoner details dug pits. This, she realized, was the battlefield, where the pyres had burned and the bones would be buried. Raien would be glad to know these things were being done.

They left the road, angling toward the broad tent camp of the southern army, a mile or so ahead. In the fields, whole cohorts played ball, a hundred in each game, or each melee. She wondered how many bones would be broken before the day was over.

Approaching camp, they sent their escorts off to the Kullvordi tentment. Her ylver would be fed there, and have tents assigned them. Then Macurdy led her to his headquarters tentment. As they approached Melody's tent, Varia felt curiosity, and a certain tension. "I hear her talking," Macurdy murmured, still in American, and halted his horse outside. He helped Varia down, though she didn't need help, and led her in as the two women inside looked up.

Varia stared startled, for one of the women was Hermiss, who stared back with her mouth open. "Varia!" she squealed, and rushing to her, hugged her hard, then stepped back to arm's length. "Oh Varia! You're so *beautiful!* As beautiful as ever. More, with your hair grown out! Where have you *been?* It's so *wonderful* to see you!"

Macurdy watched quizzically, and spoke in Yuultal. "If I had to guess, I'd say you two know each other."

"This is Hermiss that I told you about. My friend on the ride north."

"Ah! Maybe you two ought to go off and talk for an hour or so." He looked at Melody. "If it's all right with you? You and I have things to talk about, too." Melody nodded, frowning more from uncertainty and worry than hostility.

Varia and Hermiss went out into the sun, where Hermiss's horse was picketed too. They mounted, and rode northwest half a mile to a low hill. On the top, they remained in the saddle, watching the breeze riffle the grasses and wildflowers. "What were you doing in Colonel Melody's tent?" Varia asked.

The girl sobered at once. "I . . . Do you remember when I wondered what it would be like to be raped? I found out. Two nights ago. Some soldiers, Kormehri, came into town and grabbed fifteen of us, and took us to their camp." No longer animated, she described the ordeal. "But we were lucky, otherwise I might be dead now. Only three or four did it to me before Marshal Macurdy came and stopped them. All by himself in the middle of all those horny Kormehri with their breeches off! And when the Kormehri captain wouldn't obey him, Marshal Macurdy killed him with his sword! Then another officer wouldn't either, and he killed him too, and made the soldiers form ranks, and marched them off without their breeches."

She giggled with tension and the image, then hiccuped. Varia could see her quivering. "And do you know what? When he killed the second officer, there was a glowing light on the end of his sword! Some of the other girls saw it too. Then another officer took us to the Sisters, and they gave us pallets, and did magic to heal us and keep us from getting pregnant, and talked to us for quite awhile, asking us questions that seemed to help. And they gave us some of their clothes to wear, because ours were mostly torn and trampled on, and some of Marshal Macurdy's guardsmen took us home."

"And today he rides into camp with you!" Hermiss's normal animation began to return. "How did that happen?"

"A peace was signed this morning, between him and General Cyncaidh. The fighting's over."

"General Cyncaidh?!"

"He's Emperor Paedhrig's chief counselor."

"Really? That's wonderful! And—why did you come here? With Marshal Macurdy?"

The truth wasn't something Varia felt free to share. And if she started, she'd have an involved half hour of explaining to do. So she simply said, "Colonel Melody was hurt in the battle, and might have died. I've come to be sure she's all right. She's quite important to Marshal Macurdy." Varia changed the subject then. "What were you doing in her tent?"

"She talked to all of us who were raped, and gave us money taken from the soldiers who'd been there. To make up for it, or try to. She told us the marshal had had men hanged for raping women, but it still happened sometimes. Marshal Macurdy's really handsome—well, not handsome exactly, but good-looking—and so manly! I'd like to marry him! Not really of course. I'd be scared to death, he's so—*powerful!* Colonel Melody is powerful too, but . . . I mean, she's probably no older than me, or not very much, but she's a high officer in the southern army! Anyway I stayed around to talk to her more. You know me!"

My God, Hermiss! You're amazing! How long ago was it? Two or three days? And look at you, chattering and full of life! It must have helped, Varia told herself, to have been rescued and seen punishment delivered.

"I asked you some thoughtless questions, before," Hermiss went on, "and I hope this isn't another one. But—what have you been doing, Varia?"

Varia smiled at her. "I'm married, Hermiss. To General Cyncaidh. He's a very nice man—or ylf—thoughtful and loving. And we have a baby boy we've named Ceonigh. The ylver give their children names from their ancient language. Ceonigh means honor, and it sounds lovely, too."

Hermiss threw her arms around Varia, laughing delightedly and crying at the same time, tears flowing down her cheeks. "Oh Varia," she said, "I'm so happy for you! So *happy!* You *deserve* to have good things. You *deserve* them!"

They talked a little longer, of Duinarog, the Northern Sea, and Aaerodh Manor, then rode back to camp. From there, Varia, with an escort, accompanied Hermiss home. And when they parted, Varia told herself that this time she would surely write to her.

Varia rode directly back to Melody, whom she found alone. Macurdy had left, to give orders regarding the withdrawal, he'd said. Melody's aura was darkened by jealousy, but showed only a slight residual effect of her concussion, an effect she didn't feel and should be gone in another day. It also showed the usual hint of talent, but when Varia asked questions that should bring any latency to view, she found little. Even so, she decided to carry out the procedure as she had with Will, who'd actually shown more potential. It could do no harm, and if somehow it worked . . .

Melody was examining Varia as thoroughly as Varia had her. Mostly she saw physical beauty and poise, but her intelligence and power were also obvious. "Why did you come here," Melody asked, "if you're not married to Macurdy anymore? And why are you talking to me?"

Varia considered telling her, then didn't. Macurdy would, if he wanted her to know. Meanwhile she lied. "He asked me to make sure your head injury doesn't give you trouble in the future. But I'll need to put a spell on you."

Melody shook her head with no sign of a wince. "I'll be all right. I don't want anyone putting a spell on me."

"I understand that. I'd feel the same if I were you. Will you allow it when Curtis comes back? If he sits with us?"

Melody pursed her lips, her eyes intent on the Sister. "If he's here, yes. If he wants me to. It's not that I think you'd do something bad. I just don't like the idea."

Varia smiled. *Thank you, spear maiden,* she thought, *for the polite lie. I don't blame you for distrusting me.* "Fine. When he's free, I'll come back with him."

Half an hour later she did. With Macurdy there, it took only two or three minutes to relax Melody sufficiently, four or five more to put her under, and another fifteen or twenty to run the procedure. Then, on a slow count, Varia brought her back to consciousness. After directing her attention to objects in the tent, to reorient her, she asked how she felt.

"All right," Melody said slowly, as if examining how, in fact, she did feel. Then, "I feel fine," and looked at Macurdy as if uncertain what was next.

He grinned at her. "Good. The army will start south the day after tomorrow. The last cohorts will leave two days later. Jeremid will take care of the planning and coordination."

Melody looked bothered by that. "I'm your chief of staff!" she said. "That's my job!"

"Uhm. Actually I had something more important in mind for you. I thought you and I could get married tomorrow afternoon. Jeremid and Tarlok will witness it, and Asperel. I claimed half a helmetful of silver coins from a Teklan plunder wagon, and rented the house of the district governor for two days and nights. The cook and servants come with it. The governor and his wife will stay in town with their son."

Melody had listened, staring. Now, with a whoop, she leaped from the chair and embraced Macurdy, kissing him hard. Varia left without a word.

"Come back after dark tonight, Macurdy," Melody growled, "and they'll have to help you to the wedding. Loro can sleep with the Sisters if she wants to."

Macurdy laughed, disentangling himself from her arms. "Omara wants you to rest till tomorrow, and there's a lot I need to get done so I can give you my full attention after the wedding. I don't want Jeremid interrupting us with a bunch of questions and authorizations to handle."

She made a face at him. "All right, troll prince, one more day. One more day and you're mine." Her next kiss was less forceful and more sensual; he left grinning.

Varia mused in her tent, feeling vaguely jealous. Not like an ex-lover, but more like—a mother! *How dare that impetuous young woman lust for my Curtis!* she asked herself, and chuckled. *Have you forgotten when you seduced him? What a night! It's a good thing his spear maiden's strong; she may get more than she expects.*

Remembering brought a backwash of that lust, but it had little force. Tomorrow morning Curtis would come to say goodbye; they'd shake hands and probably never see one another again. Then she'd ride away north to Raien, not having to wonder any longer, and in a few days they'd be back with baby Ceonigh.

The house, known locally as Korens Manor, was not large for a governor's residence, but it was more than large enough for Macurdy's two-day honeymoon. He'd chosen the master bedroom suite at one end of the second floor, while his orderly and couriers, and two squads of guards under a lieutenant and two sergeants, occupied rooms on the ground floor. It would have felt unsafe to be there with no more than the servants.

The household staff stayed mostly out of sight. Macurdy and Melody, with the witnesses as their supper guests, were met at the door by the steward, who did his best to ignore the foreign soldiers standing guard with swords and spears. What might they do to him if something happened to their commander? Suppose a piece of meat stuck in his throat! Or some dish upset his stomach and they suspected poison!

Unlikely, he told himself, but wasn't entirely assured. After all, these people were barbarians.

Macurdy savored the last of his pudding and laid down his spoon. Excellent, he told himself, especially considering that civilian distribution of everything, food in particular, had been disrupted by his foraging parties. The wine, the first he'd ever drank, had even been cool.

"Here's to the cook!" Jeremid said cheerfully, pushing back his chair.

"Here's what to the cook?" Macurdy countered. "We need to take a collection for her. And for the steward; he's probably the one who actually got the stuff."

"The locals will be glad to see us go," Tarlok grunted. "They're on edge. Been holding their breath, afraid we'll go on a rampage before we leave. You can almost smell it when you deal with them."

Macurdy turned his gaze to Jeremid. "I'm depending on our operations officer to see that no one does."

Jeremid grinned. "I've got ears out to here." He gestured, indicating something rabbit-like. "But it's unlikely. The whole army heard what you did, or supposedly did, in the Kormehri camp. Not that the Kormehri exaggerated." He laughed. "Not having been there, I get this picture of you buffaloing a whole damn company all by yourself, pulling guys off women by the hair, gutting the company commander and first sergeant, and marching the rest of them out to the battlefield bare-assed, then running them in circles till their balls dragged."

Tarlok snorted. "Ozman, I *was* there. Not that I did anything to help; I was scared spitless. And what you just said is a pretty good description. If I'd tried it, or you, or both of us together, they'd have torn us apart. And if we'd gone in with a company of guards, there'd have been a riot as bad as the damned battle."

"That's the secret," Macurdy said. "Do it alone. Grab guys and start yanking them around. They don't know what to do then; they think you must be more than you are."

Tarlok shook his head. "If it'd been me, they'd have carved me up like a solstice ox. Besides, I saw your sword when you . . ."

Melody had been watching and listening without taking part. Now, getting to her feet, she interrupted. Firmly. "That's it! Party's over! The good guest knows when to leave, and this is when. I'm taking my husband upstairs and scrub his back for him."

"Spear maiden . . ." Jeremid began, then thought better of it. "May it be a night to remember. Macurdy, I'm glad you finally got smart. You two belong together."

Melody left then, while Macurdy walked their guests to the front door and out onto the lawn, where he shook hands with the three of them: Jeremid, Tarlok, and the Teklan, Asperel, who'd felt a little out of place with these ex-rebel comrades. They waited without saying a lot, while their orderlies saddled and brought their horses. Then Macurdy watched them ride off in the dusk before going inside and up to his suite.

He'd half expected Melody to be waiting naked, but she fooled him. She'd undressed, but put on a robe found in a closet. And with the robe, a serious face.

"Did I tell you you're beautiful, spear maiden?" he asked quietly.

"No, but I knew it anyway. Pretty, at least."

"Did I tell you I've been looking forward to this?"

Her gaze was searching. "Have you really?"

He stepped to her, put his arms around her inside her robe, and pulling her close, kissed her, then kissed her again before stepping back.

"Take your clothes off, Macurdy," she said quietly. "Unless you'd rather I did it for you."

He took them off himself while she watched. When he was naked, she dropped her robe. "Do you know what, Macurdy?"

He stared. "What, Melody?" He'd have to stop calling her spear maiden, he decided. She was too beautiful.

"I'm nervous," she said quietly. "I can't believe it, but I'm nervous. And the bath is hot. Hot enough that I closed the flue from the stove."

He took her hand. "Then let's go try it out."

They walked into the small adjacent bath. The tub was tiled and half sunken, big enough for four or five to sit. The water wasn't as hot as he'd expected, but more than warm enough, given that it was Six-Month and the room warmed by the stove. They sat not across from each other, but side by side, and within seconds were kissing again, embracing, fondling. Without either suggesting it, they got to their feet and clambered dripping from the tub. Towels had been set out on a bench, and they dried hurriedly, then went into the bedroom.

Later they donned robes and stepped out onto a balcony that overlooked fields. Dusk had thickened into twilight, and twilight into night, with the crescent moon still well up in the west. There was a cushioned bench, and they sat down on it together, for some time simply holding hands, saying nothing. At length Melody turned and found him looking at her. "I love you, Macurdy," she murmured. "I really do. I have all along, but now it's different. You're a marvelous lover. I thought you'd probably be rough the first time, like a stallion, you're so damned big and strong. And that would have been fine. But you're not. You're thoughtful and loving, and you do the right thing at the right time. It was nicer than I'd ever imagined."

She leaned and kissed him. "This is going to last a long time," she murmured. They kissed some more, and her hand slipped inside his robe. A minute later they went back inside.

✧   ✧   ✧

Private Olvi Kalister stood on the porch beside the front entrance, spear butted by his right foot, thoughts on what he imagined was going on inside. He had a wife back at North Fork, whom he hadn't seen now for—he didn't pay much attention to dates, but it seemed like a long time. A mosquito hummed beside his face, then touched down on his cheek, and absently he crushed it.

"Did you get him?" Private Malakum murmured.

"If I didn't, I scared shit out of him."

"I'll bet they're not paying any attention to mosquitoes upstairs."

"I've heard that mosquitoes don't bite Macurdy. Flies either, or cooties."

I'll bet right now they could bite his bobbing ass twenty at a time, Malakum told himself, *and he'd never notice.* "You hear all kinds of things," he said.

"I heard that when he went in and yanked the Kormehri around the other night, there was a ball of fire on the point of his saber."

Malakum said nothing; he tended to skepticism. On the other hand, Macurdy'd done some uncanny stuff, in front of people Malakum knew well.

The door opened between the two men, and Corporal Freck stepped out. "You guys thirsty?" he asked in a half whisper.

The sentries' attention sharpened. "What have you got in mind?"

The corporal chuckled. "A couple of us were snooping around the basement with a torch. Found a trapdoor in the floor, and went down in." He held out a small jug. "It's where they store their ale. We figured if the bigwigs could have a party, we ought to have one too. A little one, not enough to get drunk and in trouble. To celebrate the wedding. And the war being over without us getting killed; now there's a reason! This one's yours." He handed it to Malakum. "The stopper's out—didn't want it lying on the porch in the morning—but no one's drunk out of it yet. Just keep quiet, and bring the jug with you when you're relieved."

He went back in and closed the door softly behind him.

Malakum took a swig, exhaled a forcible "Ah!" and handed the bottle to Olvi. "Good stuff," he said. "Strong."

Olvi drank and grunted. "Better than my Uncle Loth brews. Freck is all right, bringing us this." They continued passing it back and forth, and after a bit sat down on the top step, their spears lying beside them. Olvi had been part of Orthal's Company when Macurdy first turned up, and without exaggerating much, told stories about their commander. By the time the jug was empty, each man had relieved his bladder onto a shrub, and the moon had set.

Then a woman's scream tore the air, from inside, and both guards jumped to their feet, spears in hand, unsure where it had come from, though it almost had to be . . . It was followed almost at once by a roar of anger, also inside, and a moment later another, this time from the balcony outside the marshal's suite.

"Get beneath the balcony!" Malakum snapped, then banged through the door, headed for the stairs, and bounded up three at a time. From the far wing, boots hammered down the hall, for the windows were open, and the screams had reached the guardroom. At the last door on his left, he grabbed the handle, turned it and yanked, then dashed in. The only light came from the corridor, enough to see dimly a large figure half dragging and half carrying a smaller, who was struggling and swearing. The marshal's voice shouted, "Bring a lamp, for God's sake!" and Malakum sprinted back out to take one from a tripod in the hall. By that time two more guardsmen came dashing up, one of them barefoot, and ran in.

The marshal stood naked, one thick arm across the throat of a man fully dressed. Blood ran down the marshal's right forearm, and both men were smeared with it. The bed was overturned, the mattress partly beside and partly beneath it. "Get manacles," he said, his voice controlled now. "And turn the bed over. I think Colonel Melody's under the mattress."

Malakum, holding the lamp, stared while the barefoot guard upended the bed onto its feet and threw the mattress on it. On the floor was the marshal's naked bride, bloody from face to feet, either dead or unconscious. More men came in. Malakum looked back at the marshal. The officer of the guard tried to manacle the intruder, and when he resisted, the marshal's arm tightened against the attacker's throat till he went slack.

As soon as the man was shackled, the marshal moved to his wife, swept the sheet off the bed and threw it to a guard. "Make bandages!" he snapped, and the guard began to tear it into broad strips. The marshal's hands went to two of his bride's worst knife wounds, and he began to chant. After a minute he turned to the guardsmen, his voice level but intense. "Send someone to the Sisters. Fast! Tell Sister Omara what's happened, and bring her right away. And take that—" he gestured with his head at the prisoner "—outside. But don't damage him. I'll do the damaging myself, later."

Then he turned back to his bride as if none of them were there, continuing to touch and chant while Private Malakum stood wooden with dismay.

Lieutenant Sarsli and one of the guards took the intruder out between them, the man's feet bumping down the stairs. "Be glad it's not your head," the guard said. Macurdy had dislocated the man's elbow, and the soldier jerked the arm a couple of times, making the man cry out in pain. "Stop that!" Sarsli snapped. "You heard what the marshal said." They hustled the prisoner out the front door and onto the lawn, where the soldier threw him down.

"How did you get in there?" Sarsli demanded.

"How do you suppose?" The man's voice was high-pitched with emotion. "I climbed the vines to the balcony. And I'd have killed him, if it hadn't been so damned dark in there. I stabbed his whore by mistake."

"The vines?" Sarsli turned and stared at Olvi, who'd come back to the porch.

The intruder laughed bitterly. "I watched from the fence while your so-called guards sat drinking and talking on the porch. When the moon went down, I sneaked across the lawn and climbed the vines. They wouldn't have noticed if I'd gone over and goosed them."

Oh shit! Sarsli thought, dread settling in his gut. He'd known about the ale. He should have made sure the men on watch didn't get any. No one should have; he should have stashed it till they went back to camp. The marshal would likely kill him now; flogging wouldn't be enough. For just a moment Sarsli considered killing the prisoner, but that wouldn't help. The marshal would find out about the ale anyway, and have two reasons to kill him. As it was, he might be lucky, and a flogging he could survive. Especially, he told himself, when he so richly deserved it.

Macurdy sat naked and bloody on the bed beside his bride. She had an aura, but he could find no pulse. He'd had one of the guards light the lamps in the room, and bring him wet cloths. Arbel's blood-stopping spell had worked, and now, gently but firmly, he washed the congealing blood from around the multiple stab wounds on her breasts and left shoulder, the deep and ugly slash on her left arm. But didn't bandage them; when Omara came, she'd want to see them.

He became aware that the soldier who'd brought in the first lamp still stood holding it. "Soldier," he said softly, "didn't I say everyone out?"

"Yessir."

He watched the man's aura flicker. "What is it you want to tell me?"

"Marshal Macurdy, sir, I was on guard at the front door. I'm to blame for what happened. For that guy getting in."

"I doubt he came in the front door."

"No sir, I'm sure he didn't. Nor any other door. The lieutenant locked them before I ever came on watch, and posted a guard at each end of the downstairs hall. He must have climbed the vines to the balcony. We should have seen him from the porch, crossing the grass, but we had a jug of ale, and sat there talking and forgot to watch. We weren't drunk. We were just—" he paused, swallowed—"celebrating your wedding."

Macurdy looked at him silently for a moment, and when he spoke, it was quietly. "It's done now. We'll see later what we need to do about that."

"Yessir."

"Take the lamp back where you got it and tell my orderly and couriers to stay where they are in case I need them. They're out in the hall, not sure what to do. Then go back to your post."

"Yessir." The man left.

Jesus Christ, Macurdy thought, *celebrating my wedding,* then began the healing formulas Arbel had taught him for loss of blood.

He couldn't have said how much time had passed when Omara entered with her aide. He'd heard them coming down the hall, along with someone wearing boots, but only the Sisters came in. Omara's eyes settled on Melody. "Wash yourself, Marshal," she said. "I'll see to her."

Going to the washstand at one side of the room, he filled the basin and washed, while behind him, Omara half sang, half murmured her spells. Most of the blood that reddened the wash water was Melody's, he decided. The knife gash on his arm seemed to have stopped bleeding by itself, though it was deep enough that tonus kept it open. He wondered if Varia's spell of long youth had made a difference.

When he'd washed, he pulled on a pair of breeches, then went back to watch Omara work. The Sister looked up at him. "She'll live," she said, examining him calmly. "Who taught you healing? Varia?"

"We weren't together long enough. I learned it from a shaman in Oz. I was his student for a while, but did poorly on my healing tests."

"It wasn't for lack of talent." Omara turned to her aide. "Narella, bandage her. Tightly so the healing spells work properly. We don't want great scars on the marshal's bride."

She got up from the bed, a handsome woman in uniform, managing to seem long mature, despite her youthful appearance. Macurdy wondered how old she actually was. "Let me bandage your forearm, Macurdy," she said. "Gaping like that, the scar will be large and subject to damage. Besides, the blood needs to circulate through the flesh there."

After she'd washed and bandaged it, she sang a brief formula quite different from Arbel's. When she was done, she stepped back and looked at him. "I'll stay with her tonight. Wounds and blood loss like hers shock deeply. I'll not harm her, nor anyone in my care. I was trained first in healing, and only later in other magicks."

Her aura assured him. "Thank you," he said. "I have to see about something." He finished dressing, donned boots, then belted on his knife and saber, and left. On the lawn, a whole platoon of soldiers were guarding Melody's attacker now, despite his manacles. They'd been sent for, as if Sarsli thought someone might try to rescue the man.

Macurdy stopped a few feet away and stared at the attacker. A youth, really, staring back gray-faced but defiant. "Stand him on his feet," Macurdy said. Two soldiers lifted the young man by the arms so that he cried out with pain. When he was standing, Macurdy drew his knife.

"My wife will live. She won't even be badly scarred. Does that cheer you?"

"It wasn't her I climbed the vines to kill. It was you! And if it hadn't been so dark . . . But if killing her would hurt you enough, I could still rejoice in it."

"And you like knives. Have you ever been cut by one? Badly?"

The man said nothing, but fear collapsed his aura.

"I'll show you what it's like. First I'll cut off your ears, then your nose, then your horn and balls, and then . . ."

Abruptly words burst from the young man. "And what of my father? Will you let him do those things to you? A squad of your soldiers raped my mother and sister in front of him, and laughed when he wept and pleaded with them. They took my sister with them when they left with our valuables; God knows what became of her. Afterward my mother killed herself. Will you let him cut you up for that?"

Macurdy stared a long moment. "Where did this happen?"

"In the village of Black Gum, some ninety miles south. My father is the miller there."

"How did you know where to find me?"

For a moment it seemed the youth might refuse to say more; then he answered. "I'd been here in Ternass, apprenticing as a teacher in the common school. When I heard your army had crossed the river, I went home. Too late. So I came back to avenge my family." His defiance faded, leaving him momentarily desolate, but he rallied. "When I got here, everyone was talking about your wedding, as if it was something to celebrate! Everyone knew where you'd be staying. And we apprentices had been invited to the governor's once for Learning Day. Given a tour. I could guess what room you'd be in."

"Um." Macurdy sheathed his knife. "The people in Ternass had something bigger than a wedding to celebrate. A peace has been signed."

"Peace! What good is peace to my family?"

Instead of answering, Macurdy turned to his orderly. "Bring my horse. And one for the prisoner."

With three soldiers, Macurdy took the youth into Ternass, to the jail there, and had the jailer wakened. The man went pale at Macurdy's story. "We'll . . . we'll have him tried tomorrow, I'm sure. And hanged promptly."

"No. I want no trial or hanging. Lock him up. Have a physician do something for his elbow. Keep him here for a week before you let him go. And while he's here, have him visited by the girls I rescued. His soul is scarred like my wife's body. Perhaps their stories will help him." He paused. "There's one named Hermiss that I met two days ago. A friend of the Cyncaidh's wife. Let her arrange it."

"Hermiss? I know her! Her father is principal of the common school."

Macurdy's eyes widened for a moment. "She'll be perfect. No doubt she knows this young man."

As he rode back to the manor, Macurdy told himself grimly that if this had had to happen, some good would come of it yet.

40

Squire Macurdy

Even with frequent healing attention by Omara, and by Macurdy as his skill improved, it was the fifth day after the attack before Melody was strong enough to travel safely and with reasonable comfort. (On the other hand, a physician from Farside would have disbelieved the rate of healing—been impressed that she'd even survived. Not only had blood loss been heavy; her right pleura had been punctured, and the lung collapsed.) By the time they left, the last cohorts were gone, except for their escort, the Kullvordi 2nd Cavalry.

Keeping an easy pace, they reached the Big River after the last infantry cohorts had been ferried across. And traveling more briskly, reached Teklapori eight days later, with Melody fully recovered.

Travel stained, they were ushered into the palace. Inside it had changed conspicuously, the old hangings and furniture mostly replaced. Even Macurdy noticed. It was lighter and brighter, less ornate, less of a hodgepodge. Within minutes a servant came to tell them that King Pavo was waiting for them in the guest parlor. "Two men were with him on business of the crown," the servant added, "but he has sent them away for now." Then he bowed again and gestured them to follow.

They found Wollerda in uniform, one that Macurdy hadn't seen before. The design was the same—the elegantly simple Sisterhood guardsman design—but the material had a velvety sheen, while over one shoulder was a sash that looked to Macurdy like silk, with alternating stripes of Teklan red and

Kullvordi blue. He wore a crown, though not the bejewelled ceremonial crown, and beneath it all, he'd gained weight.

Wollerda was grinning from ear to ear as he stepped quickly to meet them halfway to the throne: Queen Liiset remained in the background as the two ex-rebels gripped and shook hands. "It's good to have you back," Wollerda said, then looked at Melody. "And you, Colonel. Your husband reported your injuries, both in battle and later."

When he'd seated them, he fixed Macurdy with his gaze. "What did you do to her attacker? You didn't say."

Macurdy told him, the story bringing a gradient raising of the royal eyebrows. When it was done, Wollerda looked at Melody. "What do you think of that?"

She shrugged. "He's the commander. And when he explained it . . . The man acted in hatred, for a reason; I'd have done the same, except I wouldn't have botched it. And the story will have spread—he may even have taken it home himself— spread like the story of how Macurdy handled the rapes at Ternass. It'll give the Rude Lands, maybe even the empire, a different view of us here."

Wollerda's lips pursed, and he looked at Macurdy. "You reported some hangings earlier. What happened at Ternass?"

Macurdy told that one, too, leaving out only the ball of glowing plasma at the end of his saber, chuckling now at the memory of the Kormehri running bare-assed.

Wollerda's eyebrows had returned to the rest position. "Macurdy," he said, "I've seen wisdom from you before, but that was true genius." He turned to Liiset. "Show the colonel the changes you've made here. The marshal and I are going to talk about his negotiations with Cyncaidh. I'll send word when we're done."

"Of course, Your Majesty," Liiset answered, and smiling at Melody, led her from the room. Melody would rather have stayed, but didn't argue. When they were gone, Wollerda grinned again.

"Actually I want to talk about more personal matters: about your Varia and my Liiset. Since I married Liiset, I've looked differently at the Sisterhood. And I also understand why you were so determined to recover your Varia. Her twin is a

wonderful wife, whether we're at the table discussing matters
of state, or in bed." He grinned. "And she never demands."
His grin skewed a bit. "But then, she hardly needs to. Her
wishes are seldom far from my own, seldom far enough to
refuse. I suspect she sometimes judges how far I can be moved,
and sets her comments and suggestions accordingly." He
chuckled drily. "I've learned a lot from her; there are things I
look at quite differently now than I did."

He eyed Macurdy shrewdly. "You wonder if that's good, eh?
All in all it is. Before, my opinions were too fixed, my ideals
sometimes at odds with good sense; the Sisters have things to
teach us. Not Sarkia's ready ruthlessness, but . . ."

He changed the subject. "Your reports said nothing about
getting your Varia back, only that you'd married Melody. What
happened?"

Macurdy looked at his palms as if something were written
on them. "She was there: Varia, with Cyncaidh. She's his wife."

"Ah." Wollerda peered intently at Macurdy. "I'd like to know
more about that. There may be insights there."

Macurdy shrugged, then summarized her odyssey from
escaping the Cloister to arriving at Aaeroth Manor. "And when
Cyncaidh got her home—he told me this—he and his wife,
who was far gone in decline and died soon afterward, worked
on her until she agreed to marry him. Told her she didn't have
a chance of ever getting to me again. He said they lied to her
to break her down. *Exaggerated* is the word he used."

Neither man said anything more for a minute, then Wollerda
asked another question. "You wrote that Quaie was dead, that
you killed him yourself. How did *that* happen?"

Macurdy told him. Wollerda stared. "A ball of fire? That's
a magic I never heard of before." He shook his head. "But
you've got something beyond magic, Macurdy: beyond it and
more important. You've got a knack for doing and saying the
right thing. Or maybe that's magic. Anyway, Liiset reported
to the Dynast that you'd killed Quaie, and—" Wollerda got
up and went to a side table—"she sent you a letter we're both
curious about.

Wollerda gave a wax-sealed envelope to Macurdy, who
opened it with his dagger and removed the letter. It was brief,

and when he'd finished reading, he looked at Wollerda. "She wants me to visit the Cloister. She has an important position for me, if I'm interested."

"Are you?"

Macurdy shook his head. "Nope. I can't even imagine what she might offer."

"It could be better than I can offer," Wollerda pointed out. "In some respects, anyway. You'd have more influence from there than from here."

"There's only one Sister I ever wanted to be around, and that's over now. There are other Sisters I like, since I've gotten to know them. Liiset of course. And Omara, who was in charge of the sorcery unit with the army. She did a lot of good; among other things she saved Melody's life. And I got along with Sarkia all right, when we were negotiating. But . . ." He shrugged again. "Sarkia's too cold-blooded for me. And the things she had done to Varia—if I'd known about them earlier, I'd have killed her." He exhaled audibly. "I'll send her a message; tell her I plan to stay in Tekalos, to farm and have children."

"Maybe things will change in the Sisterhood," Wollerda said thoughtfully. "When someone else takes over."

Macurdy, seeing the aura as well as the man, looked sharply at him. "What haven't you told me?"

Wollerda shrugged. "Liiset doesn't often say what's in the messages she gets from the Cloister, but . . . Two weeks ago, when she read one, she got a strange look. And didn't put the letter away as she usually does—as if she intended to read it again first. Then I had a chance and read it myself. Sarkia asked who she'd recommend as the new Dynast, when the time came that one was needed. Asked for four names, and who she'd recommend *not* be considered.

"Later on she said to me, 'You read my message from the Dynast, didn't you?' and I admitted it of course." He looked meaningfully at Macurdy. "I asked Liiset once who she thought would eventually replace Sarkia, and she said that was one thing Sarkia never talked about. So. What caused her to think about it now?" Wollerda paused as if to stress what he said next. "Then, after her last weekly message, Liiset reminded me of that. And said, 'The Dynast has gone into seclusion.

She's at the Cloister, but staying in her suite.' " He shrugged. "Looks as if time has finally caught up with her."

Macurdy nodded thoughtfully. "Who did Liiset recommend, do you know?"

Wollerda shook his head. "I'll ask her at supper. She might even tell us."

At supper, Macurdy got a pretty good idea how Wollerda had gained weight; this wasn't the simple fare he'd eaten as a commander of rebels. When they'd finished, a light wine was served. Macurdy drank buttermilk, instead, and they talked of his plans to farm. He had in mind to try certain Indiana practices in Teklan conditions.

"I had the idea you wanted to be ambassador to the empire," Wollerda said.

Macurdy looked at his wife. "I doubt that Melody would like living in a city, especially where people might be hostile to us. She might run someone through before it was over."

"Well, if you're set on farming, I've got a farm for you. Actually a choice of two large estates. Their ex-owners were guilty of major tax frauds."

"What will the locals think of that? The neighbors around there?"

"They'll cheer. They're smallholders, and both the men I've thrown in prison were old favorites of Gurtho, arrogant and overbearing." He cocked an eyebrow. "Actually I had another job I'd hoped you'd take, if you turned down the ambassadorship. And to tell the truth, I can't imagine you being satisfied as a farmer very long, after what you've been doing."

Macurdy shook his head, laughing. "You don't know me as well as you think. I'm a farmer born and bred." He paused. "What did you have in mind?"

"Minister of Revenue. It needs a strong man, the income is more reliable than farming, and you'd have a lot of influence."

Macurdy shook his head vigorously. "No way in hell would I take that job. You might consider Tarlok though; he could do it, do it right. And Kithro's worth considering as ambassador."

"Hmm. You know, that's a good idea. Both of them are. I'll take it up with them."

"Just don't tell Tarlok I recommended him."

Wollerda grunted. "Anyone who'd want the job, I'd rather not give it to. In running a kingdom, money's a problem, but if you don't tax honestly, the whole thing turns sour."

Macurdy sipped his buttermilk, saying nothing. He was thinking about the new furniture and wall hangings in the palace, all expensive.

Wollerda's next words popped Macurdy out of his reverie. "Liiset," he said, "who did you recommend to the Dynast as dynast-designate? And who did you recommend against? Can you tell us?"

Liiset looked at him calmly. "Of the four I recommended, only two are anyone you know of. My first recommendation was Varia, if we could somehow get her back. When we were young, she was trained for the executive staff. But that's out, since she's married Cyncaidh. And my second—" She turned to their guests. "My second was Curtis Macurdy." They gawped, Macurdy especially. "You're of Sisterhood lineage," she pointed out, "and I see no reason that the Dynast has to be a woman, though who knows how Sarkia might look at it. As for recommending against someone—I'll keep that to myself. It's not someone I dislike; simply someone whose appointment would be unfortunate, a source of abrasion and conflict."

Liiset's report introverted them, killing the conversation. After a few minutes, Wollerda excused them.

Before they went to sleep, Melody lay gazing at the ceiling. "Macurdy," she said, "I'm glad you refused to be the tax collector."

He grunted. "It's a lousy job. A lot of people are going to resent whoever does it, even if he's honest. To do a good job of it, you've got to push, even throw people in jail. If I had to do that, I'd get mad every time I saw money wasted, and any government invented by man is going to waste money. Even if it's only poor judgement."

Melody nodded. "I grew up thinking there were only three honorable professions: soldier, farmer, and shaman. And I'd rather have you be a farmer. Farmers are home at night." She turned on her side, fondled him, felt him swell. "Soldiers are likelier to get killed, too." She raised up on an elbow, kissed him and threw a leg across his. "And I want us to be together a long long time."

They moved to one of the farms, into a house with eight rooms plus kitchen, pantry, cellar, and servants' wing. The field hands had kept the crops in decent tilth, and Macurdy had no difficulties with any of them. Summer faded into fall, and Melody learned about morning sickness. The corn was harvested, the potatoes dug, and fall plowing gotten under way. Farming wasn't as satisfying as he remembered it, but Macurdy told himself that would change when the crops were crops he'd planted himself. And when he learned where to get alfalfa seed, and peanuts, and other things he wanted to try.

One noon, he came up from the fields to find a large and familiar black bird perched on the roof, looking coldly at the cats, all of them interested but tentative. No doubt partly because of his size, but also because he was scolding them in a perfectly human voice.

"Blue Wing!" Macurdy shouted joyously. "It's great to see you!"

"Really! How great could that possibly be, when you keep creatures like those around?"

"The cats? There's not one who'd tackle you. They're not foolish enough for that."

"As long as I don't fall asleep."

Macurdy ran them off—as barn cats they were wary of him anyway—and Blue Wing glided down to the porch roof.

"Where've you been the past year?" Macurdy asked.

"I helped raise a pair of young, and amongst my kind, it takes till nearly the equinox before they can forage for themselves."

"Did you bring your wife along?"

"By wife I presume you mean a permanent mate. Happily we don't have such aberrated concepts." He eyed Macurdy. "Perhaps for a species like yours, that takes so ridiculously long to mature their young and tends to have more or less permanent residences, an arrangement such as marriage makes sense. But for the more fortunate . . ."

Macurdy grinned. "I'm married, you know. To Melody."

"I'm aware of that. We have already spoken, she and I. I'm also aware that she will give birth next summer. And frankly, I think she'd be much better off laying eggs than in passing something the size of a human infant through her vent. After carrying it around inside her for the better part of a year! Outrageous!"

"How'd you like to stay around this winter? I'll make you a perch in the corner of the windbreak, where the winter winds won't be so bad, and put a roof on it to keep the rain and sleet off. On top of a twelve-foot post, on a platform so the cats can't bother you, or a weasel. And nail a sheet of copper around the post near the top, so they can't get close enough to scrabble at the platform. How about it?"

Macurdy built the perch that same day, Blue Wing supervising, and although afterward the bird was off roving much of the time, over the weeks before winter they had several good conversations. Through his species' hive mind, the bird had heard quite a bit about the war, but what he learned from Macurdy was both broader and more detailed than any other great raven had learned. And when Macurdy was in the fields working, or in the woods with his men cutting firewood, Blue Wing sometimes accompanied Melody on her almost daily rides, perched on her wrist like a falconer's hawk so they could talk more easily. It was mostly she who fed him, when he was around.

Mostly though she rode alone or with Macurdy. The Green River, broad and dark, formed the south boundary of the estate, and they enjoyed exploring the woods that bordered it, both on the floodplain and the first terrace. Coons were numerous, and possums and fox squirrels. Floods were too extreme for beaver and muskrats, and deer and razorback were scarce because of hunting, but porcupines and otters weren't uncommon. Sometimes they saw tracks of bobcat and fox. And of course, cows that trailed down to drink.

Once Melody called, "Macurdy! Come here! There's something you've got to see!"

He rode over to where she sat in the saddle, pointing at a

patch of heavily disturbed ground. Something had been rooting up roots or tubers of some sort; skunk-cabbage he supposed. "Looks like a really big razorback," he said.

She shook her head, led him to the shore, and pointed to an exposed sandy mud flat. "Look at those."

He saw hoof prints, sharp and deep, far bigger than any razorback's he knew of. "I've never seen any before," she said, "and never expected to, certainly not in country as cleared and farmed as this."

Macurdy chewed a lip. A great boar could mean trouble. Something that large could hardly sustain itself on skunk-cabbage; in country without much large game, it would prey on livestock. And while he didn't believe in enchanted swine with powers of witchcraft, even in Yuulith, he could very well believe in an animal so cunning that it could be thought of as supernatural. Hopefully it was merely passing through. If it took only a calf or two, he'd call it a bargain.

They found where the tracks moved on, and leaning forward in the saddle, Melody started following them.

"Where are you going?"

"To see if we can come up on it. We'll probably never have another chance to see one."

"Hey! Wait now! They're dangerous!"

She looked at him as if to say, "So?"

"Suppose you do? And suppose he doesn't like it?"

"Then he'd have to run fast enough to catch us."

"He just might do that."

"Damn it, Macurdy! Who's the one that climbed the tree to chase the jaguar out?"

"I didn't have any choice."

"Well then, who went into the fallen timber and buffaloed Slaney? And who went into the Kormehri camp and fronted down a whole damned company?"

"I *had* to do those things, honey. I didn't have any choice!"

"Macurdy, you can be so exasperating!"

"Besides, you're pregnant. If something happens to you . . ."

She swore at him, and turning her horse, trotted across the bottomland and up onto the terrace, Macurdy trotting Hog a bit behind. He knew what would happen next, and he was right; when she got onto the firmer high ground, she kicked her horse to a gallop. The last he saw of her, she'd crossed a field of corn stubble and cleared the rail fence on the other side. He shook his head, wondering if she'd ever get over her reckless streak. *After the baby comes,* he told himself. If she didn't jiggle and jar it to death first. He wasn't going to bring that up though. Not again.

To his relief, there was no predation. The great boar passed through the neighborhood leaving no damage behind.

They had snow cover two weeks before the solstice, which everyone said was early. And when, a month later, it had deepened instead of melting, they said it was the hardest winter they'd ever seen. Finally, in mid-One-Month, a thaw arrived, with an all-night rain that took the snow out at one shot.

Meanwhile Melody had begun to swell, and not long afterward could feel the fetus move inside her. In bed, she'd place Macurdy's hand where he could feel it, and he decided he loved her more than ever. She was more affectionate than ever, too, given to kissing him without warning—or without cause, so far as he could see.

One night after they'd made careful love, she lay gentle fingers on his cheek. "Liiset calls you Curtis," she said. "Is that what Varia called you?"

"Um-hmm."

"Would you like me to call you that?"

"If you'd like. I like whatever you call me." He chuckled. "Except when you're mad at me. Some of those names I don't like too well."

"Curtis," she said thoughtfully. "Curtis. I like it." She kissed him. "Curtis, I love you. I love you very much."

And when they got up in the morning, she still called him Curtis. She stopped running her horse, too, settling for a walking gait, or an easy trot. *She's settling down,* he told himself. *At last.*

In the beginning of Two-Month, with the ground bare, the big freeze struck. The fireplaces, never adequate in cold weather, seemed almost useless now. More blankets were piled on the beds, enough that they had to wake up to turn over. Ice froze in the pail in the kitchen, and despite the fireplace, burst the ceramic pitcher on the washstand in their bedroom. Macurdy let Blue Wing perch on the mantle in the living room, though the bird suffered from claustrophobia indoors. Then, blowing on his fingers from time to time, the squire of Macurdy Manor sat down and drew plans for a brick stove, with flues to be built in the walls between the living room and the rooms adjacent, intending to build it the next summer.

The big freeze lasted for four days, cold enough that when he went outside, even at midday, the hairs in his nostrils stiffened. Something which, back home in Washington County, was taken to mean the temperature was below zero.

This time the cold broke without a storm; on the fifth day it simply warmed up. Not up to freezing—not that warm—but the bright sun felt good on his face, and the cows were let out for the exercise. The sparrows and crows were out too, those that hadn't died. And Blue Wing. After five days with only brief hours outside, he flew high and wide. "The river is frozen," he announced when he returned, and said that was something rare for the Green. The ground was certainly frozen—as hard as the new concrete pavement on Main Street back in Salem.

The next day dawned warmer than the day before. Toward noon the temperature rose above freezing, the bright sun shining on a slick of mud atop the frozen ground, and Macurdy and Melody saddled their horses for a ride. The cattle tracks went directly to the pasture above the woods, and when the two riders got there, Macurdy rode around examining what condition it was in, while Melody rode down to see the frozen river, and Blue Wing soared high overhead. The pasture grass was a mixture, and grazed-down enough that Macurdy wasn't sure what species dominated. Nor how much winter-kill there might be, given such severe cold without snow cover.

He heard Blue Wing shrieking something and looked up, to see the raven spiraling down, almost diving. The short hairs bristled on Macurdy's neck. Then he discerned the words: "Macurdy! Macurdy! The ice has broken! Melody is in the water!"

Thumping Hog's flanks with his heels, Macurdy galloped as recklessly as Melody ever had. At the river bank he pulled up. The hole was mostly full of broken ice, and only her horse's head showed, whinnying wildly. *She's gone under the ice,* Macurdy thought, and galloped wildly downstream, where eighty yards away he could see water kept open by rapids. If he could get there before she was carried through and under the next ice . . .

He got there just as she emerged, and Hog didn't hesitate when Macurdy drove him into water shockingly, deathly cold, reaching her near the foot of the rip. Leaning down, he grabbed her sodden coat with a grip of iron, then Hog fought their way across the current back to shore. Macurdy jumped down and examined her; there was no trace of spirit aura; little even of body aura.

He howled then, howled at the sky like a hound. But only once before turning her over on her stomach and beginning the artificial respiration he'd learned in grade school, at the same time chanting brokenly a formula Arbel had taught him. He pressed and relaxed, pressed and relaxed, until, soaked as he was, he was shivering almost too violently to continue. *God!* he prayed silently, *let her live, and I'll do anything you ask!* He knew that artificial respiration would be useless if long interrupted, yet feared that any life which might remain would freeze out of her, so after half an hour, his hands and mind numbed by cold and shock, he stopped. High clouds had moved in to block the sun, as if God himself had turned against him.

Almost too cold to function, he struggled the dead body across Hog's shoulders, then managed, barely, to pull himself into the saddle. At the house, he carried what had been Melody into the living room, while his houseman, who'd come into the room to investigate, melted back out in shock. There was no trace of aura now. He stripped her, dried her, wrapped her in blankets, and laid her out in front of the fireplace. Then, long after there was any use in it, he began artificial respiration again. He had only a vague notion of time, but finally was aware that her body was stiffening.

Moving woodenly, he carried her into the bedroom, washed her, painstakingly brushed her hair, and got her into clean clothes—her dress uniform, stored in a cedar chest against moths. When that was done, he called for his houseman, who came in wide-eyed and silent.

"Have Dellerd harness Socks and hitch him to the buggy. I'm taking my wife to Teklapori."

Not trusting his voice, the houseman nodded silently and disappeared. When he was gone, Macurdy wept violently for about a minute—hard racking sobs that shook his whole body, while the tears sluiced. Then it passed. Stripping himself before the bedroom fire, he rubbed his body with a rough towel till he was red and tingling with renewed circulation. That done, he dressed in dry clothes, put on a heavy coat, and carried the body out to the buggy—a sort of surrey with the back enclosed—where he lay it gently on the back seat. Then, after giving a few instructions to the houseman and farm foreman, he drove off down the road toward the capital, a silent Blue Wing flying low overhead.

PART 7
Goodbyes

41

Farewell to Melody

I took it easy, driving in to Teklapori; I didn't want to give her body any bumpier a ride than need be. It's not like I thought she was still in it or anything. It was a matter of respect. And besides, it seemed like all of her I had left.

I felt tired and empty, and kind of half conscious, as if my mind was turned off, but every now and then I'd come out of it and look around. After a while it started to get dark, so I stopped and called to Blue Wing, and asked if he'd like to ride on the folding roof. I suspected he wouldn't, on something moving like that, but he didn't much like flying after dark, either, and it seemed as if he wanted to go with me. Or with Melody, actually; him and her had gotten to be such good friends that fall and winter. Anyway he didn't say a thing, just flew up there and perched, and on we went.

After another couple hours, I stopped and put a feedbag of oats on Socks's nose, and when I got back on the seat, Blue Wing was perched on the arm rest on the rider's side, claustrophobia be darned. I didn't say anything when I sat down, but after we started off again, I reached over and stroked his head a couple of times. "Thanks, old friend," I said, and started crying again. After a while he spoke. I don't think he had the equipment to talk really quietly, but he kept it halfway soft.

"That's not her back there, you know."

"I know," I answered. "But I've got to treat her body with

415

respect. She lived in it for more than twenty years, and loved me with it, and I loved her with it."

"Do you feel her now?" he asked.

I shook my head. "No. Do you?"

"Yes." He paused half a minute, then went on. "She tells me you will too, when you go to sleep tonight."

He meant it, I didn't doubt. I didn't know whether she'd really talked to him, or if he only imagined it, but he believed what he told me. "How does she seem?" I asked him.

"Different and the same. She is herself, beyond doubt, but without appurtenances or impurities, irritations or anxieties."

"Umm." I looked at that. "I never knew Melody to have anxieties."

"Oh yes. Some of her impatience grew out of anxiety. Anxiety that she'd miss something, that it might get away. Everyone, man or raven, has a main inner impediment in life. Impatience was hers."

I thought about that. She'd been patient enough waiting for me, but overall it seemed like he was right. I wondered what my main impediment was. "Is she happy?" I asked.

"Yes she is. If you concentrate, perhaps you can sense her, even awake."

I tried it: made a picture of her in front of me, hoping she might sort of step into it, but she didn't, so I gave up on it and just drove along. After a while I got sleepy, and about half dozed. Then it seemed like there was a light floating above Socks, a sort of round glow maybe three feet across, and I stared at it, not hard, just looking. It was a spirit aura without any body, I realized, and told myself whose it had to be. Although a lot of the pattern was missing.

≋Of course, darling,≋ she thought to me. My hair stood right on end; even the follicles without hair drew up in little cones. ≋A lot of an aura,≋ she went on, ≋goes with living or comes from living.≋ I started to shake, not scared, but just . . . *It's really you,* I thought to her, and realized that along with the goose bumps, and the tears running down my face, I was grinning like a fool.

We rode along like that awhile without anything more being said. There was just a feeling of clear pure love. I don't know how long this went on—fifteen minutes, or an hour or longer. Probably longer, the way things turned out. Then the buggy hit a good bump and my eyes popped open, and the aura was gone. All that was left was a goodbye and a thought—that she loved me, and she'd drop in on me from time to time in my dreams.

I looked to see what Blue Wing had made of all this, or if he even knew, but he was perched there with his head tucked under his wing. So far as I could see, it had all gone by him, and I wondered if maybe I'd been dreaming.

Well, you big lunk, I told myself, *you'll just have to be your own witness. Whatever it was you saw, it seems to have healed your soul. Let it go at that.* Then the goose bumps came back over me, not fierce like before, but in a sort of comfortable wash, and I almost grinned my face in two. *Thank you, Melody,* I thought after her. The feeling kept on fizzing another minute, like soda water, then faded and was gone.

Another half hour or so and I could see the fringe of Teklapori ahead, a darker darkness in the night. I'd been longer on the road than I'd had any idea of.

42

Farewell to Tekalos

Melody was gone, but I still needed to burn her body. It's the way things are done in Yuulith. Lots of people there believe that ashing the body releases the soul from it; that otherwise it has to stay till the body decays. Which may be how it is, if you believe it strongly enough. I could have done it on the farm, but her best friends, along with me and Blue Wing, were Jeremid and Loro. They'd want to be there when the pyre was lit, to say a proper goodbye, and plenty of others would too. And she'd come to the ceremony, for their sake and mine, I had no doubt.

I'm getting ahead of myself though. When I drove up to the barbican, it was late enough that in Six-Month it would have been near dawn, but in Two-Month there was a lot of night left. In spite of my warm cap and coat and mitts, I felt about half froze. Overhead in the gate tower they didn't believe who it was; told me to go away and come back at sunup. I told them that somebody better get down there and at least shine a lantern on me, or I'd have their ass on a stick. It took a minute, but finally someone shined a target lantern between the bars of a view slot, and in another half minute what they call "the spy's gate" opened and a guard stepped out. The spy's gate is just wide enough for a man. It's like a ten-foot-long tunnel through the wall. In case of siege, you can use it to let spies in and out after dark. It has a small portcullis at the inner end that they can drop and trap you inside, if they want to. I

418

told the guard who'd opened it that I needed to take the gig in. He could see who I was then, and explained apologetically that they weren't allowed to open the main gate for anyone after midnight, not even a general. Said it had been the rule for a long long time, peace or war.

That not only irritated me, it felt like an insult to Melody, so I grabbed him by the greatcoat, shook him, and held him up against the stone wall.

"You go back inside," I hissed, "and find the officer of the guard, and tell that son of a bitch that General Macurdy will personally flog him right down to the bare ribs if he doesn't get his ass out here right away." And at the time I meant it, though I'd never have done it.

When I let him go, he hurried back inside leaving a string of yessirs behind, and closed the spy's gate after him. It took a few minutes for the officer of the guard to get there—he'd pulled his breeches on over his night shirt and smelled like stale beer—and after seeing for sure who it was, ordered the main gate opened, looking almost as worried about that as he was scared of me. I heard the windlass and chain grind, and watched it raise up. Then I drove the buggy through, and heard it being let down again.

The guards outside the palace itself were no problem. They invited me to sleep in the guard room, but I told them I wouldn't leave Melody. Said I wanted firewood brought out to the graveled walk, and half a dozen blankets. They'd have gotten in trouble if they'd woke up any household help, so while one of them led Socks around to the palace stable, two others brought out wood and kindling, and another came out half buried with army blankets. I laid a fire, lit it with a pass of my hand, wrapped myself in blankets with my feet toward the flames, and went to sleep on the ground.

I woke up stiff, with frost on my eyebrows. The sun had just come up and was shining in my face. The door guards had kept the fire fed, and when the household help was up and about, they'd told them where I was, and why. So almost as quick as I stood up, the steward came out and asked what I wanted done with "Colonel Melody's mortal remains," volunteering a small building used for holding bodies. Somehow I didn't want to leave it though, and asked him just to let the king and queen know. And to have something brought out that Blue Wing and I could eat. Blue Wing was awake ahead of me, and sat on the roof of the buggy with his feathers fluffed out against the cold.

The food arrived a few minutes ahead of Wollerda. When he came out, it occurred to me that I looked pretty strange— a little crazy, you get right down to it—sitting in the buggy wrapped in blankets, sharing heated-up leftovers of last night's supper roast with a great raven the size of a turkey buzzard. With the frozen body of my wife on the back seat, and the remains of my fire black and gray on his front walk. So when he urged me to come in—the guards would watch the gig, he said—I went inside with him.

Minutes later he was giving orders for a big ceremonial pyre to be built on the parade ground in eight days. That gave him time to have people sent for—officers from the march north, and especially the rebel army—and time for them to get there. I asked what if the weather turned warm, but Liiset said not to worry. Which brought to mind Kittul Kenderson putting a spell on the dead dwarves so they wouldn't spoil. The weather had been a lot warmer then.

I borrowed a saddle horse and rode north myself to tell Jeremid. It didn't seem right to send someone else. I got there in time for supper, and right away he sent a rider to let Loro know, and Jesper and Tarlok. After we'd eaten, he poured himself wine, while I drank sassafras.

"I don't know what to say, Macurdy," he told me. "I expected you two to grow old together. I'd decided early on that the best I could hope for was, she might marry me if you got your Varia back. But as long as she had a chance with you, she'd never settle for anyone else."

Grow old together. That was one thing we couldn't have done, unless Varia'd pulled off a miracle with her; I'd figured that when the time came, she'd get old and I'd take care of her. Old age wouldn't have been a problem, I didn't think, though it might have been tough for a while when she found out she was aging and I wasn't.

Jeremid hadn't gotten married. Instead, he had himself three concubines. For different moods, he said. I don't think I could be happy that way, but his aura told me he was. Content, anyway.

I hadn't planned to spend the night there, but I did. When it got late, he offered me the company of one of his concubines for the night. I told him I wasn't ready for something like that yet.

The day of the fire was mild and bright and still. There were probably a couple thousand veterans of the invasion, a lot of them ex-rebels down from the hills, plus palace staff and thousands of townfolk. The pyre was a big one, and it was me lit it off, of course. It took off quick—a small fortune in lamp oil had been poured on it—and the smoke rose straight up. Folks stood there till the whole pile burnt down; took a while. It's sort of a rule that you don't walk off early from a funeral fire. And way up high—about as high as birds fly, I guess—I could see Blue Wing soaring in big circles.

That evening I ate with Wollerda and Liiset and Jeremid. And Omara. Liiset had invited her; she'd been assigned as Liiset's secretary, lady-in-waiting, and healer to the palace.

Wollerda asked me again to go to Duinarog as his ambassador, but I told him no. There'd likely be too many ylver who'd resent me, the general of the invasion that killed so many of them. And anyway I didn't want to. Then Liiset asked if I'd reconsider going to the Cloister. She believed Sarkia was having second thoughts about a lot of things in her life. There wasn't any question now: she was in decline after more than two hundred years. I told Liiset I appreciated the invite, but I just wasn't willing. That she should send Sarkia my thanks, and my best wishes that she could wrap things up all right.

Next she said I'd need someone to look after household matters for me on the farm. And that if I wanted, Omara was willing to take the job.

For just a minute I was tempted. I already had plans of my own that I hadn't let on, and they included getting further trained in healing. She'd be as good a teacher as I could hope to have, and I liked Omara, liked how serious and honest she was. And for looks, she was scarcely behind Varia and Liiset. But I said no to that too. Making sure Omara knew that I liked and admired her.

That's when I told them I wasn't going to stay in Tekalos.

"Where are you going?" Wollerda asked surprised.

"Back home to Farside," I told him.

You could have heard a pin drop.

"When?"

"I'm leaving here tomorrow. By way of the farm, to tell the staff I'm going, and to get Hog. They'll take care of things till you sell the place to someone."

He sat there stunned, so I explained. "An awful lot has happened to me: I started a war where thousands of men died. And loved two women and lost them both. Now I need to get away, let things settle out in my mind. I can help my dad on the farm, probably log some, and just be in my own world awhile. Then . . . then I expect I'll come back. I'm not sure why, but it seems to me I will."

I didn't say anything about what I planned to do before I crossed over.

After we'd done talking, Wollerda invited me to his bath. Not Jeremid and me, just me. But when I got there, Liiset was there too. Standing nekkit like that, she'd have quickened a statue, so I got right in the water before I got a hard-on. We talked a bit, and Wollerda asked me to stay for just a few months—long enough to help him with some problems. We talked about them awhile, and I got some ideas I told him about, but I could see he really didn't need me. He just figured if I stayed around that long, I'd be over losing Melody and decide not to go.

Liiset told me that going through the other way was a lot different than coming through to Yuulith. She made it sound kind of like a hole opening in a water tank, squirting water through in one direction. Anyone could go through with the flow, the problem being whether you arrived alive or dead, sane or insane. But going through the other way, against the pressure so to speak, seemed to be possible only if you had enough ylvin blood and talent.

I didn't worry about it. I had no doubt I could do it. Anyway, after a few minutes, I said I needed to get some sleep, which was true enough, so we got out and dried off, and I left.

In my room, I'd just gone to bed when someone rapped on the door. I figured it was Jeremid, curious about what got said in the hot tub, so I called out, "Just a minute," and going over, turned the latch and opened it.

It was Omara standing there.

"Hi," I said. "What brings you here?" I was pretty sure I knew.

"Liiset suggested I come."

"Suggested? Or ordered?"

"Suggested. She is not Sarkia or Idri."

Her aura showed no sign of lying. I could feel old junior swelling, and found myself stepping back, letting her in. I watched my hand close the door behind her, turn the latch and set the bolt.

"I was glad to," she went on. "Wanted to. You are a very attractive man, Macurdy. Compelling." She stepped out of her robe then, nekkit as could be, and twice as pretty.

"Well then," I said, and peeled off my nightshirt. We put our arms around each other and kissed, then kissed some more, warm and wet. She felt good, awfully good, pressed up against me. After a minute we went to bed, and I drew the bed curtains.

After a while we got up and washed. "You are a very nice lover, Macurdy," she said. "But why did you draw the curtains?"

That kind of surprised me. "To keep the warmth in," I told her.

"I thought so. Are you unable to keep yourself warm with the mind?"

"Warm with the mind?"

According to her it was simple enough; most folks with much talent could learn. "It's limited, unfortunately," she went on. "It simply increases the rate at which the body creates heat from the food you eat, and circulates that heat. You can even concentrate it into your fingers and toes. It doesn't suffice for severe weather, though. Had you been unclothed and outside in the bitter weather recently, you'd soon have felt cold, and after a time would have frozen." She looked at me as if considering something. "There is another, very superior technique requiring more talent, but it takes careful training. As in fire starting, you do it by drawing heat from the Web of the World. The difficulty lies in control; you can easily and quickly injure or kill yourself with it. I can train you to use it safely, if you'd like."

"How long would it take?"

"Two or three days, perhaps. Or a week."

My glands were telling me, "Say yes, Macurdy, you fool," but I heard my mouth saying: "Omara, that's something I'd like to learn, and you're the one I'd like to learn it from, but—" I shrugged. "I want to go home to Farside. It feels to me like it's what I need to do, what I'm supposed to do. And if I don't go now, I may not ever."

"I understand," she said, and I think she really did.

She stayed awhile, to teach me the technique for warming the body from inside, and for me there wasn't any trick to that one at all. Then we got friendly again, and after that she put her robe back on and left.

Just for the heck of it, I left my nightshirt off and slept on top the covers that night, warm as toast. The only thing was, at breakfast next morning, with Wollerda and Liiset, I ate about twice as much as usual.

43

Vulkan

After breakfast I said goodbye to folks. A little bit dishonestly, letting them think I'd be going from the farm to Ferny Cove, in case Sarkia got ideas. Then I drove Socks and the buggy back to the farm, where I packed stuff to take with me—not very much—and went over things with the foreman and steward. I spent the night in our old bedroom; had a little spate of grief, but it passed. Then, early the next morning, rode north on Hog to the Valley Highway and headed west, taking neither remount nor pack horse. Just some silver so I could sleep at inns, and some gold coins about the size of double eagles to use on Farside, and to pay Arbel for the training I wanted. Being alone, and not caring to sit around a potroom in the evening, I generally rode late. If I didn't come to an inn, I slept in a barn. I didn't trouble to count the days.

The house looked like it had when I'd left Wolf Springs. Lamplight shone through the cracks between the shutters, and thin smoke rose from three of the chimneys, flattening out above the roof in a layer that by moonlight looked like cotton gauze. Getting down off Hog, I knocked at the door.

It was Hauser that opened it. He stood there for a minute with his mouth open, then grinned, stepped outside, and shook my hand. For a minute I thought he was going to hug me! "Macurdy!" he said. "What brings you here? I've been picturing you in a manor somewhere, or a palace! Come in!"

"I'll stable my horse first," I said. He said he'd do it, but I said I'd better, Hog being touchy with strangers. In the horse shed, I lit the lamp with my finger, hung up Hog's tack, and curried him three-four minutes, which was plenty, given the winter weather. Then I went back to the house.

I'd hardly knocked again before Hauser opened the door. Arbel was standing with him, and gave me one of his long looks. Then he grinned bigger than I'd ever seen him before; grins aren't Arbel's specialty. "So," he said, "the hero of Wolf Springs returns. It's good to see you, Macurdy." He led us to his parlor and we all three sat down. "What brings you back?"

He'd called me the hero of Wolf Springs! And his aura said he was being sarcastic! "I'm going back to Farside," I told him, "and Oz wasn't a whole lot farther than Ferny Cove. Besides, I was in Oztown twice, getting ready for the war, and never got to Wolf Springs to apologize or thank you. You did a lot for me, and I've always felt bad about leaving Oz the way I did. It must have hurt your reputation. Wolf Springs' too."

Arbel laughed. "Hurt my reputation? You became famous in Oz as the man who climbed a tree to drive a jaguar out. The man who beat up half the House of Heroes, or at least a number of them, including a sergeant famous as a brawler, and rode off with the best looking, most daring and admired spear maiden in Oz. And then became really famous for the war."

My jaw must have been down on my chest when he finished, but it didn't stay there long, because the next thing he said was, "Where is your spear maiden?"

I didn't tell him flat out; I led into it. "She and I were leaders in the rebellion that got Pavo crowned king," I said, "and she was with me all the way through the war. She was a colonel, wounded at the Battle of Ternass. Then we got married. She died about three weeks ago. Drowned." I told him how it happened, how Blue Wing had fetched me—the whole thing except how terrible I'd felt. "We burned her body outside the palace," I finished. "The king and queen were there, and a couple thousand veterans of the war. Not to mention most of Teklapori. She was well-known and much admired."

Arbel shook his head, looking sober. "A grievous loss, Macurdy," he said. "I can see the scar. I can also see you've healed." None of us said anything more right away. Then he smiled a little. "You've gotten a reputation as a wizard, too. You killed the evil Quaie with a ball of fire. . . ."

My eyes must have bugged out. "How did you hear about that?" I asked.

"The story spread through the empire and Marches; merchants carried it from there. It reached Oz this winter. And our troops brought home other stories. Perhaps exaggerated."

"Probably." It was an invitation to tell him stories, and I would before I left, but not just then. "You asked what brought me here. I told you part of it, but there's more." I stopped then. I'd been taking it for granted he'd say yes. "If you'll change your mind," I went on, "and teach me more of the shaman's profession, mainly the healing skills, I'd like to try them on Farside. I'll be glad to pay you for your trouble."

He laughed out loud. "But you're not sure I will, because I sent you to the militia. Well. I'll be happy to. But first, tell me what magicks you've demonstrated since I saw you last."

I did, not leaving out about my new teeth, though I could hardly take credit for them. It'd been Varia's spells, and from there, my jaws had taken over. I told him the luck I'd had with the healing he'd taught me, him and Omara, and about learning to keep myself warm. And about looking into the eye holes in that skull on the headwaters of the Tuliptree; to me that was bigger magic than the way I'd killed Quaie. "I guess when I was here before," I said, "I wasn't really ready to learn much."

Arbel laughed, then we sat around and talked about different things. He'd found an apprentice he liked—a twelve-year-old girl with a lot of talent, who went home before supper. That was the disadvantage of having a young girl as an apprentice, he said; you couldn't very well keep them around in the evening. Folks might get the wrong idea.

Ozians are pretty free and easy, but they don't put up with a man humping children. The punishment is, they tie you up, set you astraddle of a log, nail your cod to it, stack wood around you, and put a dull knife in your free hand. Then they light the wood. If you saw off your cod, you're a castrate, and a slave into the bargain. If you don't, you won't suffer very long, but it might seem like it.

Hauser wasn't talking, just listening, and anyway, his face, and the way he sat, and his aura all told me he was looking in, not out. It came to me that what I'd said about going back to Farside must have hit him hard. I could go because I had ylvin blood, and talent, and some training, while he didn't and couldn't.

While I was at it, I told them about other magicks I'd seen, like Kittul Kendersson "blessing" my sword, and weaving a spell so the dead dwarves wouldn't swell and stink. And about the Sisters that went with the army to heal wounds, and Quaie's shock fingers he'd used on me.

I also told him what Omara said about keeping warm by drawing heat from what she called the "Web of the World," and the dangers in learning it. That really got Arbel's interest. He said he was going to try working it out for himself.

He also told me that magic misused, even accidentally, kicked back on the magician sooner or later, and that big magic was at least as dangerous to the user as to anyone else. There'd been folks who'd set out to develop really big powers, but they died in the process.

After a while it got late, and Arbel put me up in a small guest room with a clean straw sack on the bed. I stripped, put on my nightshirt and lay down, wishing Omara would come through the door like she had at the palace. How I felt about her wasn't anything like I'd felt about Varia or Melody, but I liked her a lot. She was a good person, and just then I was lonesome, in spite of being in the same house with two old friends, and another probably perched on the roof beside a chimney.

I thought about Hauser, too. I could stay in Yuulith and be a bigshot if I wanted, in Tekalos or at the Cloister, and probably in Oz or other places. Or be Wollerda's ambassador at Duinarog. But instead I was going back to Farside, to the farm. While Hauser could probably be a professor on Farside, but in Oz he was a slave. Couldn't go back, even if they'd let him.

Then I got thinking about the dangers Arbel had mentioned in big powerful magicks, and told myself I better be careful with fireballs. Sarkia was supposed to have practiced magic for two hundred years and stayed young and healthy. And was

only now declining; something I wouldn't mention to Arbel.
But from what I'd heard about Ferny Cove, from some
Kormehri and from Sarkia herself, she hadn't used magicks
for weapons, only for protection—confusion spells, invisibility
spells, spells to raise fogs and mists. And tracking magic. Things
like that. Maybe magicks like those didn't kick back on a person.

What with all the thoughts running through my head, I must
have laid there an hour before I got to sleep.

The next day my lessons started. Like before, Arbel said I
should do other stuff too, to keep grounded, and offered to
get a slave girl sent in for me once a week, like he did for
himself. I was tempted, but instead, for a few mornings, I
saddled up Hog and rode around the countryside a couple
hours. Then I took a notion to train with Isherhohm's militia
veterans on Six-Day afternoons, for the exercise and to keep
my hand in. They'd nearly all of them been in the war, and
I'd been the commander, but Isherhohm treated me like just
another veteran.

The morning after the first workout, I was sore all over,
really sore! I'd gone soft! Never thought that could happen
to me. So I started taking an ax and trotting out to the woods
in the morning, where I'd cut logs and firewood for a couple
hours.

I'd figured Blue Wing had come along mainly to see someone
go through a gate, but he told me it was because Melody and
I had gotten to be his best friends, and now she was gone,
and pretty soon I'd be. Whatever. In Oz he didn't hang around
close all that much, any more than he had on the farm. He
even flew west once to visit Maikel. Anyway I set it up with
the local butcher to keep him supplied with cutting scraps
that otherwise would have gone to the hogs or the dogs. Most
of our talking got done in the woods, where he'd drop in on
me pretty often. But he'd be gone days at a time.

Cutting wood, I'd take a few minutes every day to practice
throwing the ax at a tree. And the knife Arbel gave me when
I went off to the Heroes. Stuck them better than ever, which
made me wonder if magic played any part in it.

Whatever. Trotting and chopping every day made me feel

good; toughened me and gave me more energy. And the lessons went really well, a lot better and faster than when Arbel had tried teaching me before. My very first day back, he'd said I was already better than lots of shamans—a late starter but fast learner. Kerin, his real apprentice, was bright and sharp, and already getting tall, but kid-skinny. And dark, with big, bright, dark eyes, a sharp curved nose like an Aye-rab, and a little narrow mouth. Lots of times he'd just give her something to do and leave her to do it, while he worked with me. I felt a little awkward about that, but he said he had years to work with her, while I wanted to be on my way. No later than Four-Month, I'd told him. Part of what he had Kerin doing was preparing dried herbs for him; and practicing to read and write, which lots of Ozians could barely do; and practicing ceremonial magic that could be used to bring rain or cancel curses—things like that. I didn't figure to learn either one; I didn't much believe in curses or rain spells. Arbel didn't seem to make much of them either, but if Ozians did, I suppose he had to go through the motions.

He took a different approach with me than before. I'd told him how Varia had taught me meditation, which she'd set me up for early on by spelling me. So he tried teaching me stuff when I was in a meditation trance, and liked how it worked. Better than just spelling me, he said, because under a spell you're less doing than being done to, while in a meditation trance you did it yourself. A matter of self-responsibility, he said.

Right from the start I did a fair job of healing injuries. Arbel was famous for his healing, and folks came or got brought to him from miles around. One guy he worked with me on had split his foot with an ax, and another'd got slashed in a knife fight, and a little girl had fallen in her ma's cookfire. Mostly what he did was refine, and strengthen quite a bit, what I could already do for wounds like those. Taught me to focus better.

Except for the little girl that fell in the fire: I didn't know anything about healing burns; all I could have done was use a sort of general spell that would give relief from the pain, and speed the healing some. He showed me things just for burns.

Where I was weakest was in healing the sick. He had different spells for different sicknesses. Some sickness, he told me, comes from the mind. Asthma was sort of like that. Some folks could get asthma from their mind alone. Others were allergic to something—hay more often than not—but get them away from the hay, they'd keep the asthma for hours or days, or even longer, because of something in their mind that held it there. It could even kill them. When someone got asthma from hay, they could come to him and he'd treat the mind, and the asthma would quit right away, instead of hanging on. After that they could still get asthma from hay, but usually, take them away from the hay, and the asthma was gone in minutes. Commonly rashes disappeared in minutes too, at least the itching eased, and the rash would almost always be gone within the day. Rheumatism might go just as quick, or take a few days, or it could hang on.

He even showed me how to make tumors shrink up and disappear. That didn't always work either, but sometimes it did, and sometimes the tumor didn't come back. And when someone got brought in that had what I'd call pneumonia, he couldn't make it go away right off, but usually they'd feel better right away, and well, after a night's sleep. They'd be back working in two or three days, instead of a couple weeks.

Like anything else, what he did had its limits. Sometimes someone wasn't helped at all—everyone dies sooner or later—and he said the shaman who couldn't live with that had better quit and go to farming, for peace of mind. For me, not being perfect wouldn't be any problem; I'd been doing it all my life.

It was a mild sunny morning in Three-Month when I met Vulkan. Or when Vulkan found me. I'd felled a tree and was chopping logs out of it when I heard Blue Wing yelling from way up high, I couldn't tell what. Then I felt someone looking at me—someone of *power*—and turned around. And almost shit myself! There was a BIG boar hog standing between two trees watching me. Not that he looked like any hog I'd ever seen, not even a razorback. I could tell he was a hog, but for size he reminded me more of a shorthorn bull; a good four feet high at his humped shoulders. He had a thick coat of bristly hair, dark gray on the sides and nearly black along the back. His tusks looked like ivory sickle blades, and I'd judge his weight at better than half a ton. There was no doubt at all that were he to meet a bear in the woods, that bear would go up a tree quick as a wink, crying for its mama.

I should have been scared to death, but after the first shock I wasn't; somehow I knew he wasn't there to rip me up. So I stepped onto the log I'd just cut, squatted there and looked at him.

≋So you are the one.≋

His "voice" was deep and hollow, like someone talking with an empty milk pail over his head, but somehow I knew there wasn't really any sound to it—that the words had come into my head without him ever speaking. "Could be," I said. "It depends on who the one's supposed to be." That amused him; I could feel it. "Sounds as if you're looking for someone in particular," I went on. "What brings you?"

≋An urge. The purpose will no doubt unfold itself for us in good time.≋ His hooves, the only dainty thing about him, brought him a few steps closer. ≋Your aura marks you as someone of power,≋ he said. ≋A ruler and magician.≋

He had an aura too, all animals do, but with all that hog to look at, I'd paid it no attention. Now I did. It wasn't what I think of as an animal aura. More like yours or mine or Blue Wing's, but different. His spirit aura showed at least as much power as that giant body. I wondered if all great boars were like him, and he answered my question without my putting it into words.

≋We are alike, they and I, in being magicians, and in essence, rulers. And in various other respects. But still we vary one from the other, though less than humans do.≋

Then he just stood there. It seemed like if he'd come looking for me, it was up to him to lead the conversation. But if he didn't know why he'd come, maybe I ought to keep things going till he remembered or figured it out, or decided to leave. "My name's Macurdy," I told him. "What's yours?"

He didn't answer for a minute. Then, ≋You may call me Vulkan,≋ he said. ≋We do not have names, but I like that one.≋

After another half minute with neither of us saying anything, I tried something else. "From what I've heard, you folks eat animals, and I've seen where one of you rooted up skunk-cabbage and ate it. But big as you are, it must take a lot to keep you fed. Seems like you'd leave more sign around than you do."

≋We are quite rare, and at any rate do not eat a great deal; we draw our energy from the Web of the World, as you think of it. But as yours do, our bodies require certain substances, minerals for example, though not in large quantities. Thus we must eat, but not nearly in proportion to our size.

≋And now I begin to see—begin to—why I was drawn to speak with you. You are from Farside, and . . . Ah yes, Macurdy! Of course. And you plan to leave Yuulith, to return whence you came. ≋

How could he have known that? Unless he read it in my mind. Or was I imagining things? No, he was there all right. I'd seen enough else strange in Yuulith that I wasn't going to doubt my eyes. And Blue Wing must have seen him; that must have been what got him all excited. It seemed like if any of this was imaginary, it was his "talking" to me. So far he hadn't moved, except early when he'd come a few steps closer, and to flick his little fly-whisk tail a few times. Hadn't even moved his mouth. But his aura and eyes told of power way beyond anything the Sisters had shown me.

I decided to ask him questions—see what he'd say. "I've heard that all of you are boars," I said, "that there aren't any sows of your kind. Is that true?"

≋Boars? Let us simply say you heard correctly: there are no sows. ≋

"Well then, uh, who births you?"

≋We are not born in the usual sense. We come from the inbetween, one might say. Inaccurately, of course. ≋

I didn't know what to make of that. "How could you come to be, without a sow to birth you?"

He chuckled again inside my head. ≋The All-Spirit provides us with bodies. There is no sexuality among us. ≋

"But then—" He seemed to be saying they got born without any breeding taking place, or any sow giving birth. I let that be. Instead I asked him: "How did you get to Yuulith from the inbetween?" Whatever that was.

≈≈We do not use gates. We once were humans, and enter Yuulith in the spirit, from the place of rest and recovery. We receive our bodies here. We are old souls, who have lived out the normal prerequisites for permanent retirement from the choices and lessons of life. And should have graduated, you might say. But instead have been sent here as volunteers, to prepare ourselves for some purpose we will remember, or discover, when it is time. ≈≈

I had no idea at all what to ask next. I just looked at him, maybe eleven, twelve hundred pounds of bone, muscle, and tusks, roaming around the back country rooting up skunk-cabbage and eating wild game, and maybe from time to time somebody's calf. All to prepare himself for he didn't know what.

≈≈And you are returning to Farside, ≈≈ he said. ≈≈Well. In time, if you live, you will return here. I will find you then, for I sense we have things to do together. ≈≈

I just stared.

≈≈And now I will grant you a favor. As a sign. ≈≈

"A favor?"

≈≈Tomorrow you will know the favor you want. It will be foremost in your mind when you waken. When you know, I will know, even at a distance. And whatever it is, it will be yours. ≈≈

Then, without another word, he turned and trotted off.

I never did go home for my day's lesson from Arbel. Instead I sheathed my ax and hiked around in the woods, a thousand thoughts running through my head, not to mention the questions Blue Wing asked. He'd lit in a tree to watch and listen, but hadn't heard any of what Vulkan thought to me, though he'd heard me talking to Vulkan, of course.

Part of what I thought about was what favor I'd get. Could Vulkan give me Melody back? Or Varia, with her and Cyncaidh's blessing? What would be on my mind when I woke up in the morning? Could he really do it?

Along toward evening my mind settled out, and I headed

back for Arbel's. I told him about meeting Vulkan, and he was impressed, but I didn't mention the promised favor. Didn't feel ready to. Besides, having spent most of the day hiking in the woods, talking in a warm room made me drowsy. I excused myself, went to bed, and fell straight to sleep, like a stone.

44

Farewell to Yuulith

The next morning I woke up with something on my mind all right: I wanted to take Hauser back to Missouri with me. Apparently that was to be my favor. Not to have Melody back, like I'd half expected; maybe because there were limits to what was possible. Or Varia, probably because it would be against her will. But Hauser. Which to my mind meant it was somehow possible to take him through. And now I'd have to tell Arbel, which I didn't look forward to. Hauser had been his slave—actually the village's, but his to use—for quite a few years.

As soon as I got dressed, I went and told Arbel what I wanted to do. He looked me over half smiling, his aura showing no sign of upset. "Why do you think I'd object?" he asked. He could read me like a book.

"I thought you might not want to let him go. He's given you some good ideas, and he's a good worker—and better company than most."

Arbel grunted. "You're right; maybe I should object." He smiled then. "In his self-chosen function as an artisan here, he has given me far more than routine service. It would be shameful to begrudge him his return."

He cocked an eyebrow. "You realize, of course, that I do not own him. He's property of the village. But if I'm willing to give up his services, the council will approve. They might, even if I weren't; you're a much bigger hero here than you

436

recognize. But the real issue is, how will you get him through? Do you have a magic you haven't told me about?"

His sharp eyes were watching my aura, I had no doubt, and I couldn't see any way around it but to tell him about Vulkan's favor, so I did. "And I take that to mean he can," I finished.

For a minute, Arbel just stared, then he turned thoughtful. "Assume he can. Assume your Vulkan has such power. Is there any guarantee that Hauser will arrive sane? Or even alive?"

I hadn't given that a thought. "Vulkan didn't seem like someone who'd send him through a gate to arrive dead or crazy."

Arbel shrugged. "Perhaps not, if he understood the problem. I have no experience with anyone coming out in Farside."

"I'm trusting Vulkan's honesty and judgement," I said. "And his power to make it happen right."

Arbel nodded. "Let's ask Hauser," he said.

I hadn't thought of that. "I guess we'd better. But let's not mention Vulkan."

We went into the kitchen, where Hauser was restocking the wood pile. "Charles," I said softly, "if you could go back to Farside, would you? Even if it was dangerous?"

He stared at me for a long five or ten seconds, while it soaked through that I was serious. Then he turned white and started to shake, leaning against the wall to keep from falling down. I could honest to God feel his feelings. Nobody said anything for half a minute; then I told him I thought maybe I could get him through. "Arbel says it's fine with him, and he thinks the council will allow it. Do you want to try?"

He nodded dumbly at me.

"Well then," I said, and turned to Arbel. "Will you ask the council?"

Arbel asked the village headman that same day. The council met next evening, and what all might have been said, I didn't hear, but the decision was that Hauser could go if the gate would take him. I went around to each councilman the day after that and thanked him. None of them seemed to think it was any big deal as long as Arbel was happy with it.

I felt pretty sure Vulkan's magic could get him through okay, but I wanted to prepare him as much as I could. Like most people's, Hauser's aura showed some talent, more than most, but nothing like an ylf, for example.

I put myself in a meditation trance and had Arbel ask me to remember everything Varia'd done when she spelled me the first two times. The drills I could remember without any trance.

Working with Hauser was good training for me. The first time I felt a little spooked to do it, and afterward I wasn't sure we'd accomplished anything. I did the first spell, and the instructions and questions that went with it, three nights in a row. Then, with him in a shallow spell again, I taught him to meditate. That seemed to pick it up. On later evenings I drilled him, and we could see him start changing.

My own training kept going along fast, even though I was giving time and attention to Hauser. Not only my training in healing, but other training I hadn't figured to do. I still aimed to leave during Four-Month, on the noon nearest the full moon, which on their calendar is always just before the middle of the month.

I felt more than ready, and Hauser seemed to have gone as far as he could. He'd even learned to keep himself warm from inside, and to start fire—way more than we'd ever expected of him. Arbel, though, figured that getting through was more a question of inborn talent than how far you'd taken it. Unless of course Vulkan did it for him. Me, I had faith in Vulkan's magic; the training was just to help Hauser survive.

Something else happened that last week, too. Unknown to me, Arbel had been experimenting on keeping the body warm by tapping into the Web of the World, and had worked out a procedure that seemed safe, if done right. Anyway it worked for him. He told me about it on my last day, and wrote out all the steps. There wasn't time to practice them under his supervision, but if I was careful, I could practice them alone on Farside. I gave them a quick look-over; they didn't seem all that hard.

That was the evening before the gate was due to open. It was also the evening I told Hauser about Vulkan and what he'd promised, and that all the work we'd done was just in case. I'd wanted him to think it was all up to him. Now he was ready as he could get, and I wanted to ease his nerves.

❖   ❖   ❖

Before I went to bed that night, I sat in front of the fire thinking about what might have been. About Melody. She'd died being what she'd always been: impetuous, reckless. She'd loved me strongly, and I'd loved her, but she was what she was; that's how the world worked. And about Varia. It still seemed as if I'd come back to Yuulith someday, and it came to me that she and I weren't done with one another yet. I shook it off. She was married to a high ylf lord, and they were happy together; had a kid, and they'd probably have more. As far as that's concerned, he was probably a better husband for her anyway, really.

I thought about Omara, too: If I'd stayed, I could have been happy with her. There mightn't ever have been any powerful love between us, but we'd have made up for that with respect and consideration, and good times in bed. But somehow, as much sense as it made, it wasn't right for me. I needed to go back to Farside.

I ended up meditating a little to still my mind. Worked like a charm. When I lay down, I went right to sleep.

And woke up fresh and confident. Had breakfast and went for a ride on Hog. I'd miss Hog; we'd been through a lot together. He'd be Arbel's now.

When Arbel's sundial said it was time, Arbel went with us. So did Blue Wing. I'd thought about what I'd say if Blue Wing wanted to go through the gate with me. Not that I thought he would, but just in case. Even if it would take him, if crossing to Farside was anything like crossing to Yuulith, he'd arrive without a feather left. And if he got there okay, some sonofabitch would likely shoot him and get him stuffed.

But he never asked, just flew along sober as a judge. After two mild rainy days, the field of buckwheat we walked through was growing strong and thick, and green as you please. The sun was out, and the day as warm as any since the fall before. I could see by Hauser's aura that he was confident, even though the dark circles under his eyes told me he hadn't slept much. He could have—he knew how to still his mind now. Maybe he'd wanted to spend the night thinking and remembering, or maybe planning. As for me—I'd wait and see how things looked when I got there, likely help Dad for a while, then maybe go wandering. See more of my own world.

In the grove, the basswood buds were opening and the dogwoods were in bloom. It wasn't noon yet; we'd left early enough not to be late. I looked at Hauser and he looked at me. He was sort of grinning, but not saying anything.

We didn't any of us know exactly how long it'd be before high noon: about a quarter hour, Arbel thought. Hauser and I each had a small pouch of Teklan silver coins in our pack, and I still had most of the gold coins I'd started out with a couple months earlier. Arbel had only been willing to take one of them for his time and trouble, and I'd given three of them to Hauser.

I felt it quicker'n Arbel, then Blue Wing gave a big squawk. Something was pressing on me, just enough to notice, from off to one side. I grabbed Hauser by an arm, and walked against the pressure, which was getting stronger fast. It wasn't affecting the trees, even the saplings weren't bending from it. I guess it only affected animals.

Arbel called out, "Good luck, Macurdy!" I knew it was him, but his voice sounded strange, tinny. I glanced back, and he looked all crooked and jiggedy. I glimpsed Blue Wing, too; he looked like three or four great ravens half mixed together, flying in a little circle, and his calling had a shrill buzzing sound, reminded me of a musical saw.

I realized that Hauser was walking against the pressure as easily as I was, but I held onto his arm anyway. My hair stood on end more than anytime in my life before. This was nothing at all like coming through from Farside. A big humming started that somehow I knew was loud, yet I could hardly hear it, and I felt like I was vibrating apart.

Suddenly everything went black as tar; blacker, as if there wasn't such a thing as light. The sound stopped, and the pressure, and the vibrating, but I still felt Hauser's arm in my right hand; I was gripping it harder than I ought to. For just a few seconds it was like that, still and absolutely black, then I felt myself drop a foot or two onto my back, a stone bruising my ribs. There was moonlight, but for half a minute I just lay there, dizzy, my stomach queasy, my eyes not able to focus. Then things steadied out, and I saw some scrawny pinetops against the night sky. Injun Knob. I turned my head and there was Hauser.

It was him that said it, sounding awed. "We're home, Macurdy. We're home."

The End